Spirits of the Land

By Mark Gomes

For Dad

PREFACE

Africa is the birthplace of humanity and therefore the birthplace of storytelling. So, as I taught African History for ten years at a college in Manhattan and told the students about the real Lion King of Mali they would be intrigued. Unfortunately, they found it difficult or didn't want to read the original versions. So, I created *Spirits of the Land* as a fictional account to feed a Western reader's interest in medieval Africa. The story of Sundjata is still told throughout parts of West Africa today. African storytelling began in the oral tradition, and the story changes through the times and the storyteller. I have read three recorded versions of the story and adapted it for a Western reader. This account is in **no way** meant to replace the original versions of the tale. Without the following books--*Sundiata* by D.T. Niane, *Sunjata* by David C. Conrad and *Son-Jara* by Jeli Fa-Digi Sisoko and John William Johnson--I could not have written this story. When I followed closely to one of the three sources I have included endnotes. *History of Africa* by Kevin Shillington, *The Way of the Elders* by Adama and Naomi Doubma, and *Warfare in African History* by Richard J. Reid were also instrumental to writing this fun and exciting tale.

Spirits puts the focus on the people. All the ways of the people and the immenseness of Africa should be celebrated. In *Spirits*, the land itself is a character. The people are intimately connected to it, and all the flora and fauna depicted were there during the medieval period and/or today.

I want to thank everyone who I pestered to read this story and who have supported this endeavor. Thank you Balenda, Gina and Paul for your editing efforts

Chapter 1

The Hunter

The old hunter's eyes darted back and forth looking for more droplets of blood or hoof prints. "Ahhh," he whispered, stopping and kicking the dirt. Losing the trail of the small sand-colored rhim gazelle was frustrating. "I am getting old," he said aloud.

"You are for sure," said a young hunter sitting in a tall tree. His legs stretched out before him, and his back rested against the large trunk. "What are you looking for?"

"I shot a small gazelle though the neck, and he ran," confessed the old hunter, motioning with his hands. "I have lost the trail. Have you seen the beast?"

"No, I have not. But I have found something more interesting."

Not in the mood for games, the old hunter put a hand on his hip. He sighed but would not bite at the question. Instead, he looked around for a sign.

"It is important," said the young hunter delighted at his secret.

The old hunter sighed again. "What is it? A pride of lions?"

The young hunter laughed. "Well, one lion. One very important lion."

"All lions are important. What's so special about one lion?"

"I saw the Lion King--King Kon Fatta--hunting with his griot, Doua."

The old hunter stopped and stood up straight. "Where? Where did you see him?"

"Well, now that you are interested, maybe I won't tell you."

The old hunter sighed again. "Don't make me pull you down from there. I have dreamt about the king and need to tell him

3

something. In the kingdom there are small troubles. Outside his domain things are falling apart, and that trouble may come here. We must be ready if it does."

The young hunter saw the serious look on the old hunter's face and sat up, letting his legs dangle off the branch. "I know. The drought, Sumaguru of the Sosso, and the trouble in Ghana; everything is crazy."

"I have something that may help him."

The young hunter knew how serious dreams were. How the spirits talk to you through them. "I saw the king and his griot that way." He pointed over his shoulder. "Follow my tracks, and you will find the king."

"Maybe find both," mumbled the old hunter as he began to walk in the direction the young hunter had pointed.

"What is your name?" the young hunter called after him.

The old hunter stopped and turned realizing his rudeness. "Bora. What is your name?"

"Oulamba, of the Traore tribe, and I believe my clan were masters, and your people our slaves." The joke was a common one between tribes.

Bora laughed. "I think it was the other way around, and what the hell are you doing up there?"

"I saw a hyena, and I decided to wait for my younger brother, Oulani, up here. He is also tracking game."

"Did you meet King Fatta?"

"No, we saw him tracking something."

Bora shook his head. "You and your brother are a long way from home."

"The drought has made farming and hunting difficult. So, we

4

are off on our own. Our mansa didn't want us to leave, but we felt it best."

"Your mansa sounds wise. Thank you for showing me the way. Good luck on your hunts, to you and your brother."

Bora shook his head and raised his right hand. He remembered looking for his first big kill. Things were easier for him. The Niger was deep, and rains came often to the grass and game of the bright country. But now he needed to find the king, the man who may have the power to talk to the spirits and make things better. The power of Sumaguru, King of the Sosso, was growing. So was the power of King Fatta. A collision of these two great men might be unavoidable. The sun was getting low, and Bora needed to move.

* * * * *

King Kon Fatta could feel the hot breeze on his face, which meant the antelope could not smell him. He dug his foot into the dirt and kept his eyes on the edge of the thicket as he waited for the beast to show himself. He waited for a clear shot to launch his attack and squeezed the smooth shaft of the spear. Feeling the weight of its iron head, he relaxed his grip. If Kon missed the target, Doua would not let him hear the end of it.

The tan oryx could smell water in the wind and gave a snort in frustration, shaking his black and white face. His skin twitched to relieve the bites of blood thirsty flies which swarmed the ragged gashes left by the lioness that had attacked him earlier in the morning. Lifting his long face and taking a deep breath, he checked the wind once more before stepping into the open.

Kon knew he had to be careful. He had seen the oryx shove both its long straight black horns through the body of a young lioness. "Spirits guide my hand. Send this spear into the heart of this great beast so the people can eat," Kon whispered. An antelope that could kill a lion was full of power and would be a great prize.

"Aim and--"

"I know how far he is…" Kon whispered to Doua.

Doua, his griot, smirked. "Well, don't miss," he said in a hushed voice. Out of the red dirt he plucked a smooth round green fruit from the karite trees that they crouched behind. He smelled it, and then slid it into a leather bag over his shoulder.

The smell of water was thick in the air, and the oryx could no longer resist; it had been more than two days without a drink. It plodded out from the safety of the thicket towards another, but there was open ground to cover. His long legs grew heavy as the loss of blood and its thirst took their toll. His hooves made ruts as they dragged through the red rocks and dirt.

Kon saw the oryx's head emerge from the tangled thicket. He paused for just a moment and took a deep breath. His powerful chest expanded as he rose from his crouched position. Holding the spear low by his leg, he took two steps and raised it; his eyes locked on his target, and then his body moved quick as lightning.

The oryx felt a blow into its side, and fear rippled through every muscle. It dug his hooves in the red dirt to jump, but all its strength disappeared. The tan antelope crashed into the ground as a cloud of reddish dust encircled its body.

Kon stood still with his arm extended, watching his spear slice into the oryx's body. The heart was the target, and the placement seemed to be perfect. It would be a quick death for this proud creature. A fine death; it would not suffer. He watched the animal make a small jump, but it crashed into the dirt. A cloud of red dust floated above the body. Bright red blood seeped from around the hole where the spear protruded. Blood soaked the smooth hide as its legs kicked in the air. Kon closed his eyes for a moment and imagined the strong heart of this animal. Life giving life, and he thanked the ancestors. He felt their strength as well as the antelope's flowed through him.

Doua watched, his hand grasping the air as the spear hit its mark. He loved to see Kon in his element. He was a great ruler, but this was where he truly belonged.

Kon opened his eyes and turned to Doua with a big smile, and their deep brown eyes locked. Kon's muscles ached to move, but he remained in place, knowing a wounded animal was capable of running. The late day sun felt good on his dark muscled shoulders, but now came that tiny bit of sadness that was produced by killing. He could feel it in the pit of his stomach; it was the ancestors telling him to have respect for life. Even though they were going to make use of this animal, it was important to keep such lessons in mind. The feeling came when he took a life. Then, as he remembered he would have to return home tomorrow, his sadness deepened.

Kon's servants and the butchers of the village dressed and prepared the meat. Before the celebration, Doua opened the ceremony. The mansa, Kon, and Doua stood in the village square in front of a large black wooden idol. Smooth to the touch, the idol was carved in the shape of a large man. In its left hand was a knife while its right hand was palm up facing the sky. The lips on the face were fixed in the shape of a word asking the ancestors to protect the village from harm. In its stomach was a hole filled with special herbs. Doua entreated, "Great mansa of the village, this meat is a sacrifice. Tell the spirits of the land, our ancestors, to make the rain fall, animals grow fat and many children to be born." He handed the meat to the mansa.

The mansa took the piece of meat and placed it in the hole inside the belly of the idol. Then he turned to take a small wooden bowl of palm wine from Doua, which he placed at its feet. The mansa stood up and saw the Oracle and the Diviner of the village, and they acknowledged the sacrifice. The mansa clapped his hands twice, and the celebration began.

The celebration fires burned brightly, and the king's guards assembled the red tents to prepare for the evening. As the sun slid below the horizon it made the sky burnt orange with long thin streaks of purple clouds. The king's camp sat in a farmer's fallow field, keeping his royal distance. Guards walked on the edge of darkness where the light of the fires dissolved. Only hunters dared to stay outside the protection of the village walls. In their garbage pits beyond those walls, wooden idols protected them from bad spirits.

"The people ate well tonight," Kon said to Doua. Listening to the people sing and dance, to the rhythm of tam tams, and the strings of the kora made him smile. It was the haunting tomes of the balafon that made him think about the future. "I prefer to sleep in the open, let's get rid of the tents"

Doua shook his head. "We will sell them back to the Arab traders we bought them from. Tonight, the village sings your praises, as they should. It has been too long since we came to visit the villages. We don't want them squabbling over silly things, or before you know it they will be fighting. Some are becoming like the Sosso - always complaining."

"The Sosso," said Kon as he shook his head. "They do complain. They are not bad people, though. We share kin, and you think that would matter, but their leaders always want their way. The mansa tonight told me that the Sosso have been talking about taking Kumbi-Sahel. They make noise about expanding their power." Kon frowned.

"They are very ambitious. I hear about their leader from the Dyulas. Sumaguru gets all the young ones crazy," said Doua, concerned. "He claims to be a great sorcerer."

"Building his musical instruments isn't enough for him. He is a great sorcerer now as well? Remember, when he was a young boy? After I became a master hunter, his father sent him to apprentice under me. He was an intense boy, and he didn't stay long."

"That's right! I forgot about that. There were several others as well." Doua remembered the eager young faces, and the serious brooding Sumaguru.

"He will probably have half his people wanting to fight, the others half-scared not to. Too many young ones wanting to fight; their Komo order needs to teach better," Kon added.

8

"There has been lots of trouble all around. We are lucky the spirits favor us," said Doua. "The drought here isn't too bad, but I don't remember seeing so many Fulani and their herds before harvest season."

"True, the mansa here is happy with his wives, but they have lost crops. If things get worse, it could change." Kon scratched his head. "You are right about the Fulani. The drought must be driving them; there might not be enough grass and water to go around." Kon's body began to feel heavy as his mind mulled over the problems that he could face. Had he angered his ancestors?

"A man of power is hard to find.[1] Niani is lucky to have you," Doua said in his reassuring way.

"I don't want the trouble the King of Ghana has. He is losing much of his power. Muslim leaders are cutting his supply routes - No gold, no salt, no trade. No power," Kon said, while poking his finger into his hand. "Look how quickly the Sosso want to take advantage of his weakness. Other clans may rise up as well."

"Sumaguru will be smart to hold fast and control his council's favor. Maybe we get lucky and he loses their confidence. Then he will be king of files and dirt," said Doua.

"I wish I could go back to hunting all day. I have waited too many moons to hunt. I have gotten rusty." He stretched out by the fire, the air cooling as the creatures of the night made their noises heard.

Dancing in and out of the flames, beetles buzzed. A male lion roared in short bursts as the crickets chirped, and wild dogs yelped and barked as hyenas laughed in the distance. Kon smiled as the hyenas mocked the creatures and the night.

"Will we start for home tomorrow?" Doua asked as he yawned and stretched his tired muscles. He picked up his kora and inspected the twenty-one strings and its long neck.

"Yes, we have been gone long enough, and you know how Sossuma is." He rolled his dark eyes. "Since she has become first wife, if I leave for more than a few days she gets angry. She will not speak to me, especially now that she is with child again. She will drive all the servants crazy. Then she will tell me how mad she is at me for being out of our bed so long." He paused. "But I do miss my son."

"I warned you about her," Doua said, "Her fruit was sweet to get what she wanted, but it turned sour soon enough. If something was to happen to you, she would soon find another. A crocodile mourns longer." He went back to tuning his kora, plucking its strings.

Kon let out a laugh. "Her fruit is still plenty sweet, old man." He paused. "And if I do leave this life, I will haunt the both of you." He worried that was Doua was right. He had spoken of her like this often.

"You worry too much about what some think." Doua replied, still plucking the kora's strings.

"I am King; I have to worry about what people think." He took a bite of the cooked heart of the oryx. The heart contained much power. It was chewy and tasty.

"I mean you are too vain and impatient, but with her, you have patience." Out in the bush Doua was forward and to the point. Back in Niani, he was careful and always respectful around the eyes and ears of others.

"You are lucky I am too tired to get up and beat you," said Kon in a mocking tone.

Doua laughed. "You are a good ruler, a good man, but all men have faults."

"Hello in camp!" a shout came from out of the darkness.

Kon and Doua sat up, looking past the fire into the darkness beyond. The heat from the flames made the darkness dance and move. Doua put down his instrument, and his hand reached for a spear but did not pick it up. Kon's hand slid to the ivory handled dagger strapped to his arm. "Aye, aye!" shouted Doua to alert the guards who seem to have not done their job. "Who's there?"

"An old hunter who would like to come and sit by the fire," replied a voice from the darkness.

"Come," replied Doua, his hand touching the spear.

From the darkness strode a tall, thin, bald man. He wore a bow and a quiver full of arrows over one shoulder, and a large well-worn leather bag hung from the other, along with a hammock. He had a sharp iron-tipped spear in his left hand, and hanging from his left hip in a hard leather scabbard was an antler-handled skinning knife. He held his right hand in the air palm up, a smile on his strong broad face. "Tell your guards behind me that I mean no harm."

"Guards, go back," Kon said.

Two guards, with their razor-sharp spears pointed at the intruder, moved back into the dark.

"Come. Sit. Have you eaten?" Kon asked. "What has you out in the dark? The lion is in my blood, but even I won't roam about in the night beyond the fires."

"Thank you. I was tracking a gazelle, but before I knew it darkness had come. I am getting old." He shook his head and sat down cross legged by the fire on a grass mat Doua tossed to him.

"I saw your fire and heard the noise from the village."

"What is your name?" asked Doua. His eyes searched the man. He was older, but he saw the long-muscled arms of the hunter, and the dark rough skin from being in the bush. Hanging off his shirt were cowrie shells, tufts of animal hair, and lion and hyena claws from his kills.

"Bora," the hunter said. The warmth of the fire felt good - as the air was cool and the mud cloth he wore was worn and tattered. "I know you, sir; you are king of Niani. You are a fair

11

king."

Kon laughed a small laugh and admired the man's tone when he said it. "I have heard worse."

"No disrespect, sir." The hunter bowed his head. Doua had a servant of their entourage bring the hunter a wooden bowl with meat and rice mixed with hot pepper. The hunter dipped his fingers in the bowl and laid the crisp meat in his mouth past his cracked lips. "I am glad to see you this night. I have seen some things about you. We were destined to meet."

"You are more than a hunter?" Kon inquired, rubbing his chin with his hand. "Men and women tell me many things." Kon ate another piece of the oryx's heart and gave some to the hunter.

The hunter took a piece of heart. "What I see is true, and it often comes to pass. I am not a sorcerer, but the spirits have given me a sight. I see you marrying again, soon, and it will change the kingdom." The hunter scooped some rice and meat from the wooden bowl. "I saw you at the palace several moons ago with the queen, and not long after the sight came to me. The air was heavy between the both of you. You should marry someone to balance what is between you and the queen. A happy king brings a happy land." The hunter ate a piece of the heart with the rice and meat.

"The land is not happy? Listen to the sounds that fill the air this night," said Kon said with confidence.

"I speak of the future." The hunter took twelve cowrie shells and a kola nut from a small leather pouch and rolled them onto his mat.[2] He asked his power object, a lion's tooth in the bottom of his leather pouch, about the king and his future. From his rough hand they spilled, and he saw the pattern they made, and the kola nut lay open. "Things change for the better, if you marry again soon."

Doua nodded his head in approval. "You are onto something." This man may be a seer, but he was left-handed, and that worried him.[3] However, hunters were full of spirit energy from the

12

animals they hunted. The signs from the ancestors always needed to be taken seriously; he knew Kon would react to this.

The hunter kept eating as his eyes looked over the older thin man. A small red hat sat atop his graying hair. He knew how much respect the griot carried with the king and was glad his sight had been well received. "A silk cotton tree grows from a tiny seed no smaller than a grain of rice. Kingdoms are like trees - some will be silk cotton, others dwarf palm. The large will shade and overgrow the little." [4]

The hunter's words hit Kon like a punch to the chest; first Doua and now the hunter both talking about his queen. She was strong, her beauty a sight to behold, but they were right: she was cold. Each season she got colder the rains were less. But she had given him a son, an heir, and was with child again. The idea of another wife made Sossuma jealous. She was scaring away potential wives, and worst of all he had not met anyone who interested him. Any new wife would have to hold their own against her. Right after his first wife died, Sossuma changed. She made him feel as if he could never do enough for her. Her love was like a hole in the ground that you could never fill. Worst of all, if the hunter could see they were unhappy what did others see?

"There is a prophecy that says a true heir can only come from happiness. Otherwise, bad feelings and bad deeds will follow," said Bora.

"I have heard of that. Destiny is in our hands if we dare to dream," said Doua. He turned to Kon. "You should sleep." He could see the worried look on Kon's face.

"I hear your words and will take them into my heart," Kon said as the hunter's words hung in the air like an acrid smoke. "Good night," he added to his small entourage before rising and stalking off to his tent. He was tired and needed to be alone. "A king's life," he muttered to himself. The tent was several paces back from the fire. As he opened the tent flap he heard yet a hyena laugh breaking the stillness of the night. Looking into the darkness he felt the hyena no longer mocked the night, but rather him.

Chapter 2

The Buffalo Woman

The small, sharp blade cut a leafy branch from a young Baforonto tree. The thin, dull, green leaves would help to heal the deep scratch from a thorn that had torn the flesh of his second wife. He cut the branch into small finger-sized pieces and dropped them into a round clay pot by his side. He then placed the knife into the smooth blue and yellow striped pot. With a sharp, black, iron bar he began to dig into the red dirt for the roots of the tree. "This is my day," he said aloud. "I will cure the fat woman's boy. Stop the shit from pouring out of him. Mansa Diarra will reward me for saving his daughter's son." He struck the dirt hard with the pointed end and small clumps flew into the air and into his face. "Ahh," he cried as the dirt stung his eyes. He stood up, clearing his eyes, and now saw his sister Sogolon. She was far enough away not to see him in the bush. As usual, she was conversing with unseen spirits.

"But I don't know." Sogolon's voice was low as the words tumbled out of her mouth. The disembodied voices tormented her today.

"Will you leave the village?" inquired the angry voice.

"Yes? No? I don't know. When it happens, when I see the signs?" she said pacing back and forth, her bent body swaying with each step. "Other villages may not accept me: I talk to the voices, and I am ugly. They tolerate me here because I make the best cures, the best poisons. I am the Buffalo Woman."

Sheka continued to spy on Sogolon. His eyes traced her curved spine that looked like a snake poised to strike. The muscles on her back tight and twisted. The right arm drooped low and swung as she walked, and her left shoulder thrust up into the air; it was hard to look at her. He shook his head and wondered about the voices she heard; they must be full of mischief. Her appearance must be the result of the bargain she struck with mischievous spirits. *I will cure the boy. I will do it before her. She thinks she is so smart, so special, not now*, Sheka thought. Feeling his body grow hot with anger he grabbed the roots he had exposed from the dirt and put them in the clay pot. He stood, his knees stiff, and with pot in hand he snuck back to the village.

"You must go; you are not welcome here," the angry voice said to Sogolon in an urgent tone.

"When the signs are right," replied Sogolon determined. She craned her neck upwards to the sky. Birds were good signs, but the canopy of trees blocked her sight. Her almond shaped eyes then squinted as a ray of light came through the canopy of green, and sweat beaded on her dark forehead as the sun heated the shimmering air. Now and then a hot breeze blew back her wild mane of hair as she walked a well-worn path that would eventually fork. One trail led to the next village, the other to the river. She hoped the crossroad spirits would lead her. As she walked, her arms swung, helping her move down the path. Sweat slid down her cheek that faced the dappled rays of the sun that climbed higher into the sky.

"Sit, stop and rest... You must wait," said a female voice in a motherly tone.

"I need signs, something," Sogolon answered the familiar voice. "I can go further."

"Wait, or go to the river," said the mother voice.

"No, I should go back to the village," she said annoyed. Then she saw the oval yellow-green fruit of the jackal berry tree. Looking around for a termite mound, she saw the tree growing out of the top of a large one. She grabbed a low-hanging branch with her left hand and with her nimble right took a small knife out of the brown leather sheath strapped to her left arm. She cut the branch off with a sawing motion and then removed all the leaves. With the branch clean, she put the knife back in its sheath, went over to the fork in the road, and began to whip the ground and bushes looking for a sign. The blood sign would make her go to the river, the milk sign back to her village. With bent knee she struck the ground, then the brush, and then the ground and back to the brush. With the next strike into the dirt, she saw a streak of blood. A good-sized, blue-brown lizard was under the dirt, and the branch struck its tail cutting it. The lizard scurried into the underbrush. [5]

"Let's to go to the river," said the mother voice.

Happy with her sign, Sogolon moved down the trail with purpose. She walked until she became tired and looked for a place to stop. A large pile of round, grey, boulders near a stand of trees would provide comfort, and they were not far off the trail.

"Watch for lions in the shade. Don't surprise them. That would be bad," the mother voice said concerned.

"I know, I know; I have been here before." Sogolon felt tired; the voices wouldn't stop, and she needed to fix her dusty wrap dress tied around her neck that cradled her heavy breasts. Over towards the rocks she limped, and halfway there she remembered the beast. Her black body - solid as rock and fast as lightning, more dangerous than a lion during the day - made her freeze. She looked into the dry brown-green brush. If the beast was close she could not hope to get away from those thick curved horns. She turned her head to listen, and the air was full of the sound of bugs and birds. All seemed clear. The tall, dry grass rustled in the breeze. She took an awkward step when she heard the crack of a branch. Her heart skipped a beat, and again she froze. She heard someone running. The sound was coming from in front of her where the land dropped off towards the river.

"Go... go... go," chanted a voice.

A tall, thin young man running as fast he could came over the top of the hill. He saw this odd-looking woman and stopped in his tracks almost falling over. Moments later came another, but as he crested the hill, he dropped to his knees, out of breath.

The man on his knees looked up, "Ahh!" he exclaimed as this bizarre woman with wild hair and dusty clothes stood before him with a smile.

"I am Sogolon Kedjou," she said looking at the two sorry-looking hunters. She knew what they were by the cowrie shells that hung from the skins they wore around their waist. Each had a large, sheathed knife strapped to a leg and carried a large bow with a quiver full of arrows. They looked too flustered to be seasoned. "Ahh… the beast," she said with a smile.

The two men gave each other a look of wonderment. They dropped their sleeping mats to the ground. "We are brothers," said the man rising from his knees. "I am the eldest."

The younger brother, now staring, spoke, "Are you a sorceress, or a witch?"

"When you say the beast, do you mean the buffalo?" added the older brother.

"Not a witch or sorceress, and in my village of Do we call that buffalo the beast."

"Yes, it is a terrible beast!" exclaimed the youngest brother. "She thinks she owns the river."

"She does," replied Sogolon.

"They are the more signs," said the angry spirit voice.

"Maybe," said Sogolon.

"Maybe what?" said the older brother. "I thought you said she owned the river?"

"She does." Sogolon's quick mind formed a plan. *The boys are young and want to prove themselves,* she thought. "Would you like to kill the beast and be rewarded?" Sogolon turned her body to be more comfortable. "Come, let's rest in the shade by the rocks; I believe we can help each other."

The group found shade among the pile of boulders and twisted leafy trees. They sat facing each other.

"What are your names?" Sogolon asked the brothers.

"I am Oulamba," answered the older brother with suspicion.

"I am Oulani, the handsome one," said the younger brother, confident in his skin.

"Ahhh, if you are talking about you and a monkey," exclaimed Oulamba.

"You remember what mother said," Oulani announced.

"Mother is not here," Oulamba replied, his response tinged with annoyance.

"My friends, I hope you hunt as well as you argue," said Sogolon with a laugh. "I have a plan that will benefit all of us."

The brothers looked at each other skeptically, but Sogolon could tell they were interested. Their family squabble was put aside for another day.

Oulamba leaned back on his hands attempting to size up this most different of women. She seemed to talk to the air now and again. Her appearance was disturbing, but her manner remained calm when she spoke. "How can you help us?"

"I can give you poison to kill the beast, and you will be rewarded by my chief. Gold, wives, kola nuts and song will be yours." She brushed some stray hairs from her face.

"All that for us, but what do we do for you?" asked Oulani.

"Kill the beast, and tell the mansa I helped, that's all."

"That's all?" inquired Oulani.

"That's it?" remarked Oulamba.

"That is all. I need the mansa to have confidence in me," Sogolon said sitting up. "My brother has become jealous of me. He tries to convince them I am a witch, and he feels that I have embarrassed him by curing people he could not. He thinks I use evil spirits because of the voices I hear." Her tone was not pitiful, but filled with determination.

The mother voice jumped into her head. "Quiet or they will leave. Don't say anymore."

Sogolon shook her head and said aloud, "quiet you."

Oulamba laughed, and Oulani looked at Sogolon strangely. Oulamba spoke first. "With whom do you speak?" Oulamba was amused, feeling that if she had a special gift she could help them. Oulani, however, was a little frightened by her ways, though he would not show it. He wasn't sure what to think but being with his brother gave him courage.

"I speak to the voices that speak to me."

"Voices?" asked Oulani, concerned.

"Yes. Several."

"Do they tell you the future?" asked Oulamba hopeful.

Sogolon let out a laugh. "They can give good advice as they guide me, but they also annoy and torment me."

"Oh," said Oulamba, wishing Sogolon could always tell the future. "Well, they are a gift."

"It is one of my gifts. Now let me show you another gift. Give me time to make you some poison - very strong poison that will kill the beast. However, the trick is getting close enough to get the arrows to stick into her hide, which is like iron. If you do then just be patient, and promise me you will both be careful."

"Easier said than done." Oulani put his hand to his chin. "Why hasn't anyone from your village used your poison?"

"Two hunters using my poison were killed by her. They never got the arrow through her skin. One of them was married to the mansa's daughter. Everyone now is too scared. Then my brother made everyone think I cursed them." Sogolon shook her head, visibly sad about her brother.

"There are trees we can climb where she can't see us and hopefully not smell us. She will be close when the herd goes down to drink in the morning," Oulamba said with confidence.

"Yes, they should use the trail where she almost got us. Brother, I know the tree you speak of." Oulani felt better about their developing plan. "I can get a shot at her neck."

"I will go make the poison, and you men make a fire." Sogolon rose in her awkward way.

"We will get something for us to eat tonight." Oulamba watched their new friend rise to her feet and wobble off.

Oulani was quiet till she moved off. "She scares me, but I like her."

"Yes, she is odd, no doubt, but she is easy to be around, like we have known her before." Oulamba smiled.

"Would you lie with her?" Oulani asked.

As Oulamba thought, his brow became tight. "Hmm, I'm not sure." He tried to demonstrate with his hands. "It might not work." His one hand bent the other straight, and he crashed them into each other. The brothers laughed.

Sogolon awoke to red glowing embers surrounded by grey ash in the fire the brothers had made. To her they looked like red angry eyes. A small trail of smoke twisted into the air, and she looked over to the empty mats where Oulamba and Oulani had slept. She was fast asleep when they left to claim their perch in the tree above the trail to the river.

"They must get there before the herd moves from their night place," said the mother voice.

"They did," said Sogolon rising in her awkward way from the mat of leaves she had slept upon. She took a sip of water from a bladder bag and then cleaned her teeth with a stick she cut from a tree. The sun was rising steadily, and the daily heat began to

21

build.

"They are dead... dead," said the angry voice. "The beast has broken their bones."

"Shut up," Sogolon said. "No, they are capable. I gave them amulets off my wrists to protect them." Doubt began to creep into her mind, and she bit her lip. She sat back down on a mat and waited by the dying fire as the sun rose into the clear blue morning sky.

"Oyyyy yeah!" Sogolon heard a shout and turned towards the river. Over the crest of the red dusty hill came Oulamba and Oulani. Between them was the head of the beast. Each brother held a thick curved horn in one hand and a bloody knife in the other. Bright blood dripped and trailed in the dirt as they walked. The tongue of the Cape buffalo hung from its open mouth, and it flopped as they walked. Large toothy smiles filled the brother's faces.

"Your poison worked, it worked," said Oulamba excitedly.

Sogolon was so happy she clapped her hands. They were alive, safe, and the beast had been killed. Then she saw Oulani's upper arm had been slashed, and blood was running down his dark arm to his wrist. "No, you are hurt," she said looking into his eyes.

Oulamba laughed. "He fell out of the tree and cut his arm." The beast began to chase him. Lucky for him he can climb fast, and I managed to get several arrows into the beast before it got him."

Oulani looked skyward for a moment a bit embarrassed. "True, I fell out of the tree. Let's put this head down - it's heavy."

The thick, black, horned head lay in the dirt. Its eyes were lifeless, and now it didn't look like a beast anymore. Sogolon, Oulamba and Oulani embraced each other laughing and smiling. "The beast is dead. The beast is dead. What mighty hunters are we," sang Oulamba and Oulani, while Sogolon clapped.

"You did it!" exclaimed Sogolon. She clapped her hands together touching the tips of her fingers to her chin. "We must take this head to the village."

"We must hurry before the meat spoils and the animals get it," said Oulamba.

"I will run ahead to the village and bring back others." Oulani turned and sprinted off towards Do.

"Come, Sogolon, I will begin to butcher the beast, and you can watch for any lions that may come. Oulamba raised his eyebrows at her. He looked down at the head as blow flies began to buzz around it in a mad dance to eat and lay eggs.

The afternoon sun was now low in the clear sky as the butchered body of the beast was cooked by the servants. Mansa Gnemo Diarra of Do, his council, and his wives stood in their place at the front of the entire village. Several paces away stood Sogolon, Oulamba, and Oulani. The village was in two long lines, several people deep on either side.

Oulamba was looking over the mansa and his council. One man, in particular, wearing a hat adorned with a large bird's skull glared back at them.

Oulamba leaned back to Sogolon, "Is that your brother?"

"Yes, that is Sheka. I don't like the look on his face."

"Me either," replied Oulamba keeping his eyes on Sogolon's brother.

Oulani's attention was on an eligible young woman in the front of the line.

The mansa raised his hand and the lines went quiet. "These two great hunters have saved our village and many lives." The people burst into cheers and applause.

Sogolon saw Sheka lean over and whisper into the mansa's ear.

"She is a witch and called the spirits. Our two best hunters died. Now these two skinny fools come and kill the beast," Sheka hissed into the mansa's ear. "I know her magic. I will protect you. I saved your daughter's son."

The mansa raised his hand again, but now his griot raised an iron spear with bells attached in a circle. He shook it to bring quiet.

"We will reward these two brave men with what they deserve." The mansa clapped his hands, and two men came forward, one going to Oulamba, the other Oulani. The brothers each received a small nugget of gold and several red heart-shaped kola nuts. The brothers bowed and thanked the men as the people cheered. Then they were presented with pieces of the heart to eat.

"Ahh... Wait and the best for last," exclaimed the mansa. The crowd hushed.

Oulamba looked at a tall, longed-limbed girl with a big smile and small firm breasts.

"I award these two great hunters... Sogolon Kedjou."

Oulani and Oulamba turned to look at the mansa who had no smile on his heavy face.

"Sheka," said Sogolon.

"Kill him, kill him," cried the angry voice in her head.

"No, run," said the mother voice.

Tears ran down Sogolon's face as she looked at her brother.

Oulamba looked back at Sogolon and saw her tears and a faraway look. He reached down, took her hand and began to notice the crowd's cheers had turned to laughter.

Chapter 3

Niani

Kon lay behind Sossuma with his hands on her shoulders; she was soft and wet. She knew he was close, and she quickened her pace as he pushed hard into her. He admired her soft brown skin as he peaked. Sossuma's breath was heavy and sweat ran down her back. He closed his eyes when the feeling of pleasure washed over him. Moments later, he opened his eyes and admired her curvy shape; being with child agreed with her. It was the first time in a week since his return that they had made love. The child had grown too big for him to be on top.

"I missed that," Kon said rubbing the back of her long neck.

"Then don't stay away so long," Sossuma said, turning her head and moving just enough away that he fell out of her. "We are not supposed to do this now anyway. It's taboo. It's bad for the baby."

Kon stretched his long powerful arms and yawned. "Yes, but we did; you know how it relaxes me. We did it sometimes when you carried Dankaran, and he is fine, but this is another reason I should marry again."

"You did have another wife, and she is with the spirits now. You are not ready to marry again. Will you stay here today?"

Kon thought of his very first wife, an older woman who was kind and sweet, but they produced no children that lived. "You know I must visit the people; they must see me."

"Make them come here inside the palace to see you. If they don't, tax them more. Teach them. After all, you are king and I queen." She turned to face him, her belly making the turn difficult. Holding his face in her hands she said, "They love and respect you, and they will do as you command."

He admired her swelling breasts and thick dark nipples, and his finger traced them. "But the people outside of Niani work hard and demand respect in return. Besides, it is how it's been done since my father's father. It's tradition, and there are good spirits in the tree."

"Tradition is important, but you can make new ones." She kissed him, and their full lips pressed together. As she pulled away she looked into his eyes for agreement.

"Maybe, but I will do what I feel is right." He thought about the hunter and his words. He got out of their bed and put on a pair of light white cotton pants. "I have to wash up; I am hearing people's complaints today."

She looked at him with her big brown eyes, frustrated. "Then you will not feel my favors till the baby comes. After all, it is tradition." She turned away from him, pulling on a sheet, which floated down, covering her long body. "And if you marry again too soon, she won't be as good as me. The signs are not right; you should wait."

Feeling frustrated, Kon left the bed chamber to a room where he washed. He put on clean clothes, and around his wrist placed a leather loop connected to an elephant hair brush to shoo flies away. He needed to find Doua, and he made his way out of the palace and headed for the courtyard. The smooth, brown mud walls shaded him. When he stepped out into the open, he squinted as the sun's rays hit his eyes. In the courtyard sat seven men from the seven largest villages, arguing. The council men sat on ox hides under several mid-sized trees, and these tree branches formed arches that delivered relief from the hot sun. The high, smooth, tan, mud-brick walls that surrounded the royal palace kept the men out of sight of the village.

The council men turned towards him and bowed, becoming quiet. He acknowledged them, and they returned to arguing.

"Ahh, sir," said the shortest man, stepping away from the group. He was a sorcerer. "I believe that you must heed the warning of the hunter. He is a seer. It is a sign, and the signs I read in the kola nuts agree with him." The little sorcerer always wore red.

The largest man of the council was tall and thick. He was from Sossuma's village. "Don't listen to this little man, ahh." He waved his hand and gestured as if he was waving away a fly. "You need to do as you have always done. The queen is all you need for now. Just look at her beauty, and she gives you children."

Doua walked around the corner to see Kon and the council. He shook his head in disgust. "You fight like old women," he said aloud.

Kon looked up to see Doua. "I need to see the blacksmith. Maybe he can help me with my puzzle." Kon looked at Doua shaking his head. "All the signs confuse me."

"Don't let them; have patience. Let it work itself out," said Doua as he put his hand on Kon's shoulder.

Kon had heard enough from the council and so requested that Doua join him on a ride. They took two light brown mares with jet black manes from the royal stables. Kon and Doua loved horses and often went on rides, racing any challenger.

The blacksmith's workshop was south of the city closer to the river. The river made it easier to bring the needed hardwood and ore to the smith, and he lived where he worked. Five mud huts with thatched roofs sat behind a great workshop. Mud brick forges with bellows glowed red and produced smoke. It was here he kept the secrets of the iron.

Once Kon and Doua got to the wide muddy river they raced towards the smith's. The hooves of Kon's horse splashed water and mud, causing him to slip a bit as Doua stayed to the dry red dirt. Doua's horse was a step faster, and he beat Kon to the forges. Doua turned and smiled while Kon furrowed his brow; he hated to lose. They tied their heavily-breathing horses to wood sticking out of the roof of a nearby hut.

"Ahh!" cried Kon as a sliver of wood pierced his finger as he tied up his mount. He tried to bite out the offending piece of wood but could not. The blind smith was sitting on several skins instructing a young apprentice.

"Nounfairi," acknowledged Kon as he approached the old man, before kneeling and hugging him. The old shirtless man hugged him back. The heat was intense in the open room with half a roof as the large forge glowed red. Nounfairi's workers stopped and bowed before the king.

"Kon, it has been a while. Doua, you are here; I can smell you," said Nounfairi with a laugh.

Doua laughed in return. "Burn your wrinkled old manhood off - if you can still find it," Doua said playfully.

"Sit, sit," Nounfairi said, shooing away his young apprentice. "Get some water," he said aloud. The two sweaty, muscled men working at the forge took the chance to remove their clothes and left to cool off by the river.

"I need advice, old friend. You know the secrets of the iron," Kon said leaning on the wall alongside Nounfairi as Doua sat on the opposite side of the old man. "Doua and I were out hunting and visiting the other villages when a hunter came out of the dark. He claimed that for the good of the kingdom I should marry again very soon--someone different than Sossuma. He could tell that I am not happy. This drought also seems to be connected to all of this. The river is low, and the streams are dry. Herdsmen, the Fulani, come sooner than usual. There is trouble all around Niani."

"Are you not happy?" exclaimed Nounfairi, wiping his head with a cloth.

"Sometimes. I have a king's life - can I be happy?" asked Kon, swatting at a fly from the side of his sweaty face with his elephant-hair brush.

"You can take another wife. That is not the issue. But finding the right one is. The drought will cause problems. The things certainly all seem to be connected."

"I want to do what is right for the kingdom while also keeping peace in my house. You know Sossuma - she is stubborn and jealous; she can be cold and distant, until it suits her. She has given me a son, and for that I forgive much. I also have not found anyone that interests me, but I feel the signs may be right."

"What does your council say?"

"Most are for it, and one is cocksure. He says, as the hunter did, that I should choose someone very different to balance the household."

"And what do you say, Doua, oh great griot?" Nounfairi reached out a shaky, wrinkled, and yet somehow heavy hand.

Doua reached out and took the shaky hand, the grip still strong from pounding iron. "I agree with change."

"You have your answer then. Find another wife soon! Make it one that will balance your house. Remember to tread lightly as you need your council." Nounfairi shook his head and wiped his brow again. "Now, let's get out of here; it is just too damn hot."

They took Nounfairi to the river to be with his students, and then Kon and Doua rode back to the palace. When they returned, the council was still debating. Female servants were putting out food and passing out water from a clay pot with a calabash. Kon and Doua washed the dust off their hands and joined them. The men grabbed fingers full of spicy goat and cous cous. There was still time before people would come to be heard.

Kon asked the men, "Have you agreed on anything?"

"Only that you have the prettiest servants of all the villages," said the councilman in red. Everyone laughed, and he waited for them to quieten once more to speak again. "It's a prophecy - a hunter in the night brings you a message to marry again, soon. You must not ignore signs, the voices of the ancestors." Three other council members now held a piece of red cloth to show solidarity with the short sorcerer.

"Kings must make decisions on clear, strong signs," the tall advisor said. "These are weak; they could even be a trick."

"The hunter was sure," said Doua. "He found us and read the shells."

Kon chewed a mouthful of crispy goat. He felt as if a force was pushing him. Swallowing the meat, he asked, "What does my council say? Who thinks the signs are strong?"

"Strong," agreed four men.

"No," said the two largest shirtless members from Sossuma's village. The other two men said they weren't sure, but to be safe it should not be ignored.

Kon shook his head. "The signs are strong for me." Like a bolt of lightning the solution struck him.

Doua noticed a sudden change in Kon as a strong smile broke across his dark face. Doua made eye contact with him and gave him a look of concern.

Kon rose. "Council, thank you for your words." He started to stride away, but then he stopped and turned to Doua. "I will meet you by the front gate and tell you my plan."

Doua stood still. He'd seen Kon like this before. Kon would be determined to carry out any plan on his mind.

Kon strode back into the palace and saw a young woman who was one of three who tended the queen. She saw her king and bowed. "Go find the queen and bring her to our bed chamber," he ordered.

The soft rays of the late afternoon sun brought the city back to life again with the hottest part of the day now over. Shopkeepers put out their slabs of brown and white salt, bolts of blue and brown cloth. Beaded and gold jewelry sat next to guinea hens in cages, and baskets of ginger, root and rice. Women balanced red clay pots of water on cushions on their heads as the smells of food and spices filled the air. A massive silk cotton tree, the largest for many a day's ride, stood outside the gate to the palace. Its reach shaded a large area, and its broad trunk was like a wall. Four people sitting side-by-side would fit in comfort. The grey-colored bark gave the tree a look of invincibility, and many spirits were said to inhabit this ancient tree.

Kon sat on a small, low, backless chair under the great tree, watching as people hurried about. His council sat on either side of him. "Dankaran!" he called to his son. "Come," he said, with outstretched arms.

Dankaran looked up with a dusty face and ran into his father's arms. He held several silk cotton seeds that were bursting with yellowish fibers.

Kon kissed the boy on the forehead and gave him a hug. Dirt smeared his lips from the boy's head, so with the back of his hand, he wiped his mouth. Kon laughed and looked into his son's face, which was so much like his mother's. He was a handsome boy of eight years. "Sit for a bit, and then you can go play. Give those seeds to your servant, and she will put them in your mattress. They will bring you good dreams."

Dankaran sat on the soft hide and crossed his legs. "What are we doing here?" It was his first time at an official meeting.

"I make myself available to the people in case they have any problems, and then I try to fix them. People must know who is in charge, and who they can come to."

"Can you always fix them?" asked Dankaran looking up at his father.

"Haaah!" laughed Kon with a big smile. "I wish that was so, but we will do our best."

Doua stood just in front of Kon and would filter those who'd speak to the king. "No, no!" he exclaimed to two men who came often in dispute, this time over several goats. "You must see the man with the red robe," he said moving them towards the short man. When Doua turned back towards the crowd, two men and a strange-looking woman stood before him. One of the men held the leg of a small antelope on his shoulder.

"Great griot, I felled a gazelle not far from here, and we come to give the king his portion of which he is owed," the oldest male of the group said. [6]

Doua was happy to see someone not with a complaint, but he couldn't help but look at this strange bent woman. "Yes, come see the king," he said. Slowly taking his gaze from the woman, he turned towards Kon. "King Fatta, these men were hunting not far from here and have brought you your royal share." Turning back to the ragtag group, "What are your names?"

Kon saw the bent woman and was puzzled by this strange vision.

"I am Oulamba," the elder man said as he bowed. "This is my brother, Oulani." Oulani bowed. "Our sister here is Sogolon, the healer." Sogolon was looking at the council but turned towards Kon when she heard her name. She attempted to bow, but only turned a little sideways. "My king, my king," she said twice.

Doua signaled for a slave who came forward to take the gazelle leg. That's when he noticed Sossuma was standing behind the great tree, watching.

"Where are you from?" Doua motioned for the party to sit on the soft hides brought to them by servants dressed in white.

"Oulani and I are from the Traore tribe, but hunting brought us to Do."

"Are you the two who killed the buffalo at Do?" asked Kon.

"Yes, sir," replied the brothers in unison. On their shirts, large tufts of hair from the beast were sown. They pointed to them.

"Excellent. You both are very brave and honest. It is good to have you here."

"Our sister provided us with a strong poison to fell the beast," said Oulamba.

"What is your story, Sogolon?" Kon asked quite interested.

"Lie. Don't tell him the truth. They won't want you here. They will mock you and be afraid of you," hissed the mother voice.

Sogolon paused. She could feel all eyes on her. She did want to run but took a deep breath. "I am from Do." She focused on Kon's deep brown eyes and handsome broad face. "I was a healer there."

"And your poison killed the buffalo; very good."

"And she has begun to heal my arm." Oulani raised his arm, showing the gash from his fall.

"Welcome, everyone!" exclaimed Kon. "I know well your mansa there in Do."

Covered in a long, dark-blue wrap, Sossuma stepped from around the silk-cotton tree. She seemed to glide over to Doua. She whispered in his ear. His eyes went wide, and he took a step back turning towards Kon.

"The queen has an announcement!" he proclaimed raising his hands. "The path is clear. These two hunters have brought us someone special. This woman will become the king's next wife." Sossuma turned towards Kon with a self-satisfied smile on her face. Shocked, the crowd and council went quiet.

Kon's eyes locked with Sossuma's.

Chapter 4

The Union of Two

Doua and Kon walked side by side around the outside of the palace.

"It was brilliant," said Doua shaking his head. "She did it in front of everyone; you can't go back now. You don't want to shame her and anger her family. Their family has too much influence. Her village grows the most crops. You need to keep the confidence of the council."

"When I gave her the choice to pick the next wife I thought there would be a search. I thought giving her some control would make her feel better, show her my trust. I try to make her happy, but it is impossible." Kon folded his arms, feeling a mixture of anger and betrayal. "I'm tired of playing games with her."

"You need to marry this girl, and who knows what will come of it," Doua said, wanting to sound positive. "This is why men have roles and women theirs. You should never mix them. You broke the rules, and now you pay."

"She is a bit strange," said Kon, making a face of concern.

"And a bit strange-looking," Doua added, breaking into a small laugh.

Kon could not help but also laugh. "That is not a lie, my friend. The smith said to find someone not as pretty as Sossuma. I expected plain, not, not this."

Doua and Kon walked around the palace yard till they came to the gate. "Goodnight, Doua. I will certainly dream about this day."

*****

Sogolon woke up in the palace, not able to comprehend what was going to happen. Things were happening so fast. She looked out the window in her new quarters, its brown clay walls were cool and the room well lit. The voices in her head were arguing.

"You have never been with a man," said the mother voice.

"It will be terrible. It will hurt. You must refuse," said the angry voice.

"How can I refuse? He is king and I am to be his wife. And the first time with him, I KNOW it will hurt, but I also want to know what it will be like," Sogolon said aloud.

Kon stood behind the door of Sogolon's room, listening to her talk. He knocked on the door but heard her say, "Quiet." He paused, knocked again, and then he heard, "Enter." He opened the door and strode in expecting to see others, but it was just her. He looked around, puzzled and left the door ajar.

"Sir," said Sogolon with a head bow.

"Please call me Kon. You are alone?"

"Yes, my kin-." Sogolon stopped in mid-sentence, "Kon."

"So, it is true. I hear you speak to those that can't be seen. You are visited by spirits?"

"This is true," Sogolon said. She noticed she felt calm in his presence; the voices were quiet. Her eyes traced his broad, strong shoulders and muscled body. His dark skin glowed.

"I hope they guide you well." Looking close at Sogolon he noticed her skin was smooth and dark, and she had a bright smile. Her bent body looked stiff, but her breasts full. He smiled at her wild and tangled hair. He felt relief when he looked into her bright eyes as they were full of life.

Sogolon looked at Kon and noticed he held the finger on his left hand. "Does your finger hurt?"

"I had a sliver of wood in it. I couldn't get it all out."

"Give me your hand," said Sogolon. Kon didn't hesitate and put his hand in hers. She pulled him towards the window to see his red swollen finger. "I will fix this." She moved over to a bag on the floor and brought it to the window. She pulled out a small knife and cut into his finger.

Kon winced as blood and pus oozed from the wound, but he felt relief as he saw a small piece of wood on the tip of her knife.

"Got it." She put down the knife and took some salve made from karite tree fruit. She spread it on his finger and wrapped a piece of linen around it. "Leave it on for a day or two and let the spirits work."

"Thank you. You are a good healer." He paused. "I hope." He smiled at her.

Sogolon looked but saw him smiling and broke into a grin. "You will find out."

Kon smiled and wiggled his fingers." The wedding will be on the first new moon."

"I look forward to it," said Sogolon.

"Refuse him," said the angry voice.

"No," said Sogolon.

"No," Kon inquired?

"I mean, yes," replied Sogolon.

"Good," said Kon.

"No," said the angry voice.

"Yes," said the mother voice.

"Quiet," said Sogolon.

"You want me to be quiet?" asked a confused Kon.

"Sorry my kin-, I mean Kon. The voices, the spirits, speak when they want."

Kon raised his eyebrows amused. "How many voices are there?"

"Two."

"Two... What do they sound like?"

"One is a woman, like a mother, an older voice. The other is angry, deep, urgent, a man's."

"Interesting." Kon was sincere. If they spoke to the right ancestors it could help him rule, and she could be very interesting to talk to.

Sogolon watched Kon's face for a sign of fear or disgust but saw sincerity. "You mean that don't you? I can feel it. When you look and act like I do, people can be afraid, or make fun."

"If you were born like you are now, how did you survive? You weren't killed after birth as is custom."

"My mother's sister hid me. They felt I was special. There was a long drought, and as I was born it began to rain. If my deformities were the price paid to bring the rain, my aunt felt I should live."

"Let's see if she made the right decision," he said with a smile. He bowed and went through the door with his eyes still on Sogolon.

*****

Sogolon had only to wait ten days before the wedding. Kon gave her Fanta, a servant girl, who attended to her needs.

Sogolon was amazed by Fanta's body: thin, almost no hips, tiny breasts yet her small bottom high and round. She was a woman.

"My mistress, have you married before? Have you known a man?" inquired Fanta.

"No, men make fun of me. I was a joke. Most often they asked me to heal them or make amulets and charms. The hunters wanted poison."

"That is good that you are a virgin. The king will be happy. Tomorrow you will be a virgin no more. I will get you something to eat. You're going to need your strength." She left for the kitchen.

"The king will be happy," said Sogolon shaking her head. "I'll be happy after tomorrow night."

*****

It was early morning of the wedding day, and Sogolon was in the house of the best hairdresser in Niani. The hairdresser started at first light, untangling and braiding the rat's nest that was her hair. Kon's aunt who had come with his sisters and other relatives for the wedding sat with her. Kon's two sisters teased her as was tradition.[7]

"No more going where you please, talking to just any man," said the eldest sister with a wry smile.[8]

"Say goodbye to being no one," the youngest sister added mischievously. "The boys will leave you alone."[9]

Sogolon's head was in the hairdresser's lap as the voices and the sisters tormented her. "The boys never bothered me," she admitted.

"You are not welcome here," said the angry voice. "From the beginning you were not welcome. They will make fun of you, taunt you."

"They may not be mean, but for sure it will be hard for you. Queen Sossuma chose you but won't speak to you. She looks at you with contempt," said the mother voice.

Sogolon felt dread and fear drain the strength from her body.

"Now, now, child; the girls are only doing as custom permits.

You must not fear." The aunt knelt down and placed a small dry wrinkled hand on Sogolon's cheek. She wiped away some tears. "Your new life will be wonderful. You will have children, you will live in the palace, and you will also be a queen." [10]

The hairdresser made Sogolon sit up, and she said, "Let's just shave it all off."

Women griots and poets stood outside the door of the hairdresser. They chanted Sogolon's name and poems of love and happiness. Rhythmic drums continued to beat through the day to call people to the celebration. Drums from near and far beat in response to announce their coming. [11]

Kon and his court were dressed in their finest clothes. They sat under the great silk cotton tree on soft cow hides over mats of fresh thatched palm. Doua stood, an iron spear in his hand. He sang a song reciting the names of the kings of the Mandinka. [12]

Each village sent a troupe of musicians and dancers for the ceremony.[13]They wore gold and copper jewelry with colored beads and silver bracelets. [14] Their faces and bodies painted with lines, dots and images, and there were many masks and costumes to bring good luck. Each troupe was trying to outdo the other, which made Kon smile as he sang and clapped along. Doua guided mansas and elders to him as they paid their respects and passed on congratulations.

Sossuma and Kon's brothers and sisters stood in a line handing out gifts of gold, grain, and clothes. [15] People all over Niani sang happy songs, danced and ate.

Once the sun began to sink low and the drums stopped, Kon went back to the palace to prepare for Sogolon. The wedding procession formed in front of where Kon's aunt was staying. Fanta was by her side all day helping to get her ready. The aunts and sisters along with Sossuma led her out of the house towards the palace. She wore a long black dress with green lines and patterns, and her head was adorned with a bright multicolored beaded headdress. Around her neck she wore a polished gold necklace, and down her back ran a long strand of yoroo beads with two cowrie shells on the end. Over the dress was a black robe with a hood that hid her face from sight. As she was led along she wondered what everyone thought.

"You look beautiful," said the mother voice.

"Best you've smelled in a while," said the angry voice.

"I know," said Sogolon with a little laugh. It was dark. Only when she passed someone with a torch could she see faces. Some were smiling, some skeptical, and some were laughing. She thought she saw Oulani and Oulamba, but she wasn't sure.

Behind Sogolon were Kon's relatives and a choir of young girls clapping and singing her new-bride song in their high voices. [16]

She starts a new life (clap, clap, clap)

We will have another queen (clap, clap, clap)

New children will be seen

The land will prosper (clap, clap, clap)

All hail the new queen!

The procession stopped outside the palace, and all grew quiet. Kon was sitting on his royal stool with Doua and the council behind him, and he now watched the doorway. Kon's sisters put their heads inside the door and smiled, and then they pulled them back out. They did it once more with large grins. On the third time they moved Sogolon through the door. [17] She walked over and sat next to Kon, Doua, the council, and other family members. The large altar loomed before them for the final ceremony, and the sacred wooden idol of a man and a woman sitting side by side sat atop it. The man wore the cap of a hunter; the woman had a baby on her back. The eldest villager, bent and frail, would perform the ceremony. His clothes hung on his thin frame.

The elder was surprised at how pretty Sogolon's face was when the hood was lifted. Her shaved head with the bright beads, her bright eyes, and her full lips brought a smile to his face. Kon and Sogolon stood in front of him as the room filled with the rich haunting sound of a balafon.

Kon was pleased - at last he was able to see Sogolon's almond shaped eyes and how soft and deep brown they were. Her lips were full and her cheek bones high.

The elder handed them broken kola nuts to eat. [18] Then he said the words, "Guide and protect one another. Make a shrine together to honor the space in which you live. Make the appropriate sacrifices to the spirits. Have many children and follow in the tradition of our people. Love one another."

Kon and Sogolon turned, knelt and bowed before the large idol.

When Kon and Sogolon rose, the crowd cheered as the new royal couple hugged.

Sossuma leaned over to her handmaiden. "She looks funny all bent. You can leave a boat in the river, but it won't become a crocodile." The maiden covered her mouth and laughed.

Everyone enjoyed the ceremony, and Kon and Sogolon greeted all well-wishers. They became separated, and Kon's sisters sneaked through the crowd. The sisters carried Sogolon away to the wedding bed, an upper room in the palace. [19]

"Your bride is being abducted," Doua pointed out to Kon. "It is time to find out what many have thought about. How do you feel?"

"A little excited." He paused, before adding, "And a little nervous."

"Life is full of mysteries, and you are about to uncover one." Doua shook his head.

"This will be interesting." Kon made his way through the crowd and left the party. He made his way upstairs to the chamber and stopped by the door not knowing what to expect. He felt the door on his palm. Part of it was smooth and part of it was rough. *It is like my new bride,* he thought as he traced the door with his fingers.

"What will you do?" asked the mother voice.

"I don't know. I'm not sure."

"Stop acting innocent. You want him. You desire him," said the angry voice.

"How could I not?" Sogolon smiled. "But I am ugly; look at my body. He may not desire me."

"Blow out the candles," said the mother voice. "Don't let him get a good look at you."

"He is not blind!" the angry voice said. "He will reject you."

"The candles, yes, the candles," exclaimed Sogolon. She blew out the beeswax candles except for one. She had taken off the robe but still had her wedding dress on.

Kon opened the door, and the room was dark except for the light of one flickering candle. He couldn't see much till his eyes adjusted. He saw an outline of Sogolon sitting on the mattress bed on the floor. He closed and bolted the door, then walked across the room feeling anxious. A strong breeze blew through the window blowing back the cloth window covers.

"You look beautiful. Tonight, I can see your face." Kon sat next to her in the dancing light. His eyes were adjusting, and he could see she was scared.

"Thank you," Sogolon said feeling embarrassed. She felt her face warm up and kept her high left shoulder turned away from him. She wanted to pull herself inwards until she disappeared altogether. She was not used to this kind of attention, and she could feel his energy, his eyes watching her.

"I have been so busy. I realize we have not spent much time together. I know you have never been with a man before."

42

"No… How did you know?"

"It's your first time. I will be gentle."

"So, next time you won't be gentle?"

"King's choice." He smiled.

"Good," she said. "Or maybe queen's." She became nervous and had made a joke. "Men never paid much attention to me. I just concentrated on the healing arts and taking care of my parents till they died."

"I understand. It's not easy being different," said Kon. He could still feel her nervousness, and he put his hand on her shoulder.

"I would like to blow out that candle," Sogolon said attempting to get up, but he held her there.

"I would like to leave it lit; don't be afraid," he reassured her.

"I would like to cover myself. You don't want to see me."

"Well, we need to see something." He laughed as he touched her neck. "I fear we are thinking too much." Kon then reached over and touched her chin, turning her head towards him. He turned his body to kiss her, and their lips met. At first, she didn't kiss him back, but then she began to. After a few minutes they stopped and hugged. Her breathing was fast. "Remember the servant girl Fanta attending you?"

"Yes, she is sweet. She said you are a very brave and good king."

"Well, she said you were very sweet also. I've had her watching you from the day after you fixed my finger. I bumped into one of Sossuma's handmaidens. Fanta has kept them away."

"I am glad you did that." She paused, "The queen does not like me much, I can tell. Yet, she chose me. Why did she try and embarrass you with me?"

"You are very perceptive. I needed to take another wife, and she is very jealous. I figured if she had an active choice in the matter it would make her feel better. But, as you see, she likes to always have the upper hand."

"I understand if you leave then." Sogolon pulled back.

The angry voice hissed, "See, you were brought here to be made fun of. You must leave."

"Maybe you should leave," said the mother voice. "It will be dangerous for you. He already has a son by the queen. You must refuse him. You must leave."

Sogolon's body tensed up. She stood and began to pace in the room.

"She is your first wife, and you have a son, an heir. You can never choose me, "she said to Kon.

"Besides your body will disgust him," said the angry voice.

"He will humiliate you to prove his love to the queen. Run, child. Leave this place," urged the mother voice.

"I must leave. It isn't safe for me here, and when you see my body you will not want me," Sogolon said and headed towards the door.

Kon was surprised by her sudden reaction. "Wait," he said and got up, grabbing her by the arm.

"He will hurt you, child. RUN!" shouted the mother voice.

Sogolon tried to pull away, but he was too strong. "No, it is not safe here!" she yelled.

"STOP, STOP!" he shouted, then lowered his voice as he let go of her arm. "Stop. Please stop." He put his hands in the air. "You have my protection. I want you here. The spirits have brought you here."

"But they are telling me to leave."

"That maybe so, but we are so often tested. You must trust me." He took a step back from her and put his hand on hers. "No, I am not embarrassed by you. Tonight will be ours and you are welcome here. Let's give Sossuma something to talk about." He laughed. "I need you to balance this household against her suspicion and anger. Be the sweet, gentle person that you seem to be."

She was happy to hear those words, but the thought of Sossuma still frightened her. She took a deep breath.

"Come, sit on the bed. Relax," said Kon.

Sogolon went back to the bed and sat on the edge. Kon left the room, came back with some water and sat behind her. She drank it and felt the tension leaving her body. "I am sorry for how I acted. Sometimes, I can't help myself."

"It's okay," Kon said as he pulled her into him. "Just relax. We have all night."

She felt her back against his chest and she closed her eyes. They were quiet for a while. She felt his chest rise and fall.

After a bit, Kon broke the silence. "You know what relaxes me, is when I take a horse and ride along the river. I watch water birds fishing as long pointed boats move through the water; fish jumping as crocodiles sun themselves. But hunting, that truly makes me feel at peace."

She listened to his story and felt her tense back muscles relax. "I love walking through the bush collecting plants for healing or charm making. It always relaxes me, and making amulets for the children of the village while they play. I love to hear them laugh."

"Will you make one for me, to ensure good hunting?"

"Yes, of course, I will."

"You feel better now?"

45

"Yes, I will stay," she agreed.

"Good, then it is settled. I want you to know this is your home now." Kon felt her body relax as he sat her up, and she turned to face him. He leaned in and kissed her. She kissed him back, and he felt her sudden urgency.

Sogolon felt relief and warmth spread through her body. The feeling of being wanted was overwhelming, and she wanted to climb into his lap. She took his hand, put it on her breast and kissed him hard.

Kon was surprised when she took his hand. He felt her small, dark nipple respond to his touch. He pulled close to her and swung her legs onto the bed. The tension between them rose, and he felt himself grow. His worry about her body slipped away. He took her hand and guided it to him. They sank down onto the bed in unison.

Sogolon's head was spinning and between her legs grew wet. He touched her, and his hardness in her hand was exciting. It was as if she were floating. Her fears disappeared, and even the voices were quiet.

*****

When she woke, Kon had gone, and she gave a great stretch and yawn.

"That wasn't so bad," said the mother voice.

"No, it didn't hurt too much. The second time it felt even better," said Sogolon, pleased with herself.

Kon came into the room first, followed by Fanta carrying eggs, rice and some fish on a large plate. The smell of the food filled the room, and Sogolon realized how hungry she was.

He smiled at her. "Good morning."

"Yes, it is," she replied.

Chapter 5

The Messenger of Death and War

"You look well today, my queen," said Fanta. "I am glad the king chose me to take care of you."

"Me, too," said Sogolon, looking at Fanta who wore a tight blue wrap-around dress and matching head scarf.

"Your baby is beginning to show," Fanta said as they walked through the market.

It was early morning, and the sellers were putting out their goods on cloth or reed mats in the rickety stalls. Thin square slabs of salt were being stacked, and fresh brown and grey catfish lay in shallow baskets. Bright white rice, brown oval sorghum, and tan balls of millet stood mounded in tall clay jars, and cotton cloth of yellow, red and green were being folded and arranged.

"Let's get some fish," said Sogolon. They went to the fisherman they liked the most. Today they found him at the end of a row, with no stall, just baskets. The man was short with broad shoulders, a narrow face, and kind eyes. Fanta called to the fisherman.

He was barefoot and naked from the waist up--taking fish from a tall woven basket when he heard the new queen and her servant call to him. "Morning, my queen." He paused, wiping fish slime off his hands with a dirty rag. "Fanta, you must love my fish; you keep coming back to me."

"Don't try and sweet talk us; don't raise your price, fisherman," Fanta said with a finger in the air.

"Your fish are usually the fattest," replied Sogolon. "For the king's daughters' celebration your fish were the best. Who are your people?"

"I am Borzo." The fisherman smiled. The second queen had become known for her kindness and her appearance was no

47

longer an issue for most. "Fanta, why don't you trust me? I would not cheat you."

"Hmm," said Fanta hands on her waist. "I hear your prices rise when the queen comes to market."

"No, no, these are my fattest fish." He held up one in each hand. Sogolon and Fanta inspected the plump, smooth brown-skinned fish. The fish's mouths were showing just the hint of a smile. Their whiskers hung limp until one of them took a gulp of air. The women pulled back and laughed.

"He likes you; he wants to kiss you, Fanta," the fisherman said with a smile.

Fanta gave him a cross look.

"Yes, those will do fine," said Sogolon. "Fanta, his people are expert fishermen."

Fanta smelled each one before sliding them into a straw basket. She gave the fisherman four kola nuts.

"Thank you." He gave a slight bow to Sogolon, who smiled in return. He smiled at Fanta, who just ignored him with a quick head turn.

Several stalls away at the end of the market, Sossuma was with two of her handmaidens and was kept hidden by a stand of trees. They could hear Sogolon talking.

"She struts around here like a water bird," whispered one of the maidens.

"Her back looks like the neck of an egret," Sossuma said.

Her youngest maiden started to laugh but caught herself.

"She is too lame to strut. Look at her, so clumsy," Sossuma said with contempt.

"So many people say how kind she is," said the other older

maiden.

"She is pretending to be nice because she frightens people. She doesn't want them to run away. I know women; believe me. She wants to be first wife. If she has a child she will want him to rule, but my Dankaran is the rightful heir." Sossuma stepped out from her place to watch Sogolon and Fanta walk away.

Fanta noticed Sogolon looking worried as they walked back to the palace. "I don't think the sun is too high; the spirits aren't roaming yet."

"That is not it; I am worried about Kon fighting. He has been gone a long time."

"Yes, but the king has gone to war before. He has the blood of the lion in him. He will be fine," said Fanta with confidence.

"Kon said there is trouble in the kingdom of Ghana. There has been a lot of unrest with tribes raiding caravans by men who cover their face. Fulani people coming when they don't usually. Muslims who say we don't worship right, that we have too many gods. He fears that this trouble may spread. But who he says is the most dangerous is the Sosso tribe."

"There is always trouble somewhere. I go about my business, and my business is to take care of you and your child. Let the kings, the warriors, and the elders fix those things."

"I know you are right, but I worry," Sogolon said as they made their way back to the palace.

*****

Sossuma left the market place, walking past several round thatched huts to a string of camels. A long rope hung from the camels' halters and ended tied to a stake in the ground. There a man with a white turban and black robes worked on a camel saddle.

Sossuma's maidens hung back while she approached the man.

"So, you got my message?" She asked of the sorcerer who often traveled to Niani by caravan.

"Yes, it will be quick, and no one will be the wiser," the sorcerer said with confidence. He fixed his white cotton turban. "I've not failed you before."

"That is true," replied Sossuma. "Please, as soon as possible."

The sorcerer stood up, fixing his black pullover outfit. "Payment after." He nodded.

"Of course." Sossuma nodded back.

"She lives in a house on the end corner of the palace away from the gate."

"Good, that will do."

"Then you have much work to do." Sossuma turned and walked away as her blue dress and white robes blew in the dry morning breeze. She walked back past the round houses with thatched roofs into the market place. Wearing orange and yellow dresses, her two handmaidens followed. "We must get back to feed Nama," Sossuma said. "I'm leaking."

The sorcerer watched Sossuma disappear between the huts, and then he turned his head to shield his eyes from the blowing dirt. He took a step but felt his sandal become loose. He checked the sandal on his right foot and thought he should get a new pair when he heard the sound of hooves. He looked up to see the king and a dozen riders coming fast. They galloped down the dusty street. He felt the ground shake and heard the sound of leather and metal in motion as they thundered by. He lost sight of them when they went through the open iron gate into the palace.

Kon and the riders all wore leather vests over dark-brown mud cloth, that had a zig-zag pattern of black and white lines. While on their heads they wore tight leather helmets with metal rings sewn into them. Their small saddles creaked as the men dismounted in the courtyard. They were the heaviest armed cavalry he'd seen this far south of the Maghreb.

Sogolon was washing herself in her house in the palace courtyard when she heard a commotion. Fanta was helping but stopped and removed the small wooden door to see the king in the courtyard.

"He's back. The king is back," Fanta said in excitement.

Sogolon began to fumble, attempting to dry herself and wrap her body in an orange and yellow dress. Fanta helped get the dress on her under one arm and then over the hump. Sogolon's hair had grown back, so Fanta pulled her braids up and wrapped them together with a piece of cloth. Now they were ready to see Kon.

Red dust hung in air as three young servant boys in shorts gathered the horses to bring them back to the stables. Kon and Doua stood in the center of twelve men. They shook hands and hugged. One by one the men left to go back to their nearby farms as people from the village began to come through the gate.

Sogolon watched the men say goodbye as Fanta followed behind her.

"They are the king's guard. He chose them himself. They are his most loyal men and protect him when he goes to war," Fanta explained.

As the dust cleared, Sogolon could see Sossuma standing by the gate opposite to Kon. She stood wondering what she would do.

Sossuma stood with her maidens behind her as the king's guard acknowledged her when they walked by tired and dirty. She bowed and smiled back, then saw Kon and noticed Sogolon on the other side of him. She looked at him and out stretched her arms.

Sogolon looked at Kon and put out a hand.

Kon realized his position and looked at Doua. "Three months

we were in battle and this is the most dangerous situation I have been in."

Doua smiled, "But you were shot with an arrow."

"Yes, like I said, most dangerous."

Doua laughed and put his hand over his mouth.

Kon stood still, then spread his arms each one pointing at a wife. With his hands he motioned for them to come. He gave each a smile and noticed Sogolon started towards him first with her awkward gait. He then turned towards Sossuma, who had a smile on her face that attempted to hide her aggravation.

As Sogolon approached Kon she hesitated and let Sossuma get to him first, as she was first wife.

He hugged them both and gave each a kiss.

"I am glad you are back safe," said Sogolon, putting her hands together and touching her fingertips to her chin. Looking at his face, his eyes showed a deep tiredness. Something was wrong.

Sossuma held his hand. "I knew you would come back safe. You must see Nana. She has grown so much."

"What happened out there?" Sogolon looked at him puzzled.

Sossuma got angry at Sogolon's question. "You look like my servant in that dress. Don't question him." This low-born fat woman interfering, Sossuma wanted to say, but stopped herself. In an instant it hit her. She wasn't fat; she was with child. She spent most of her days ignoring her, so she hadn't noticed.

Sogolon and Kon looked at Sossuma's maidens dressed in orange and yellow like her. Sogolon didn't know what to say; she was surprised by the attack. Not wanting a fight on his return, Kon spoke: "I was hit by an arrow, but I am healing well."

"I should take a look at it," Sogolon said, concerned.

"I suppose you should. I have things for you both." Kon paused and looked at Sogolon. Her dress was tight in the belly, her breasts were fuller, and Sossuma was angrier than usual. "Are you with child?"

"Yes." She smiled.

Sossuma's heart sank as her fears were confirmed.

Kon hugged Sogolon, and then his lips pressed against her forehead and lingered.

Sogolon felt his lips and smelled leather, dust and sweat on him.

After the kiss he turned to Sossuma, "Isn't it wonderful?"

"Yes... wonderful," she said without emotion.

"We must celebrate; I will have three children soon. I have presents for you both."

"The king, the king has returned." Voices of the villagers began to be heard as more people came to the gate. They began to clap and sing.

> The King is back
>
> We are safe
>
> It's a great day
>
> The King is back
>
> We are safe
>
> Today is a great day

Kon put his arm around Sogolon and they made their way to the palace. The people bowed and knelt, and he waded into them. Some of the women began to cry in happiness.

Kon and his entourage made it into the palace, but only after the people were addressed.

In the main hall, servants helped Kon off with his dusty helmet and battle-scarred leather vest. He winced taking off his shirt, and on his left side a healing wound was visible.

"How?" Sossuma asked with concern.

"We were ambushed in camp," Doua said with anger. "They slipped past our guards."

"I didn't even feel it at first." Kon laughed. "Even funnier is I was about to put on my vest."

Sogolon inspected the wound. It didn't smell and was closed nicely. "This is good, but don't reach or pick up anything heavy. You don't want to tear it open."

Sossuma was glad to hear that Kon was alright, but not happy that Sogolon had this knowledge that she did not possess herself. She wore a jealous smile and hoped the man she hired would succeed and do it soon. If he succeeded, she would be getting two for the price of one.

The next morning, Fanta came early to cook breakfast for Sogolon. The air was still cool and the sun beginning to rise as she knelt in the dirt by the hut. She lit a fire using some dry grass to help the wood to burn. Blowing on the flames, the larger sticks began to catch. She walked through the garden checking the ground she had prepared and wondered what plants her mistress wanted to grow. She turned and saw the fire wasn't catching and went to fan the flames.

The sorcerer, now wearing a black turban, had noticed the guards by the gate did not move, and the street was empty. He would drop three black mambas over the wall near the house - their black mouths delivered a bite of instant death. He also had a dozen death stalker scorpions. The snakes would seek the hut to live, and the scorpions he would throw on the roof near the opening on top. The bag was small and the color of the grass roof. These beasts were common to the area, so no one would question what happened. He could see the top of her hut above the wall, and a tree was next to it. He grabbed the lowest branch and was able to pull himself into the tree. The bags were tripled so he would not fall prey to an accidental bite. Two branches up and into the leaves, he was near the top of the brown wall. He saw a woman by a fire. Her back was to him as he untied the bag with caution, leaned over and the snakes dropped to the ground.

Fanta was blowing on the flames when she heard a small thump. Turning around she saw three black shapes writhing on the ground. She took several steps forward and felt as though something squeezed her heart. She gasped and took two steps back. What she saw next both amazed and frightened her.

Perched in the tree above Sogolon's house with the sun just coming over the horizon, the large desert eagle owl knew food was still around. Its large orange-yellow eyes darted back and forth looking for movement.

Fanta watched a large owl pounce on two of the black snakes. The owl's head disappeared for a moment. Then with several mighty flaps of its wings it rose off the ground, and it all happened with almost no sound. The owl was a terrible sign, but it just saved her life.

The sorcerer was untying the scorpion bag and couldn't believe his eyes as he watched this messenger of death and war ruin his plans. He saw the young woman run to the side of the hut. Not wanting to be seen, he stepped down, and his sandal broke.

Fanta watched the owl propel itself into the air, and it snapped her into action. Running to the side of the hut she picked up a digging tool. Within a few steps, Fanta was close to the third snake that had not moved from the wall until the owl left. The mamba rose up as high as it could and hissed before lunging at her. Fanta side-stepped the bite and swung the tool, hitting the snake, and sending it into the wall of the hut. The powerful snake coiled and lunged at her again but bit the tool. In a hacking motion, Fanta chopped it to pieces.

The sorcerer felt himself falling, and his breath left his body in a rush when he hit the earth. The bag of scorpions lay open on the ground. For several moments he couldn't breathe. A sharp pain came from his shoulder. Now his breath was coming back in gasps. He realized the scorpions were lose and needed to move. He got to his feet feeling angry. He looked down to see the scorpions scattering in every direction. One was on his foot, and he kicked it sending it into the air. In an instant he felt a sharp pain in his heel. His foot felt on fire, and that fire began to move up his leg.

Later that morning, Fanta was showing Kon, Sogolon and Doua what had happened.

"I can't believe the owl is still here." Doua pointed at it in the tall tree. "They are very shy." He wondered if this was bad magic at work - it was confusing this messenger of death and war.

"If any of us were bitten by this snake there is nothing I could have done to save us," Sogolon said with the snake head in her hands.

Kon turned to Doua. "Have some men check the wall for openings, so no more snakes can get in."

Sossuma was standing behind everyone observing with her arms folded. She turned and went back into the palace. "Go find the sorcerer," she said to her youngest handmaiden. The maiden bowed and scurried off, and Sossuma went back to her room and lay on the bed, feeling defeated.

"Mistress, you worry too much. You are beautiful, your family is powerful, and your son will be king," said the older of her young handmaidens.

Sossuma propped herself up on her elbows. "Seers, hunters and his advisors are telling the king nonsense. They are misreading the signs. Dankaran may be cheated out of what is rightfully his."

The maiden was sorry now that she said anything and looked at her small feet. She admired the bright copper ring she wore on a toe of her right foot.

"It is my responsibility as a queen and a mother to make sure Dankaran is king, and what will be best for the people. Not the half-royal child of some deformed Buffalo Woman. Now go find the sorcerer."

"But you sent--"

Sossuma cut her off in mid-sentence. "Ahh, go make me some Jala tea." She dismissed the maiden with a turn of her head, a flick of her fingers and sucking her teeth. She watched the maiden leave. "Stupid girl," she said, lying back down. She scratched at her scalp under her blue wrap. "Let this child be born," she said. [20]

*****

As the moons passed, Sogolon was less able to move as her child grew. The weight on her bent spine caused her pain, and Fanta barely left her side. Kon gave Fanta a servant to make things easier, but Sogolon's time was now near, and as she squatted and leaned against a wall in her hut the muscles in her back ached. Kon was called. He knelt next to her.

"Do you think the child will be like me?" Sogolon said to Kon.

"Have big eyes and talks to spirits? Definitely." Kon laughed.

"No, deformed," she said, a little annoyed. "I am scared for our child and for me. Can I give birth?"

"I have all the best midwives from Niani and the surrounding villages here tonight. [21] Don't worry; you will be fine." He lied but did it with a big smile.

"You don't think those nights we made love the past few months could have hurt something?"

"No," he lied again. "You are the healer; I thought you would know." Now he felt guilty.

Sogolon shook her head and squeezed Kon's hand. A muscle in her back twisted in a knot, and she let out a small moan.

Kon noticed that far-away look in her eyes. The firelight in the room flickered, casting shadows as the sun outside sank below the horizon.

"It's time you left," said the eldest midwife to Kon as she entered the hut. "It's our time now; no room for men, even kings. This is a battle made for women."

Kon laughed as he rose from Sogolon's side. "How can someone so sour bring so much life into this world?"

"Ahh, you weren't so funny when you tried to come out ass-first from your mother! And when you had your first son you were sweating as a man too close to the fire."

Kon laughed again. "Yes, yes, I know, and you never let me forget." He smiled at the old woman and touched her drooping face. He wondered how old she was. Her bottom eyelids drooped, showing red. The lines extending from the corners of her eyes like leafless branches of a tree made her seem eternal.

She touched his face with a still, steady hand. "Now go." She smiled, took his hand and kissed it.

"She is going to be alright?" asked Kon.

"I don't know. I've never delivered a baby with the mother like this before.

"Do your best," said Kon.

"I always do."

Doua stood just outside the doorway. "What did the midwives think?"

Kon came out of the hut. "They weren't sure," Kon answered as he shrugged his shoulders. "I hate this feeling of helplessness."

"It's the will of the spirits I'm afraid. We must trust in them," Doua said, putting his hand on Kon's shoulder.

"As the Imam at the mosque would say: It is written."

Doua and Kon turned around to see Abdul-Azeez, the Muslim man Kon had Doua hire to keep account of his gold, fonio, rice and herds.

"Our destiny is written by Allah, the most high."

"The most high?" asked Kon.

Like your Spirits or Nyama," explained Azeez.

"Which is in everything," Doua replied.

"Yes," Azeez acknowledged. "My king, there is plenty of food for the celebration of the birth."

"Excellent," said Kon.

"I was purchasing goats from some locals. I came by to tell you that we are ready."

"Very good. If all goes well we will have a great celebration." Kon looked back at the hut.

The young midwife with the bright face, big eyes and braids stuck her head out of the hut. She said, "You men can go into the palace. We will get you when it is time."

The three men, led by Kon, turned and walked into the palace.

"What you said earlier about it being written... do you think things are meant to be?" asked Doua.

"Nothing will happen to us except what Allah has decreed for us. He is our protector, and on Allah let the believers put their trust. That is a passage from my holy book." Azeez took a handful of rice and fish that servants were putting out.

"The Mande people - our clans - believe that one must read the signs and act. If one misses their chances then one can fail, but if one moves too fast or tries too hard they may be consumed by their desires." Doua took a drink from the calabash and then took some rice with peppers.

"There is much to learn between our ways," said Kon.

"True, the city has its places for everyone now. The blacksmiths, the leather makers, the fisherman, the sellers, the Dyula," explained Doua. "They all have their part of the city, and now there is even a mosque."

The men ate and talked on for a while. Rumbles of thunder rolled in the distance, and the men all looked at each other.

"This is good. The birth and rain, together," said Kon.

They fell asleep on their mats to the sound of the storm.

"King Kon, you must come."

Groggy from sleep, Kon wiped his eyes, and the three men sat up. "What is it? How are the child and the queen?"

A mid-wife paused, "My king, you have a son."

"How is his back?" asked Kon.

Chapter 6

Blood of the Lion and the Buffalo

"I hope this is the last celebration for a while," Azeez said to Kon and Doua. "We had just recovered from your daughter Nana's naming celebration."

They stood under the silk cotton tree looking across the street. They watched ten women in pairs of two using long, smooth, dark, wooden pestles pounding rice into flour in wooden mortars. Up the street muscular oxen and black and white goats were being sacrificed by elders.[22]

During the celebration, Kon, Sossuma, Doua and his family made their way to Sogolon's hut. Men and women poets, griots, and singers followed the royal procession.

Sossuma's mood was sullen, but she did the best she could while paying attention to Nana in her arms.

"I hear his back is straight," said a council member from her village to Sossuma.

"Yes," she replied without emotion, watching Sogolon.

Sogolon and Fanta stood outside the hut. Fanta held the boy child.

Doua turned to the crowd and said, "This child has the blood of the lion and buffalo. His name is Sundjata. Tell all that a new king has been born." [23]

Sossuma cringed when she heard those words.

The griots began to recite his name. Singers sang

> Blood of the lion
>
> Blood of the buffalo
>
> The new king will rule the land

Sogolon looked around at the crowd and couldn't believe how her life had changed

"You have come far," said the mother voice. "Your son will be king one day."

"No one will accept him. Queen Sossuma will hate you even more. She will act like your brother and turn people against you. You can't stay here," said the angry voice.

Sogolon looked around at the happy faces and saw Sossuma staring at her. Their eyes met, and Sossuma looked at her without emotion. She wondered how such a beautiful face could be so cold. Sossuma turned away towards the palace, and Sogolon felt a shiver filter down her curved spine.

"That woman is going to kill you," said the angry voice.

"She is scary; we need to watch her. She means you harm," agreed the mother voice.

"I won't let her harm my son or me," Sogolon said aloud.

"Whom, my queen?" asked Fanta. She turned to see that faraway look in Sogolon's eyes. "Come, you look tired."

Azeez had been looking at Sogolon and noticed the exchange of looks between her and Sossuma.

Doua had also been watching and noticed the reaction of Azeez to the scene. His eyes met those of Azeez.

Azeez acknowledged Doua and made his way to him. The two men walked off from the crowd.

"Tell me what you just saw?" Doua asked Azeez.

"I see a struggle between two very important women. One protecting what she has, and one up and coming," said Azeez.

"You are brave to speak your mind so clear."

"I know that you are King Fatta's man no matter what."

"You are very observant," Doua said, impressed. "Things have been changing all around Niani, and we need to stay aware of what's going on. Remember, if we are not stable here at home we could lose everything."

"Agreed, that is why I am in your employ. I heard about King Fatta, and I have observed him for a while now. All that they say is true."

"So, even though in your eyes he is a pagan, you don't mind working for him? Will you stay loyal to him if, say, a Muslim leader wages war against us?"

"My allegiances are to the man who is my employer." Azeez paused. "If I felt the king was bad or a cruel man I would leave his employ."

"That is good to hear," said Doua as he shook his head in approval. "Have you ever been employed by a pagan before?"

"No, but I have done business with Jews and Christians. They are not pagans, still many would not approve. I have seen evil things done by all types of people."

"This child is very important, and we must watch him." Doua looked into Azeez's eyes till he knew he understood.

"I'm sure we won't be the only ones watching him." Azeez smiled.

"Correct," Doua said. "Now, I must meet your uncle. I would like to do more business with him."

"You will like him. He is man of many talents." Azeez and Doua walked back towards the celebrating crowds. "He will be in town soon."

*****

And watched Sundjata was, as everyone took great care in overseeing his development. No child in all of Niani had more eyes upon him. For that first full growing season with the aid of

63

Fanta, Sogolon was a dutiful mother. Kon visited often as did the wives of Azeez and Doua, as well as Queen Sossuma's handmaidens.

"He moves fast," Fanta said smiling as Sundjata crawled around exploring their hut.

"He has lots of energy and a great appetite. I am surprised I have any breasts left," Sogolon said with a laugh, her hands on her chest.

Fanta laughed and looked at her small breasts, "I am glad I don't have to feed him. You certainly have breasts to feed a king."

"Yours are good for a fisherman's son." Sogolon poked her.

Fanta made a face. "Ahh, don't say that." She was embarrassed. "He does not even like me."

Sogolon loved joking with the oft-serious Fanta. "He does. Very much. You should entertain him; he seems like a good man."

"I am busy with you and Sundjata. I can't."

"You can do it. I won't mind, and Sundjata is getting easier to take care of."

"We shall see. I will check the garden." Fanta went out of the hut.

*****

The days of a full growing season passed, and Sundjata kept crawling and spoke little. He was no longer at Sogolon's breast, but his appetite was fierce.

"We need to get some extra fish today. Kon is eating with us tonight," said Sogolon.

"Okay, we need to get six then; the king has a big appetite." Fanta carried Sundjata on her back as they made their way

64

through the market.

They found their fisherman as usual at the end of the market. Fanta put Sundjata down, and Sogolon watched him crawl on the ground around her feet.

"My queen... Fanta," said the fisherman. He bowed at Sogolon and gave a long look at Fanta.

Fanta looked back remembering two nights ago floating down the river in one of his boats as the sun went down. They made love with the boat tucked into the reeds on the bend of the river away from prying eyes. After they finished, mosquitos forced them from their spot. The memory started the bite on her right arm to itch, and she began to scratch.

The fisherman smiled watching Fanta scratch her arm, and the bites on his shoulder began to itch. He remembered the softness of her small body and the wet warm snugness that greeted him when he entered her. They stood there smiling, scratching in silence.

Sogolon watched Fanta and the fisherman and realized the cause of Fanta's good mood these past two days.

"Dog, dog, dog," Sundjata said as he crawled towards a skinny, light-brown dog with a black muzzle, lying in the dirt. Sundjata loved playing with the dogs at the palace.

Sogolon heard Sundjata and turned to see him close to a skinny dirty dog. She turned almost tripping. "Sundjata," Sogolon moved towards him.

The dog heard a disturbance and looked up to see a small animal heading towards him. He lifted his black lip showing pink gums and gave a long slow growl.

Sogolon heard the growl, and saw the dog show his teeth. She quickened her pace.

Determined, Sundjata crawled faster and squealed with

delight. The dog was now standing, head down, hair up.

Fanta heard Sogolon and Sundjata and turned to see the trouble. She looked down and found a rock, snatching it from the dirt. Stepping sideways to avoid Sogolon, she threw the rock at the dog.

Sogolon reached for Sundjata, and her toes caught a depression in the dirt.

The rock hit the dog square in the side, making it yelp and jump sideways before it ran off.

Sundjata reached for the dog when his world went dark and his face slammed into the dirt. Pain in his back was intense.

"No!" Fanta yelled. Watching Sogolon fall on top of Sundjata, she rushed to their side. She grabbed Sogolon and flipped her over. Sundjata lay there, mouth wide open, and Fanta held her breath. Then a piercing scream came from his mouth.

Light returned to Sundjata's world - the pain was so strong he tried to scream, but nothing came at first. He took a deep breath and screamed.

The fisherman yelled, "Don't move him; leave him." He picked up a reed mat and brought it over.

Sogolon lay on her back, tears in her eyes, panic gripping her body. She raised herself up, relieved to hear his cry.

"You could have killed your son. You have hurt your son. You are a bad mother!" yelled the angry voice.

"You must be careful. You must be careful!" yelled the mother voice.

"Gently put him on the mat," said the fisherman. "Don't roll him over yet." Fanta helped lift Sundjata as Sogolon got to her feet, tears in her eyes.

"Is he alright?" Sogolon said, fear in her voice.

*****

The days and nights went by after the accident, and healers tried to help Sundjata. They chanted, sprayed water and palm wine from them mouths, and blew smoke on him. They asked the ancestors to intervene in their plight. Sossuma reveled in the constant bad news. Back at the palace in Sogolon's house, Kon paced with his arms wrapped around his chest. "How many full moons has it been since the accident?"

"Six," said Fanta.

"And still he does not walk?" asked Doua.

"No," Fanta said looking down at the floor.

"Your fault, your fault," said the angry voice. "You should go; you should go and never come back. The boy is ruined."

Sogolon sat in the corner immobile with a blank stare. Her face wet from tears.

"You did a bad thing, but you should not leave," said the mother voice. "You should be still. Be still."

Sogolon listened to the voices, frozen, not feeling anything anymore. Her eyes were full and tears spilled down her face.

Kon could feel his anger building. "Sogolon, you are a healer; you must do something."

Sogolon stared without a word. She listened to the voices, trying to feel, not able to answer Kon, her muscles locked in place.

"She has gotten worse. She says less and less." Fanta looked at Sogolon and wanted to yell at her to get up, but she knew that would not work. She recognized the look on her face and knew she would not respond. She hoped Sogolon would not wet herself. She could feel the anger building in Kon.

"So, she hasn't been able to try anything on the boy?" asked Doua.

"No, but in the beginning she did. Day after day, but nothing has worked. I still rub shea butter and ntoro on his back, but it is still sore to touch. He has drunk roselle, jala and kolebe. We have sacrificed hens, goats, even a bull."

"Yes, the bull was big," said Doua. "I watched it done."

They all looked at Sundjata who was crawling again, but he dragged his legs using his arms to move, a charm made of white string around his waist. Seven knots were tied into the string, and each knot had red, white and black strings attached to them.

"That charm he wears now is from the best healer in a village not far from here." Fanta wore a stern look on her face. She was frustrated by the whole situation. She was getting angry at Sogolon for being still and Kon for getting angry at what was an accident.

Doua sensed Kon's frustration. "Come, we have business to attend to. We need to think about strengthening alliances remember."

"Ahhh," said Kon frustrated as they walked out of the house. "The prophecy may have been wrong. I may have done something wrong." He thought about the taboo he broke, of making love to Sogolon and Sossuma while they carried his children. *Had he angered the ancestors? Is Sundjata paying his price?* He tried to push those thoughts out of his mind.

"Maybe, maybe," Doua said. "It all won't matter if we don't check the power of Sumaguru. I know what you are going to say next, but you are wrong. The spirits don't favor him."

Kon managed a smile for a moment and marveled how Doua often knew what he was thinking. "Are you sure?"

"Yes... I am very sure. It's your presence that will keep the people with us; they trust you. We need to go meet Azeez and his uncle. They say they have found out some interesting things. You are impatient, my friend. Things don't grow overnight. All things must grow. Trees come from seeds; even an elephant starts small. Be patient."

"I finally get to meet his uncle."

Kon and Doua packed for several days and were met at the palace gates by a rider sent from Azeez with two fresh horses.

The rider was a small and skinny young man.

Kon's mood was sullen, and the look of the skinny man angered him. He snatched the reins from his hands. "When was the last time you ate? I've seen hens bigger than you."

The rider looked at Kon and was about to answer back, but Doua interjected, "My horse." He shook his head at the rider, saving the man some punishment.

They mounted their horses and broke into an easy gallop as Kon turned to see the great hill that overlooked Niani. He hoped that the forces dwelling within would protect the city. Kon pulled up alongside Doua. "Where is the chicken rider taking us?"

"All the way to the Niger," Doua said. "Things are getting bad there, and Azeez says his uncle thinks the Sosso are making it worse."

"If he's right, we need to settle things down and keep the Sosso on their side of the Niger. "Chicken rider where are you from? You are not Mande and not Berber."

The skinny rider took a deep breath and remembered the words of Azeez that he was bringing a king. "I come from Taghaza."

"Ahh, the place of salt; is it true you have houses, even a mosque, made of salt?" asked Kon.

"Yes, it is true."

"And flies, lots of flies," interjected Doua.

The skinny rider took a deep breath. "Yes. That is true as well."

"You speak our language well for a slave," Kon said.

"Amed Salem bought me because of my ability with languages. He has freed me from digging salt for the rest of my days."

"Is this Salem a good, honest man?" Kon inquired. "Is he right about this trouble?"

"Yes. He is a just and honest man of God. The trouble is real, very real; that Sosso ruler is an ambitious man."

Kon was quiet, his body rocking to the rhythm of the horse. "I will call you...Salt."

They followed the wide Sankarani River along the bank where the rocks were small, the ground flat. Near the river, life was fresh and green, but when they moved away to higher ground, the countryside was dry, twisted, and dusty. Each day they watered the horses in the river where they found clear, fast-moving water. They washed the red dust off their arms and faces and out of their throats. On the morning of the fourth day, they moved away from the Sankarani and into the bright country. The village of Selefougou was near the Niger River. By late afternoon, they approached the mid-sized town. Surrounded by a low stick-and-grass fence, a rider came towards them.

From afar, Salt recognized the rider and waved at him. The rider waved for them to follow and kicked his horse into a fast gallop.

"No rest for the weary," said Kon.

"Not today," agreed Doua.

The group followed at speed but was careful not to push their mounts too hard as they were traveling most of the day. The late afternoon sun was still bright, and the rider didn't get too far ahead. He moved toward a hill.

Kon and Doua did not like the idea of going over the hill without knowing what was on the other side, so they looked at each other with concern. They had trusted Azeez this far and hoped that their trust would be rewarded. The rider, then Salt, disappeared over the hill, but Doua and Kon got to the top and stopped.

"We should have brought the army," said Kon.

"You will need to be a great king tonight," said Doua.

Before them were almost a hundred men, and their center of attention was a dead cow in the middle of a farmer's field.

"There seems to be as many farmers as there are herders," said Kon.

"I see Azeez by the mansa. Where is his uncle?" He saw Azeez involved in a heated conversation. A mansa and several Fulani herders were trying to explain their version of what happened.

Kon noticed the mansa's guard stood behind him. He hoped that the situation wouldn't change before he got there. "That big guard wants to fight. If he kills one of those Fulani, war could break out against the farmers."

Salt stopped half way. He watched Doua and Kon, feeling impatient until they kicked their mounts forward. He called out to the men below, who turned to notice the riders. Kon rode past him first, and he rode alongside Doua. "I thought you were waiting for an invitation."

"You are impatient," Doua said, dismissing him with an indifferent tone of voice. "Smart men think before they act."

Kon road up to the mansa and the herders but dismounted a few feet before the group. The mansa was surprised by his sudden appearance and the Fulani were not sure who he was. He strode towards them and bowed to the mansa. "As-salamu alaykum," he said to the Fulani herders.

"Wa alaykumu s-salam," they replied.

"This is King Kon Fatta," Azeez said to the Fulani.

The tallest and eldest herder shook his head. "Ahh, from Niani; we know of you."

"What goes on here? What happened to your cow?" Kon knew it was best to let the men express their anger and frustration.

"We were passing through to the river, and the farmer who owns this land killed my beast." He kept eye contact with Kon while pointing at the body.

Kon turned to the mansa. "Is that true?"

"No, but the cow was eating and trampling his crops. The crops are having a hard time as it is, and we can't have this. It has happened too often. They have come and dirtied the water upstream, drinking precious water from our well that we need." The mansa's anger was visible. "We have every right, but the farmer claims he did not do it."

Kon turned to the elder herder. "You have arrived early again this year. Why is this?"

"The lack of water is the problem. The cattle and goats need to drink, then they need to eat, and if they die my people suffer. That I cannot have what kind of leader I would be if I do nothing."

"But you show us no respect by coming here like this, doing as you please," said the mansa.

"Ahh, we come as we have, but you do not have to kill our beasts," the herder's voice rose. The other herders agreed. "What are we to do? Besides, we have had more cattle missing and killed as we passed the hills yesterday."

"This is not my people doing this," said the mansa. "If you would come at the right time of the season we would leave the edges of the fields for your animals to eat. But you are early... worse than last season."

Azeez jumped in. "The Sosso are beginning to raid across the Niger. They may be responsible for those killings."

"This man claims to be yours?" inquired the herder.

"This is my man; he keeps track of my needs," Kon said.

The herder observed Azeez and turned back to Kon, "It is true that you are a king to many. Allah works through all," he said his right-hand palm up in the air.

"We must work together while the spirits test us; our stories are intertwined." Kon clasped together his hands linking his fingers. "This cow has been sacrificed; whoever did it we will find out. Now, we should all share it. I believe we should work on making paths or spaces for the cattle to go through. How about working a new well and planting some Balanzan trees close to the river? The tree's leaves can be used to feed the animals and help the fields. It will benefit both."

Doua interjected, "We could send some men to help dig." He looked at the herder. "Could you leave some men behind to help dig?"

"Some young ones we could spare," agreed the herder.

"We must not let this trouble grow, otherwise things will be bad for us all. Let's be like the Balanzan and help one another. What about the Sosso?" Kon turned to Azeez.

"My uncle is up in those hills tracking a raiding party as we speak," Azeez said.

"Are we going to be able to find him?"

"Yes, I know how to find him," Azeez said, shaking his head.

"How are the crops in the other villages near here?" Kon asked the mansa.

"Closer to the big river, they are better, of course."

"Then strike a deal with these herders to let them have some of your crops in return for some cattle, milk and leather. In turn, you trade to other villages for grain. Meanwhile, you get started on a new well," Kon said.

Doua and Azeez had stepped back from the mansa and closer to Kon to protect him in case fighting broke out. But they relaxed when they heard Kon's words.

"He has a way of saying things with authority without making you mad," Doua whispered to Azeez.

"He is a persuasive man; I grant him that." Azeez took his hand off his sword and relaxed as the tension in the air dissipated. He saw the farmers and herders relax; even the Mansa's guards seemed less tense.

Kon approached Doua and Azeez. "Things will be okay here, but we must find both your uncle and the Sosso raiding party. "

"It is getting dark; we should leave at first light," said Azeez. "It's too dangerous, and there aren't many of us in case we run into more raiding parties."

The cow was butchered, and the village ate well that night. The herders gave the village three cows and took their beasts to a night pasture. Thorn bushes were cut to keep the cows in and the lions and hyenas out. Kon, Doua and Azeez sat around a fire by a round house they would spend the night in.

"It's important to establish if the Sosso are beginning to raid across the Niger or anywhere else. There are two larger villages towards the Niger. If this one isn't protected and stays loyal they can be out-flanked easily. We can't let that happen," said Kon to Azeez.

Out of the darkness and up to the group strode a woman with two handmaidens on each side of her a few steps behind. The men stared at her beauty, and she radiated strength that was obvious in her posture. "My father says if you need anything he will leave a servant to tend to you tonight."

"Thank you. His hospitality has been perfect. Please tell him that we will be gone early, but we shall be back. It may take a few days."

"I understand. There is a lot of change about, and the people are worried. Is it wise that you have come here with so few men? It is important that you stay safe. My father believes you are the one who can get us through these troubles."

"Well..." Kon paused. "I needed to move as quickly and as quietly as the trouble has come."

"That is wise. I... We are glad that you are here. Are you not afraid of the power of Sumaguru?"

Kon bowed his head. "Thank you. No, the spirits favor us, and I have many good people protecting me." He looked at her full lips and liked the shape of her clean head. She wasn't as short as Fanta and not as tall as Sossuma. It made him wonder for a moment how tall Sogolon was. This woman was thick and curvy.

"Good night." She bowed and turned with her maidens in tow.

Kon watched her walk away. With the help of the night fires, he noticed how her fullness moved the cloth to her wrap dress. When she was out of sight, he turned his attention back to Doua, who was looking at him. "Don't say a word."

Doua just smiled at him and thought *wife number three. He's going to keep trying to fulfill the words of the hunter; he must feel it pushing him.*

The group bedded down in the hut provided by the mansa, and all but Salt slept a fitful night. As the sun began to crack the darkness, the rider that had come out to meet the group the day before awoke them - their horses were saddled and ready.

"We will ride along the river, then head towards the hills where the Fulani had trouble. The trail they took runs on the other side. We will come up behind anyone that is up there," Salt said to the group.

"That is where my uncle will be," Azeez said.

They rode their brown mounts at a gallop towards the red hills that rose from the rolling plains. They hoped if anyone were up there they would be looking at the trail. They made the base of the hills by mid-afternoon, and out of a group of flat-topped acacia trees that stood at the base of the tallest hill rode a man. He rode an enormous black horse with a long flowing mane. Salt and the lead rider raised their hands when they saw the man.

"That is my uncle," Azeez said.

Ahmed Salem rode up to them. "As-salamu alaykum."

"Wa alaykumu s-salam," replied the men. Azeez rode alongside Ahmed, and they hugged and kissed on the cheek. "You are safe. God be praised," said Azeez.

"Why are you worried, nephew?" asked Ahmed.

Azeez laughed. "Because I know you and how things happen around you."

Ahmed smiled. "You give me too much credit. I am just a vessel of God."

Azeez laughed again. "Uncle, this is the King of Niani, Kon Fatta, and you remember Doua."

Ahmed bowed at Doua and rode up to Kon and extended his hand. "I hear much good about you."

Kon had to reach up because Ahmed's horse was so tall. He grasped his hand in return and held it firmly. "I hear much good about you as well. That is the biggest, most beautiful horse I have ever seen."

"Thank you. I brought him from Andalusia. I can get one for you, if you like?"

Kon smiled. "Yes, I would, very much, very much." Kon looked at the strong muscled body of the horse, its large black eye looking at him. He noticed how the horse danced and jumped and how Ahmed had to play with the reins to contain its vast energy.

"A horse fit for king," Ahmed said. "When we settle this business and I make a trip north, but for now there is a group of Sosso on top of this hill."

"How many," Kon asked?

"Ten men; not many," Ahmed said.

"How many do you have?" asked Doua.

"Five, plus me and the four of you, so we have ten as well," Ahmed said.

"I want to take at least two alive. One to send a message to Sumaguru, and one to bring back to show the mansas what is happening here," Kon said, his horse moving sideways.

"We can do that; let's move into the trees and plan." Ahmed turned his horse with a jump and made for the trees. There they dismounted, and Kon smiled, surprised to see he was taller than Ahmed. His horse made him appear so large. He also wasn't a skinny man; he was stocky. It kept him from looking small with a head of thick black hair with streaks of grey. All the men gathered under the stand of tall Arcadia trees. Kon and Ahmed knelt facing each other, and everyone else gathered around in a circle.

"When the sun is close to going down, we shall attack the men on top of the hill. My scouts say that they are all up there now," Ahmed said.

They waited till the sun was low, and they crawled on their bellies up the large hill with bows, spears and swords. They left their shields down below with the horses and moved in single file till they got to the top. When they reached the top, the light was dimming fast, and the Sosso men sat around a small fire. There was plenty of cover from bushes and small trees. Ahmed sent two of his men to the right and two more to the left with bows to catch them in a cross fire.

"I count six around the fire," Salt said.

"That means a few on guard," Doua replied.

"The wind is blowing in our faces; luck," said Ahmed.

"What about the guards?" asked Kon.

"The four archers will hold their position to protect us while we rush in. They will either run away or attack. We will find out," Ahmed said with a smile.

Kon nodded his head in agreement; he liked Ahmed's attitude.

The men began to eat. Ahmed hoped that the guards would come in and reveal themselves. It was getting late, and he didn't want any of them to escape into the darkness. He knocked an arrow, pulled back the bow, took a deep breath and held it. He released the arrow, and it flew with a hiss and struck a man in the neck. The man let out a scream; clutching his throat he fell sideways. The other men froze for a moment and more arrows flew into their camp. Two other men were struck in the chest and side and they fell moaning. The raiders not struck yelled, grabbed their swords, and began to run towards the other side of the hill. Ahmed leapt from his position and ran after them with Kon, Doua, Azeez and Salt fast on his heels. The lookout guards ran towards the attack. The men running away stopped and turned towards their attackers. Now feeling safer together, they turned to fight. As Ahmed ran past the fire, he grabbed a flaming stick and threw it at the man nearest him holding a spear. The spearman knocked the fire stick away, but that was all the opening Ahmed needed, and he jammed his sword deep into the man's chest. The man standing next to the dying spearman swung his sword at Ahmed who pushed the dead body at him, and the sword struck the body of the spearman with a thud. Ahmed removed his sword and pushed the body at his attacker making space between them.

Salt yelled in Sosso to surrender, but the men fought on. Doua, Kon and Azeez each swung their swords in the dim light attempting to subdue but not kill the men--keeping their thrusts short and parrying oncoming slashes. The men attacked, yelled and cursed at them.

His attacker came at Ahmed again with a long swing. Ahmed stepped sideways, and with a swift motion he chopped off the man's hand. The hand still holding the sword hit the ground, and the man let out a long scream. In an effortless motion, Ahmed's sword came back and sliced the man's throat, and the scream turned into a bloody gurgle. Ahmed twirled the sword and pointed it at the men.

Again, Salt yelled for them to surrender. Surrounded and outnumbered, one by one their weapons fell into the dirt. The darkness of night fell in around them.

Chapter 7

Of Alliances and Gold

Fanta cleaned the hut as Sundjata played in the middle of the round room with several sticks and a calabash. She knelt next to him; her hand caressed the top of his head. "Sweet boy, sweet boy... so much trouble for someone so young. Where does all this trouble come from?" she sang.

"From Sossuma, she calls trouble for us," said Sogolon.

Fanta was surprised. Sogolon had been silent since before Kon left. "Mistress." *The iron must have worked,* Fanta thought. She looked at the iron rods Nounfairi had crafted for Sundjata. "How do you feel?"

"Better. Come to mother," she said, stretching out her arms to Sundjata, who crawled over to her.

Fanta felt light as if she could fly. She was beginning to wonder if her mistress was ever going to talk again. "I feared that Sossuma had cursed us for sure."

"Where is Kon?" Sogolon asked.

"He went to the Niger with Doua to meet Azeez and his uncle." Fanta paused. "The Sosso."

Sogolon felt as if she had been away, but now she felt firm, in place. She looked around the house and at Fanta looking at her. "It's good. I am here now."

"I was very scared. I thought you would never be back. Have you ever done that before, for so long?"

"No, that was the longest. I was with the voices, and we talked and talked. We argued, we laughed, and it was as if I were here but not here." Sogolon looked down at Sundjata. Other than not walking, he seemed healthy, and that was Fanta's doing. She smiled. Tears welled in her eyes, and she reached out to Fanta. "I owe you so much; you are more than a servant."

Fanta came over to Sogolon and knelt at her feet, bowing her head. "It is my pleasure to serve a queen so kind and good."

Sogolon put her hand on Fanta's head. "It is I who owe you."

*****

Sumaguru's large village sat between hills in a valley. Walls stood were there were no hills, and the road into the village was protected by a tall iron gate. Made of dark stone, his palace stood above everything. The palace tower was where he spent most of his time. At the top was his sanctuary where few were allowed entry, and where he practiced his power. He was playing his balafon. The soft notes filled the round room when he heard a knock on the door and the voice of his guard. [24]

"My king, you have a messenger needing your attention," the guard said through the wooden door.

Sumaguru put down the mallets of the balafon and opened the door. "What is it?" he said impatiently. His eyes went wide when he saw the man with the message.

"My king," said the messenger. He was kneeling but had his eyes on a large spotted hyena that Sumaguru's guard held on a short, thick black chain. "I need to speak to you alone." He could feel bursts of hot breath that smelled like rotted flesh on his face.

"Don't fear my pet; he protects me and does what I say. Come inside."

The man rose as slowly as possible. As he moved through the doorway, the hyena extended his head as black nostrils opened and closed to smell the man. The guard tightened his grip on the chain, and the man jumped through the doorway into the room.

Sumaguru smiled and closed the door. He liked to see the fear. "Why are you back here so soon?"

The man was now relieved to be away from the spotted beast.

But now he realized he was in a room where few went and even fewer left. He saw an owl with a large round white face on a perch and two human skulls on the floor under them. He stepped back and saw the balafon and several other instruments, all next to a basket. "We were attacked in the night by many men. We fought back, but it was no use."

"Did you disrupt the Fulani as they passed? "

"Yes, we were able to kill several cows that slipped away from the main herd, and in the night, we ran some others off."

"But why do you have a message for me?" asked Sumaguru. He took a long, thick brown python from the basket near the balafon.

The man stared speechless. The owl, the snake, the hyena, and the skulls, it was true that their king possessed great power. "What is this message for me?" Sumaguru said impatiently.

"We weren't attacked by just anyone; we were attacked by Kon Fatta of Niani."

Sumaguru was surprised; he put the snake back in the basket and covered it. He knew Fatta was brave, but this was unexpected.

"He was there with his men, trained soldiers. He said not to cross the river and raid the Fulani or anyone else."

"Are you the only survivor?"

"No, he spared me to send you this message. He kept three others that survived."

Sumaguru was silent and began to pace the room as the man watched nervously.

"Will you ransom them back or leave them as slaves?"

"What did you tell them? Did you say why you were there? What you were doing?"

"I told them we were hunting. But the Fulani told them about the attacks. They looked at our tracks up and down the hill we camped on," said the man with regret in his voice. We had no fresh-killed game with us."

"Were you dressed as hunters at least?" Sumaguru's anger was rising.

The man hesitated. "No, we left right away. We were going to move quickly from hill to hill." The man looked at the floor.

"Why didn't you move?" Why did you stay there?" Sumaguru said throwing his arms wide.

"Once two groups of Fulani passed there was another group a day behind with goats. The farmers were almost at war with the herders the night we were attacked, but King Fatta calmed them down. We figured we could scatter and kill some goats, and then have the goats eat some crops; we hoped fighting would break out," the man said with hope in his voice. "But the—"

Sumaguru interrupted him, "I know King Fatta. He is powerful, and his family is strong. People follow him, and he has a way of uniting them."

"He has Islamic men fighting with him. The Fulani took it as a sign. One of them might be Jinn. We never heard them coming when they fell upon us. They must have used magic."

"I am a sorcerer King; the spirits listen to me." He took a deep breath, "However, these jinn may have strong magic of their own."

"I trust in your power, your control of Nyama." The man knelt and bowed his head, hoping this show of deference would spare his life. "Command me, my king."

Sumaguru walked over to the window of his tower and looked out on his city. Killing the man may show others not to fail. But this appearance of the King Fatta and his magicians was not foreseen, not even by him. "I want you to slip back over the river and get the other raiding parties to return. If you are caught do not come back. We will direct our efforts elsewhere for now. Fatta has a way of uniting the other people, and we don't want to be outnumbered. We will take another direction." He paused. "For now."

✳✳✳✳✳

Salt hung back for most of the day to assure that no one followed the as Kon, Ahmed and Azeez rode ahead together.

It was the second day out, and Kon was riding Ahmed's giant black stallion.

"You see you need to pull hard, but not too hard, and use your knees more!" Ahmed yelled as he rode up to him.

"Yes, I can feel it." Kon had to rein the horse with force and turn him as he jumped and wanted to run again. "How do you like my mount?"

"A fine animal, a fine animal…" Ahmed leaned forward and patted the horse on its neck. "Very well trained. She responds fast, and she is nimble."

"That she is. I have done lots of work getting her right. Shall we race to that baobab tree?"

"If you don't mind losing," said Ahmed with a smile. "On three… one-two-three!" Ahmed kicked the horse, and it jumped with a burst. There were clumps of grass, small shrubs, and uneven ground. He liked his chances, even against his own muscled beast.

Doua walked alongside the king's new wife, finally getting a moment to talk to her in private. His horse trailed behind him as he held its reins in his hands behind his back.

"Wouldn't you rather be racing than walking along with me?" Nama asked Doua as she watched the two horses kick up clouds of dust into the hot afternoon sky.

"I would just beat them both, and then the king would be in a bad mood for the rest of the day. He hates to lose," Doua said, looking down at the red ground. "You will find out soon enough."

"I am sure I will." Nama looked to see who was winning the race, but she couldn't tell. "Will I like Niani, do you think?"

"I do. It is a lovely place. They will accept you rather easily I suspect."

"I am going to miss my family so." Nama paused. "I hear stories that Queen Sossuma is…" She paused again. "Rather strong willed." Nama was looking at her feet as they walked.

Doua did not answer right away. He let out a deep breath. "You could say that. She is from a very strong and proud family. She has very strong opinions."

"And Kon's other wife, Sogolon? Kon said she is a hunch back."

"Oh, yes, but a kinder gentler person you will not meet," Doua exclaimed.

"How many wives and children do you have?"

"I have three wives now, four daughters and three sons."

Nama smiled. "Seems I have an interesting new home."

Doua smiled and looked at her bright brown eyes and soft mouth. She was very pretty, and it was a good sign that she asked the right questions. "Yes, you will be very happy."

"The uniting of our cities will keep them safe. King Fatta surely has the spirits with him." Nama looked up at Doua into his dark eyes and noticed his graying hair and a slight smile on his lips.

After their race, Kon and Ahmed trotted back towards them.

Nama walked out towards Kon. "You won?"

"Yes, I did." Kon smiled and dismounted to walk with her, ahead of Azeez.

Ahmed rode up to Azeez with a smile.

"You let him win; I saw you pull up at the last minute," he said in a hush.

Ahmed laughed. "You are too observant."

"You taught me well."

"Better one happy king than one happy subject. And, he may buy some horses." Ahmed smiled.

*****

"The rider claimed they were close," Fanta said as she tied a bright yellow wrap around her head. She picked up Sundjata and followed Sogolon outside. They made their way to the gate and the enormous silk cotton tree to shade them from the afternoon sun. They turned the corner to find Sossuma sitting with Nana in her arms, flanked by her handmaidens. Dankaran played at her feet.

Sossuma was talking to Nana when she felt a presence and saw Sogolon with her servant and crippled child. She sucked her teeth softly and continued to play with Nana.

Sogolon smiled at Sossuma, her braids tossed by a hot breeze. "Sossuma," she said.

Sossuma smiled. "Sister," she responded and then turned to look for Kon.

It didn't take long until Kon, Doua, Azeez and Ahmed came into sight. Sogolon, Sossuma and everyone present stood up.

"I see a woman," Fanta said.

"Hmmm," Sossuma moaned in a low tone when she too noticed the young woman sitting behind Kon with her arms around his waist. Then she noticed women behind Azeez, Ahmed and Doua.

Kon smiled, seeing his wives and children waiting for him. Nama felt nervous when she saw how beautiful Sossuma was. She was tall, dark and strong, but the look on her face was stern. Sogolon was bent over with a bright smile, full lips and big eyes. She was much prettier than Nama imagined. Kon dismounted with a jump and helped Nama down.

Fanta began to clap and sing,

"What a great day.

What a great day.

The King returns today.

Oh hey, oh hey.

What luck comes our way."

Sossuma's maidens joined her. Sossuma looked at them, but they were caught up in the moment.

Kon hugged Sossuma, then Sogolon and his children. Nama stood back, and her handmaidens assembled behind her. They took the dusty blue head wrap off her - revealing her clean-shaven head - and adjusted her dress.

"Sossuma, Sogolon, I would like you to meet Namandje of Selefougou. She is our new wife."

"Call me Nama." She bowed and smiled.

Sogolon bowed, stepped forward, and took her hands. "Welcome."

Sossuma stepped forward and offered her right hand which Nama took.

Kon turned to Doua. "Get the council together so we can let them know what has happened by the Niger."

Doua nodded his head in confirmation and turned to see Sossuma examining Nama with her eyes while Sogolon watched

Kon. *Nama will have her hands full here,* he thought.

*****

A pit was dug, and the fire burned brightly. It chased the shadows from under the stand of silk cotton trees on the palace grounds. The council sat around the fire on grass mats as Kon, Doua, Azeez and Ahmed addressed them. Kon sat on a short, two-legged, wooden stool.

"The Sosso have sent raiding parties across the Niger. They attempt to cause a fight between the farmers and the Fulani. I caught a group of them in the act. With the help of Azeez and his uncle, Ahmed, we were able to stop them. We even captured a few," said Kon as he rose from the stool.

"I gave one of them a hand," Ahmed whispered to Doua.

Doua smiled and put his hand over his mouth. Azeez was sitting opposite his uncle and shook his head in disapproval.

"Sumaguru is trying to extend his power by starting a war between the Fulani and the farmers. When there is chaos he will raid. With everyone weakened by war, he could take what he desires," said Kon with concern in his voice.

"Why do you believe this is so?" asked the large council representative from Sossuma's village. "We hear that the herders have been rough with the farmers."

"This is true, but not to cause a fight. We found other raiding parties," Ahmed said, sitting next to Doua. "My men engaged them as well."

"Again, proof of this?" said the large man.

"Several of them are coming to us as slaves. Both the Fulani and the farmers claimed not to do anything against the other," Ahmed responded.

"I have taken a daughter of the Mansa of Selefougou as a wife, as a show of alliance between our cities and clans. They also believe in this threat and know our clans should stand together. It will allow us to listen and follow the traditions of our ancestors."

"What is to be done then?" asked the large councilman.

"We need to be ready if word comes from Selefougou; we need to fight to protect our farms and homes. We will send some men there to help build a well and to keep an eye out for trouble."

The men of the council began to talk amongst themselves. Kon went with confidence back to his seat to let them deliberate.

*****

"Are you happy with your space in the palace?" Sossuma asked Nama. They walked through the courtyard with their oldest handmaidens trailing behind them.

"Yes, thank you. It's been tough adjusting, but it's getting easier," Nama said, running her hand over her smooth head. "I miss my family, my clan."

"Of course, you do, child. It's only natural. It's been good having someone else around I can talk to," said Sossuma as she gazed into Nama's dark eyes.

"Thank you. Do you not have Sogolon to talk with?

"Well, she... she is different. She doesn't understand the responsibility of being a royal. To have your people talk to the ancestors, to guide the people. She is common."

"Hmm, I see. I have heard many things about sister Sogolon," Nama said. "I've heard she is a witch, yet many say she is kind and a fine healer."

Sossuma sucked her teeth. "I too believe she is a witch. The voices she speaks to cannot be the same as our fathers, who are mansas."

"How does she live with that back?" Nama shook her head.

"You have good points."

"It must be evil magic that keeps her alive. The drought persists since she has been here and has given birth to that crippled boy. I wouldn't be surprised if something happened to him someday."

Nama shook her head. "It is all very strange. She is a bit frightening to look at. How does Kon sleep with her?" Nama's eyes went wide at the thought.

"There goes that wretched handmaiden, Fanta," Sossuma snorted with disgust.

Fanta saw Sossuma from far off and avoided eye contact. She ignored her and stomped by.

"Ugh, she is more angry and rude than usual," Sossuma huffed, watching Fanta pass. "She sleeps with a Borzo fisherman."

"I suppose they are made for each other," Nama said. "She is quite small."

"I know why he can stand her - he is used to being with foul-mouthed creatures all day." Sossuma laughed.

Fanta entered Sogolon's home. Sundjata, dragging his legs, crawled over to her. She picked him up, and he burst into laughter as Fanta put her face close to his.

"Lay him down by the window here," Sogolon said. "I've noticed that sometimes he does move his feet. Lay him on his stomach."

Fanta brought him over, and Sundjata squirmed. "Shhh, lay still my boy." Looking into his eyes, she knelt before him and began to sing.

Sogolon knelt opposite the window. The light bathed over Sundjata's smooth brown skin as she ran her hands up and down his spine.

"What do you feel?" Fanta asked.

"Where I fell on him it doesn't feel right." Sogolon's fingers could feel the bones in his back were not straight. She got up and limped over to her store of shea butter, put some in her hands, and began massaging it into his back. Then she pushed and Sundjata gave a cry. Sogolon knew this was the problem. She had to somehow straighten his spine. The right side of the bone was higher than the other, and she pondered what to do. "I need to see some bones. Play with Sundjata."

Sogolon got up in her awkward way and left her house. She went through the gate and to the edge of town where they butchered the animals for food. The sun was on the wane, and the heat of the day beginning to break. The men worked under a large tree as bald red- and grey-headed vultures hovered and perched.

Several men were charged with cutting up meat for the day and were getting back to work. "Is that the queen?" the tallest man of the group asked.

"Do you know anyone else who looks like that?" replied the elder of the group.

The others laughed but contained themselves when then queen got close.

"Greetings," said Sogolon as she waved her right hand at the men--standing before them in her bent way, braids swaying back and forth.

"They were laughing at you," said the angry voice.

Sogolon ignored the voice. "Good men, I need to see the back of a beast you have cut up."

"My queen?" the elder asked, confused.

"The back bones, I need to see them, all together if possible, from a goat or a cow. I think a chicken would be too small."

"I have them in large pieces," said the elder. He turned to the tall man and snapped his fingers. The tall man went to a pile of meat with bone.

"Here," he said as he handed her a long section of a goat spine. "You are lucky; we were about to cut them up into pieces for the soup."

Sogolon held the spine in her hands and noticed how it fit together like a puzzle. First, she shook it, then twisted it and rocked the pieces back and forth.

The men looked at her wondering if it was magic she was attempting or trying to casting a spell. They gave each other concerned and confused looks.

Sogolon then bent the spine in half till it broke with a pop. She noticed how the bones did not break but the things that held it together had let go. She gave a great smile and handed the pieces back to the elder.

"Bring water for the queen to wash her hands!" the elder barked.

*****

The midwives of Niani handled Sogolon as she gave birth for a second time. She had a beautiful daughter with a straight back. Her name was Kolonkan. Sundjata was happy to have a sister and played with her often, and Kon was proud to have a daughter. Fanta, always the bundle of energy, was happy to have new life in the house. Sogolon's breasts grew larger again, and she rubbed shea butter to keep her dark nipples soft. She nursed Kolonkan, making her healthy and strong. The voices were supportive, most of the time, and she reveled in her motherhood. Sossuma complained at the attention the new baby was getting. Nama brought presents and lent a servant.

Chapter 8

Farakoro

"Pull," grunted Sogolon. "Not too hard. Steady."

"I know!" snapped Fanta. "We've been doing this for many seasons now."

"Mother, Fanta knows. Please stop. You are going to fall again," Sundjata said, straining his neck to look back at Sogolon. It had been several seasons they were doing this to him, and it felt good.

"Don't talk back to your mother," Fanta said.

"Okay, let's stop," Sogolon said but lost her grip of Sundjata. She fell onto the floor of her house and began to laugh. Her slip sent Sundjata hard to the ground and Fanta onto her backside. This made Sogolon laugh even more. Sundjata wiped dirt off his lips, and even Fanta gave a chuckle.

"How do you feel?" Sogolon inquired.

"Good," Sundjata answered. Rolling over onto his side, he was slow to get up.

"Try to straighten up," Sogolon said, getting herself off the floor.

Sundjata began to stand, but he could not straighten up. Fanta was on her feet and moved to help him, but Sogolon shook her head.

He stood bent over but now higher than his mother. "It feels better," Sundjata said, and he took a step and limped, then limped again.

"It gets better a little each time," Fanta said. She went over to a servant Nama had lent to them and took Kolonkan from her arms. She kissed the baby's forehead.

They all went outside into the bright morning light as the dusty heat began to build.

Kon, Doua and his son Balla were crossing the courtyard. They approached Sogolon, Fanta and Sundjata.

"Does he seem to be standing straighter?" Kon asked Doua.

"I would say yes," Doua replied.

"But he still limps." Kon shook his head.

"It's getting better; he couldn't walk a few seasons ago. Let me talk to Balla." Doua stopped Balla, who turned and looked into his eyes. "You have one of the most import jobs in the kingdom. It's you who will be his advisor; he will trust you most. You keep the stories and the lineage of the kings. You decide who shall learn and hear the words."

Balla looked around his father to see a stooped over boy. "But father, how could he become king?"

"Don't let his looks deceive you. Don't always trust your eyes but trust your heart. He may very well be king someday. The spirits may well be testing him... and you. Don't butterflies come from caterpillars?"

"But so do moths. I fear he is a moth, Father."

Doua made a face, not knowing if he was angry because of the joke or happy because his son was quick witted. He took a deep breath. "I give you this job. It is your duty, and you are capable. Aren't some moths as beautiful as butterflies? Right now, he is a caterpillar."

Balla looked past his father and again at Sundjata, taking a deep breath. "Yes, Father, I will do my best."

"Good, then let's meet your caterpillar."

Sogolon saw Kon coming and smiled.

"Father!" Sundjata exclaimed and gave him a hug.

"Sundjata, I have a present for you." Sundjata turned to see a thin, muscled young man, older than he was, standing next to Doua. He looked like a younger Doua.

"This is Balla, Doua's son and your griot." Kon walked over to Sogolon.

Balla stepped forward. "Hello."

Sundjata looked up at him into his bright brown eyes and wondered what Balla thought of him.

"Kon, that's wonderful and such a surprise. I thought you felt he wasn't special," Sogolon said.

"I may have been rash in my decision. The drought seems to be over. You have him walking. You have not had any spells in many seasons now, and we have kept the Sosso contained. The ancestors may favor him yet." Kon looked at Sogolon and saw a bright, wide smile on her face. "You know patience isn't my strongest quality."

"Tell me about it," Sogolon said. "Did Doua help change your mind?"

"Of course. He is always in my ear, and now that Sumaguru has raided Ghana, Sundjata must grow up faster."

Sogolon nodded her head in agreement with her husband's judgment. She looked at him and took his hand as they watched Balla and Sundjata.

"My father says I am to help you become great," Balla said to Sundjata.

"Great? I never thought about being great," Sundjata pondered.

"You are the son of the king, right?

"Yes."

"Your mother is a great healer, right?"

"Yes."

"I am your griot now, right?"

"Yes." Sundjata paused. "My mother would tell me one day I would be great. Fanta would tell me I will be king. But everyone else laughs at me, or thinks I am crazy, just a cripple. It makes it hard to believe."

"Well, now you are hearing it from me. Our families are special, and we will continue the work our fathers are doing. Who cares what others say? Do we ask them how to farm, or how to make iron? It's not their place to rule. They have their place, and we have ours. In the end, we all work together to survive."

Balla's words filled Sundjata's head, and he felt a surge of pride. "Then I will try to be great. I know I want to make my father proud."

"Then you must keep trying to stand straighter. You have come a long way since you used to crawl around."

"Yes, Mother and Fanta stretch me, push on me and rub shea butter on my back."

"You must try to get stronger; keep working at it. I know you can do it, Sundjata. The spirits will help you."

"Thank you," Sundjata said as he reached out his hand. "I will do my best."

Kon came over to talk to the boys. "Sundjata, listen to Balla's council, and work together. Balla, your father says you learn fast. You are a good young man. If you are half as good as your father, then you will help Sundjata become great. You both need to work together... and trust each other. The kingdom may someday be in your hands."

"What about Dankaran, father?"

"He will be king. He is my first son, but the gods and our ancestors may have other things planned for you. We never know. There are a great many mysteries in life."

Sundjata couldn't stop smiling. A while ago he had dirt in his mouth, lying face down on the floor, and now he had his own griot. His head and chest felt light.

Fanta moved next to Sogolon. They entwined arms, both with tears of happiness filling their eyes.

"You two, get to know each other. I have things to tend to." Kon gave Doua a look, and off they went out of the palace into the growing city to meet Azeez and Ahmed in the market place.

Azeez and Ahmed stood by the gold trading house of the men from Bure. Two large guards protected the door.

Azeez saw Kon and Doua making their way through the crowd. "Uncle, they are here."

Ahmed was talking to a tall, dark pretty woman with large gold rings hanging from her ears, her eyes bright with life. She gave a flirtatious laugh and touched his arm. "I will see you again, my sweet," Ahmed said as he touched her cheek with the back of his fingers.

"Men," Kon said, noticing the display.

"Walk this way," said Azeez, pointing to an opening away from that part of town towards a growing Muslim quarter. After a short walk, they entered a place with a thatched roof, low walls and carpets covering the ground. Azeez motioned to the party, inviting them to sit down.

"Tea," Ahmed said, his hand making a circular motion to a man who came up to them as soon as they began to sit. "Do you like the horse I got you?" he asked Kon.

"Yes, very strong and active like yours. Now, do I have to ride him into battle?"

"Well, Sumaguru has been busy. He did try to force our friends from Bure to work with him on his terms, but they did as they promised. They stopped mining gold and disappeared. I hear they even harassed his men as they left. Sumaguru raids where and when he can. The villages who are aligned with us keep him out, so he raids around us."

"You can bet he wants to pay us a visit," Doua said.

"Yes, it seems he is expanding what he tried to do before, but now he sends raiders in small bands on horseback," Azeez said.

"And he doesn't try to hide it anymore," Kon added.

Several men in turbans and long shirts silently entered the room and served them strong, dark tea in small glass cups before leaving once more.

"My spies tell me they have seen his men headed towards Farakoro," Ahmed said, taking a sip of his tea.

"That is where I was born," Kon said with concern. "How sure are you of this?"

"I heard this yesterday, and the source is very reliable," confirmed Ahmed. "Niani is growing bigger every day. Sumaguru can't attack us, but he can still cause trouble for people coming here."

"We may need to gather a larger army to keep him in check," Kon said rubbing his chin. "I prefer not to go to war; it is so costly and destructive."

"The alliances we have made over the past season will keep him wary. Gathering a large force might not be a bad idea for show, though. Then negotiate," Doua said, looking at the group.

"I think we should visit Farakoro. Doua, gather the cavalry. Ahmed, can you spare any men?"

Ahmed pondered for a moment. "I have two caravans out, and most of my men are with them. I can spare about ten to fifteen men."

"That will do fine. You are bringing much business to Niani. If it continues, we will grow happy and fat. Azeez was right about you. Even the drought seems to have come to an end, all appears to be going in the right direction."

Ahmed bowed. "Thank you. He was also right about you. Under your leadership, Niani will continue to grow. The word is spreading about you, and people know they can do business here and that your taxation is fair."

"And you gain wealth as well," Doua said to Ahmed.

"There is no harm in that. I am but a poor man looking to find his way in this life," Ahmed replied with a smile.

The group laughed.

"We will leave in the morning," Kon confirmed.

The group finished their tea, and Doua sent out the word to gather their cavalries. Then he went to see his wives. Ahmed gathered twelve men and prepared them to leave in the morning. Kon decided to eat with Sogolon and Sundjata, spend some time with Sossuma, and then spend the night with Nama.

Kon, Doua, Ahmed and their men left as soon as the sun began to push the darkness out of the sky. They rode hard through the heat of the day on their new black or brown mounts purchased from Ahmed. Kon now rode on a horse even larger than Ahmed's. They stopped when the sun was at its height and rested in the shade of several large barrel-trunked baobab trees.

Days later, they arrived on the hard bank of the Niger River. It was too dark to cross; they would have to wait till the morning. They set up camp far away from the water to keep safe from crocodiles and hippos, but most didn't sleep well so far from home. Kon was restless, but his dreams were of Sogolon's smile and of Nama's soft skin.

Salt crossed the river at first light. When he came back across he woke up the rest of the group. Sleep hung in their eyes, and their limbs and backs were stiff. Kon was still dreaming of Nama when he was roused.

"They are not far. If we cross now we can catch them before they get to Farakoro," Salt said to Ahmed.

Ahmed was on his feet, stretching, and listening to Salt. "How many are there?"

"About as many as us, I believe. I followed them for several hours and saw no others."

The group had camped by a high area of the river and found a spot that was easy to cross. They drove the horses into the brown rushing water and held onto the horse's manes or tails as they swam across. The top of the water was warm, and cooler currents from deep rose up to give them a chill. This refreshed the men such as Kon, Doua, and Ahmed, who could swim. But it terrified those who could not, Salt most of all. Their imaginations raced with images of tiger fish, crocodiles and water spirits. A group of hippos stood in the smooth, flowing river. Their eyes, ears, and nostrils were hard to see poking above the surface. A large male moved towards them, making a splash and several grunts, not happy with their presence. One-by-one, the horses rose out of the deeper water, and the riders slid back into their small saddles. They splashed onto the shore, taking the reins once again.

Farakoro was not a large town. It was surrounded on three sides by a large swampy area with tall reeds that stretched as far as the eye could see, and fishing and trapping were the mainstays of the people.

"There is but one main road in and out," Kon said to Doua, Ahmed and Salt. "It's easy to trap anyone coming down into the village, as that road comes down off a hill into a valley. That would be the place for an ambush."

"Why are they raiding this place? It sounds none too wealthy," Ahmed asked.

"There is a fair amount of gold here from people coming to get turtle shell, furs and fish. I grew up with the love of fishing from this place."

"What about fever in such a place?" Ahmed asked with concern.

"It's worse in late summer when the water is low. Since it has been raining a lot as of late, we should be fine," Kon assured them. "Salt, see how far away the raiding party is? If you follow the main trail back, you will find us."

Salt wheeled his brown mount around as its long black mane lifted into the air. He took off on his mission while Kon led the rest to the ambush point. Their horses climbed the terrain as it rose from the river and changed from grass and brush. The ground leveled out, and they were in groves of tall trees. At the edge of the grove a trail ran below them. Doua, Ahmed, and Kon surveyed the ground.

Ahmed was quick to assess the situation. "May I suggest catching them from both sides?"

"Like up on the hill by Selefousou?" Doua asked.

"Yes. Have archers hit them from the sides, and then we will charge them from the front and the back."

Kon pointed away from the village. "Doua, there is a spot not too far from here where you can take about ten men and hide. Towards the village there is a turn in the trail where we can hide. When you hear the signal, we attack."

"If they send scouts first, let them come down the bend. We will stop them. Doua, you pick ten men and take them to your spot. Ahmed, position your men in the trees with bows on either side of the trail, and take ten of mine with spears. When they get in the middle, have them let loose, and give a scream. That will be the signal for our attack." Kon looked around, hoping Salt would return soon.

The sun was close to being at its highest point in the sky. Salt galloped up, sweaty and breathing hard, his clothes loose on his skinny frame. "Be ready. Be ready," he said, breathing hard.

"Did they see you?" Kon asked. He pulled on the reins, attempting to contain the energy, wanting to burst forth from his huge black mount.

"They are chasing me," Salt said without panic.

Kon gave him a look of frustration.

"It wasn't my plan," Salt shot back.

"Doua, take your place!" Kon yelled. "Come with me," he said, looking at Salt.

Ahmed stood above the trail, listening. He made eye contact with Kon before they turned to go to their spots. Turning to his group, he said, "Okay, men, down and wait till the signal. Hand me that spear," he asked the man next to him. He looked across the trail and signaled to the men, and they went out of sight. Ahmed jumped down onto the trail and stood in the middle of it where it began to open up. He could hear hoof beats coming fast. He tilted his sword, so he could pull it out fast, and he wiped sweat from his forehead, pushing back his salt-and-pepper hair. He smiled as he saw three men on horseback ride fast into the trail, but they pulled hard on the reins to stop. He had learned some Sosso from Salt. "Men, if you want to pass you must pay me a toll."

Three shirtless sweaty men looked at each other and laughed. The largest of the three spoke: "Old man, get out of the road. We don't want to ruin our horse's hooves on your old bones."

"You must pay or turn around and go home," Ahmed said with a smile and a laugh. "I'm just poor old man looking to make a living."

"Did you see a skinny, hungry-looking rider? We were chasing him."

"No. If I had I would have turned him away if he had no money."

The riders grew impatient and angry. "Move now and let us through unless you want to die today. No rider has passed us."

"You must be blind," replied Ahmed, goading the men into action. Then he heard horses coming, and the rest of the raiders came down the trail. He watched their leader ask the scouts why they had stopped, and there was much yelling. As he expected, the large man charged him. Waiting till the rider was half way to him, Ahmed threw his spear. It struck the man in the chest, knocking him off his horse and to the ground. "Now!" he yelled and stepped back into the turn of the trail, drawing his sword.

The raiders began to move down the trail after Ahmed. Then the bow and spearmen rose up and rained arrows and spears into the men. The group attempted to ride forward but was met by Kon and his riders. The raiders had no saddles and were easy to knock off their horses. On the ground they were easy targets.

Kon rode hard into the group, and his huge horse knocked down the first rider he met. He swung his sword downwards, left and right, cutting deep into bodies.

Doua heard Ahmed's signal and launched his own horse onto the trail, his men close behind. It wasn't long before he met three riders attempting to escape the ambush. Doua noticed they had reins in their hands, so he swung and cut deep into the leg of the lead rider. Blood splattered over his clothes, and he rode on till he saw the raiders locked in battle in the tight pass. From behind, Doua and his men began cutting into them.

Ahmed stabbed a horse as a raider broke free from the pack, the horse reared up, dumping the rider hard to the ground. He rushed over and stabbed the man in the chest. He looked up and watched the battle rage on, seeing terror in the raider's eyes. Kon looked magnificent on his tall black stallion. And his bright eyes

103

shone fiercely from his dark face. A raider attempted to run down the trail, but Ahmed stood in his way. The man dropped his sword, and Ahmed motioned for him to lie in the dirt.

"Surrender!" Salt yelled several times. "Surrender to King Kon Fatta!"

Now that the raiders realized whom they were fighting, their situation grew desperate. They looked to see the man with the leather vest and helmet. Their fear got the best of them, and one-by-one they gave up.

They took the surviving raiders into Farakoro. Kon's brothers and sisters were both happy and surprised to see him. The village celebrated when they learned they had been saved from a raiding party. Again, Kon sent one man back to Sumaguru with a message: To be mindful of where they raided. They stayed two days to take care of their wounded and to rest themselves, and then they left early in the morning of the third day, making it to the Niger as the heat was building.

"To see Sumaguru's face when that messenger you sent him arrives." Doua laughed as he scratched the bites on his arm. His head was hurting, and he didn't feel right. "I thought you said the mosquitos weren't bad in Farakoro."

"They are not. I can't help it if you have sweet blood." Kon laughed. "Well... sweet for you."

"Better than the sour stuff that runs through you!" Doua laughed in return.

"You two argue like husband and wife," Ahmed said with a smile.

"After dealing with Sossuma, he is a delight," Kon said.

They made it to the river as the sun baked the red dirt, and the heat shimmered in the air. The heat made them sleepy, but the sight of the river gave them strength. The horses began to gallop, for they were as thirsty as the men. Once there, the horses gulped at the river's edge with their hooves in the mud. The riders wiped away sweat and dust while drinking from bladder skins and refilling them.

"Salt, stay behind till we are all across," Kon said as he nodded to Doua to begin the crossing.

Doua turned to four men and nodded at one, in particular, "You first."

Ahmed was off his horse, kneeling riverside, and washing his face. He ran his wet fingers through his salt-and-pepper hair and watched as the men crossed the river. "I will cross with Salt!" he yelled to Doua. He then looked across the river to the other side, which danced in the heat. In the middle of the river not far from the crossing he saw hippos and heard their snorting.

The hippos stood in a group with their nostrils above the water. Some had little birds standing on their heads, picking parasites from their ears. The females didn't mind the odd creatures in the water, but the male was angry; they were too close. He splashed and snorted, but they didn't notice, and more of them were getting in the water.

Doua felt light-headed and hoped the water would refresh him. As the water rose, he hung onto his horse's mane and dipped his head in the water, feeling a little refreshed.

Kon's horse, being so large, was catching up to Doua. Out of the corner of his eye he saw something move. The top of the water was showing rings where something submerged. Kon could see a gigantic dark shape moving just under the water headed straight towards Doua. He tugged on his horse's mane to go faster and the huge black stallion responded. "DOUA!" he shouted drawing his sword.

Doua heard his name and turned around to see Kon close to him on his left. Suddenly, the water exploded, and a giant mouth was hovering over him.

Chapter 9

Namugu

"We are now getting what is rightfully ours!" Sumaguru addressed his council of the village elders. He spoke with his tower behind him as the sun sank, making the sky a fiery red and orange. He watched the elders shake their heads in agreement as they sat on mats and shooed away flies. Brushes made of horse, buffalo and prized elephant hair flicked in the air. "We have gained allies since we raided Kumbi-Sahel and other villages."

"When shall we raid across the Niger? There is much wealth to be had there. They grow more crops than us," said an elder. The shadows of night began to grow, and the darkness was descending.

"Soon. You all know of Kon Fatta and his influence on that side. He is strong, but our people and my magic are much stronger. When the signs are right we will strike." Sumaguru paced back and forth with confidence, meeting the eyes of the elders. "Soon no more humiliation from those who have no place taking what rightfully belongs to us. The gold trade will be ours. The salt trade will be ours. No kneeling to rulers and sprinkling dust on our heads. My father bowed and crawled, but no more." Sumaguru's words were said with a deep, steady tone. He had the council in the palm of his hand. He could feel it. "My magic and sacrifices have ended the drought. The spirits know we deserve this happiness."

The elders nodded their heads. "Yes, yes," they said aloud, first in pairs, and then in unison. Sumaguru folded his arms and stood before them tall, straight and strong. Then one of his guards stepped from the gathering darkness and whispered in his ear. The guard pulled back into the darkness, and he stood there silent. Taking a deep breath, Sumaguru said, "Hear my words. Go back to your homes, your wives, your children and your farms to prepare for what is to come. Make sacrifices, and have them adorn your altars." He turned and went into his tower, climbing the stairs in the dark, his hand on the warm rough wall. He was looking upwards to the lit area outside his chamber. As he entered out of the dark, the two hyenas held by two large guards let out a growl. Sumaguru spoke to them, and their growls turned into high-pitched barking laughs. They recognized him, as they had known him since birth. He turned away from his beasts and went through the door into his chamber. A man stood before him and now took a knee.

"My king, we were ambushed just outside of Farakoro. Our entire group was defeated." The man dared not lift his eyes. He knew his life hung in the balance of the next few moments.

"Who?" Sumaguru asked.

The man was silent and remained bent over, afraid to answer. "King Kon Fatta." The man remained bowed, expecting a sword to pierce his body. Sweat dripped from his face, drop-by-drop from his broad nose. Maybe a spell was being cast to punish him. He looked up to see Sumaguru standing by the window.

"I want people to know that Fatta attacked our men. We need to go to war," Sumaguru pondered.

"We will need more men, more horses. Fatta said he was defending the place where he was born."

"I will need my nephew's cavalry to accomplish this. Before you go and spread the word of this attack, summon my nephew, Fakoli, and tell him come as soon as possible. If I hear anything different I will come to you. I will feed you to my pets beyond that door. Trust me; you will be quite alive when it happens."

"Yes, my king." The man rose and left the chamber.

Sumaguru lit several more oil lamps, and then he went to his small seat near a table where he kept his beasts. He opened the lid to a small woven basket, and with great speed he picked out a mouse and threw it onto the floor. His owl flapped its wings and pounced in silence. In a great gulp, the mouse disappeared into the owl. Then Sumaguru took his rock python from his tallest basket. He admired the deep bronzed spots along its brown and grey body. He then spoke to it in a soft tone and felt it wrap its tail around his arm. Its smooth scales felt cool on his skin. He enjoyed these beasts almost as much as making his musical instruments. This gave him more power and control of nyama. He put the snake down and moving a nearby palm oil lamp he took a pellet his owl had thrown up after digesting one of its meals. He unraveled the pellet and saw the perfect skeleton of a mouse. This was a good sign. When the skeleton was perfect, it was a sign of things going his way.

✶✶✶✶✶

Sundjata and Balla were outside of the villages of Niani in the bush at the edge of the forest. Before them lay a wide-open field of grass and dirt and they knelt looking at tracks.

"See the edges?" Balla pointed to tracks in the red dirt.

"Yes, they are sharp. I see solid shapes," Sundjata said.

"Good. What tracks might have made these prints, and which way was this beast going?"

Sundjata pointed across the open field. "That way." The direction was easy, but what made the tracks was a harder riddle. "Uh... hmm... a duiker?"

"What does it look like?"

"Small. Light brown with a black stripe running from its nose to between its eyes. The horns are short like spikes."

Balla smiled. "Yes, yes, you are getting good. When you are able to stand up straight you will hunt and become one with this land. Which way is the wind blowing?"

Sundjata took a handful of dirt and sprinkled it into the air, and it fell straight to the ground. "No wind."

"Yes. Good. What would you use?"

"Well, I would use a spear, of course, like my father."

"This is a small beast remember."

"I would--"

Balla interrupted him, "Think!"

Sundjata paused. "Bow--with poison."

"Excellent! And remember to appease the bush spirits. Where do they live?"

Sundjata thought for a moment. "Rocks, forests and slopes."

"Which animals possess the greatest nyama?"

"The Duiker, the antelope we are tracking, anteater and hippopotamus."

Balla was impressed. "You remembered. Very good, now, how do you protect yourself against bad nyama?"

Sundjata thought before he spoke. "Amulets, charms worn on my clothes... and sacrifices."

"Good. Enough for now, let's go back," Balla said. This moth was becoming a butterfly - if he would only stand up straight. The boy was smart, had a way about him like his father, and was kind like his mother.

They turned back into the forest and walked down a trail that led into another that would take them to the main gate.

"Do you think I will walk straight someday?"

"Yes, I believe in your mother's magic. If anyone can do it, it will be her."

"Do you think I will be a great hunter?"

"Yes, I do."

"Do you think I will be a king some day?"

"I think you ask a lot of questions." He laughed. "And yes, I do, but why do you keep asking the same questions?"

"It keeps me going, gives me hope," Sundjata answered.

"I know it can be hard, but remember, your people may someday look to you. Give them hope. You belong to them, and they to you." Balla looked him in the eye to make sure he understood this most important lesson. "We can play mancala when we get back."

"I am going to beat you this time," Sundjata said with assurance.

"Ha, you think so?"

"I beat you."

"You beat me one out of every ten games."

"It is a start."

They walked through the forest with its deep greens shading the sun, but still felt the day's heat building. The forest changed to scrub, then to grass land and finally to farmers' fields. Sundjata pondered Balla's words and his role with his people. He felt a well placed silence made a big impression on Sundjata. Not everyone was worthy to learn, but Sundjata was proving so. The fields ended and now began the mud brick walls with grass roofs of houses. Niani was growing, and narrow twisting streets were becoming common. Smells of food, people, straw and smoke filled their heads. As they got close to the gate, people were shouting and running towards the palace.

"What is happening?" Balla asked a passerby.

The man running by looked at Balla, and his eyes went wide. "Come, come quick."

"Sundjata, come," Balla said as he quickened his pace. Sundjata limped close behind.

A crowd had gathered and was blocking the way past the gate.

Women were crying, and men were shaking their heads. "Clear the way; make a path!" Balla shouted. People closest to them turned and bowed their heads with sad expressions on their faces. One by one, they looked at them and stepped aside, making room, creating a path.

Sundjata was confused and became scared when he saw two bodies on the ground. One was moving and the other still. He moved closer and saw his mother, Nama, and Sossuma standing around them.

"Come," said Balla, taking Sundjata by the arm.

Sundjata gasped as he saw his father motionless, his eyes closed, and his mouth open. Dried blood was apparent through his clothes. He then noticed Dankaran and Fanta, tears in their eyes as Sogolon took his arm and hugged him.

Balla knelt down next to his father who was sweating and shaking, and his left arm was bandaged. "Father!" Balla cried. "What happened?"

"Hippopotamus," said Ahmed, who had pushed through the crowd after he found Azeez. "We were crossing the Niger when a huge beast burst from the water and attacked Doua. Kon charged the huge beast and saved Doua, but it grabbed him. There was nothing we could do." Ahmed shook his head, upset, reliving the scene. "Then Doua came down with a fever less than a day later."

Sogolon put her hand on Balla's shoulder. "Go tell your mother; we shall bring your father to your home."

"He has a fever. It's not just his arm. He is not well," said Ahmed.

"I shall prepare to take down his fever," Sogolon said.

"Kon is dead; Kon is dead!" cried the mother voice. "He was such a good man."

"We are in trouble now. Trouble I tell you," said the angry

voice.

Sogolon nodded her head in agreement with both voices. Her love was gone, and she felt lost. He was the first man to love her, and he changed her life forever. Whatever would happen now would be cold without his love.

Sossuma looked down at Kon, feeling sadder than ever before. Tears rolled down her beautiful face as she looked at her husband's broken body. Dankaran came to her side and hugged her, his eyes and nose wet.

Nama knelt down and kissed her fingers then touched Kon's cheek. This man had given her children, had made her a home, and had been so kind to her. It wasn't fair that he was now gone. His children needed him; his wives needed him.

Fanta stood with her arms wrapped tightly around her small frame. Her tears fell to the ground, staining her round cheeks. *This can't be, this can't be,* she thought, over and over. Fanta watched Sogolon and could see her heart breaking.

Azeez rubbed his forehead, looking at the scene. The air was heavy. This was a good man; sometimes Allah's plans seemed too harsh to take. "Uncle," he whispered, as he touched Ahmed on his shoulder.

Ahmed turned to see his nephew and rose. He led Azeez away from the crowd and towards the palace. "It was written; there was nothing I could do. I was standing on the shore. We killed the beast with spears and arrows, but it was too late."

"I can see you had true affection for those men, as did I," Azeez said, surprised to see his uncle looking so forlorn.

"Yes, they were good men. Good as I had ever met. Kon was a true leader with fairness in his heart. Doua was his right hand, advisor, confidant and friend. To lose both..." Ahmed said.

"But Doua lives?"

"He has the fever. I have seen this before: he is weak, and his arm broken. The fool attacked the beast trying to save his friend. He's lucky he's alive. I fear he will not last long. Men of this quality, we do not meet often," said Ahmed as he put his hand on Azeez's shoulder.

"Our position here is now in jeopardy. All we have worked for could vanish like smoke in a breeze again," exclaimed Azeez as he waved his hand."

"True, Dankaran is young, but when his mother becomes his regent events may not favor us. She is a stubborn woman," Ahmed said with concern.

"Stubborn and spiteful if she does not get her way, and I fear we will lose the favor of this council." Azeez rubbed the palm of his hand against his chin. "I have dealt with her. She is not like her sister queens, Sogolon or Nama."

"What about Sogolon's son? Is there a chance of him being king? Is he walking?"

The people began to sing the death song. The air was heavy with sadness. It was as if they were under water.

*****

Fanta looked in the basket. "Ahh," she said, aggravated at finding it empty of namugu.

Sogolon sat outside her hut watching Kolonkan play with Sundjata and heard Fanta. "What's the matter?"

Fanta stuck her head through the window. "We are out of baobab leaves. I need namugu to make sauce."

Sogolon watched Sundjata follow Kolonkan around the back of the house. "Go to market," she said to Fanta. It had been two full moons since Kon's death, and everyone was having a hard time dealing with it, but Fanta was almost unbearable. Doua's passing soon afterward only further cast a dark mood over Niani. As for

113

Sogolon, only her children made things bearable. Evil spirits seemed to be everywhere.

Sossuma was out walking with two elder first wives from the surrounding larger villages of Niani, their servants close behind. The wives brought their first-born sons as commanded by Dankaran at his mother's urging. She was enjoying her position of regent and the power she now wielded. Hosting the first-born sons at the palace would ensure village loyalty.

Sogolon saw Sossuma and her entourage passing by her house. "Sister," she called and waved.

Sossuma heard Sogolon and ignored her at first until she was called again. Acting surprised, Sossuma turned and came closer as the entourage followed.

"Sister, do you have baobab leaves to share? I am all out, and Fanta needs to make sauce," Sogolon said with a smile. She rose in her awkward way and acknowledged the other women.

"Why don't you have your son get you leaves, or are you afraid he may fall over?" Sossuma asked sarcastically. She turned and dismissed Sogolon. "Her son is quite crippled; very embarrassing," she said for all to hear. [25]

Coming from behind the house with his sister, Sundjata stopped when he heard Sossuma talking. He hated the glares she threw at him. It was then he heard her embarrass his mother. He poked around the smooth wall of the house and saw all the women.

Sogolon smiled, shook her head and called after the group, "Much thanks, sister. Much thanks. The spirits will fix you someday," she said for no one to hear but herself.

Fanta heard the exchange and came out of the hut like an angry bee from a hive. "Ooh, I want to slap that woman. I don't care if she is queen. She walks around here..." Fanta imitated her by putting her right hand on her left shoulder and stuck her nose in the air.

"Let her be an ass; she will get her comeuppance."

Sundjata came from around the hut, angry, feeding off Fanta's energy. "Mother, I will get baobab leaves for you today." He came over to her, and she touched his cheek.

She smiled and looked up at him. He was bent over, but not so much anymore. "Thank you, my son. I know you will, someday."

"Today, Mother, today," Sundjata turned and went off to find Balla.

Sundjata never felt such energy and anger. It was as if a spirit had invaded his body. He knew Balla would be home, and he walked with limping determination.

Balla saw Sundjata from afar and could tell right away something was wrong. "What's the matter?"

"Sossuma, argh... She is so mean. What she has done to my mother shall not stand!" Sundjata was breathing hard.

"What?"

"My mother asked her for some baobab leaves, and she made fun of her and me in front of lots of others. She joked why don't I get the leaves, but I might fall over."

Balla shook his head. "So, you are ready then?"

"Yes, let's do it today. Now."

"Let's go then," said Balla as he held his arm up in the direction of their rendezvous. They walked away from Niani under the blue sky streaked with thin, white clouds--their destination a stand of dense balanzan trees in the middle of a farmer's field. In the middle of the stand was a small circular clearing. No one could see through the trees. It was a hot and sweat dripped from Balla's brow. He dug up several different size dark metal rods and smooth wooden sticks just under the red dirt. He laid them out on the ground from smallest to the tallest.

"Which should I start with?" Sundjata asked.

"Let's do smallest to tallest. Your mother said this could work."

Sundjata knelt in the dirt, and Balla handed him the smallest iron rod. He put both hands on the rod and began to reach out in front of him. At first his back was tight, but he did it again and again. His muscles warmed up, and his back became a little more flexible. Sweat beaded on his skin and rolled off his body in streams. After several times Balla would change the size of the rod and then give Sundjata a stick. The sticks allowed Sundjata to stretch his back out better. Sundjata's hands began to hurt, and his back ached. Then he remembered Sossuma's words, and the pain turned into determination.

"Arch your back as you reach out," Balla said. "Push, slow and steady."

Sundjata reached out again and again, and the more he reached, the more he began to feel movement in his spine. It hurt but felt good at the same time.

"How do you feel?"

"Good. I feel loose."

"Stand and take this iron rod."

Sundjata stood, breathing heavily, sweat pouring off his body. He put his hand on his back and could feel the bones move a little more, and he stood a little straighter. He took the iron rod and put one end on the ground. He slid both hands down the dark smooth iron and arched his back, pushing the metal forward. The spine moved. *This is it,* he thought. *I will be straight.* But it was as if his spine was stuck on something. "Balla, give me the tall custard apple branch." [26]

Balla handed him the branch, and the iron rod crashed to the ground.

Sundjata pushed his back outwards and bent the stick. With a pop his back was loose, and he felt a sharp pain. "Oww!" he yelled but stood straight as tears ran from his eyes and mucus filled his nose.

"Ahh," Balla said as he saw Sundjata stand straight. Balla lifted his arms in the air; he couldn't contain his excitement. "'The spirits and iron have intervened! You are well!"

"Oooh." Sundjata rubbed his back and noticed he was now standing straight. His back was sore, but he felt good.

Balla could not believe his moth had turned into a butterfly before his very eyes. The power in the iron and the wood had worked. The boys hugged each other and began to dance and sing.

Sogolon sat in the shade of her house making charms for Sundjata and Balla. The charms would protect them as they moved outside the safety of the city and the farmers' fields. Fanta had gone to the market to get baobab leaves and had taken Kolonkan with her. Sogolon could see out the open gate and looked at the passing people. In the distance she saw two familiar figures, but one moved different. She couldn't figure out what it was. She shrugged it off and went back to tying colorful threads to a copper rings when it hit her like lighting to a tree. It was Sundjata and Balla, but Sundjata was standing straight. She was enchanted watching her boy walking straight like an iron rod. Joy filled her heart and swelled in her chest. Her prayers to the spirits had been answered. She clapped her hands together and touched the tips of her fingers to her chin. Sundjata got closer, and she could see that he was carrying baobab leaves. Today was the day. She rose in her awkward way and began to sing and clap with tears in her eyes. "Something wonderful has happened today. The spirits have made this a triumphant day. My son walks like his father's way, oy yeah, oy yeah."

Sundjata could see that his mother was looking at him, and a large smile filled his face that he could not get rid of. "Mother, these are for you, and I did not fall over."

"Oh, my son, you are so straight and kind. Wait till Fanta sees you. It will even bring a smile to her face."

"Give him the bow now; give him his father's bow," said the mother voice.

"Yes, it is time," Sogolon agreed.

Fanta turned the corner from the gate and saw two boys with Sogolon. She recognized Balla, and the other boy seemed familiar. She held Kolonkan's hand, cooing, "Baby, who is the child? I know that child."

"Brother," said little Kolonkan.

Stopping in her tracks, Fanta gasped, "Oh, my. Come, child." She began to run, pulling Kolonkan into her arms and dropping the leaves she got in the market. "Sundjata! Sundjata!" she yelled, unable to contain her excitement.

Sundjata, Balla and Sogolon turned to see Fanta running towards them.

"Yes, yes, yes," Fanta said, hugging Sundjata. His little sister hugged him as well. "It is done. Your power is great, Sogolon. So great. I've waited so long for this day."

"Thank you, Fanta," Sundjata said, the smile still huge on his face. "You can make namugu now," he said, and he gave her the baobab leaves.

Chapter 10

In the Hands of God

During the night, Sundjata's back was sore, causing him to shift around on his mattress of straw and feathers. The morning sun found him tired. He rose and found Fanta up and preparing food.

"Stretch yourself. Walk if you must, but don't go far," Fanta advised. "Let's keep this quiet a little longer, till we know this is permanent and not a trick by the spirits. I'll be right back."

"Yes, Fanta," Sundjata agreed. He went around to the back of the house to keep out of sight and took his father's bow with him. His mother had given it to him after dinner. Thoughts of his father flooded his mind. He wished he could see him now and listen to Doua exclaim the lineage of his relatives. He felt sad, but then it must have been his father's influence with the spirits which helped him stand straight. He stood and felt pain, but he knew he must endure it. He pulled the string on the bow and winced. Balla taught him how to make a power object, and he made his father's bow his power object.

Fanta made her way to the growing square-housed Muslim quarter of Niani to Azeez and his uncle's house. She knew he rose early. When she knocked a tall, dark, bright-faced woman opened the door and took her to a room where Azeez was finishing his morning prayer.

"What are you doing here so early? Everything alright?" Azeez rose from his prayer rug with a concerned look on his face.

"Oh, yes, something wonderful has happened. You must see," Fanta said, her smile stretching her dark face.

Azeez could not help but smile back. "Give me a moment to dress, please." Azeez changed from his night clothes and put on a long shirt. He then tied a sash around his waist and slipped on a pair of sandals. "Lead the way."

Fanta was out the door, walking so quickly she was almost

running.

"How is your fisherman?" asked Azeez, trying to slow her down.

"Good," she said, keeping her pace through the dusty streets. Now back to the round houses of the original people.

"This better be good. Why the secret?"

"Oh, it is. Sogolon thought it would be best kept a secret."

They went through the gate as the palace was coming to life, and the servants and slaves were cleaning, cooking and completing their daily chores. The bright sky seemed to go on forever, Azeez noticed, just before he reached the back of Sogolon's house.

Sundjata had the bow stretched and pointed at the sky. He jumped with surprise when Fanta and Azeez were standing behind him.

Azeez's mouth hung open when he saw Sundjata pulling the bow and standing upright before him. "Allah be praised!" he exclaimed as he held his right hand in the air.

"See. The spirits have intervened. Sogolon's magic is strong," Fanta said.

Sogolon came up behind Azeez. "Isn't this wonderful?" she said, clasping her hands together and touching her fingertips to her chin.

"This is a miracle," Azeez agreed.

"It is. But I fear Sossuma will see this as a threat," Sogolon said as she shook her head.

Azeez's smile left his face, and in an instant, he knew she was right.

Sundjata looked at his mother, and then Fanta frowned.

"Mother, why is that?"

"She fears you want to overthrow your brother," Azeez said, assessing the situation. "She is a stubborn and jealous woman."

"Yes, she is," Sogolon agreed. "There have been complaints from the surrounding villages. They don't want to have to send their sons here."

"Yes, I have heard the same thing. I also hear that they are not finding satisfaction when they come to Niani to settle disputes. Kon was very good at this, and they know now what they have lost."

"I fear for the unity of the villages and Niani," Sogolon bemoaned as she shook her head.

"There is much talk in the market as well and--" Fanta stopped when she heard drums.

"There is trouble," Sogolon said, making her way to the courtyard with the group following.

Dust was rising into the air mixing with shouts and screams, and the sound of hoof beats.

Azeez heard people shouting about riders and strange men. "Close the gate!" Azeez yelled to the guards and ran to help them.

"Sundjata, get inside the house... and stay bent. Understand? Do not stand straight," Sogolon said after him.

"Yes, Mother," Sundjata said as he turned away with Fanta.

Sogolon made her way into the palace. "Sossuma, Sossuma!" she called up the stairs.

Sossuma lay in her bed dreaming. In her dream she was dancing to unseen drums when she heard her name, again and again. Then she heard screams and yells, her eyes opened, and anger rose in her.

Her handmaiden raced into her room. "My queen, we are under attack."

Sossuma jumped up naked and covered herself in a yellow and red wrap. She heard Sogolon downstairs calling her name, and her anger mixed with fear.

"How many guards are there on the palace grounds," Azeez asked a guard as they locked the gate with iron bars.

"About ten," said the guard with a worried look on his face.

Azeez wished his uncle and his men were in town. Then he realized besides the gate the most vulnerable spot was by Sogolon's house because of the tree by the wall. He turned and ran to her house, dodging arrows as they began to fly over the wall. Inside he found Sundjata, Fanta and Kolonkan. "Come! Inside to the palace. Hurry."

"I want to fight," Sundjata said with his father's bow and quiver full of arrows in his hands. "But mother says I should be bent again."

"Yes, yes, she is right. You must not pose a threat to anyone. Pretend until this danger has passed. Give me that bow."

Sundjata, with great reluctance, gave Azeez the weapon.

"Now, limp towards the palace--and tell any guards to come here to me."

Sundjata was first out the door. Then Fanta followed, holding Kolonkan tightly to her chest.

Outside, Azeez slung the quiver over his shoulder and knocked an arrow. Stepping back from the hut and seeing a man at the top of the wall, he let the arrow fly. It hit him in the middle of his chest with a thud. Blood flew into the air, and the man fell into the courtyard. Azeez knocked another arrow and saw a head pop up above the wall. He drew the bow and waited as a man pulled himself up, and now the whole body was exposed. He let the arrow go, catching the man in the side. The man yelled and fell backwards.

Sogolon appeared in the palace doorway and an arrow struck the wall. She winced but out stretched her arms to Sundjata and Fanta. "Come, come." Sundjata was running but everyone was too busy to notice. Fanta was close behind still clutching Kolonkan tight. Sogolon grabbed Sundjata's arm and pulled him through the door. Now Fanta was in the doorway. She slammed into Sogolon, and they both fell to the ground. Sogolon was on her side looking up at Fanta. Fanta was on her knees, still holding a screaming Kolonkan with an arrow sticking out of her back.

Sundjata rushed over to Fanta and took Kolonkan from her. "No, Fanta, no," cried Sundjata through tears.

An arrow was deep into Fanta's lung, and she struggled to breathe. Sogolon crawled over to Fanta. She put her hand on Fanta's face, their eyes locked, and Fanta fell onto her side, her breathing getting shallow.

"I'm sorry," Fanta said in a gasp.

"No, no never. You are my sister forever," Sogolon said with tears in her eyes.

Now three men in the tree climbed onto the wall. Azeez looked at his quiver and counted ten more arrows; he would be in trouble soon. He dodged an arrow, then fired one that missed his target but hit so close that the man lost his balance and fell. The second arrow pinned a man's arm to a branch, and he screamed in pain. The third man jumped to the ground, and Azeez ran to the side of the house. The man jumped to his feet, and Azeez shot him in the throat. More arrows rained down onto the courtyard. One landed inches away from his foot, and Azeez ran for the safety of the palace. He could hear arrows hiss as they passed his head. He ran through the door to see Sogolon leaning over Fanta. Sundjata was crying and pacing back and forth with a screaming Kolonkan in his arms. Sogolon was holding Fanta's face. Azeez knelt next to Fanta and saw the arrow protruding from her back. "Damn it!" he shouted, shaking his head and touching her arm.

Sogolon lay Fanta's head onto her lap and stroked her short curly hair as tears dropped from round cheeks. "I owe you so much."

Fanta struggled to breathe, and she felt herself slipping away to join the ancestors.

Azeez was angry and went back to the doorway. No more men attempted to breach the wall. He saw the gate guards with their backs to the wall, blood staining the ground where they had stabbed men trying to get through. Several servants and a few guards were lying in the courtyard. They were pierced with arrows, their blood seeping into the dirt.

Sossuma came down the stairs with Dankaran. "Who is doing this to us?"

"It has to be Sumaguru," said Azeez. He noticed Sundjata was standing straight, and he motioned to Sossuma. "Come see."

Dankaran saw Sogolon and Fanta on the floor and went to them. He put his hand on Sogolon's shoulder.

Azeez called to Sundjata; he mouthed and motioned at him to bend.

Sundjata frustrated understood and hunched over.

"I don't see anyone," Sossuma said, aggravated.

"Look at the gate," said Azeez, seeing a man on the outside talking to a guard. He saw Sossuma's youngest handmaiden, took her by the arm and stepped back into the room. "Take this bow and take the royal chair and hide it in your room. Go now. Don't let the queen see. We mustn't let the Sosso get them... go."

The guard saw Sossuma in the doorway and ran over to her.

"My Queen, Sumaguru says if you will surrender there will be no more fighting," the guard said with concern in his voice.

Sossuma stepped back from the door and paced the room. "We can't fight them; we weren't ready." She looked at Azeez.

"No, we were not prepared, and I am sure he has attacked other villages as well to keep everyone scattered," said Azeez.

"How do you know that?" Sossuma asked.

"Because it's what I would do," Azeez said. He hoped that Sumaguru would be a man of his word, and they seemed to have no choice. He and his uncle told her to prepare, but she wouldn't listen. Now it was too late; it was written then. He knew he was in the hands of God.

Sossuma approached the guard. "Open the gate." She knew what she would do to appease Sumaguru. She knew how to melt him, whether he was a great sorcerer or not, he was still just a man.

"Poor, poor Fanta," said the mother voice.

"We are all going to die," said the angry voice. "You killed her; it's your fault."

"No," Sogolon said. She gently put Fanta's head on the ground and got up in her awkward way. "Sundjata, come." She took Kolonkan by the hand to comfort her.

Azeez watched the guards open the bloody gate. Raiders began to walk in, many of them shirtless. He saw others holding their horses just beyond the gate. They were lightly armed with small shields and their horses with no saddles. He hoped they were here to strike fast and raid, not meaning to stay. He looked around to see if Sumaguru was near, and sure enough the only man to ride through the gate had to be him. He was a large muscular man. He wore a blue sleeveless shirt and loose brown pants with sandals that went up to his ankles. A sword in one hand and a knife on his arm, his face was strong and his expression one of confidence. Two men walked on either side of his mount. He gave an order to stop anyone from the village from entering the palace.

"Where is the first son of Kon Fatta? Where is the new king?" Sumaguru asked in a deep, calm voice while his chestnut brown mare pawed at the dirt. He could feel the excitement of his men. They lined up behind him, excited at this victory. This raid was their biggest since the sack of Kumbi-Sahel.

Sossuma stood in the doorway, "Dankaran, come."

Dankaran rose from Fanta's body and went to his mother. "We should fight."

"No, not now, my son, we must wait; right now we must just get through this. Let me lead you through and we will be alright."

Sumaguru summoned one of his commanders and spoke to him. He was shirtless but wore leather straps over each shoulder holding a sword and a knife. He stepped forward. "Sumaguru demands the court of Niani to come before him."

Sossuma stepped out of the doorway with Dankaran beside her. "Go ahead. Today you will bring no shame to our clan."

Dankaran felt fear and anger, his stomach tight. Sumaguru and his men were fierce-looking. He must protect his people, but words stuck in his throat. He swallowed and stepped forward. "I am him."

Sumaguru smiled and spurred his horse forward and rode around Dankaran.

Sossuma attempted to step forward, but Azeez grabbed her arm. "Wait," he said to her, wanting to see what Dankaran was made of. "If we appear afraid, Sumaguru may grow bolder. We need his respect if we are to survive this. I have hidden the royal chair. We will not let him have it. If he asks, tell him we buried it with Kon, and his body is in a secret place."

Sogolon was behind them. "Listen to him, sister."

126

"Why do you come here?" Dankaran asked. He stood still, only turning his head as he was circled.

"To take what is rightfully mine," Sumaguru said. "My people where denied land, gold and a say in what happens in that land," he said as he stopped his mare in front of Dankaran.

"Who has done this to you?"

"First, the king of Ghana, and then your father," Sumaguru said.

"My father was a great king."

"He attacked my people and in doing so made me angry. He is dead because of my magic."

Dankaran was angry and clenched his fists. "That is not true!" Dankaran yelled, taking a step forward.

"Sumaguru, the queen regent and I would like to help guide the young King in resolving this matter," Azeez said hoping he would take the bait. They had walked out of the castle and stood behind Dankaran.

Sossuma stood next to Azeez and attempted to step forward, but Azeez took her arm again.

Sumaguru turned his head and horse towards Azeez and Sossuma, leaving Dankaran. "He speaks for you?" he asked Sossuma.

"He speaks when I want him to speak," Sossuma said.

Sogolon watching the scene rolled her eyes at Sossuma's words. But what bothered her most was the expression on Sumaguru's face. He seemed arrogant and dismissive, even worse than Sossuma. She turned away to get Sundjata.

Sumaguru smiled and dismounted. He put his sword in its scabbard. "Your husband was a thorn in my side, but he was a brave leader. Bring your court here and have them sit before me."

"Come into the palace, out of the sun," Sossuma said pointing the way.

"I like to be in the sun; the light can show you many things," Sumaguru said, looking around, impressed by the palace. "You can show me the palace after we conclude business here.

His commander cleared the area of people. "Bring the king something to sit on. Where is your royal chair?" He clapped his hands and paced the courtyard.

Azeez stepped forward. "I shall have the council brought here. However, we do not have a new one. We buried the old one with King Fatta. It is our custom to wait a full season before we make a new one," Azeez said a smile.

"Where is your uncle?" Sumaguru turned his attention to Azeez. "You both are very well known when it comes to buying and selling... and fighting as well."

"We only fight to protect what is ours, when we have to. We are just humble merchants working through the grace of Allah."

Sumaguru laughed a smug laugh. "You know what you are, and you will bring me lots of gold soon. Are you sure you are not telling me lies to stay alive?"

"My life is in the hand of God, and I never lie." Azeez felt relief that Sumaguru was interested in gold. "Excuse me," he said, and then went into the palace to get the servants to put down mats.

Sumaguru was mulling over Azeez's words when he saw the famous Sogolon standing by the palace door. The stories he heard were true. He couldn't believe how bent she was and wondered about her magic and her voices. She seemed too strange to be a threat. He was even more amused when a boy who was bent over came out of the palace and she touched his arm. Even her son wasn't right. How could these people ever have given him trouble?

"Go to the courtyard," Sogolon said to Sundjata. She turned to see Fanta's body on the floor and her heartbreak began to turn to anger. She turned away and went to join her children.

"We are all going to die," the angry voice said.

"Fanta can never be replaced," said the mother voice.

"I know," Sogolon said aloud.

"You know what?" asked Sumaguru, who had walked up behind her.

"I know nothing except that sometimes life is cruel. It bends and twists us," Sogolon said, holding back anger awash in sadness.

He smiled. "I see. Is that why you are the way you are?"

She took a deep breath and looked at him in a sideways glance, wanting to lash out. She took another breath, again her braids moving across her face. "I am like a tree that grows crooked because it is always being pushed by the wind, but it makes me ready for the storm."

Sumaguru weighed her words, looking for insult but found none. "How can someone so ugly be so smart?"

"It's the same way someone can appear to be so strong and yet act so weak."

Sumaguru felt that insult and slapped Sogolon across the face with the back of his hand.

Sundjata stepped between his mother and Sumaguru and looked into his eyes. He continued to play a cripple but would not allow another strike.

After the slap, the people of Niani outside the open gate began to yell and push. Azeez was coming through the door and saw what happened. He reached for his sword but forgot he left it home and hurried to Sogolon's side.

Sumaguru laughed. "I'd kill you both. I'd kill you all, but I'd rather people see the weakness of this clan. Obviously, you are cursed, and I will not anger the spirits by interfering in their schemes to make you suffer. People will see who is strong." He turned to Sossuma. "Where is your court? I am growing impatient."

"They will come," Sossuma said. "You caught us by surprise." Then she felt strange as for a moment she felt bad for Sogolon.

Men came with mats to cover the ground, and Sumaguru sat while his men stood behind him. Dankaran sat opposite of him. Sossuma sat to Dankaran's right with Sogolon, Sundjata and Azeez to his left. The council of representatives, the sorcerer in red, and the large men of Sossuma's village filled in around them. The first sons of the surrounding villages stood behind them.

Before Azeez sat down he saw a palace guard and instructed him to bring Fanta's body into Sogolon's house. He counted fifty armed men behind Sumaguru. He saw many others outside the gate as they held back a gathering crowd of villagers. None of their cavalry or soldiers had attempted to help them; this was a large force for sure. He knew now they were on their own.

"I am now the force that will rule the bright country from the Niger to Niani. We will now take what is rightfully ours when we need it. I am very generous, but as you have seen my magic is strong and the ancestors favor me. Do not oppose me or my retribution will be swift and terrible," Sumaguru warned.

"If you let us know how much you want we can provide it for you. Remember, we are used to taking taxes not giving them," Azeez said.

"Does he speak for you, this man of Islam? This man of one God," Sumaguru asked in his dismissive tone. The control he felt swelled his chest, but he always knew he would wield this power someday. The feeling was intoxicating.

Sossuma waited a moment to measure her tone. She saw what had happened to Sogolon. "He is our factor. He doesn't speak for me but because of me." She smiled a confident smile.

"Then we will expect gold and salt every three full moons. During harvest season rice and grain as much as ten camels can carry. Azeez, you and your uncle will bring this to us. We will pay you a fee to do this, as I am a reasonable man."

"Ten camels are a lot. What if it does not rain? What if the miners find less gold? How will this amount of gold and salt be determined?" Azeez inquired.

"I will send some men here to see what you have and what we should take."

"These amounts need to be flexible," Azeez said.

"It depends."

"On what?"

"On how much we need," Sumaguru said with cold eyes.

Dankaran sat there wanting to speak, confused by the way everyone was paying this man homage. He killed many of his people and now wanted to take things from them. He leaned over. "Mother I--"

"Not now," clipped Sossuma, cutting him off.

Dankaran frowned and sat back feeling frustrated and angry.

Sumaguru saw the exchange between Dankaran and his mother. "Son of Kon Fatta, I see anger in your eyes, and you need to see my power. Who are these boys behind you?

"They are the vassals' sons of the many villages," Sossuma said. "It is a show of their loyalty."

"Which are from the biggest villages?" inquired Sumaguru.

Sossuma pointed to three shirtless boys on the verge of manhood standing behind her. Two stood with heads down, but one looked straight ahead with defiance on his face.

Sumaguru shook his head. "Good, they will come with me to

Sosso as a sign of their new loyalty."

"I can watch them. You won't have to bother yourself with them," Sossuma said, tilting her head. "Let me show you the palace. Your factor can talk to mine, and we can strike a bargain satisfactory for all."

Sumaguru made a face of approval. "I have something in mind. Now, please show me your palace." He turned to his captain and whispered in his ear and rose to his feet.

The captain with the leather straps motioned to Azeez to come to him. "Bring these sons of kings to me."

Sossuma said, "I know we can work together."

"Perhaps." Sumaguru noticed Sossuma's beauty. Her tall lean body and deep brown, almost black eyes that stared a bit long into his.

Dankaran sat there feeling lost.

Sogolon watched Sossuma lead Sumaguru inside. "Careful, sister," she said to herself.

"How long will you stay in Niani?" Sossuma asked, leading him into the palace.

"Not long. Until tomorrow, I think." Sumaguru's eyes searched the main court room with a high ceiling. He saw the two-step altar adorned with the large wooden statue of a man, woman and child. At its feet were many sacrifices of food, plants, and small carved wooded idols from the death of Kon and Doua. "Your palace is very beautiful." This palace was much smoother than his; the bricks and stones were covered by mud plaster. He felt himself becoming jealous, but then he smiled knowing that he could destroy it if he so chose.

Sossuma turned to her handmaiden. "Bring palm wine, water and some food. Set it up down here." The maiden bowed turned and scurried off. Sossuma turned to Sumaguru. "You must see the view from above; come." She turned, and they went up the stairs.

Sumaguru put his hand on the smooth tan wall and watched how Sossuma's body moved under her wrap. He felt a rush in his chest. The stories of her beauty were not exaggerated. He laughed at the thought of the two opposite-looking queens.

"From my window you will see most of the city," Sossuma said, leading him through the door. As he passed through she closed and locked it by pushing a bar into the wall.

Sumaguru looked out over Niani at its many round and square houses. It was bigger than he expected; the city was growing fast. The market place was large and open, and he smiled while watching his men taking by force the goods from the sellers. "Your city is large and rich. Azeez and his uncle serve you well. There are many things to have here."

Sossuma walked up behind him, whispering, "There are many things to have right here." She pressed her body onto his. She ran her hands across his stomach and then down his legs. She laid her head on his back below his neck and smelled the sweat and dust on his skin. She laid her hand across the front of him and felt him grow as it filled her palm. She felt his body stiffen as he became more excited.

He pushed into her hand and closed his eyes taking a deep breath. This would be the ultimate victory to take Niani and take the queen of his enemy.

Sossuma held him in her hand. When he turned around she let go. She watched him untie her dress. She knew he couldn't wait to see her, and it excited her. She spread her arms as he dropped the dress to the floor. She stood there feeling her power, knowing it was she taking him. She liked how his eyes moved over her naked body. He unbuckled his belt, holding his sword and let it drop to the floor. Then she lowered his pants and pulled him to the floor as she was about to climb on top of him.

Sumaguru realized Sossuma was moving him towards the

floor. He couldn't wait. He grabbed her hard and spun her around, forcing her down.

Before she realized what was happening, she was on her hands and knees, and he was inside her thrusting fast. She wanted to control him. She tried to turn around, but he held her there. She tried again, but he pushed back harder his right hand now on her back.

She submitted, now he would desire her even more with this taste.

He had been out for weeks raiding and hadn't had a woman in a while, and his pace made him climax fast. This feeling was of ultimate triumph. No clan, no queen would resist him now. He reveled in it with a deep moan, holding her tight to him.

Sossuma held his weight as he lay on her back breathing heavy. She hoped a child would come of this. She tilted her body, and he slid off to the floor. "I have food and drink downstairs."

Balla stood outside the gate blocked by the spear carrying Sosso guards. He was looking for a glimpse of Sundjata or Sogolon. He strained his neck and was worried about what might happen to his lion butterfly. He noticed Dankaran's new griot standing close to him.

"Have you seen the king?" asked the griot.

"Not yet." Balla saw Azeez and called out.

Azeez started to walk back towards the palace worried about the vassals' sons being taken. He heard his name and saw Balla and Dankaran's griot. "Let them through," he said to the guards, pointing at the boys. "They work for me."

The Sosso captain nodded his head. The spears were pulled aside, and they entered the courtyard.

Dankaran's griot ran towards the palace.

"How's Sundjata? Is he okay?" Balla said concerned. "Is this the Sosso?"

"He's fine. He's with his mother." Azeez pointed them out. "Yes, Sumaguru has come."

Balla breathed a sigh of relief; he could see them through the crowd. He walked up to them touching both on the shoulder. "Good to see you. I was worried."

"Balla," said Sundjata to his great relief.

"How's your family?" Sogolon asked.

"Good, safe, I hid them in a stand of trees in a farmer's field. What is happening here?"

"We are at the mercy of these people; we have to pay them." Sogolon paused and looked at the palace.

"And?" Balla asked.

"Hmm, well Sossuma is dealing with their leader in there."

Balla looked at the palace, concerned and alarmed to see Dankaran with his griot going inside. "Dankaran is not part of the negotiations?"

"Sossuma has her own special negotiations," Sogolon said smiling.

Balla felt sad for Dankaran. He could see that the griot his mother gave him was weak.

Dankaran went inside the main hall looking for his mother. He saw her and Sumaguru descending the steps.

"The food is ready, my king," said Sossuma's handmaiden. She moved close to him and whispered in his ear, "Your royal chair is hidden away in my chamber. Azeez did not want them to take it."

Dankaran looked in the direction of the altar and realized it was gone. He nodded his head, acknowledging the good idea.

Sossuma came down the steps feeling victorious. Seeing her son turned toward Sumaguru, she said to him, "You must be hungry."

Sumaguru's captain entered the palace. He walked over to Sumaguru, whispered something in his ear and then went back outside.

"Sumaguru's face broke into a grin. "Yes, let's eat."

Servants placed bowls of food on the floor and encircled them with palm mats. Servants handed Sossuma, Sumaguru and Dankaran each a calabash with water.

"To the ancestors," Sossuma said, spilling a little on the floor.

"Yes," Sumaguru said and held his calabash high, spilling a little then taking a drink.

Dankaran looked at his mother, not believing how she was acting. He turned to his griot, a thin young man with a weak chin and small mouth. "It looks like she's having fun. I don't understand."

"She is securing the peace. What's done is done. She knows what she is doing," the griot replied.

As the group ate, an odd feeling filled the silence in the room. A growing tension and uneasiness was in the air.

"I like your palace; it's very well made. It's nice and green down here as well. I was here as a child."

The captain came back inside and motioned to Sumaguru.

"Ahh, young Dankaran, I have a lesson of my power for you. Come outside," Sumaguru commanded, rising from his mat.

Outside, Sundjata, Sogolon, Balla, Kolonkan and Azeez stood against the wall in the shade of the palace. They could not stand to see Sossuma put on an act for Sumaguru. From beyond the wall and gate they could hear people talking, crying and some shouting. Then, through the gate a raider led a brown horse covered in bright red blood that dripped down its body. The blood did not come from the horse but from the body hung across it. The body was bright red, the muscles exposed with the skin peeled off. The dark, wrinkled, wet skin was next to the red body. It looked like leather.

Sogolon first thought it was an animal, but horror gripped her. It was a person, a boy. Tears filled her eyes.

Azeez had seen skinned people before and recognized it right away. "Cruel," he said aloud.

Sundjata, transfixed by the terrible sight, could not turn away. It was the worst thing he'd ever seen.

"Ahh," Sumaguru said, spreading his arms wide. "My new coat," he exclaimed.

Sossuma let out a shriek when she realized it was a boy on the horse. The boy's blood was thick and sticky on the horse's coat. Flies were buzzing around the horse, making him shake his long mane. She put her hands to her mouth.

Sumaguru picked the dripping skin off the horse. "This is one of the vassal boys; you can keep the other two with you. I only need this," he said as he held the dripping skin in the air.

Chapter 11

Lions versus Cheetahs

The blinding sun turned the pale sky of the morning into a deep blue. Sundjata, Balla, Bory, Fran and Kama were lying in the grass on a hillside shaded by trees. They were waiting for cheetahs to come and rest.

"So, tell me again about the look on Sossuma's face when she saw you stand up straight?" asked Manding Bory, Sundjata's half-brother. He looked like his mother, Nama, with a small nose and flat cheeks.

"Ahh, not again," said Fran, vassal son from Tabon. You've asked that every moon for almost a full growing season.

"She keeps getting meaner, and anytime she gets upset it makes me happy," Bory said with a smile.

"She is strange - one minute smiling, the next yelling. She has no patience," Kama, vassal son of Sibi, said.

"She made a face like she smelled shit and then a sound like a goat," Sundjata said, imitating her.

Bory laughed hard and rolled in the grass. The others laughed at both the story and Bory's reaction to a story he had heard often.

Balla noticed that since Sundjata had begun standing tall he was becoming a force. He was persuasive like his father and kind like his mother.

The laughter died away, and the boys returned to watching for the cats.

"Are you sure they will come?" Bory asked impatiently.

"They have been coming almost every day," Sundjata said with confidence. "They will come."

"You have the blood of the lion in you; they will listen to you,"' Bory said.

Balla gave Sundjata a sideways glance.

Sundjata had stumbled upon this place by accident while out hunting. He walked right into four young sleeping cheetahs. They were lying in knee-high, brown and green grass. Their sleek chests were rising and falling, and the tips of their black-capped tails curled, waiting for the heat of the day to wane. When he was not attacked he knew his power was growing. His father's blood of the lion and his mother's buffalo blood were fierce; no wonder the cheetahs were afraid of him. He wanted to impress the others. Since his secret was out, and now that he was standing straight, he never wanted to be laughed at again.

"I have the blood of the lion in me as well. I can go with you," Bory said.

Balla and Sundjata looked at each other and thought for a moment. "Not a good idea," Balla said.

"Right, but I have the blood of the buffalo as well. It gives me an edge," Sundjata said winking at Bory. "When you get a bit older... and bigger.

Bory was disappointed, but he understood. He was the youngest of the group, much smaller than the others. Balla was the oldest, and Sundjata and the other royals were close in age.

"Look. Here they come," said Fran. The group ducked down, as where they lay was higher than the shady open spot the big cats strolled onto.

One by one, the cheetahs strolled into the shade with their mouths open. Their pink tongues panting hard and their shoulders shifting their coat back and forth. They moved in their silky-smooth gait. Out of the sun, they dropped their thin muscular yellow and black bodies onto the grass.

The boys waited for the cats to settle and become drowsy.

Balla whispered to Sundjata, "Are you sure about this? You walked among them only once before?"

"Yes, they were scared of me; they won't attack," he whispered to Balla. *"I think,"* he added, more to himself.

"Are you afraid, Sundjata?" asked Kama.

"He is not afraid," Bory said in his brother's defense. He turned to Sundjata. "Are you afraid?"

"No," Sundjata said with confidence.

"Their heads are small," said Fran.

"But their teeth sharp," Kama replied.

They waited until each cat had its small but sharp-toothed head on the ground.

Sundjata took a deep breath and stood up straight with his father's bow over his shoulder. He left his quiver of arrows on the ground.

Balla's eyes looked to the quiver then to Sundjata, imploring him to pick it up.

Sundjata gave a small shake of his head.

Balla's eyes did it again.

Sundjata rose and began to walk down the hill. After a few steps, he began to sing in a soft voice.

"Blood of the lion

Blood of the buffalo

Make me strong

Blood of the lion

Blood of the buffalo can't go wrong

Blood of the lion

Blood of the buffalo

I have my father's bow."

The boys looked on in amazement. Sundjata with nothing but a bow walked down the grassy hillside to the resting cheetahs.

Balla was holding his breath.

"They are going to eat him," said Kama.

"No. Cheetahs don't eat lions. It's the other way around," Bory said with both hands grasping thick grass blades between each finger.

The four young male cheetahs heard something moving towards them. One by one, they lifted their heads and rolled over. Their chests low to the ground with legs outstretched. Their backsides high, tails twitching left then right.

Sundjata kept singing in soft tones, watching each cat, careful not to move too fast or get to close. "Hello, my friends. We meet again. Remember me?"

One cat hissed, but the others growled in low deep tones.

Sundjata got as close as he dared and stood his ground still speaking in soft tones. "Now, I am part lion, so you are afraid of me."

The cheetah nearest to him swatted the ground. The paw landed close to his foot; he could feel the ground shake from the blows. Sundjata felt fear and excitement flash through his entire body. He took a few steps to the right, and the cats turned their bodies to follow him. Each time he moved, they adjusted to stay aligned with him. Sundjata felt confident and took a step closer. The cats growled, inching their coiled bodies backwards, ready to spring into action.

Balla was in awe. Bory and the others were mesmerized. They

held their collective breath, feeling dizzy, scared and excited.

Sundjata took half a step closer, and the closest cheetah lashed out like lighting. He felt the weight of its paw on his foot. Its claws were not out, yet Sundjata felt as if lightning had struck him. He raised his arms in the air, and jumping as high as he could, he swung his father's bow over his head and screamed, charging the frightened cats.

The boys jumped at Sundjata's scream and could not believe their eyes. The cheetahs scattered, running away in different directions.

Sundjata was now laughing as hard as he could.

Balla was smiling and shaking his head at his brave lion butterfly.

The boys walked home side by side with Sundjata in the middle. They laughed as they each retold the story. The sun was getting low in the sky, streaked with wispy, thin white clouds, as the boys entered the palace. After a drink of water, the other boys took off to their homes eager to tell what they had witnessed.

Sundjata entered the hut to find his mother sitting with Kolonkan on her lap.

"What did you do today?" asked Sogolon. "You look happy."

Kolonkan went and hugged her brother.

"Not much. Just teaching some cheetahs not to play with a lion," he said with a smile.

*****

Sundjata and his usual entourage hunted along the Sankirini River. After hunting, they played mancala for a time, making pits in the dirt by using stones from the river. Sundjata and Balla had beaten them. After several rounds Sundjata then bested Balla. With mancala over, the boys began a stone-throwing contest which Balla was winning.

"Watch this," proclaimed Kama. He raised both arms high in the air. "This rock may land on the other side."

Bory looked across at the wide swift-flowing river to the far bank. "Ha!" was his reply.

Kama held tight a rough, sharp-edged red stone he had found not in the water but on the edge, half-buried in the dirt. Feeling its heavy weight in his palm, a look of supreme confidence appeared on his face as he leaned as far back as he could and with great effort thrust his arm forward. But he held on to it much too long, and it gave a mighty splash not far from where he stood.

There was silence for a moment before the boys began to laugh. The laughter got stronger as they looked at each other and the disappointed look on Kama's face.

Kama shook his head and saw in the water a good-sized grey rock. He knelt on the bank and plucked it out of the warm clear water. He then took several steps back from the river bank. He liked the feel of the smooth round stone on his fingers. He took a running start, and as he made it to the edge of the river he let the smooth stone roll off his finger. He launched it from where he stood. It flew high and far. The boys stopped laughing as they watched it sail in the air. It made a small splash and floated down through the rushing currents to settle on the sandy bottom. Kama's face showed confidence again, and now the group nodded their heads in approval.

Balla had a large round stone, and from where he stood he launched it as far as he could. When it landed he yelled, "I've won again!"

"No!" Fran yelled. "Kama's went further."

"No, no," Bory proclaimed. "Balla's for sure."

Balla turned to Sundjata, "Mine, right?"

"Honestly, your throw surprised me. I was looking for a rock." Sundjata held a small red stone in his fingers.

"I've won," said Fara, the blacksmith's youngest son, suddenly as he approached them from behind. He held a rock and with a violent throw sent it further than Kama and Balla's stones.

"That's a winner for sure," Sundjata said with envy. Fara's muscles were tight and solid.

"Sundjata, is it true that you walked among cheetahs?"

"Oh, yes; I saw it with my own eyes," Bory exclaimed.

Fara turned to the others. "All of you?"

"It was the most amazing thing I'd ever seen," Kama said.

"I wouldn't have believed it if I hadn't seen it," Fran said.

"You are getting quite a name for yourself," Fara said as he turned to Sundjata.

Sundjata laughed. "I don't know about that."

"Your name is on people's lips. Many are not happy with your brother's rule. You have settled a dispute between two farmers, and you saved a girl from the river," Fara exclaimed.

"That's right. You did all those things," Bory said.

Balla felt proud of Sundjata.

"My brother is king, and rightfully so. He will get better. Much better when Sossuma has less influence on him."

This is very bad, Balla realized.

"Dankaran will be fine, and the people will learn," Sundjata said with confidence.

"Well, my father doesn't think so." Fara shook his head. "I must get back to the forges." He turned to walk away.

"Fara," Sundjata called after him.

Fara turned around.

"I never thanked you for those iron rods you made for me. Thank you. Their power helped me; I am sure of it. I could feel it," Sundjata said with gratitude.

"Good. I am glad to have helped you. The iron is powerful indeed," Fara said making two fists and squeezing them tight. Fara looked at Sundjata, sensing that someday he would be an important man. He held his tongue and said nothing. His power came from the secrets of the metal. Sundjata's hunter's power was different; it came from the animals, and he did not know those forces. He raised his right hand and turned to return to his forges.

The boys watched Fara leave, and Sundjata felt like going home. "I'm hungry and a little tired," Sundjata said with a stretch. He began to walk home, and the boys followed.

Balla was walking alongside Sundjata. "You realize if those words get to Sossuma's ears she may do something against you and your mother."

Sundjata smiled. "She is a miserable person, but I don't think Dankaran would allow it. He is my brother."

"I would be careful," Balla said as they walked back towards the palace in silence.

"I am going to my mother's big garden; there might be things to pick," Sundjata said to Balla as they reached the palace.

The other boys went off to a stand of trees to take a nap in the soft grass.

"Since your father's death, Sossuma has cut the amount of food you and your mother receive. Now she has to plant and tend the garden. Almost by herself since you no longer have a servant," Balla said trying to convince him to be wary. "You are lucky that Nama lends her servants."

"True, Sossuma can be nasty, but that is her. I do not fear her," Sundjata said.

Sogolon's big garden sat at the edge of a field. A farmer had given it to her after she healed his youngest wife from the bite of a small brown and red scorpion.

"Well, I am going to the garden. Do you want to come?" he asked Balla.

"No thanks. No farming for me, but I will see you later." Balla touched Sundjata's shoulder and turned for home.

Sundjata walked on, not believing Balla even though he was right about many things. The walk was long, and he hated that his mother had to do it so often. He practiced moving through the fields and forest with as little sound as possible. The garden was separated from the farmer's crops by indigo bushes. Sogolon had planted them for their medicinal uses. Sundjata would surprise his mother with what he could pick today.

Chapter 12

Rivals

Sossuma walked to the market place alone. The heat of the day was over, and night was falling. The town prepared for the evening meal, but she was restless and needed to walk. Every attempt to get rid of Sogolon or Sundjata had failed, and Sumaguru never returned. It had been over a growing season and their coupling did not produce a child. His demands for gold, salt and food only increased. She walked along a line of large thick trees behind the last row of stalls. She wanted to hear what the people were saying. She hid behind the widest tree in the stand. It wasn't long before she heard the grumblings of two salt sellers and a man who sold cloth.

"Are you finding it hard to sell your salt?" asked the cloth merchant. He was a heavy-set man putting out rolls of brown mud cloth with black and white patterns of zig-zags and stars.

"Yes, less people come to the market. It's been getting worse and worse." The heavy-set man wiped the sweat from his brow with the bottom of his tunic. "Same for you, I guess?"

"Yes, there are less caravans coming this way. Less gold as well," said the tallest of the salt sellers. There is more trading being done in towns near the big river."

"The king is too young; he listens to his witch of a mother too much. He must become a man," said the shorter salt seller.

"Ahh, we all miss his father. He was growing this place. There is too much arguing now; the people are scared. There is no fear in the Tuareg," the cloth seller said. "It's not as safe as it once was. I have heard of many raids on the caravans."

"True, the caravans don't come as much since," the tall salt seller said in a sad voice. "This king has caught no one nor taught anyone a lesson."

"Sundjata should be king. I hear many good things about the

boy," the cloth seller said. "More like his father. He would teach the Sosso and the Tuareg a lesson."

"Yes," both salt sellers agreed.

The tallest one added, "Even though his mother is strange, she is kind."

Sossuma had heard enough; her face felt flush and hot. She balled her fists together and stormed off. She needed to get back to the palace. It was what she feared: Sogolon had to be spreading lies and this discontent.

*****

Dankaran's spear didn't stick into the light brown Dorcas gazelle that Kama, Fran and his griot had helped him track.

"The blood trail is still easy to follow," Dankaran said as he picked up a leaf with a splatter of fresh blood on it.

The others held back allowing Dankaran to track his kill.

"He's not bad at tracking," Fran said to Kama in a hush.

"True, but he's not as good as you know who," Kama responded just as softly.

The griot heard Fran and Kama whispering but couldn't make out what they were saying.

Dankaran knelt down, scanning the bush and looking for more signs. He crept forward, following splashes of blood and hoof prints till he saw a large bush with broken branches. The trail of blood led straight into it. Dankaran looked back at his group and shook his head, a smile on his face. He stood up straight and walked to the large, dark-green bush and pushed it back to reveal his prey. When he pushed the bush out of the way a wild dog barked at him and stood over the gazelle. Startled, Dankaran jumped backwards, and his heel caught a low branch. He tumbled backwards to the ground.

Fran and Kama watched Dankaran fall to the ground, and a wild dog run out of the bush. The griot was startled and jumped back. Fran and Kama began to laugh. The griot stepped forward to help his king.

"I guess that dog didn't know who you are." Kama said through laughter.

"Don't laugh at the king," his griot said with anger.

"We meant no harm; we are but from the same caste," Fran said controlling his laughter.

"All men fall, but it's how they get up," Kama said.

Dankaran rose, dusting off, embarrassed. "The dog was just watching my kill for me."

"You should take lessons from your brother. He makes cheetahs run away," Kama said picking some grass off Dankaran's tunic.

"That story is true?" Dankaran asked in disbelief.

"I saw it with my own eyes," Kama said.

Dankaran looked at Fran.

"Yes, me too," Fran acknowledged.

"I heard the story from Bory, but I didn't believe him. He is young and prefers Sundjata over me," Dankaran said. "He walked right into them?"

"Yes, into a group of them and made them run away." Fran shook his head.

Is he a better hunter than I am?" Dankaran asked.

The griot folded his arms and looked hard at Fran and Kama who now were caught off guard by the question.

"He is… good," Fran said.

"Yes... good," Kama agreed.

Dankaran looked at them, suspicious of their answers; their voices betrayed them. "Let's get this gazelle back to the palace," he said feeling jealous of his brother and embarrassed about his fall. Now even the royal caste was talking about Sundjata.

They butchered the gazelle and divided it up between Fran, Kama and himself. Through the entire walk home Dankaran could not stop thinking about Sundjata. His mother kept telling him how Sundjata was jealous, wanting to be king, but he didn't believe it. But now all the castes were talking about him in special ways. This was not the first time, yet they never said good things about him. Dankaran gave his gazelle parts to the palace cooks when he returned.

His mother saw him enter the main hall with that look on his face. She knew that look, and her son was unhappy. "What troubles you, my son?"

"Fran and Kama said I should be more like Sundjata, and that he is a better hunter." He dropped his head.

Sossuma had calmed herself down from the marketplace, but last night came rushing back. "I also heard people saying bad things about you and praising Sundjata. I am sure it is he and Sogolon spreading rumors. She is using dark magic, poisoning people against you. Don't we do the best we can for our people?"

Dankaran thought for a moment feeling anger surge through his body. "Yes, yes we do."

"Wasn't your father a great and loved king? And you are his son, his legacy."

"My brother needs to be taught a lesson."

"And see his reaction when it comes to him; it will be strong, and he will be angry," Sossuma said. 'It will show you his deceit."

*****

It was early morning with the sun creeping above the horizon, lifting the veil of night. Sogolon was rising when she heard horses outside. She took the wooden square out of the window and saw the figures in the dull blue morning light. She thought she saw Balla.

"Wake up, Sundjata. Wake up." Sogolon touched his shoulder.

Sundjata's head was full of sleep, but now his mother's touch and the sound of horses outside made him rise. "Mother, what is going on? I am tired." He rubbed his eyes and stretched, waking his sleeping muscles.

"Hello," Balla called through the window. I'm sorry to wake you, lazy boy, but I have something important to tell you.

"Ha, lazy, but I can outrun you," Sundjata replied. He rose, took the wooden door out of the opening, walked outside, and stretched again. "What is this? Where are we going?"

"Not we, me," Balla said with a concerned look on his face.

"Why not me? You are my griot."

"I'm afraid I am being sent on a mission. King Dankaran is sending me to Sumaguru."

"What! Why you?" Sundjata was growing angry.

"I don't know why; it's what the king wants. Maybe because I am capable. He says I must try to change the terms of the bargain that was struck when he invaded us."

"Well, of course you are capable, but you were given to me by my father," Sundjata grew angrier.

Sogolon was listening and came outside. "Sundjata, it's probably Sossuma making Dankaran do this."

"Well, he is king and a man now; he must make his decisions," Sundjata said clenching his fists.

"I must be off before the sun gets high," Balla said. He put his right hand on Sundjata's shoulder, looking into his eyes. "You have grown much and will be fine without me for a while. Just promise me you will leave the cheetahs alone." Balla smiled.

Sundjata put his right hand on Balla's shoulder. "You must be careful without me to protect you."

Balla smiled. "True, I will." He turned and mounted his deep brown mare.

"Why don't you take one of the big black ones from Ahmed?"

"They drink too much water, and they don't like me. Behave," Balla said. He turned his horse and galloped towards the gate as two other riders followed him.

Sundjata watched him gallop off, and he turned back, looking at the palace. He saw Dankaran and his mother in the doorway. "Brother," Sundjata said with anger in his voice, walking towards him.

"See his anger. If he is faithful to you, why?" Sossuma whispered in Dankaran's ear. "He knows he spreads lies."

"Why do you take my griot?" Realizing now that he and Balla had not been apart since the day they were introduced.

"He is off to Sumaguru to tell him he takes too much. We don't have enough stores in case there is drought again," Dankaran said with confidence.

"Why send him?"

"Because he is a griot, and Sumaguru will be less likely to kill him," Sossuma interjected.

"It is my decision," Dankaran said.

"Is it?" Sundjata asked. "Is it?" He turned away and kicked and stomped at the dirt in frustration, slamming his hands together.

Dankaran saw Sundjata's anger, and he knew his mother was right that his brother was a threat. He had become a rival.

*****

Sumaguru's captain rode alongside him in the early morning sun. They followed a trail through tall green hills, some with exposed red-rock faces. The air was fresh and light with small flies buzzing by them. They were going to talk to Sumaguru's nephew, Fakoli, whose village was only half a day's ride away.

"You are sure Fakoli is in the village?" Sumaguru said to his captain.

"Yes, he's there; our scouts have spoken to him. Are we going to use his cavalry again?" the captain asked.

"Yes. I want to raid along the Niger to the land of the Do. We will expand our power to wherever we can reach."

"No one is able to stop us," the captain agreed.

"We are united while everyone is squabbling. We are strong and will get stronger," Sumaguru said, feeling flushed with power.

The trail opened up and dropped down into Fakoli's village. Sumaguru and his ten men rode down into the village.

Fakoli was alerted of his uncle's presence, and he met him in the council area. He was waiting for him under a large, circular, brown, thatched grass roof held up by four large tree trunks. Grass mats were arranged underneath the open-air structure. Fakoli swatted at a fly with his elephant hair brush. He wore a red and blue shirt with no sleeves, his shorts exposed his strong, thick, muscular legs, and he rose and came out to welcome his uncle. They hugged warmly.

"Welcome, Uncle. It has been a while since you have come here. It's usually I who come to you," Fakoli said, motioning with his arm for Sumaguru to sit under the roof.

Sumaguru sat near the center. "Nephew, I come to you to talk about the future."

Fakoli sat across from his uncle and noticed his powerful arms and solid shoulders. "How can I assist you?

"Your cavalry is the fastest and strongest, and I want to expand my reach towards Do and the surrounding area. Come the next harvest season, I plan to bring in more food and goods," Sumaguru said with great confidence. "With your men I can reach far and keep other forces that may oppose us from attacking. It worked so well when I took Niani."

"Yes, it did. We were unstoppable that day." Fakoli wasn't surprised his uncle had come because he had not gone on the last two raids. He grew tired of raiding. Since he had found a beautiful young woman to marry he wanted to stay home a while. "Uncle, why don't you use saddles on your horses? Then your cavalry would be almost as good as mine."

"Since I rid us of Kon Fatta, the Sosso have taken their rightful place in the bright country. I will not let us fall," Sumaguru said with determination. "It is because I stick to the old ways and do as our ancestors did."

Fakoli felt his uncle's power and a level of confidence he'd never heard from him before. His power had grown unchecked since Kon Fatta had gone. Every undertaking his uncle had attempted had succeeded; his magic was growing stronger. "You are right, Uncle, and I will raid with you. I know that region well."

Sumaguru smiled. "Good. I was afraid you were growing soft. You got married again and were beginning to act like a woman," he teased. "Where is this new bride of yours? Is she a local girl? You married her while I was away."

"That's the thing, Uncle. She came from another tribe with her brother, a hunter," Fakoli said. "She was drawn to me from the start. Her name is Keleya."

Sumaguru began to laugh, low and slow at first, and it built until he couldn't contain it. He said, "It is so because I made it so."

Fakoli was confused. "Uncle, did you use your magic?"

"My power... I made a deal with a mansa; I took one of his daughters for you in exchange for not destroying his village. Keleya is my gift to you."

"Thank you, Uncle."

Sumaguru stopped laughing, and his expression changed. He became very serious. "You are welcome, and the next time I ask you to raid you don't stay home," Sumaguru said.

Fakoli was surprised by the seriousness of the tone. "Yes, Uncle."

*****

Sundjata and Fran were stuck in their stone and grass hunting hut. They built it on the edge of a local farmer's field furthest from Niani. Rain poured down hard, and sometimes droplets would drip through the thatched roof and splat onto the dirt floor. The air inside smelled like wet grass and dirt. They hung in their hammocks listening to the din, drifting in and out of sleep,

"How many moons has it been since Balla left?" Fran asked.

"Five," Sundjata said with a mix of anger and disappointment.

"Are you sure we can't hunt in this weather?" Fran asked. "Nothing would be able to hear or smell us coming."

"It would be impossible to track anything, and you should try to throw a spear or shoot an arrow with wet hands. You would be lucky to hit an elephant."

Below them, snoring rose up and annoyed Sundjata. "Why did you bring your slave? How did you find me out here anyway?"

"You have been in a bad mood since Balla was sent away. Where else would you be? The slave was sent to me by my father, so he follows me around.

"He annoys me," Sundjata said.

Fran smiled at Sundjata's bad mood. "Balla will return. Sumaguru has all the griots he needs I'm sure."

"Eh, when the rain stops get this snoring dog out of my sight," Sundjata said turning in his hammock and pulling a blanket over his head.

Once the rain had stopped, five shirtless men with clubs walked single file down a narrow trail. The sun was beginning to set, and the air was cool, giving the men goosebumps. Some began to shake, and not just from the damp air or the cold droplets of water hitting them as they brushed wet plants. They shivered because they knew what they were about to do would change the course of Niani.

"Are you sure this is the way?" asked the second man in line.

"Of course. I've been on this trail before. When Dankaran asked me to do this I made sure of where it was," said the first man in line who was their leader. He wore a tense look on his face as he clenched his jaw muscles. To kill the son of Kon Fatta was a serious thing.

They walked on in silence as the rain made everything on the trail soft. Some men slipped in the mud caused by the deluge. The sun was setting, but there was just enough light to see. The trail turned a corner, and before them stood the hunting hut. The leader took a deep breath and led his men to the opening of the hut. A blanket was used as a door, and he pushed it aside. He rushed through the hole with several men holding their clubs ready to strike. Inside the hut was dark; a man lay in a hammock.
27

"Who are you?" asked the dark shape in the hammock.

The leader brought his club down. He heard a crack and could feel warm blood splash on his face and chest. The other men began to chop downwards with their clubs. Each blow produced a dull thud or sharp crack when it hit bone. They circled the man in the hammock, and their blows knocked him to the floor. The man moaned a little, but this made him easier to strike and seemed only to excite them. They grunted as they hit him until they were breathing heavy and became tired. It was as if they used up all the air in the hut.

"Enough!" said the leader. "Go!" Each man lingered for a moment and then walked out of the hut. The leader was the last to leave. The excitement was gone, and nobody spoke as they walked back down the trail to Niani.

Sogolon woke and stretched her tight and twisted muscles the best she could. She needed to pee and rose seeing Sundjata not in his place. She removed the wooded door and stepped into the courtyard smelling the fresh morning air. In the blue grey morning light, she noticed a tall shirtless man enter the palace.

The shirtless leader saw a servant in the main hall and called to her, "Wake the king."

It was Sossuma's youngest handmaiden, and she was startled by the man's voice. She was cleaning things off the altar with the tall wooden idol. She hurried up the steps to bring the king.

The leader watched the steps for the king who came down in a hurry. He was also shirtless and rushed up to the man.

The handmaiden stayed on the steps but out of sight and pressed her body against the cool mud stone wall.

"Is it done?" asked Dankaran.

"It is done," said the leader. "You have a rival no more." He turned to walk out of the palace but paused to look at the large wooden idol. He felt intense fear. He left with his head down not wanting to make eye contact with anyone.

The handmaiden's eyes went wide with what she heard, and her heart began to race. She knew if she was caught listening she would suffer the same fate as Sundjata. She turned to run up the steps being as quiet as she could, but each step she made seemed loud.

Sogolon returned from relieving herself, and at the gate she passed the man she saw earlier. She looked at his face with his troubled expression. She thought it odd for such a strong man to seem so scared. But she was sure Sossuma and Dankaran had something to do with it. Sogolon could not worry about their schemes. She had to make breakfast for herself and Kolonkan. She started a fire outside and began to make her food, and every once in a while, she looked out the gate.

Chapter 13

The Fox in the Hills

Dankaran felt free and light as he had not felt in a long time. "Bring more food," he called to a servant.

"It is good that you listened to me," Sossuma said with confidence. "Now people will listen to you without distractions."

Sossuma's youngest handmaiden could not believe her ears and knew she had to tell Sogolon--but not be discovered doing so.

"I think I shall go for a ride today," Dankaran said.

Nama was puzzled by Dankaran's mood. He had done nothing but sulk around for days, and yesterday he walked around not speaking a word. "You seem in an exceptionally good mood today," Nama remarked.

"Ahh, well the skies have cleared, and the rain has stopped. The rain always brings in good things and washes away the bad." Dankaran stuffed more food into his mouth.

Nama gave a look of doubt. Her handmaidens stood behind her, and she turned to them. "One of you go see if Sogolon needs anything today."

They both nodded their heads and said in unison, "Yes, my queen."

"Ahh, I don't know why you bother with her," Sossuma said.

"She is our sister, is she not? She is kind, is she not?" Nama retorted.

"You waste your time; she is crazy.... and dangerous. I wouldn't be surprised if something bad happens around her. Bad spirits move about her," Sossuma said with great seriousness.

Nama was used to Sossuma's moods and ways. She learned to ignore them... most of the time. "Hmm, I don't believe that. I've spent plenty of days with her."

"Too many," Dankaran said with a full mouth.

"Don't talk with your mouth full," Sossuma snapped at him. "Eat like a king, not like a vulture."

"Yes, yes," said Dankaran. He got up, still chewing. "I am going for a ride." He strode out of the palace and headed to the stables with his griot close behind.

Sossuma's handmaiden wanted to leave, but she had to wait to clean up. Once Nama and Sossuma got up she would go, but then she saw Azeez enter the palace.

"Is the king here?" asked Azeez.

"Come with me," said the handmaiden. "Come." She walked out the door into the courtyard. The other two handmaidens looked up at her for a moment but kept on working. She looked around to see if anyone was watching and led him straight to Sogolon's house.

Sogolon was inside her house tending to Kolonkan when she heard a voice call out to her. "Queen Sogolon, may we enter?" "Yes, of course," she replied. She saw Azeez enter with Sossuma's handmaiden.

"My queen, I believe something bad has happened to your son. I heard a strange man talking to the king early this morning, and he told the king that he no longer has any rivals."

Azeez looked at the handmaiden in disbelief. "Are you sure that is what you heard?"

"Yes."

Azeez was worried. He still hoped for Sundjata to take over from Dankaran someday. If Sundjata was dead or crippled again all hope would be lost. "Where did Sundjata go?"

"He went hunting, of course, but he got caught in the rain," said Sogolon.

"He's dead; he's dead for sure," said the angry voice.

"No, but we need to be careful," said the mother voice.

"Do you think he went to his hunting hut during the rain?" Azeez asked.

"I would think so. He can't hunt in the rain; that is why he built it," Sogolon said.

"I will check. You stay here and be watchful." At a brisk pace, Azeez walked to the royal stables and chose a light brown mare he favored. He saddled it himself, as the smell of horse, manure and dust filled his nose. Flies buzzed around, but he ignored them and mounted up, taking off for the hunting hut. Once out of town he followed a trail he knew well and trotted at a steady pace. The closer he got to the hut the more his heart began to race. Between the heat of the day and his nerves, he began to sweat. He then broke into a gallop, branches hitting his body, stinging him, but he didn't care. One branch cut his cheek and drops of blood ran down his face. He saw the hut, stopped short of it, and dismounted. He tied his mount to a strong branch and walked down the trail. The closer he got to the hut, the more he could hear movement inside. He paused to listen. It sounded like an animal. He looked down to find a large stick and threw it at the hut. The stick hit the wall with a thud, and the noise inside stopped. He found another stick and threw it again. This time two jackals burst out the door and ran at full speed into the brush. Azeez drew the dagger from his belt, just in case, and moved towards the door. He poked his head inside. The room smelled of death, and he saw a body on the floor. Blood and bits of flesh covered the floor. The body was in terrible condition. The face of the person had been smashed in, and the jackals had chewed chunks of red flesh from the arms, legs and torso. The bones of the arms and the legs lay broken. It looked like it could be Sundjata, and Azeez's heart sank. This was a disaster. He gave a sigh and left the hut, walking back down the trail crestfallen. His uncle would be upset as well as they both liked the boy and had hopes of recovering the kingdom in his name. He untied his horse and trotted but did not pay attention to where he was going. He was lost in thought and wondered what he could do for Sogolon. Without Sundjata she wasn't a threat anymore, but she wasn't important either, regardless of her healing skills.

Dankaran rode along the river as fast as he could and felt the hot wind on his face. He could not stop smiling. His griot was a poor rider, and every time Dankaran turned to see where he was he laughed at his griot's awkwardness. He turned from the river and onto a trail that led to a long stand of trees. He pushed his mount faster, and the stand grew closer as he galloped over the red ground and tall grass. He began to laugh, and the faster he rode, the more he laughed. Dankaran was almost at the stand when he turned to see that his griot again was almost off his horse. Dankaran turned back to slow his mount, but something burst out of the trees and scared him. He pulled on the reins too hard and too fast. His mount tried to adjust, but the bit dug hard into its mouth making it stop short--losing its footing so both rider and mount fell hard into the dirt.

*****

Balla sat on the edge of the grass-roofed meeting spot--his back in the hot sun-- as he watched Sumaguru address his council. He stopped listening to Sumaguru brag about his powers, threatening those who dare stand against him. He looked at the faces of the council members. Some hung on his words, shaking their heads, clenching their fists and shouting. A few swatted flies and looked around at the others their mouths upturned in agreement. The oldest two elders nodded in and out of sleep, their grey heads bobbing up and down. And who would oppose him anyway? Everything he had attempted, he had done, and that bothered Balla most. He knew this must be temporary, that the spirits of his ancestors would not allow this. The trickster spirits must have them confused. Try as he might, he could not understand. Kon was a great king, a good man who treated all well, and this sorcerer king could be cruel, using his power to hurt people and taking without asking. Sumaguru stopped talking, and

Balla rose to follow him as he turned to go into his tower.

"Sir, may I ask when I can go home?" Balla walked behind him.

Sumaguru stopped and turned. "Why? Are you not happy here? Have I not treated you well?"

"Sir, you have. I have no complaints, but I miss my family." He wanted to say he missed his lion butterfly.

"I need you for some things, and I need you to teach one of my sons. He could use a man like you. Then maybe..." Sumaguru shrugged. "You are very smart but remember who is smarter." Sumaguru stared into Balla's brown eyes, raised his eyebrows and turned away.

Balla let out a sigh and hung his head as that was no answer at all. He didn't want to be the griot of anyone else. He began to walk back to his house--he needed to consult with his power object-- when he heard Sumaguru call to him. He looked up and saw Sumaguru motioning him to come. With reluctance, he followed him into the tower. Entering the rough-hewn walls, he could not see, so he used his hand to guide himself up the steps. As he reached the top step, Sumaguru was bathed in flickering light from palm oil lamps.

Sumaguru watched Balla rise up from the dark, and he moved aside and opened the door. Behind him was his guard with the hyena. He watched to see fright on Balla's face, but there was none, and he tried not to show his disappointment.

Balla watched Sumaguru step aside and saw a muscular spotted beast on a chain held by a guard. He felt fear run through him. He'd seen these beasts from afar, but now they were close. The beast lifted its lips, showing dagger-like teeth. Balla swallowed hard and kept close to the wall away from the danger until he was through the door.

Sumaguru smiled, "You like my pet?"

"Very..." Balla paused.

"You didn't show any fear."

"You just said you needed me. I didn't think you'd kill me so soon."

Sumaguru shook his head impressed. "You are right. So soon...You think I may kill you?"

"If someday it pleases you, you might."

"Give me no cause, but you are right again—if it pleases me. But give me no cause and you may live to be an old griot."

Balla then noticed the owl on the perch. Fear rose in him again. It was one thing to see them in a tree, but to be locked in a room with them was another.

This time, Sumaguru saw the fear on Balla's face and was happy. "So, you will help one of my sons. He is lazy and not very good at hunting. I want you to teach him."

Through the door came a large young man. Balla could see the resemblance to Sumaguru. He couldn't be worse than Sundjata in the beginning. He smiled and thought I always train the tough ones.

*****

Dankaran let out a scream before he and his mount went down. Several small gazelles had burst out of the trees, and he had reined his horse too tight. His head hit hard on the ground, and he saw stars and let go of the reins. The horse got to its feet and wandered away.

The griot watched in horror as his king fell into the dirt. He tried to ride faster but again almost fell out of his saddle. He saw a group of gazelles, they were running as if chased; it scared him that a lion or a leopard might be near. They might have to get away in a hurry. He rode over to capture the king's horse. "Easy boy," he said as he grabbed the reins. He turned the horse back around and saw two people standing over the king. He couldn't make out who it was in the bright sun as he shaded his eyes.

Dankaran's head spun, and his ears were ringing. Sweat stung his eyes, the sun blinded him, and muffled voices caught his attention. He shaded his eyes as his sight began to return. "No!" Dankaran shouted when his eyes focused. "You are a spirit. This cannot be!" He began to crawl away when he heard hoof beats and turned to see his griot as he got on his feet and stared.

The griot was confused as to why Dankaran was crawling away as if he were scared because all he saw was Sundjata and Fran. He rode up to the scene relieved. "Was it you hunting those gazelles?"

"Yes, but we spooked them," Fran said.

"We chased them for fun. Are you okay, brother?"

Dankaran was now on his feet realizing Sundjata was not a spirit. His head pounded, and his knees felt weak. He took his horses' reins, and after several awkward attempts he pulled himself into the small saddle. "My head... yes, I am fine. I must get back to the palace." Dankaran turned his mount and rode off.

The griot nodded at Sundjata and Fran and followed his king.

"He is strange--and rude," Fran said. "He is your brother."

"Unfortunately," Sundjata said shaking his head with a laugh. "But still my brother."

They turned to move back into the bush but heard movement and stopped to listen.

"Hear that?" asked Fran.

"Yes, it sounds like a horse," Sundjata said.

From the trees rode Azeez. His head down.

"Azeez," called Sundjata.

Azeez raised his head. A large grin grew across his face, and he sat up straight. His body, once drained, now filled in an instant. "Allah be praised." He looked at the sky, then back at Sundjata. He jumped out of the saddle and ran up to him. He hugged Sundjata, lifted him off the ground, and then spun him around.

Sundjata laughed. Fran looked at Azeez and laughed as well.

"You missed him!" Fran said.

Azeez put Sundjata down and looked at his body while touching his arms and legs and then his chest. "You are well!"

"Dankaran runs away from me, and you can't stop hugging me," he said with a laugh.

Azeez looked up to see two riders galloping away in the distance. "Was that Dankaran?"

"Yes, he ran like he was on fire," Fran said.

In an instant Azeez's chest was gripped with fear. "You need to come with me, now, and listen."

"What is the matter?"

"Your brother tried to kill you!"

"He just ran away from me."

"Not him, he got someone else to try. Come back to your hunting hut, and you will see the body. I thought it was you. We were warned by a servant from the palace. Come now." He led them back into the trees and to the path, pulling his horse by the reins.

Sundjata couldn't believe it; his heart felt wounded. He loved his brother and would never dream of hurting him. Between Sumaguru's magic and Sossuma whispering bad things in his ear he was crazy.

Fran's mind was racing wondering what was happening. *Can this really be happening? It all seems very frightening and exciting,* he thought.

No one spoke. They walked down the trail towards the hut. The air was alive with the sounds of birds, insects and the breathing of the horse and its hooves in the wet red mud. The three were tense, almost holding their breaths.

Azeez's mind raced with plans and schemes to protect young Sundjata.

The hut came into view, and the air became heavy. They could hear buzzing flies and could smell the sweet and sour mix of death mingling with the usual smells of wood, dirt and grass.

"Look inside," said Azeez. "But mind your stomach; it is a terrible sight."

Sundjata and Fran moved towards the hut, and both looked inside holding their breath. They saw the broken body smashed, chewed and twisted on the floor. Flies buzzed, and beetles gnawed their way into the body.

"That's my slave!" Fran said. "He must have stayed, even after we left."

Sundjata's heart sank. He turned around to Azeez. "I can't believe it."

"Believe it! It has happened. You are in danger," Azeez said. He put his hands on each of Sundjata's shoulders and looked into his eyes. "You need to leave Niani."

Sundjata looked at the dirt, not wanting to acknowledge the truth. "What have I done to anger the spirits?"

"It is a test... and you will pass," Azeez said. "But first we must get you safe." He looked over at Fran and back to Sundjata. "We must get your mother, and sister and leave."

The trio walked back to Niani in silence, each wondering what the future would hold, what the spirits would allow. Sundjata held on to his father's bow, his power object, and asked it for help, for guidance.

Sogolon was outside, sitting in the shade of her house. She crushed some plants, making a healing potion. Nama watched her and glanced over as Bory played with Kolonkan.

"It will ease my stomach?" Nama asked.

"Yes," Sogolon assured her with a smile.

"Do you still think of Kon?" Nama asked.

"Often, I miss him, and I think about him every day."

"I know," Nama replied.

Kolonkan and Bory laughed as they chased each other around the house.

Sogolon looked up through the open gates and saw three people walking down the road towards them. She recognized Azeez, Fran and Sundjata. She stopped and put the tips of her fingers to her chin, her face breaking out into a great smile. She felt light as relief spread through her body. *Thank you, Kon,* she thought.

Nama saw Sogolon's face and turned to see what she was looking at. She broke into a smile when she saw the trio coming down the road.

Bory chased Kolonkan around the house, and his eye caught his big brother walking towards him. "Brother!" he shouted and ran towards him. Kolonkan chased behind him with a stiff-legged gait.

Sundjata hugged Bory as he ran into him. He felt better seeing his little brother.

"What did you kill?" Bory asked.

"Nothing," Sundjata said.

Bory noticed the look on Sundjata's face. "What's wrong? Are you sad that you did not get anything?"

"Yes, that is it," Sundjata said.

Little Kolonkan now ran into Sundjata. He knelt down, hugged her, and then scooped her up into his arms.

Sogolon rose in her awkward fashion as Nama helped her to her feet. She noticed the look on her son's face and then the look on the others.

Nama sensed that everyone was upset, and she looked at Sogolon who nodded at her. "Bory, come. We need to do something."

"But, Mother!" Bory cried.

She sucked her teeth and gave him a look.

He stomped his foot and lowered his head, knowing he was defeated. He followed behind his mother, kicking the dirt. His mother paused for him to catch up, then gently put her hand on the back of his head.

Azeez turned to look at Fran. "The less you know the better."

Fran looked at Sundjata. Sundjata put his sister down, and the two friends hugged, not knowing what was to happen next.

"We will meet again, my friend. I'm sure the spirits will bring us together." Sundjata's eyes filled with tears.

"Yes, I am sure. Be safe. When I am king we will meet again, and I will help you." Fran's eyes filled with tears; he wiped his face, turned and walked away.

"You don't need much. I will supply you with what you need, but you need to leave now!" Azeez looked around and saw no one watching them. "I will have Salt guide you to Ahmed who will take you someplace safe."

"I hate to leave. I hate to give Sossuma what she wants," said

Sogolon as she turned to look back at the palace.

"Yes, we all do, but Sundjata is very much in danger and so might be you and Kolonkan. You know I am right," said Azeez looking at her children, then her.

Sogolon looked at him hard wanting to be stubborn. But this attempt on Sundjata's life was too much. She was pressing not just her luck but that of her children's as well. "You are right, we must leave."

"You will…"

"Shhhh," Sogolon said to quieten the voices. She had been getting more control over them the older she got.

Azeez smiled, used to her behavior. "Gather what you need. What you can carry. I will send Salt to meet you on the old trail that leads to the hills. You will be safe for now. There are too many people around." Azeez turned and left.

"Come, let's pack up," Sogolon said.

Salt walked right through town as if he owned it. He held his head high, walking with a swagger as he pulled his brown mare behind him. He seemed uninterested, but his eyes searched for trouble. He was ready for a fight. He hoped no one would follow Sogolon to their meeting spot. As he walked the trail he looked down into the red dirt and saw nothing but a few old footsteps. All the trails around Niani were used less and less these days. Looking up he could see the hills he would have to cross with Sogolon and her family. He walked till he no longer heard noises from Niani. When he saw a large tree off the trail he went over and tied his horse to a low-hanging branch. He took some water from a bladder skin and propped himself up against the tree in the shade. The heat was building, and it kept many off the trails. He watched black heavily-armored ants marching up the tree besides him. They were on some quest. He smirked as he was going on a quest himself. He felt a hot breeze on his skinny face and wondered if young Sundjata was as special as everyone said. Azeez and Ahmed were good judges of character. After all, they did choose him from the heat and flies of the salt mines. He laughed to himself and heard someone coming. He stayed against the tree and saw Sundjata.

Sundjata walked down the trail lined with chest-high brown grass. He felt sad about leaving home. He missed Balla, and now he had to run away. This feeling of shame was great, and he blurted out, "I will never forget this feeling of running away. I hate it." He wondered if his brother would send anyone else to try and kill him. He turned around but saw his mother and sister far away. He stopped so they could catch up to him. He adjusted his leather bag. As they got close he started walking again.

"Don't worry, my son. There are others who have it worse than we do."

"True, mother." His mother could always calm his heart. He walked on until he heard a horse whinny. There was an opening in the trail ahead of him. He took an arrow out of his quiver and put it in the bow. When he got to the opening he saw Salt leaning against the tree. They had met on several occasions, but Sundjata did not know him well.

"Are you going to use that on me?" Salt asked.

"I heard your horse. I am not very popular of late," Sundjata said, putting the arrow back in the leather quiver.

Salt smirked and stood up. "Let's try and keep you alive for a while."

"I would appreciate that." Sundjata looked back to see his sister and mother catching up.

Salt looked the boy over, appreciating his readiness to fight. "Is it true you walked into a pack of sleeping cheetahs and made them run away?"

"Yes, it is."

"Were they young males?"

Sundjata smiled. "Yes, they were. Ahh, so you know my secret then."

"They are young; they aren't that aggressive at that age. But my friend, you are kind of small. It was still a brave thing," Salt said impressed.

"That, and they ate earlier in the day when I led my friends there. Full-bellied cheetahs are happy cheetahs. You won't say anything, will you?" Salt had his usual sour look on his face, so Sundjata couldn't tell what he was thinking.

Salt looked at him with a sideways glance and was silent for a bit. "Hmmm, I think I will keep your secret. I don't want your mother casting any spells on me."

Sundjata laughed. "She isn't a witch, just different. She's a kind and-"

"Okay, okay..." Salt broke into a smile. The spirit of his father was strong with him. Salt liked it even though Sundjata's father once called him 'chicken rider'. He turned to get his horse, then turned back to Sundjata. "Cut me a large branch with leaves on it."

Sundjata was surprised by Salt's smile. It was the first time he'd ever seen him smile like that. "A big one?"

"Not too big. You are going to tie it to my saddle, and I will drag it behind us. I don't want anyone following our tracks. This trail isn't used much."

Sogolon and Kolonkan caught up to Sundjata. She knew Salt a little and liked the grumpy man. He reminded her of Fanta. She looked at him and bowed her head.

Salt looked at Kolonkan. "I have water for the little one. We won't move too fast; I don't think anyone is following us. Did anyone see you leave?"

"The gate guard did but we walked as if we were going to the market. I am not carrying much, so I believe no one noticed," Sogolon said.

"Good. I'd hate to have to move fast with the little one."

"Where are we going?"

Salt turned and pointed to the hills that rose above the plains. "Over those hills to Tabon."

Sogolon smiled. "They should be friendly."

"They are not happy with Dankaran. He keeps trying to get more crops from them to give to Sumaguru."

"Where is Ahmed?"

"He will find us."

"Do you think they will send anyone after us?"

"I hope not," Salt replied.

Sogolon nodded her head in agreement. "True, as they say, 'If you want to move fast, go by yourself; if you want to go far, go with company.'"

Salt nodded at her wise words.

Sundjata came to Salt with a large branch.

"Tie it to the saddle; use the rope that is there. Make sure it drags behind us and covers our tracks," Salt said.

After Sundjata tied the branch onto the saddle, Salt watched Sundjata, Sogolon and Kolonkan walk in front of him. Anyone on the trail would see just one set of footprints. From time to time he would look back but saw no dust, heard no hooves, and would smile at the sight in front of him: Sogolon's wobble, Kolonkan's quick gait, and Sundjata's easy stride. *This is still better than the salt mines, or crossing the desert,* he thought.

Sundjata walked ahead as the trail became wider and grass

much shorter. Sometimes, he carried Kolonkan on his shoulders. Sometimes, she would ride on Salt's horse with her mother. Sundjata studied large groups of red-fronted gazelles. He noticed their red foreheads and the cream-colored patches around their eyes. Near a patch of forest, he saw a huge thick-bodied, reddish-orange Bongo. He admired its thin vertical white stripes as it browsed on a shrub. He wanted to hunt it, but Salt said no. They couldn't carry all that meat, and most of it would go to waste. Instead, his arrows found several plump, furry, pig-nosed hyraxes for dinner. Before they knew it, the light was growing low, and Kolonkan was getting tired. They would have to stop for the night.

"That stand of trees on top of that hill," Salt called out to Sundjata. "See if that is a good spot to stay tonight."

Sundjata saw the thick stand of trees on the little hill to his right; he waved at Salt and left the trail. He walked through the grass and grasshoppers jumped out of his path. As he climbed the hill he began to hear voices. Low-hanging branches blocked his sight and as he got to the trees he looked through the small spaces between the smooth trunks. Two men were surrounded by fist-sized stones in the dirt arranged in the shape of a box. They pointed down at the dirt and were deep in conversation. He watched them and sensed they were not a threat. Their brown shirts with black circles and white dots blew in the late afternoon breeze.

Salt saw that Sundjata was looking at something. He took his sword out of its scabbard and gave the horse to Sogolon. His light frame ran without making a sound. In an instant he was behind Sundjata. He put his hand on Sundjata's back and peered through the trees. When he saw the men, he whispered in Sundjata's ear, "Not to worry." He turned to Sogolon and motioned for them to come. He then went around the tree to address the men.

The two men looked up at this skinny fellow who came towards them.

Salt raised his right hand and spoke to them in their tongue. "Se-o, what is to happen, friends? Can you tell me what the fox in

174

the hills says?"

Sundjata followed Salt and wondered what the men were doing.

The taller of the two men responded, "It says we have to leave."

"I know the feeling," Sundjata said.

The two men stood up straight. Their eyes went wide when they saw the famed Buffalo Woman, and they bowed. She left the horse behind, worried about what was beyond the trees.

Sogolon put her hands together and touched the tips of her fingers to her chin.

"Who are they, Mother?"

"They are the Dogon. This group is the last one down here. They have been moving up past Segou by my homeland of Do and building into the cliffs."

"What are they doing?"

The men bowed again. "Queen, would you like to see the prints?" the men asked in unison.

"I would." She turned to Sundjata. "Come, we are going to read the signs of a fox that has walked through their pit."

Salt picked up Kolonkan. "We will get the horse."

Sogolon took her son's arm, and they walked over to the stones. The fist-sized stones had two rows of smaller stones in the middle the length of a small man's foot apart. "See the prints between the middle stones," she pointed.

"Yes. What does that mean?"

She looked up at the men. "What do they say to you?"

"It says we have to leave," said the taller man. "The Dogon

people will not be harassed anymore by Dankaran. And we will not convert to Islam. We don't want to fight, but we will if we are pushed."

Sogolon closed her eyes and let the voices speak to her.

"They are true, and all must leave this area," said the mother voice.

"Stay and fight; fight to the death," said the angry voice. "Never give in."

Sogolon opened her eyes. "Yes, I see how the prints are on the outside of the inside rows of stones. They don't fall in the middle."

The men nodded in agreement.

"May we spend the night with your people?" asked Sogolon.

"Of course, you may stay," the shorter of the two men spoke.

"Thank you. That is most kind. Go tell Salt," Sogolon said to Sundjata.

Chapter 14

The Gates of Tabon

As the pale, yellow rays of the sun peaked over the horizon, Salt, Sundjata, Sogolon and Kolonkan left the Dogon village. Kolonkan rode on the back of Salt's brown mare. She waved the arm of a jointed, wooden puppet given to her by the elder of the village. Salt no longer dragged the branch behind them as they walked through the brown and green grass. They would walk until the sun was strong and overhead. They tried to avoid people but did not stray too far from the trail. The movement of gazelles, warthogs and buffalos would cover their tracks. When the sun reached its peak, they went back to the trail and took a break to rest in the shade of a giant baobab tree. The tree trunk was wide enough for everyone to lean against on the same side.

"See if there is any fruit on the ground, although it's not the season really," Salt asked Sundjata.

Sundjata nodded in agreement.

"I don't think they sent anyone after us," Sogolon said to Salt as they leaned against the grey trunk.

"Probably not. We have moved at a snail's pace. A one-legged man could have caught us," Salt said.

Sogolon smiled, "You never knew my servant Fanta, did you?"

"I saw her, a small thing."

"Yes, but like a bee, small with a big sting."

"More like a wasp I heard," Salt said.

Sogolon took a wooden buffalo out of her leather bag which she kept over her shoulder. She placed it at the base of the tree. She knelt and asked the spirits for assistance on their journey. "Do you talk to the spirits?" she asked.

"Yes, and Allah. I don't take any chances."

Sogolon nodded her head in agreement. "I understand."

"There is no fruit," Sundjata said coming around the tree with Kolonkan. "But I got a snake." He held up a long, fat black snake with an arrow through it.

Sogolon gave him a look, "A cobra! You couldn't find a less dangerous one?"

While Kolonkan gathered wood, Sundjata pulled the snake skin off the pink white meat. He gave the head to his mother who removed the fangs and absorbed some of the poison in some herbs. He then started a fire putting the meat on sticks. It didn't take long to cook. The flesh smelled like smoke; it was crispy on the outside but firm and sweet on the inside. It filled their bellies and made them sleep. They lay against the tree in the afternoon heat that made them sweat, even as they sat and dozed.

Sundjata dreamed of bringing down the huge Bongo he saw yesterday. His father was guiding him, telling him where to shoot his arrow. He pulled back on the bow, but the Bongo became spooked when the sound of horses' hooves got closer and closer. He turned to talk to his father, but he was gone. The sound got closer. He rose out of sleep, opening his eyes to a blurry world. He rubbed his eyes and saw two figures on a large black horse. In an instant he recognized Ahmed but holding on behind him was his brother. "Bory!" Sundjata yelled and ran towards them.

Ahmed stopped his horse and lowered Bory to the ground. He smiled seeing Salt and the rest safe and sound.

Sundjata and Bory hugged. "Why have you come?" he asked his brother.

"Mother felt I also may be in danger."

Ahmed rode up to Salt and Sogolon as Kolonkan ran to her brothers. "Salam," he said to them.

"Salam," they said in return.

"Anyone care that we were gone?" Sogolon asked.

"You can be sure Sossuma and Dankaran cared. Most people were sad that you are missing."

Salt asked, "You think anyone is after us?"

"No. No one is following us," Ahmed said, getting down from his horse.

"Why did you bring the boy?" Salt asked. "We move slow already."

"Nama came to us when she couldn't find you, and so we told her what happened. She felt as Bory grew Dankaran will see him as the next threat. And I have to say, Azeez and I agreed with her, so I brought him."

"He is a fine boy," Sogolon said. "I am glad he is here, poor Nama."

"She cried, but she felt she would see him again." Ahmed took a bladder skin off his saddle and took a quick drink. "She is leaving, going back to her village; she will be fine."

Sogolon looked at Ahmed and realized something was different. Then it struck her. "I have never seen you wear a turban before."

"I only wear it when I travel far, and Tabon is far enough. Shall we be on our way?"

"Come, children," called Sogolon. "We must be on our way."

"Ride ahead and find a place to stay for the night," Ahmed said to Salt. He turned to Sogolon. "May I walk with you?"

Sogolon bowed. "Of course."

The children ran ahead as Sogolon and Ahmed walked side by side.

Ahmed looked at Sogolon's rounded shoulder, but when he

saw her face he thought it looked like a beautiful mask: round cheeks and her wide, flat, triangle-shaped nose. White teeth flashed a bright smile through large soft lips, and her dark-brown eyes glowed with life. She had shaved her head many days before they left, and soft, tight curly hair filled her well-shaped head. "You look very beautiful for a woman who had to flee her home."

Sogolon smiled and nodded, "Thank you. And thank you for protecting us. Aren't you afraid of Sossuma and Dankaran retaliating against you for helping me?"

"Well, that is why I am here and not my nephew. No one so far knows of our participation in your leaving. We wanted it to be a secret, so we could stay in Niani for now, and keep you safe."

"Are you going to leave Niani?

"I fear we have to… move our base closer to the Niger. Less and less trade comes our way; raiding has become more common. Azeez and I don't want to work for Dankaran either. He is not like his father. Kon was a great leader; he was fair and able to persuade people to follow him."

"Yes, he was a great man. Sundjata will someday be like his father. But we have to be patient."

"Yes, I hope he does take after his father. In the meanwhile, we must find a good place for him to grow." He looked at Sogolon's body and her heavy breasts against her green wrap dress. "I think we will be at the Niger in two days."

"I hope so. Tabon isn't far after that. Will you leave us after we reach there?"

"Let's see what is to come. Just because Dankaran and Sossuma aren't chasing us it doesn't mean they aren't going to make things difficult for us."

"True. But I expect the king of Tabon to receive us well," Sogolon said. "May I have some water?"

"Of course. A queen should drink whenever she desires," he said with a smile. He stopped the horse and handed her the bladder skin from the ornate saddle.

Sogolon raised the skin and squeezed the warm water into her mouth. She swallowed but then splashed water onto her chin, and she lowered the bag laughing.

Ahmed couldn't help but smile as water dripped off her chin. "Don't drown, my lady," he said with a laugh.

She wiped her chin and handed the bag back to Ahmed. "I am clumsy."

"Queens are allowed to be clumsy." Ahmed then tilted his head up and took a drink.

"I'm afraid I am not a queen anymore."

"Nobody can take that title from you. You may not live like one, but one you shall be."

Sogolon smiled and bowed at his words. "You are too kind. Your saddle is larger than I've ever seen," she noted.

"Ahh, thank you. It's called a La Jineta, from Cordoba." He attached the skin back on the saddle, and they began to walk again.

"That is far away from here, I am sure."

"Very far north of here, more than twenty-four moons to get there. You have to travel over nothing but sand, sometimes so hot you can't touch it. If you get lost... you die and shrivel up like a fish left on a river bank. There are men who cover their face with blue cloth - The Tuareg - who ride camels like the wind and will take all your belongings and leave you to die.

"They sound fierce. Is Salt a Tuareg?"

Ahmed smiled. "No, no, his people mine salt from a place in the middle of the dessert. The Tuareg never rest; they are always on the move. But if you make it past the sand and the Tuareg, you come to some mountains, and over them are plains filled with wheat. Then you can stand on the shore, you can look across the water and you can't see the other side. Have you ever seen the ocean?"

"No, just the big rivers. And on the other side is Cordoba?'

"Yes, in a land called Al Andalus."

"It sounds like an exciting trip and a wonderful place."

"It is, my lady. You would like it, as there are many great Muslim healers there."

Sogolon smiled. "I would like that very much."

"I'm afraid, though. There is fighting and turmoil like what has been happening here."

"Hopefully, Sundjata will grow up like his father and make things better," said Sogolon with a smile.

"Hopefully," Ahmed said. "But for now, you and he must stay safe."

Sogolon looked at Ahmed, and her voices were about to speak. "Not now," she said aloud.

Ahmed smiled.

*****

Inside the main hall of the palace sat Sossuma, Dankaran, and Nama. The captain of Dankaran's guard and all the servants stood before them.

"Where did they go?" Dankaran asked the captain of his guard. Exasperated, he turned and looked at his mother and then back to the captain.

"I do not know. She walked out of the palace grounds and to the market the guards thought. No one was told to watch her." The captain kept his head down to mask his frustration.

"True, but I can't believe no one saw them leave," Dankaran demanded, shaking his head.

"They are gone. Doesn't that make you happy?" Nama asked.

Sossuma looked at Nama for a long moment. "Does it make you happy?"

"You know it doesn't make me happy. I like Sogolon and her children," Nama said.

Sossuma looked at her again. "Even if you did know, you would not say."

"Maybe she went to visit her people in Do? She hasn't been exactly treated well the last few seasons. I would not blame her."

"You be careful," Dankaran said to Nama.

Nama looked at him and gave a slight smile. *I will leave this place and never look back,* she thought.

"If Sundjata wasn't looking to overthrow you, why would he flee? He is being controlled by his witch of a mother," Sossuma said.

Nama shook her head.

"May I go?" asked the captain.

"Yes... But, wait. Send some people to find them," Dankaran said. "Let it be known that they are banished and send out riders to tell people not to help them. I will pay if someone finds them."

The captain nodded and turned to leave.

Nama shook her head and sucked her teeth in disgust. She hated to see Dankaran act like a petulant child, and it was Sossuma's fault. She abused her power over the council, keeping them on her son's side, and making him stay around the palace. "If your father could see you now," Nama said. She walked out the door and decided to leave that night.

*****

It was dark when they got to the Niger River. They made camp by a stand of small trees; the weight of sleep was heavy in their limbs. Salt made a small fire as they bedded down for the night. They lay down on slabs of flat rocks still warm from being in the sun all day. Their sleep was hard from the travel, and no one woke till they were bathed in the soft morning light. They stretched, yawned and shook the sleep out of their heads. When the heaviness of sleep was gone, they made their way down to the river to clean up after days of travel. Salt found a spot on the river where the bank had long ago been separated from the main channel. A tall green wall of wavy reeds hid them from the swift, deep, tumbling current of the river. The small channel was clear and not too deep. The current slow but steady. Herons and ibis patrolled the shallows, frogs jumped, and turtles scrambled for cover as they approached the bank. Sogolon made a small offering prayer to the water spirits before wading in. Sogolon, Bory, Sundjata and Kolonkan bathed and cleaned their clothes in one spot. Salt and Ahmed went around a bend and found cover by some tall weeds. Flowers and long-bladed leaves with tufts of brown fluff at their tops mixed with the weeds.

The water felt good on Sogolon's body. She sat in it deep enough for her breasts to float as she held her dress under the water and rubbed it together. "Mind your sister, boys. Be careful not to go too deep, and watch out for crocodiles!"

Sundjata, Bory and Kolonkan sat in the water up to their waist. They laughed as small fish pecked at their toes and legs. "Yes, Mother," Sundjata called in reply. His mind wandered to crocodiles, and he still laughed but also kept one eye on the water.

Salt was the first to finish. He could not swim, and he was afraid of water. It scared him to cross deep rivers. He climbed the narrow rocky trail to tend to the horses. His wet clothes in his hand, he would dry them on the rocks above.

Ahmed sat in the water and would lean back, submerge his head and scratch his hair. He wished he had some soap, but the water was refreshing. He could swim and so paddled around a little, but he preferred to float. His clothes he draped over short green plants on the bank to dry in the morning sun. He leaned back as his head became hot, and when he raised it he saw Sogolon standing on the bank. He gave a big smile.

"I see you can swim." Sogolon stood there in her wet wrap dress which clung to her shapely but crooked body. She stood crooked; her breasts were full, and her hips made a nice shape through the clinging fabric.

"Would you like me to teach you?" Ahmed said.

"You will not let me drown?"

"I promise," Ahmed said with a smile.

"Are you not afraid of the water spirits?"

"No, I think they like to watch if you can swim, but if you can't...swoop," Ahmed pulled his hand under water.

Sogolon unwrapped herself and put her wet dress on the leaves by Ahmed's wet clothes. "I don't disgust you?"

Ahmed smiled. "You are not ugly, just different." He looked at her high and rounded left shoulder, but then his eyes went to her lovely dark skin and full breasts. He stood up out of the water and extended his hands as she splashed towards him. "The women in this part of the world are the most beautiful."

She watched Ahmed rise out of the water, and she laughed. She had never seen such pale skin before; his member hung down and was surrounded by black and grey hair. She smiled.

He took her hands in his, and they sat down in the water. "Now, relax and we are going to swim like a dog or a horse would.

It will please the water spirits to see someone like you."

Sundjata, Bory and Kolonkan ran naked, clothes in their arms, laughing as they raced up a trail to the top of the hill where they camped. Their bellies rumbled with hunger. They were now getting dressed in the grass, wiping sand off their bodies and damp clothes.

"I have collected some wood. Get more," Salt said to Sundjata. "There are some embers you can start up again." Salt turned away, and then turned back. "Take your bow," he added, motioning with his hands.

"I will get some small dry twigs to bring it back to life and maybe get us something good to eat."

Salt nodded his head in approval and realized he liked Sogolon's children and Bory. Most children he couldn't stand to be around, but they were pleasant to be with. Ahmed brought a few provisions, and he was going to get them. Salt wondered where Ahmed was and if Sogolon was able to make it up the hill. "Those two," he said aloud, finding one of the trails that led down to the river. Going down the steep trail a rock in the dirt came loose. "Shit," he cried, his skinny arms flailing in the air. He righted himself, his heart beating fast. A large tangle of tall bushes and vines ran along the sloping hill, hiding the river, and different trails cut through the wall of green. When Salt got to the opening he stopped in his tracks. He watched Ahmed and Sogolon in an embrace moving rhythmically in the water. "That old man," Salt said with a big grin. He turned around and marched back up the hill.

Later, Ahmed came up the hill sideways, holding Sogolon's hand as she slipped going up the rocky trail. "Careful, come." He took both her hands as they reached the top. He looked at Salt who was shaking his head at him. "What's to eat?"

"Birds… Bory and Sundjata caught some birds." Salt leaned on his saddle as the children cooked the birds, each on a stick.

"Wonderful," Sogolon said and walked over to Kolonkan and
186

sat down behind her. She touched her head and hugged her. "How long till Tabon?"

"Tonight, as long as we find a good crossing." Ahmed turned to Salt. "There is one not far from here if I remember?"

"Yes, not far. There is a man with boats who will take us across."

Ahmed shook his head and noticed the look on Sundjata's face; the boy was usually smiling.

"What's the matter, Sundjata?"

Sundjata was lost in thought, staring into the fire when he heard his name. "Hmm, well I was wondering how this all happened." He felt a surge of sadness in his chest and held back tears.

Sogolon reached over and touched his shoulder. "Things happen that we don't understand. We must understand the signs and try to find out what the spirits are telling us. Things change, and our lives will eventually unfold. Not to worry."

"That is true; Allah has many mysteries, and he tests us," said Ahmed. "You will learn through all of this."

"I did nothing wrong. I did not want my brother's crown! I just want to hunt."

Sogolon smiled. He sounded like his father. He was growing fast and would soon be of age. He must learn the secrets of his clan, but they were far from those who would teach him. For now, she was confident the spirits of the animals he hunted would guide him. "Hunt, you will, and you will learn. You are special."

"Balla used to tell me that all the time. I always thought he'd return to me."

"He is a wise griot, and he was right," Sogolon said with a big smile. "Remember, you grew up in the palace. Your destiny is different from those who are farmers or blacksmiths or leather makers."

"That is true. The farmers are afraid to go too far from their village or farm. The blacksmiths stay by their forges."

"You will learn as you hunt and travel," Sogolon said.

"I travel everywhere, and I learn new things all the time. Keep your eyes open, and your life will be richer for it," Ahmed said looking at the boy. "I had to give up lands and leave my home, and I have been traveling ever since. I was hoping to stay in Niani, but I will be moving again."

"But why is Dankaran acting in this way?"

"It's his mother who believes she is doing right. It's her attempt to control him, and the nyama, that is turning everything upside down," Sogolon said. "That is what helps to make Sumaguru's magic so powerful and work against us."

Salt nodded his head, agreeing with Sogolon's understanding of life. She was a wise woman. He was glad he was protecting her and her children.

"The land will be rising; we will be moving through hills and forest. While we will be closer to the Sosso, it will be easy to hide if we have to." Ahmed reached over and took a piece of cooked bird off a stick. "Salt, I want you to go get five of our men and bring them to Tabon. They should be heading back from Sijilmasa."

"Why?" Salt said with impatience. "You and I can do this."

"I'm not sure if we are going to stay in Tabon, and word will get out that we are there. If we leave, we may need some protection."

Salt's anger dissolved as Ahmed's words hit him. He smirked, realizing Ahmed was right. "Yes, once we cross the river I will go."

"Let's get moving as soon as we finish eating," Ahmed said, smiling at Sogolon and noticing her gazing at him.

After they'd eaten breakfast, they saddled the two horses and traveled along the river till they found a boatman that would carry them across the Niger. They rode up as he was coming to shore.

"I will take both horses across," Ahmed said to Salt. "I know you don't like water. This morning your clothes got wetter than you did."

Annoyed, Salt looked at Ahmed but considered his offer. He did not want to be teased, however. He gave Ahmed a sideways glare and dismounted, handing Sundjata his horse's reins. Approaching the boatman as he rowed ashore, he called out, "How much to take this lady and her three children across?"

The shirtless boatman rowed the boat in an effortless style. He landed the boat onto the hard, sandy shore and splashed up to Salt to negotiate a fair price.

Ahmed rode next to Sundjata. "I will race you across the river."

"Race? What will I win if we race?"

"How about a horse and saddle of your very own."

Sundjata looked across the smooth surface of the river. Its current was swift. He was scared at first, but the thought of his own horse made him feel brave. He looked up at Ahmed.

Ahmed gave Sundjata a big smile and gave a nod of his head towards the water. "Come on, before your mother has a chance to say no. Just think of the look on Salt's face."

Sundjata's face broke into a smile, and he turned and gave Bory his father's bow and quiver. "Don't drop them in the river!"

"I won't." Bory was excited to hold such a powerful bow. "Good luck."

Sundjata slipped his foot into the small metal stirrup. He

jumped up and grabbed the small saddle horn and pulled himself into it. His feet left the stirrups, and his legs dangled free.

"Hold on with your legs, then squeeze them into the saddle and the horse's side. If you get in trouble grab the mane, but don't let go. When the water gets deep slide off the horse and grab the tail. Better yet, hang onto the saddle, and keep your head up. Ready?"

Sundjata gave a nervous smile. "Yes."

"Just give him a kick."

Sundjata's heels hit his mount and moved forward into the water.

"Okay, you, the lady, the boy and the little girl. Give me four kola nuts," the boatman said to Salt.

"What? Who? Not me, the boys."

"There is only one boy. The other boy is already going," said the boatman as he pointed at Sundjata on Salt's horse halfway into the river.

Sogolon and Salt looked towards the river. Sogolon put her hands together. With the tips of her fingers touching her chin, she held her breath.

"Ahhh, quick, take us across. I will pay your price," Salt said to the boatman.

The man turned sideways and motioned with his hand. "Climb in." He then bent down and held the boat steady. Salt picked up Kolonkan and placed her in as Sogolon threw her leg in over the side of the carved canoe. She almost lost her balance but caught herself at the last moment. Bory splashed into the water and flung himself into the canoe. He had a death grip on Sundjata's bow and quiver full of arrows.

"Can he swim?" Salt asked Sogolon.

"I don't think so?" Sogolon looked at Bory.

Bory shrugged his shoulders. "I've never seen him swim, but is there anything he can't do?"

"Hurry," Salt said to the boatman as he knelt in the canoe.

The boatman pushed them off before he got in. He plunged the paddle into the water and moved them forward with a smooth stroke.

"There isn't much current here, and it's not too deep," the boatman replied.

Salt looked at Sogolon. "My horse is an excellent swimmer."

"I hope so." Sogolon would not take her eyes off her son.

Ahmed watched Sundjata and saw the smile on his face. "Good, relax and hold on."

Sundjata laughed and looked around, seeing the boat with his mother. He made eye contact with her.

"Don't look at me. Hold on." She shook her head. "Watch the shore."

Sundjata looked back at the shore and heard the deep breathing of Salt's horse. He imagined its legs running underwater. The body of the horse pulsed with each kick.

Ahmed held the reins of his horse to slow it down. He then pulled on the right rein and moved himself closer to Sundjata. Ahmed looked behind him, and then ahead, and saw they were past the half way point.

Sundjata felt a bump as his horse began to touch the bottom of the river. He pulled himself back into the saddle as his horse rose out of the water. He looked to his left and saw that he was ahead of Ahmed, and his smile grew larger.

"Go, Sundjata! Ride it hard!" Bory exclaimed and clapped,

rocking the boat.

Salt swung and slapped Bory in the back of the head. "Sit still."

Bory laughed.

The boatman repeated paddle strokes two to the right then one to the left. Sometimes he turned the blade straight to keep them going to the place his eyes fixed on the shore. They weren't too far behind the horses.

Sundjata had let go of the reins to hold onto the saddle. They hung down in front of the horse. He grabbed the mane and gave two kicks into the side. "Go, go." He looked behind him; Ahmed was close on his tail.

Ahmed moved the horse closer but gave a slight pull back when Sundjata wasn't looking.

Sundjata lifted his hands in triumph as his horse cleared the river first.

Ahmed laughed. "You've won."

"When will you give me a horse? Can I have this one?"

"Ha, if I did Salt would never speak to me again. Which might not be so bad." Ahmed laughed.

Sundjata's smile shrank, realizing he had asked for Salt's horse. He liked Salt. "Oh! Oh no. Don't tell him I tried to take his horse."

"I won't, and you will get one soon enough."

The boat hit the shoreline and stuck in the hard sand. The boatman jumped out to push the canoe further out of the water and held it still for everyone to get out.

Ahmed rode over and took the dangling reins of Salt's horse and gave them to Sundjata.

"I won a horse!" Sundjata exclaimed to his mother.

"You didn't give him my horse, did you?" Salt gave Ahmed a look of concern.

Ahmed laughed. "I thought about it. We will buy him one when we get to Tabon."

Salt turned to Sundjata. "Get off my horse."

Sundjata said to Salt, "He is an excellent swimmer."

Salt took the reins. "I know. Get off and walk. You will dry faster."

Sundjata felt embarrassed. He turned sideways and slipped to the ground. Bory was waiting for him with bow and quiver.

"Here," said Bory as he proudly held out the bow and quiver of arrows. "Was the water cold?"

"A little."

"Were you scared?"

"It was fun." Sundjata realized he had been scared but excited.

"Let's get a move on. We have a way to go to Tabon," Ahmed said. "Queen Sogolon, would you like to ride?"

"No, thank you, but Kolonkan could."

Ahmed dismounted and picked up a giggling Kolonkan and swung her into the saddle. Sundjata and Bory ran ahead of the group.

Salt rode up. "You want me to go get the men?"

"Wait till we get to Tabon. Keep an eye on those two," Ahmed motioned with his head.

＊＊＊＊＊

"Take all of them!" Sumaguru yelled to his captain.

The captain stood in front of ten men, who looked scared and bloodied. They all stared down at the ground except for one proud man who stood and glared at the captain. The captain met his glare with equal strength, and when the man would not break the captain turned to Sumaguru. He sat mounted not far away. Sumaguru nodded, and the captain turned back around and walked towards the man. The man stood motionless, not showing any fear. When the captain was close he raised his sword and brought it down hard where the man's neck met his shoulder. The man grunted as bright blood flew in an arc through the air. He crumpled to the ground as his life flowed into the dirt. The other men were now even more frightened and dared not look up.

"That's not how I would have handled it," Balla said to Sumaguru's son.

The son couldn't stop staring at the man dying in the dirt.

"What would you have done?" Balla asked.

"I...I don't know." The son took a glance but turned away again.

"How do you think the people of the village now feel about Sumaguru?"

"They are afraid. They know who their leader is now."

"Yes, true, but if they get a chance to take revenge what will they do?"

The son paused and furrowed his brow in thought. "Take it?"

"Yes, very good. So, what should he have done?"

The son furrowed his brow again and stared blankly at Balla.

Balla tried not to be impatient, but this was a common occurrence with his student. He gave a heavy sigh. "If you cannot even give some answer maybe you are not worthy to know."

The son looked skywards for a moment. "Just punish him?"

194

"Yes, that was one way. There may be hope for you yet," Balla said.

Fakoli rode his horse hard onto the scene. "Uncle," he said as he rode up to Sumaguru.

Sitting tall and straight on the bare back of his horse, he turned to see his nephew.

"Uncle, are you taking all these men from this village?"

"Yes, I am going to give them to the villages that are supporting me."

"There has been sickness here, and there is a shortage of men. If you take these men, the village will be in trouble."

"That is not my concern. They fought back and would not cooperate with me, so now they must suffer the consequences. Make sure nobody tries to follow us. Hang behind in case anyone escapes and tries to return." He turned away and rode off.

Fakoli sat there and shook his head. What was happening to his uncle? He was changing with each success, each raid. He saw Balla standing close to him and gave him a look of disapproval.

Balla had walked closer to listen to Sumaguru and Fakoli. He didn't like the look Fakoli gave him before he rode off, but he wasn't ruthless like his uncle. "Things are getting interesting," he said aloud. He turned to see his charge picking his nose and staring into the distance. "Why me? I just want to go home."

*****

A lone guard sat in the dirt in front of the closed gate. He traced figures in the dirt with his finger. It was hot, and he felt sleepy, but it was his turn for guard duty. Up the road he saw shimmering figures that approached at a slow, steady pace. As they came into focus the sight intrigued him. At first, he thought they were villagers. Then he saw an Arab pulling his horse with a little girl riding on its back. Next to the Arab was a skinny man

195

wearing what seemed like rags. There was a horse trailing behind him, and two young boys walked before them. What confused the guard most was an odd-walking woman. He rose as they got closer and moved to the side of the road.

The thick, dark gates of Tabon were strong and secured to walls made of stone and mud brick. The walls encircled a large city. One could see over the gates if one was on a tall horse.

Ahmed was glad to see the dark wood and smiled as he and his ragtag group walked up to them. He laid his hand on the wood. "This would bring much gold if I were to sell them," he said to Sogolon.

She smiled. "You have sold this wood before?"

"Yes, but it is in a large forest many days south of here. It is hard to cut and very, very heavy."

The guard asked the group, "Have you come for market?"

"Of course," replied Ahmed.

"They will start later, but you can get something to eat most likely. Open up!" the guard yelled to unseen people.

"Why is the gate closed in the middle of the day?"

"Raids, Fulani, Sosso. You can't be too careful these days," the guard replied to Ahmed as the gates swung open.

The boys ran through the gate, and the others followed. "That should be the king's palace over there," said Ahmed as he pointed towards the large rectangular mud brick building surrounded by other smaller round structures. Many servants moved about preparing for the evening meal.

"Have you met the king?" Sogolon asked.

"No, I have not."

"Should we introduce ourselves now?"

"Now would probably be best. Have a look around. Keep an eye on these three while we make our introductions," Ahmed said to Salt. He plucked a smiling Kolonkan from the saddle and placed her on the ground.

Kolonkan ran to her brother while Salt handed his reins to Sundjata. The little group walked off to the market place.

"Have you met the king?" Ahmed asked Sogolon.

"He has come to Niani on occasion. I am sure he will remember me."

"Good." Ahmed smiled. They walked towards the large rectangular building and stopped the first servant they saw. "Go find your king and tell them the Queen of Niani is here."

Sogolon smiled. "Thank you. But please stop saying that. I *was* the queen. Besides, he might think it is Sossuma."

"Well, once you were. And maybe he will come faster if he thinks it's her."

Sogolon laughed. "I hope he isn't too disappointed when he sees me."

"We should not be here," said the angry voice.

"No, we should stay," said the mother voice.

"We shall see," Sogolon whispered. "Now hush."

Ahmed heard footsteps and turned around to see a man his age and height followed by several servants. He had a concerned look on his face.

"Ahh, Queen Sogolon, how wonderful to see you," said the king relieved.

Sogolon bowed, and he bowed in return. "King Aflia Banda, meet Ahmed Salem."

The king stood up straight and tall. "Salam," he said, holding up his right hand.

"Salam," Ahmed said in return, giving a bow.

"Your name, I know it. You are well known."

"Thank you. About half of what you hear is true."

The king smiled. "Half. Then you are a great man; most men's stories are all lies. My factor has told me about you. Half is about right."

Ahmed smiled. "He and you are too kind."

The king turned to Sogolon. "Do you have my son with you?"

"I am afraid we do not. We had to leave in rather a hurry."

The king's face became sad. "Then I am afraid you can't stay here very long. You see Dankaran has given the word that anyone aiding you will not be welcomed, and they have Fran still."

"I understand. I am not surprised by this. We had to flee for our lives, and if it wasn't for Ahmed and his nephew we would be in grave danger still--unfortunately, like Fran."

"Stay in the palace; you can leave tomorrow. You must rest and eat. I will keep your whereabouts a secret. I do not trust Sossuma."

"My son Sundjata and his brother are in the market with one of Ahmed's men."

"I suggest you stay here. I don't think anyone will know your son. But he should not speak much."

"I will go and talk to them. We will be gone in the morning. Thank you," said Ahmed.

Chapter 15

There is No Beauty but the Beauty of Action

Bory stood off the trail behind Ahmed and Sundjata rooting for his brother. Since they left Tabon, Sundjata and Ahmed had been having constant contests.

"I bet you can't hit the branch," Ahmed challenged Sundjata after he put an arrow into the center of a dead tree.

Sogolon sat with Kolonkan further off the trail, cooking the evening meal.

"Ha!" Sundjata kept both eyes open and focused on a small branch. It stuck out over the path from a lone twisted leafless tree. As he lifted the bow he took a deep breath and pulled the bow string as far as it could go. He held his breath and released the arrow. The smooth shaft sliced the air, and the iron tip smacked into the branch where he aimed.

"Ahhh, a fine shot, a fine shot." Ahmed laughed. "I would not want you to shoot at me on the battle field. You remind me of your father. I fought with him."

Sundjata smiled at his marksmanship, and Ahmed's compliment made him beam. "Yes?"

"Yes, and you are confident and strong like him. The way you stand. You look just like him." Ahmed paused for a moment. "Go get a long straight stick, about the length of your arm and thick as two or three fingers."

"Bory, please go get my arrows." Sundjata ran off to find his stick.

Ahmed walked across the trail and over to his saddle, which was close to Sogolon. He knelt, picked up his sword and pulled it out of its scabbard. He looked up at Sogolon, who was now watching him. "He should learn this," said Ahmed as he shook it.

She smiled at him and nodded her head in approval, then went

199

back to tending the meal and playing with Kolonkan.

Ahmed walked back across the trail and watched Sundjata return with his stick. He held out his hand. "Let me have it." Sundjata handed the stick to him. Ahmed took a dagger from his belt and started to knock off the knobs and rough spots.

Sundjata watched him, wondering what he was doing.

"You can ask. It is always good to ask questions."

"What are you doing?"

"It is important to be good with the bow, but eventually you run out of arrows and have to defend yourself. You must be good with the sword, otherwise..." He raised his eyebrows. "You will get to meet Allah." Then he paused. "Or, your ancestors."

"I won't meet Allah?"

"Well, yes, yes you will. We will talk to your mother about these things someday soon." He smiled at him, looked at the long stick, and began to strip off the bark. "Any more questions?"

"Where do you and my mother go in the mornings?"

Ahmed stopped cleaning the stick but didn't look at Sundjata. "Ahh, well, she shows me about healing herbs and how to read signs."

Sundjata nodded his head. "Yes, she is very good at that."

Ahmed nodded in agreement and went back to cleaning the stick.

"Was my father good with the sword?"

"Oh yes, very good. I saw him best many a man."

"Will you teach me?"

"I am going to start. It takes some time, so be patient. You should always be learning."

"My griot, Balla, used to tell me the same thing."

"He was wise for his age. He was like his father as well. You miss him, don't you?"

"Yes, yes I do. I miss all of them."

"Well, if it is written, you will see him again." The stick was now clean, and he handed it to Sundjata. "Stand over there."

Sundjata took the stick, walked a few paces away and turned to face Ahmed.

"Always face sideways if you can. Never stand with your shoulders facing your enemy. You don't want to be a big target." He pointed his sword at Sundjata. He poked at the middle of his chest the sharp point almost touching Sundjata's smooth dark skin. Then he poked at his shoulder, then his stomach, then his leg. Understand?"

Sundjata smiled and turned sideways. He watched as Ahmed poked at him again, and this time the steel blade missed him.

"Now, as the blade comes knock it aside." Ahmed thrust the blade at him.

Sundjata pushed the blade away, but he put no strength behind it. Ahmed stepped in, pushed the sword into him and broke his skin.

"Ouch!" Sundjata yelped and jumped back.

"Weak defense will get you killed. Push it away like it is a snake that wants to bite you."

Sundjata rubbed his side where the blade cut him and rubbed a small droplet of blood into his skin.

"Hurts? It would be a lot worse; don't ever forget that."
Ahmed lifted his shirt and showed Sundjata a large scar where the skin was darker and rough. "See this?"

Sundjata moved closer to look. Bory had run up with the arrows and also moved closer.

"I wasn't paying attention, and I got stabbed." Then he pulled up his sleeve and showed his right arm which bore a long, crooked scar from his elbow and down his forearm. The skin was the same color, but it sunk in. He held his arm out and the boys ran their fingers up and down it.

"Did it hurt?" Bory asked.

Sundjata made a funny sound. "Of course, it hurt." Then he put his hand on top of Bory's head.

Bory shook his head, realizing what he had asked.

"Yes, it hurt very much. When you fight you will get cut, but you must not panic. Otherwise you are dead for sure. I have killed each man who gave me these scars. Bory, go get a stick the size of your arm, you should learn this as well."

Bory ran off to find a stick.

"You two will practice; it is important to have someone you can trust. Bory will be that for you. I can tell. Treat him well, and he will be at your side forever."

Sundjata nodded. "Yes, yes I will."

Bory came back, thick stick in hand, just the right size.

Ahmed took it and cleaned it up like he did Sundjata's. He handed it back to Bory. "Now, like this." In slow motion he brought the sword down towards Sundjata's head. "Block it, strong."

Sundjata raised his sword, met Ahmed's blow and stopped it.

"Good, and now like this." He swung at Sundjata's side. "Take a step back and block it. Strong."

Sundjata did as instructed and blocked the blow.

"You two practice that back and forth with each other until you are tired. Then, do it some more. If you don't have your breath, again, you will die. Remember, if things are in your favor, attack; if not, no harm in running away." Ahmed turned and walked away towards Sogolon. He listened to the click and clack of the boy's sticks hitting each other, and he smiled to himself. As he got closer to Sogolon his smile grew wider.

"You will make proper warriors out of them yet," Sogolon said without looking up at him as she checked to see that the bush meat was ready to eat. She pulled some off, put it in a large leaf and handed it to Ahmed.

"Thank you, my queen." He blew on the hot meat.

"How long do you think it will take Salt to return to us?"

"I'd say about three or four days. He is very resourceful."

"How will he find us?"

"We will continue along the Niger, more or less, until he does. He has an uncanny way of finding me, even when I don't want him to."

Sogolon laughed and handed some meat she had cooled off to Kolonkan. "Eat, child." She took some meat for herself. "I am so tired of just this plain meat. I cannot wait to have some sauce and vegetables."

"Do you think you might want to go back to your hometown of Do?"

Sogolon thought for a moment. "No. The last I heard my brother was still there, and I would not be welcome."

Ahmed shook his head. "Ah... family can be a blessing and a curse. Is there any place you want to go?"

"Not that I can think of. Niani had been the place where I wanted to be buried. Is there anywhere you think we should go?"

Ahmed thought for a moment. "I think, wherever is safest. We don't know the reach of Dankaran and when Sumaguru and his friends may show up."

"As long as I'm with my children," Sogolon said looking at Ahmed.

Ahmed noticed a look on her face; she was thinking of something. "What's the matter?" he asked as he pulled a small bone out of his mouth, sucked it clean, and threw it into the fire.

"I was thinking of Sundjata and Bory. Soon they must go through the ceremony to become men. They must be cut. What if we are with people who do not do such a thing? I will have failed them."

Ahmed laughed. "Don't worry. It is common practice. My people do it as well, but we do it just after birth."

"The ceremony must be done to move into adulthood; the blood of childhood nyama must be released. We must do it after twelve full growing seasons. He must do it in two more seasons."

"It will get done. I know you will make it happen," Ahmed said. "You are a survivor, and you saved Sundjata. You will never fail him."

"You must stop, old man. You will get what you want, you flatterer." She laughed. But it did make her feel better.

"You want the same," he said with a smile.

"Boys, enough; come eat." She picked up a small stick and tossed it at him with a laugh.

The small group had a good night's sleep except for Bory and Sundjata when ants crawled over them and they had to move. They were sleepy in the morning, and it made it easier for Ahmed and Sogolon to sneak away. They got a late start but stopped, as usual, when the sun was overhead. A stand of tall trees that were almost in the trail was the closest shade. Ahmed stopped a small

204

caravan going by and was told about a large village not far away. It was in the red hills covered in green. Even the castle of the Mansa Konkon was built into the hill he was told. This he wanted to see. Sogolon said that it was true as Kon once told her about it. They ventured off to see the castle in the hill.

"Are we there yet?" asked the impatient Bory. "It's been so long."

"It should be just around this hill," Ahmed replied.

"Be patient," Sundjata said. He was on one side of Ahmed and Bory on the other. He turned to see his mother and Kolonkan riding just behind them.

"It's getting dark. What if we don't make it?" Bory asked.

"Then we will make do, like we have since we started this journey," Sundjata said with assurance. He knew Bory was still afraid of the dark and the noises that came with it. He had not found the full lion in himself yet; it was still a cub.

"Your brother is right. We will be fine. Besides, I can hear people. Listen," Ahmed said. "The hill in front of us is blocking most the sound. Once we get to the top you will see."

Night was starting to fall, and the orange purple sky that glowed bright was fading. It was that transition time between day and night, and the night noises began. The crickets, the beetles and the night birds chirped, buzzed and clicked. Lightning bugs flashed and floated in the coming night air. The group climbed the steep path as the sun sank lower, and their tired legs felt the strain of the steep incline.

"I see lights," Bory exclaimed.

"Yes, yes," said Sundjata, and he and Bory ran ahead to get to the top. Their young legs pumped through the strain as they reached the top of the hill first.

Ahmed looked behind to see how close Sogolon was. When he

reached the top he saw lights, and a hill in front of him looming in the growing darkness. There were lights coming out of the hill itself. Below stretched out before him were the evening's cooking fires and houses of the village. A large circular wall of wood and stone surrounded a large compound and built into the hill was the king's castle. It looked like a face with its mouth open and large eyes of flame. "I must say I've been around, but I have never seen anything like this."

The boys stood silent, taking in the scene as the sun slipped down below the horizon.

"What is the name of this place again?" Sundjata asked.

"It is called Djedba, and the mansa's name is King Konkon," said Ahmed.

The group moved aside as Sogolon, still on horseback, topped the hill. "Oh my!" she exclaimed. "This is a place of power."

"What kind of power?" asked Sundjata.

"Dark power," said both voices to Sogolon.

"Yes, yes, dark power," Sogolon said.

"Should we not go?" Ahmed asked.

"We should go there," Sogolon said.

"But if it is dark magic it will be dangerous," Ahmed said. He felt Bory take a step as he was against his leg. He put his hand on the boy's head.

"I will protect us." She reached into her leather bag on the saddle and pulled out five bracelets of grass and cloth she made on the trip. She held them up and reached for the bladder water bag. She took a mouth full and spit a shower over them. Then she held them up to the sky. "Here. Put them on." Ahmed took them from her and gave one each to the boys. She slipped an extra small one on Kolonkan's slight wrist. "Don't take them off, even when you are sleeping. I will make a sacrifice tomorrow to strengthen the protection."

"Alright then, let's go meet Mansa Konkon," said Ahmed leading the group down to the village. The sun had set, but the moon was full and round, and it hung in the sky. The trail turned right and then left making it easier to come down the hill. It straightened out, and at the end two guards met them at the wooden gate. A large fire on the right side of the gate threw shadows, spat and popped.

"Do you seek shelter for the night?" asked the smaller of the two bald-headed, muscular guards—iron-tipped spears in hand and knives strapped to their arms.

"Yes, we do, and food as well."

"You may enter. You are strangers but are welcome." The guard looked at his taller counterpart. The man leaned his spear against the wall and pushed open the gate.

"I think I have met the mansa," Sogolon said. "He came to my wedding."

"Let's see how he feels about you now," Ahmed said, leading them past the gate and to the castle in the hill. They walked to the hill past many round houses, and then a courtyard opened before them. The roofed meeting place was in the middle of the open space. They walked around it and met an older female servant. She was the head of the servants for the mansa and wore a look of confidence. A large yet sturdy frame wrapped in blue and yellow.

The servant to the Mansa had been to Niani many times and recognized Sogolon in an instant. She was surprised to see her. She collected herself. "Queen Sogolon." She bowed. "You have come for a visit."

Sogolon bowed in return. "Yes, may we find a place to sleep and some food?"

"Of course. I will tell Mansa Konkon."

"What do you think?" Ahmed asked Sogolon as they waited.

"He was never one of Kon's favorites. He tended to stay to himself, but that was a long time ago."

Sogolon dismounted, and Sundjata tied the horse to the meeting place. Bory kept Kolonkan busy.

Two young girls came out of the castle. One was Bory's age, and one a bit older than Sundjata. They came out giggling and whispering but stopped when they got closer. The youngest girl went up to Bory while the oldest to Sundjata.

Bory didn't like girls much, although he liked his sister. They were always so serious and always had secrets. It made him uneasy. He stared at the youngest girl.

Ahmed watched the scene unfold and turned to Sogolon. "Bory is speechless and still. That is a first."

Sogolon smiled. "The power of a woman," she said.

"You'll get no argument from me."

"Why do you stare?" asked the young girl. "Is that your sister?"

Bory started to say something but couldn't. It was as if a spell were cast upon him. He looked at her face, her wide mouth full of bright teeth and small but shiny eyes. He felt something stir inside him and swallowed hard. "Yes."

"Yes? That you stare or yes that is your sister?"

Bory went inside his head to remember what he said. When it came to him he felt his body grow warm with embarrassment. He caught himself not wanting further embarrassment. "Yes, she is my sister. I don't stare. I am just looking at that piece of grass in your hair."

The young girl reached up but missed the blade of brown grass. Now she was embarrassed.

"No. Over, up more."

She now felt the blade in her fingers and pulled it out and dropped it to the ground. "Thank you. Are you staying long?"

"I don't know?"

"You don't know much, do you?"

"Go away," Bory said.

She laughed. "What is your name? Mine is Latali."

Mansa Konkon came through the castle door, followed by two small wives and several servants. Although most people in his presence seemed small, he still moved rather fast. His wrap-around garment was green and yellow, and it held his weight. "Welcome, welcome, Queen Sogolon. It has been too long." He noticed the others in the party and stopped and looked. "Who might these be with you?"

Sogolon bowed. "My sons Sundjata and Bory, my daughter Kolonkan, and this is..."

"Abdul Hakeem. Salam." Ahmed bowed. "Your palace is magnificent. I've never seen anything quite like it."

Sogolon paused and followed Ahmed's lead. "Yes, I used to hear my husband speak about this place."

"Salam," the Mansa replied. "Are you a dyula?"

"Yes. Yes, I am, but a small one. I have but a few camels and horses. Queen Sogolon hired me."

"Maybe we could do business someday."

"Maybe. Thank you."

Konkon turned to his wives. "Take care of them. Get them a place to sleep and some food."

The wives turned to their servants, and a look put them into action. They scurried like ants. They took them all, except Ahmed, to a large empty round house outside the castle but still inside the compound.

"The horse you can put in my stable." The mansa grabbed one of the girl servants by the arm and commanded, "Go get a boy and take this horse to the stable." He watched the girl run off, and then he admired the saddle. "That is a beautiful saddle. Not many ride with a saddle, especially one that big."

"Something I picked up in Kumbi-Sahel." *That damn saddle,* thought Ahmed. *Everyone looks at it and admires it. It could give me away, but it is too late now to worry about it.* He took the saddle off that would go with him. A young boy ran up to Ahmed and held out his hand for the reins. He untied the reins and said, "Take good care of him."

The shirtless, dirty-faced boy took the reins. He had never seen such a large horse before and was a little scared.

"Show him who's the boss and he will act like a kitten at your command," Ahmed said. He watched the boy take the big black horse away. Ahmed turned to the king. "I will see you later or tomorrow."

"You rest. I am sure you must be tired. Niani is a far walk from here."

"I did not come from Niani. The queen hired me in Selefougou. I have not been to Niani for a long while. Not since Mansa Kon Fatta ruled there. It is too far south for me to operate and still make profit."

"Mansa Kon Fatta was a great man, a great king! I will see you tomorrow then."

Ahmed bowed and watched Konkon turn his bulk and leave. He saw his little group go into a house not too far away, and he could see through an open window a fire burning inside. He strode towards the building with his saddle over his shoulder and his sword swinging from it. He had to bend to pass through the door and turn the great saddle sideways to get it inside. Inside the round room, the roof was tall coming to a point far above his head. The boys played with the fire in the fire place. "This must have belonged to one of his wives. That fire pit is quite large and inside..."

"Well, Abdul, what do you think?" asked Sogolon. She sat on the floor against the wall.

"Who is Abdul?" Sundjata asked.

"You all must call me by that name while we are here," said Ahmed. "We don't know what Mansa Konkon knows, and we don't want my nephew endangered by me helping all of you. As far as Dankaran and Sossuma know, you escaped on your own."

Sundjata and Bory thought about Ahmed's words and nodded in agreement.

Sogolon picked up Kolonkan and put her in her lap. "Can you do that? Can you call Ahmed, Abdul?"

Kolonkan nodded her head and smiled.

"Say it, baby."

Kolonkan looked at her mother and chanted, "Abdul, Abdul, Abdul, and Abdul."

"Very good," said Sogolon as she hugged Kolonkan.

"He seems welcoming, but we shall see what happens."

Ahmed heard something outside and put his finger to his lips, whispering, "Shhhh."

Two servants came in with food and water for the group.

"Thank you. We will be fine for the night." The servants left, and Ahmed watched them leave to make sure they walked away.

*****

"How many moons has it been since we arrived?" Sogolon asked Sundjata.

"At least seven, I think."

"How have you felt here?" She noticed he was still wearing his amulet bracelet.

"Good. Everyone has been kind." He looked through the trees as they walked through the forest. "Listen, over there." He was looking for a hunters meeting which he could attend. He walked fast and through the trees to find a group of men sitting and talking. He sat down behind the older men.

Sogolon could sit outside the circle, but she wanted to go back to her house. She was feeling uneasy and could not understand why. She walked back through the trees. As she got back to the house she saw Bory, Kolonkan and Konkon's youngest daughter, Latali, playing. Latali had been a constant visitor. She had taken a liking to the impulsive Bory.

"Where's Sundjata?" Bory asked.

"He's with the other hunters. I will take Kolonkan, if you wish?"

"Thank you," said Bory. He turned his attention to Latali. "What do you want to do?"

"Would you like to play hide and seek?"

"Where?"

"In the castle. My father is out, and we can play inside. There are many places to play."

"Yes!"

Latali took off towards the castle with Bory close behind. There were buildings on each side of its entrance. She ran around the buildings, her skinny young legs moving fast. Bory ran hard to keep up. He couldn't believe how someone in a dress could run so fast. She ran close to the building's round walls, making her hard to see. Bory ran away from the wall because she kept disappearing. Once, when he saw her, he pushed off the wall, his foot slipped, and he fell hard into the dirt with a thud. Latali heard the thud and stopped when she realized Bory was no longer chasing her. She walked back, looking around the house to see Bory getting up from the dirt. He cut his elbow, and blood was smeared on his arm.

"Ouch." Bory stood up looking at his blood. He touched around the wound and smeared blood on his finger. He looked up at Latali and with a smile ran towards her.

Latali laughed and turned on her heels in delight. She sprinted towards the castle door with Bory close behind. She knew during the day most of the lamps and fires would not be lit, and she would lose him in the dark. Once inside the door she ran towards the wooden altar and lay down behind it. The carving of a man with a large head and pointed chin with crossed arms was upon it.

Bory came into the room, and it was dark. His eyes betrayed him; he could not see a thing. He stood still, trying to listen for Latali.

Latali lay flat against the stones laid for the floor. Dust filled her nose. She tried to breathe as little as possible, but it made her sneeze. She sprang to her feet and ran for the back of the deep chamber room.

Bory heard her sneeze and ran towards her. His eyes gaining sight, he saw her figure running. He gave chase, but again she disappeared. As he walked he turned his head to listen. There were now rooms within rooms in the back of the large chamber. The light from the door only penetrated so far, and these rooms made of stone and wood, were black.

Latali hid in the second room and curled up in a ball against the back wall. She knew no matter how long he stared the darkness would hide her. She again smelled dust, but it was mixed with the musty odor of dirt. She heard Bory's footsteps as he paused in front of the room. Once he moved far enough away she would make a run for the back staircase. She felt something crawl over her foot. It was long and broad. As it moved she could feel its many legs on her skin. Panic hit her. She kicked her foot forward and screamed, sending the creature flying through the dark.

Bory heard her scream, spun around and ran back to the room he had just left. Running out of the room was Latali, as Bory grabbed her arm. She was shaking and scared. "What's the matter?"

"Something big crawled over my foot!"

"Hah hah! Well, I got you. Afraid of a bug?"

"Do you want to find it?"

Bory paused. "No, no, I believe you."

Latali caught her breath. "Let me show you the rest of the castle. Wait here." She ran to the door where there were smooth clay lamps holding palm oil. Each was round enough to fit in the palm of a hand. Part of the lamp extended into a short spout where a twisted cloth wick poked out. She ran outside and lit the lamp at the nearest fire. She then walked back in holding the lamp in her right hand, shielding the delicate flame with her left. "Follow me." Bory followed close behind as they climbed the carved stone staircase against the back wall. Up through the dark they climbed, the small lamp giving just enough light to see. "I have been up and down these steps so often I could do it in the dark. Want to see?"

"No, no, I believe you.

Downstairs, the light from the doorway gave him courage, but now upstairs he was scared. The light of the flame was dim, and its flickering cast ominous shadows. They entered a room where tiny slits of light poked through a wooden window cover. Bory recognized this as one of the rooms that looked like an eye coming out of the large hill. He could smell smoke and burnt wood mixing with the dirt and dust in the air. Dust particles floated in the small beams of light.

"They will remove the wooden doors and light the fires in here just after dark," Latali said. "Upstairs is another room which room opens to the top of the mountain."

"Can we go now?"

"No, no, you will like it. Come on, don't be scared."

"I am not scared. You are scared."

Latali laughed. "Come on."

She led him to another set of stone stairs and again they climbed upwards. Bory put his left hand out to steady himself and touched the stone wall as they entered another room. This room was as dark as death itself, and the little flame made the room dance. "What do they do in here?"

"They perform rites of passage. The sorcerers see the future in here. That is why it must be dark, my father says." She moved to a corner and knelt. "See." The little flame showed several knives, bones and kola nuts on an ox hide. "I sneak in here when my father, the sorcerers, and the diviners are away. Only they can come in when in the company of someone with royal blood. Like me."

Bory shook his head, looked around the room and wanted to leave. This was a place of magic, and he feared bad spirits lurking in the dark. He felt all the hair on his arms and the back of his neck stand up and chills ran down his spine.

"Come on; one more room. Hold the lamp."

Bory watched her disappear into the darkness. She came back with wood and a rope ladder. She placed it against the back wall. He kept looking behind him, wanting to get out of the room.

Latali climbed the ladder and turned to Bory. "Come on; climb."

Bory climbed the ladder while holding the lamp.

Latali knew there was a secret doorway in the ceiling. She pushed up, and it gave way.

Bory was surprised when dim light appeared above him. He watched Latali climb through a large opening in the ceiling. "Your father fits through this?" He handed the lamp to Latali and went through the opening.

"Shhhh," Latali said.

Bory stood in a small room that was lit only by light coming through the slits in a wooden door which looked like the eye in the room below. But this was opposite of the eyes. He could hear voices coming from the other side of the door. He and Latali crept on bent knees to the door to listen. She knelt down, and he was right behind her.

"I have traveled fast to deliver this to you" said one of the voices.

"I appreciate that, but I hope Dankaran appreciates what I am going to do for him."

Bory and Latali looked at each other as that was the voice of her father.

"Not everyone wants them dead you know. Sogolon and Sundjata are well-liked. Her magic is strong; she talks to spirits whom I do not want to anger."

"I have brought some gold dust and some nuggets. The rest you will get when you complete the deed."[28]

Bory and Latali looked at each other. He noticed she had tears in her eyes. She couldn't believe what her father was saying. She turned and pushed him. She whispered, "We must go, now!" She was so close to his ear he could smell her breath and sensed the panic in her voice.

Bory crept to the hole. He climbed down the ladder, not afraid of the dark room anymore. She handed him the lamp and kept moving downward.

Latali picked up the ox hide to lay it over the trap door in the floor so that no one would know they had been there.

Bory stepped down the ladder fast, but halfway down his foot slipped. His chin hit a rung, and his teeth clacked together hard. The lamp jumped, shook and started to slip from his fingers. Still, he held on, but the flame went out.

Latali was putting the door back in place when she heard Bory slip. As soon as the door was back in she looked down as the flame went out. "Are you alright?" she whispered as loud as she dared.

Bory's teeth and head hurt, and now he was in complete darkness, frozen in fear. "Yes, yes," he groaned.

"Just climb down, and when we get to the floor I will lead us out. I can do it in the dark."

Bory took a deep breath and felt for the next rung.

"Come on. Hurry or we will get caught."

Bory searched for the rung and found it. With his foot secure, he took his next step and then another until he reached the floor.

Latali got to the bottom and took the ladder off the wall and placed it back on the floor. She took Bory's arm and pulled him to the stone steps. She had done this many times. She knew each step, each stone under her bare feet. She could feel him hesitate and sometimes stumble, but she held on to his arm. Her head was spinning, and tears still flooded her eyes. She wiped them away with her other hand.

Bory tried not to fall as they descended the staircases. He was scared, and he had to tell Sogolon. They were now into the lowest main chamber. He could see out the door and started to run. He grasped Latali's hand and pulled her.

Sogolon and Ahmed were with Kolonkan in the house. Bory and Latali came running in out of breath.

"We have to leave. NOW!" Bory exclaimed, still breathing heavy.

"He is right. My father is going to kill you and Sundjata," said Latali with tears down her cheeks.

"How do you know this?" Ahmed asked.

"I was showing Bory the castle in the hill. I thought my father was gone, but he was not. He was on top of the hill. No one is allowed up there but him. He was up there with some man. We heard them say it."

"Dankaran is paying her father some gold now. After he does it he will get even more gold. But Konkon is afraid of Sogolon's magic. He says many people like you and Sundjata."

"He should be afraid of me. My magic has grown stronger over the years. I am tired of this foolishness."

Ahmed turned and looked at Sogolon, not used to seeing her angry. "Where is Sundjata?"

He went out hunting with some locals this morning," Sogolon said.

"Bory, go find him and bring him back," Ahmed said.

Bory turned on his heels and ran out the door. He knew a spot that Sundjata said was a good place to hunt. He turned his head to look at the castle door and stopped dead in his tracks. Lalati came up behind him. He was watching Sundjata hand a small antelope to a personal servant of King Konkon. "No!" Bory shouted and ran towards him.

Sundjata heard Bory yell and he turned to see his brother running towards him.

Bory grabbed Sundjata and started to pull him away. "Come,

come now."

Sundjata laughed. "Yes, yes, alright. He allowed himself to be dragged by his little brother. Latali grabbed his other arm, and his bow began to slide down his arm. "Why is your ass on fire?" Bory just pulled and pulled until they returned to their place.

"I am going to see if I can find anything out," said Latali as she turned to leave.

Bory pulled Sundjata into the house.

"Sit down, son," Sogolon said. "Bory has heard that King Konkon is being paid by Dankaran to kill us."

Sundjata was surprised. "Why are we always in danger?"

"I was hoping we were far enough from Niani and that your father's good will would aid us," Ahmed said.

"I have been invited to play mancala with the king tonight. His servant just invited me."

Everyone looked at each other concerned.

"Do you know how to play mancala?" Ahmed asked.

"Of course. I am good at it. Balla taught me."

"Let him win, most of the time. Nothing makes a person happier than to win."

"What if we run?" asked Sogolon.

"Well, we don't run very fast. I am afraid we would be easy prey if we just run now. Unless we get to the river and hire or buy a boat." Ahmed rubbed his chin, weighing their options.

"Your horse will leave him behind?" Sogolon asked.

"I will buy and train another. Let me think. We will act soon. If you play with Konkon tonight do not eat or drink anything. Say your stomach is bad. Try to get him to play outside."

"Can you buy another horse or two? We can move faster that way. I am getting better at riding. Hopefully he stays hesitant to kill us." Sogolon went over to the fire and took a burning stick and some small twigs. She knelt down in her awkward way and made a small fire in front of her shrine with a carved wooden buffalo. "Sundjata, come." Out of her bag she took a tuft of fur from an antelope Sundjata had taken and a porcupine quill.

Sundjata went to his mother and knelt down beside her. He watched as she took the finger of his right hand.

"Relax, I need some blood." She took the quill, poked the tip of his middle finger and dropped the blood onto the burning fur. "This will protect you."

Sundjata put his finger in his mouth to stop the flow of blood.

Ahmed purchased food from the local market for the evening meal to be safe from being poisoned. "Now, I will purchase two more horses. When we leave I will ride with Kolonkan; she is small, and I can hold her well. Sundjata and Bory, ride together. Sogolon, you can ride your own horse. If something happens, then I will put Kolonkan down and you boys will give her to your mother. Everyone ride ahead. I will catch up with you. I will take care of any problems, right? We will head for the river."

Everyone agreed, and Ahmed left to purchase the horses. Sogolon packed the things they needed to travel while Sundjata and Bory went to the hill castle. Latali met them before the servants came out.

Bory whispered to her, "Have you found anything out?"

"No," replied Latali.

"No matter," Sundjata said.

"He wants you to meet him in the main chamber inside," Latali said to Sundjata. "We can't go in," she said looking at Bory.

"Be careful," Bory said. He and Latali watched Sundjata walk into the main entrance of the hill castle. Above them the doors covering the eyes had been removed and fires lit. Bory thought his brother was walking into the mouth of a monster. From the doorway he could see inside. Many palm oil lamps were lit, and he wondered if he would ever see his brother again.

Sundjata walked into the dome-shaped chamber. Palm oil lamps, some big, some small, were placed about the room. Their combined flames lit the rock and dirt. He realized the room was actually a cave. Outside the wind started to blow in strong gusts. Flames flickered, and this made the room appear to move. He noticed to his left a wooden idol on a raised altar, then a stone staircase running up the back wall. In the center of it all lay King Konkon on several oxen hides. Behind him were rooms that looked like horse stalls. Sundjata thought he saw someone moving in one of them. Was it a killer, a shadow, or a cave spirit? He was glad he had his hunting knife strapped to his arm with his mother's amulet on his wrist. He felt her magic protecting him, but he wished he had his father's bow.

"Come. Sit," said Konkon, sitting up and shifting his weight to be more comfortable. He liked this young man; he was like his father whom he had admired but had found arrogant. Latali would not shut up about Bory. Sogolon was always with a smile, but the gold... all that gold was so enticing. He needed that gold to buy more food to then hide it from Sumaguru who took so much.

Sundjata sat cross-legged on a soft brown ox hide. He looked down at the ebony mancala board. "Is this board new?"

"Yes, I had it made not long ago. This will be the first time using it."

Sundjata looked at the rectangular board and admired its smooth finish. He ran his finger over the edges and into the deep round pits and long, wide finger-shaped wells at each end. He'd never felt anything so smooth. It was the same style of board he had seen before with six pits on each side and wells at each end.

221

"Shall we start? Did you eat? Are you thirsty?" King Konkon asked eagerly.

"Yes," Sundjata replied but then paused. "No, I am sorry, my stomach." He suddenly noticed a servant standing behind. He didn't see where he had come from. The servant then turned and left after Konkon dismissed him.

"Okay, pick up your seeds and start," Konkon said. He had to shift his bulk again to lean forward.

Sundjata picked up his twenty-four river stones. He ran them over his fingers, feeling their cool smoothness and admiring their colors of black, red and brown. He then put four in each of his pits and laughed.

"What do you find amusing?" Konkon asked.

"Well, we are using river stones, but when you play the game you call them seeds. I just realized I've never used real seeds to play the game."

Konkon though for a moment, "Neither have I. Well, I guess if we were farmers we would."

"Yes, yes, true."

"You can go first since you are my guest."

Sundjata remembered what Ahmed said. Instead of picking his stones out of the fourth pit, he put the last one in his empty spot, so he could go again. He took them from the one before. He scooped them out and dropped one smooth stone in each well until his hand was empty. Then it was the king's turn. Sundjata watched Konkon who scooped out his stones from the fourth pit and gained another turn. Konkon gained the advantage. Sundjata kept the game close, but he would always make a small mistake giving the king the upper hand. The turns flowed back and forth, but, of course, the king was first to have all his stones in the well and his pits empty. The stones for each side were counted.

"Ahh, I have won. Good job, young man." Konkon was pleased and liked that Sundjata did not get angry at losing. His sons would always get mad when he beat them at anything.

"Ayeee, we can play again. I will beat you next time," Sundjata said smiling and with a laugh. He noticed the king's round face happy at his victory.

They played again, but this time Sundjata won. The third game the king won, and Sundjata took the fourth game, each game close. But as they played Sundjata noticed the king's mood began to change. After the king won the fifth game they took a break.

"Let's make this last game interesting. Would you like that?" The king said shifting his bulk again.

"Sounds good," said Sundjata as he stretched his stiff muscles. The games took a while, it was getting on in the evening, and he was feeling tired.

"For this last game we will do two things. First, we will recite poems. Second, if you win this last game, I will let you leave here with gold! But, if you lose I get your life. I will kill you; it will be quick. If you win you can use the gold on your journey.[29]

Sundjata tried not to react, but his heart began to race. This was a bit of a surprise. He was hoping that Konkon had changed his mind. This snapped him out of his sleepy feeling. Sundjata sat up straight and looked Konkon in the eyes who was staring intently at him. "I will let you go first."[30]

Konkon was taken aback at Sundjata's relaxed manner. He had just threatened his life. His eyes went to Sundjata's wrist, and he saw the amulet charm. The offer of letting him go first surprised him. It was such an advantage to go first. Maybe he was arrogant like his father. Had he been pretending all along? "Yes, yes, let's begin." He picked up his stones and filled his pits. Before he began, he looked at Sundjata and tried to decide if the boy was arrogant or brave. He took the first stone from the fourth pit and began his poem. [31]

I am mansa

I have absolute rule

I have power that stretches from river to hill

Konkon made his two turns, and Sundjata started his.

I have the blood of the lion

The blood of the buffalo

I can make cheetahs run

I can hunt from sun to sun

He finished his turn, dropping the smooth stones into the pit. Then Konkon recited his next poem.

It is the spirits of the land

My family is the connection through my hand

I will rule far and wide

The people will be by my side

Konkon took four stones from his third pit and placed a single stone in every pit to the left and then in his well. He turned the corner on the board and put a stone in Sundjata's pit. Out of stones and no empty well, his turn was over.

Sundjata knew it was time to spring his trap.

I have the blood of the lion

The blood of the buffalo

I can make cheetahs run

I know the gold from where it comes

It comes to kill from my brother's hand

My mother's magic will not let this stand!

He took his stones from his last pit near the well and put his last stone in an empty pit capturing all the stones in the opposite pit.

"How do you know that, how?" Konkon was angry, but then fear flooded his body. 'Your mother is a witch! I knew it! The stories are right!"

"Yes, they are! Unless you want to be cursed you will forget about killing me and my mother!" Sundjata knew he would lose count on the board now, if he finished the game at all.

Konkon stared at the boy, trying to decide what to do. The lure of the gold was strong, but a curse could end his reign and bring constant misery. "If I let you go, without any gold, will your mother still curse me?"

Sundjata smiled, "Maybe. I will tell her how kind you were here tonight."

Looking down at the board, Konkon said, "In the morning you must leave at first light. Now go."

Sundjata rose and looked at Konkon. It was all he could do to keep from laughing. This king was afraid of his mother who would never curse anyone. For once he was glad for the stories and rumors whispered about his mother. They used to anger him, but now they had saved his life. He bowed to the king, turned with a smile on his face, and walked out into the night and the blowing wind.

Bory and Latali were waiting for Sundjata to come out of the castle. They hid in the meeting place in the dark and ran up to him on his way back to their house. They couldn't decide if the blowing wind was a good or a bad sign.

Sogolon was burning herbs in the fire and praying that their plans would unfold in their favor. Kolonkan slept on the floor next to her. She smiled as Sundjata, Bory and Latali walked through the door. "Latali, come here." Latali came to her and knelt down. "Thank you for what you have done, but it's best if you don't know our plans."

Latali knew she was right. "Yes, I know. "I will go back to my mother's house."

Sogolon gave her a warm hug. "Go now and don't be seen."

Latali rose. As she passed Bory she looked at him. Tears flooded her eyes as she realized she would not see him again. He had to leave; he could not stay.

Bory looked at Latali as she left. His eyes began to tear and he fought hard to hold them back. Still, a few escaped and ran down his round cheeks.

Ahmed entered the house as Latali left. "Ahh, you are here," he said with a smile. "What has happened?"

"We played many games of mancala, and things were good. But suddenly he wanted to play a last game and with poems. Then he said if I won he would give me gold, but if I lost he would kill me."

"And you won, of course," Bory said.

"I didn't even finish the game. During my third turn in my poem I told him that I knew about the plan and the gold. He was so scared that I knew. He thought it was though my mother's magic, and then he was afraid of being cursed by her. He was so afraid he wants us to leave at first light."

Sogolon laughed. "See! And you always get angry at those stories. See how the spirits work!"

Ahmed laughed. "A wonderful turn of events. Well, that explains why more people have not taken Dankaran's offer. I will have the horses ready for the morning."

The group slept well, except Bory who was sad to leave Latali. They rose as the dawn was breaking the night, chasing the dark spirits away. The other horses Ahmed had bought were smaller than his, of course, and they rode off in the twilight. Bory kept looking back hoping to see Latali, but she never appeared. When they rode far enough away and could no longer see the hill castle everyone began to relax.

"I have a new plan," Ahmed announced. "I know where we can go and be safe. It came to me this morning. We will meet up with Salt and his caravan. Then we will go to Ghana. I know the king there very well, and it is far outside of Dankaran's reach."

"What about Sumaguru?" Sundjata inquired.

"I don't think he is concerned about us. With Ghana losing much of its power and wealth, I have a feeling he doesn't visit there often. The king probably pays him enough tribute to keep him away."

"Is it a far ride?" Sundjata asked.

"Yes, but it will be worth it to not have to look over our shoulders all the time." Ahmed nodded his head.

*****

"They are here; we can take them!" Dankaran shouted. He spurred his horse forward. The forest in front of them was getting closer. There was a clearing to open ground with low grass to the left. Dankaran pointed at his captain who was riding next to him. He signaled him to keep pushing the bandits towards the trees. Dankaran then moved left and he signaled for several men to follow. He had to keep them from escaping to open ground. In the trees the men would be separated and couldn't fight together. They would be as easy to defeat as they would be outnumbered.

The captain road hard, looked at Dankaran, and then nodded his head.

These bandits had to be stopped. There were too many caravans being attacked, and Niani was feeling the pressure.

Dankaran shouted, "Go!" and kicked his horse. Four men followed close behind. He had never ridden so fast before. With his feet firmly in the stirrups, his body moved in time with the galloping horse.

Azeez rode in the group that split off with the king. He went along this time to see what was wrong with Dankaran's methods. Why was he only stopping a few raids? Was there no fear of him? He counted ten bandits. He was impressed with the speed Dankaran was riding.

Dankaran now occupied the open space close to the trees, and the bandits entered the forest. He smiled and said aloud, "I've got you now." He slowed his mount to see what his next move would be. He must hold them in place. Turning his mount, he moved towards the trees.

Azeez caught up to Dankaran and was close behind him when he saw some of the bandits. "Look!" He shouted and pointed. Three bandits rode out of the forest.

Dankaran and three men took off after them. Azeez stayed in place watching them ride off.

One lone bandit burst out of the trees and saw Azeez. He stopped his mount and wheeled it around to return to the safety of the woods.

Azeez saw the lone bandit. Their eyes locked together even as he turned his horse. The bandit was so distracted he didn't see a low thick branch. It smacked him in the face knocking him to the ground. Azeez let out a laugh at his good fortune. He stopped his mount and leapt off. He looked up to see Dankaran and his men in hot pursuit. Azeez drew his curved sword and pointed it at the man rolling around in pain on the ground. The sword shone brightly in the morning sun. He admired it while waiting for the bandit to stop holding his face. Azeez began to feel sorry for this poor bloody young wretch. His pants were torn, and he looked skinny. "Come on, get up. You will live." The bandit groaned and took his hands off his face to reveal a long, ragged cut across his cheek bleeding profusely. "Why do you raid here, so close to Niani?"

As the skinny bandit got to his knees, he felt as though he might throw up. The pain in his face was intense, and then his left hand felt it as if it were on fire. He looked at his hand. His pinky was sticking away from his hand. It was badly broken. Now the boy did vomit into the short brown grass.

Azeez shook his head and turned away from the sight. "Ugh, you are not having a good day, my friend. Just sit down."

The skinny bandit sat down and looked up in a daze at Azeez. Spit hung from the corner of his mouth and vomit on his chin.

"Why do you raid so close to Niani?" Azeez repeated.

The bandit spat then wiped his mouth and chin with the back of his hand. He replied, "Because it is safe now."

"Because King Kon Fatta is dead?" asked Azeez.

"Yes, and because Queen Sogolon is now gone."

"What do you mean?'

"Everyone has heard about her. Even Sumaguru wouldn't kill her. She is a witch and talks to the spirits every day. Everyone knows King Dankaran catches few who raid. "

"He caught you."

"That tree branch caught me!"

Azeez could not deny that and said nothing.

*****

"There he is," remarked Sogolon with surprise.

"I told you he always finds me." Ahmed smiled pulling his great black mount behind him.

"He found us after we left Djedba and now again. He left us for four days and we've been on the move."

"He was trained by one of the finest trackers that was ever in my employ. Unfortunately, the tracker took ill and died. However, he taught Salt everything he knew - except how to smile."

Sogolon laughed. "I hope he brings good news. I am getting tired of traveling."

"Well, I don't blame you. Even I like to settle down awhile after a long trip. But then I must be on the move. I am going to miss you when this is over." He turned to look at her face. He wanted her to see his eyes. She had shaved her head at the beginning of the journey and kept it clean ever since. Her skin was luminous from the sun.

She felt him looking at her and she dropped her head first. She then turned to look at him. "I will miss you too. I hadn't even wanted the touch of another man since Kon. You brought something out in me. I can't thank you enough for helping us."

Ahmed could not help but smile. "You are a special woman. I will return when I can."

"Between wives and the others, you will be tired." Sogolon laughed.

Ahmed smirked. "Perhaps... unless you want to become number three?"

Sogolon was quiet for a moment and thought about it. "I would not mind it, but in my heart, I can't. Still, I do hope you will return when you can."

Ahmed felt a little sad. "Hmm, I understand, and I will. But if you change your mind, I will marry you."

Salt rode up alongside them but did not dismount. He was closest to Ahmed whose horse gave a snort at Salt's horse.

"The road to Wagadou is clear, and the king awaits us with open arms," Salt said.

"Wagadou?" Sogolon asked.

"Another name for Ghana," Ahmed said.

"You will be able to speak their language; it is like the tongue spoken in Niani," Salt said to Sogolon.[32]

"Any raiding by the Sosso?" Ahmed asked.

"No. It is as we thought. He pays his tribute, and Sumaguru stays away. But, I heard the strangest story. Sumaguru saved a village of Bamana from attacking Fulani. In some places they are calling him a hero!"

"Ahh, a leopard gives birth to a leopard," Sogolon said.

"True," Ahmed said. "How many days away are we?"

"Three days at the most." Salt looked at Sogolon and a smile broke from his dour face.

"How come you don't smile when you look at me?" Ahmed asked.

"There is no beauty, but the beauty of action," Salt said, and his usual look returned to his face.

Ahmed shook his head. "The guinea hen's prayer does not affect the hawk."

Smiling at Sogolon again, Salt said," I will find a place to camp tonight," and rode off.

Sogolon was laughing at the exchange. "It is as if you two are married. I think he is your third wife."

Ahmed laughed. "It feels like it sometimes."

"You should give him his freedom."

"I did many years ago. A Muslim can't enslave another Muslim. But we laugh about it now. A man like him should never be a slave."

Sogolon smiled at Ahmed's wisdom and generosity. While the voices in her head argued about his marriage proposal; she just smiled and listened as they walked on.

Salt found a good spot by a stand of trees with lots of wood. To guard against beasts and bandits the caravan was kept close together. The twenty-five camels and twenty-five horses were tied on two long ropes, and the men on guard duty tended fires. Some laughed, some talked about the past, and others dreamed of the days ahead.

After dinner, Sundjata, Sogolon, Ahmed and Salt sat around the evening fire. Bory and Kolonkan were fast asleep on soft skins. Soft wool blankets brought by Salt with the caravan covered them.

Sogolon sat quietly, calming the voices in her head. She was able to control them better with each season. It pleased her to make them apologize to her. She looked at Bory and felt sad for Nama, not being with her boy. Yet she knew in her heart that they would be together again someday. She saw Sundjata staring at Ahmed who was holding pieces of paper stuck together. He looked at them with great concentration.

"What are you doing? I forgot what you call this?" asked Sundjata.

"Reading. You may have seen Azeez doing it."

"Yes, I have. Azeez said he was always reading about numbers or things. He called them lists. Are you reading lists?"

Ahmed smiled. "No, I am reading about Allah. It's good to do that from time to time."

"How come I only see you pray in the morning when you get up and at night before you go to sleep? I see other men like you pray often during the day?

Ahmed smiled at the boy's mind. "Well, some would say I am bad for not praying as required by this book I am reading. It's called the Koran. But, only the Most High can judge, and judge me he will. I pray in the morning because He allows me to see another day. What happens the rest of the day is written. If it is to be, it will be. Allah knows my heart. So, twice is usually enough for me."

Sundjata shook his head as he thought about it. "Some say that our gods and spirits don't mix with your God and that they shouldn't."

"Well, there should be no gods or spirits other than Allah, but I see many things. I am of a tolerant mind. If Allah does not mean for me to see and feel them he would not let them be. He is all powerful. So, I treat them all as part of him."

"I like that you see them all as part of one. Like Nyama that flows through all," Sogolon said.

"There are many mysteries in life. Often the fun is to discover them and find out about them." Ahmed held up his Koran. "This is called a book. Men who discover things write what they know down in books, so others can learn about them. It's like a griot, but in this shape."

"One day I hope to get my griot back. I miss Balla. I miss him every day," Sundjata said in a sad tone.

"There are those among my people, who don't like what you bring. They say books are evil, and only the word passed from lips to ear is what should be. Our ways should be followed. I don't believe that. I think many paths are the way to follow," Sogolon said.

"Sumaguru is one of them. He doesn't like the ways of Islam, but I know men of Islam who think only our ways are best," Ahmed said with sadness.

"Are they afraid?" asked Sundjata.

"Yes. Their souls are afraid. Afraid of life."

"And their hearts are small as well?" Sundjata asked.

"Yes, small and shriveled like piece of dried fruit." Ahmed laughed.

The group drifted off to sleep and was up with the sun to make their goal of arriving in Wagadou by sundown. They pushed the animals hard that entire day. The camels took it all in their stride--just moving faster than usual--but the horses had to be pushed. White foamy sweat gathered around the edges of their saddles and on their necks. The flow of people became steadier as they got closer to Wagadou. They were ignored like any other caravan and Ahmed was happy about that. They arrived at the gates as the sun began to set.

"I'm glad we are finally here. The hunting has been terrible for the past few days. Balla would hate it," Sundjata complained." His brown mare still seemed strong even though she was breathing hard. Kolonkan sat in front of him.

"It's so dry here," said Bory. "Where are the trees?" His black and white stallion was dripping foamy white sweat.

"I see some way over there," Sundjata replied as he pointed to a grove of thorn trees in the distance.

"That is where they bury their royals," Ahmed said.

"They cut all the rest of them down. The spirits are not pleased," said Sogolon. "One cannot speak to them." Her back hurt from the hard pace, and she could not wait to dismount.

"The buildings are all made of those smooth, square yellowish stones. Where is the mud covering?" Sundjata had never seen so many square buildings and smooth stones. "Salt, you said there was a gate. I don't see one."

"Well, there used to be one, but Sumaguru commanded them

to take it off. Now the city is beginning to fall into disrepair. Parts of the walls are weakening."

They rode through the hole in the wall where the gate once stood. The wall was taller than a man on horseback, and in some places, the stones had fallen and lay strewn on the ground. Small towers rose along its corners.

The group rode up to a large square building that rose above all the round houses surrounding it. Several bald, shirtless servants approached them. They wore gold bracelets around their wrists and ankles with long necklaces of gold. They came out to take their horses. Salt took the rest of the caravan to the unloading area.

Sundjata helped his mother off her horse. She winced as she stretched her twisted back and limped a bit. Ahmed started to go over to her, but she waved her hand. "I'm fine."

Ahmed smiled at her but stayed near.

"This way, please," said one of the gold-adorned servants as he waved his hand toward the doorway. The group followed him into the great room where King Moussa Tounkara sat on a large stool.

"Welcome, Ahmed. Welcome, Queen Sogolon of Niani. Your husband was a great king; he is missed." He turned back to Ahmed. "Your man says you have bought me things."

"Yes, yes, you will be happy. I am sorry I have not visited in a while."

"I understand, my friend. You must go where the trade is. Things have become difficult for me."

Sundjata watched as the king stood up. He was surprised how tall and thick-bodied he was. The king wore clothes made in a way he'd never seen before. Gold bracelets adorned his wrists. He moved with a slow sadness like a man weighed down by something heavy. "You may stay here, but not for long."

"Where should we go my friend?" Ahmed asked.

"You will stay with my sister, a day's ride from here. Neither Sumaguru nor Dankaran will look for you there."

Chapter 16

Even the Dwarf Palm Grows

Salt could see the village on top of a small rise. He saw not a soul the entire ride from Wagadou to here. The village was a mid-sized affair but easy to miss as it was not on any well-traveled trails. He rode into the village looking for Sogolon. His eyes searched the many round houses and low walls. It had been six full growing seasons since he'd been back, and he wasn't sure where her house might be now. He was glad to get out of Wagadou. The king wandered around in his empty kingdom. Just a few servants and a few families roamed around the empty buildings. There were more dogs than people now. Salt looked up at the sun and saw it was mid-day. Most people were resting and waiting for the heat of the day to break. In this place he felt life. This far north it was much hotter and drier than in Niani. He wondered how Sogolon was adapting to such a dry climate; the young ones probably didn't care.

"May I help you, friend?" said a shirtless man with a sword in his belt. "We don't get many visitors."

Salt heard a voice and turned to see a man behind him. *I am getting old, letting this man surprise me,* he thought. "I am looking for Queen Sogolon. Tell her Salt is here to see her."

The man looked hard at this stranger and then he remembered. "Ahhh, I remember you. You are slave to the Islamic man."

Salt made a face. "I am slave to no one. I have been freed. Your people were slaves of mine. Go find the queen." He dismissed the man with a face of disdain. A sense of pride filled his chest. He did not have to wait long.

"Salt, Salt!" Sundjata and Bory came running towards him from a house. He couldn't help but smile.

"You have returned!" Sundjata said with glee.

"He has returned; he has returned," Bory began so sing. "Has Ahmed come as well?"

Salt looked at the two boys. "My, how the dwarf palms grow; I can't believe how big you two have become. Yes, he follows."

"Come. Come see, mother," Sundjata said. He led Salt to their house.

At Sogolon's house, Salt took the saddle off his horse and put it on the low knee-high wall surrounding it. He tied the horse to a stick that protruded from the wall.

Sogolon came from inside the house and put her hands together, touching the tips of her fingers to her chin. "It is so good to see you. It has been too long." She walked in her awkward way towards him.

Salt could not help himself from smiling even harder at her. He admired her so, and he walked into her open arms to receive a hug. He bent down a bit and hugged her back. "I know it has been too long."

"Does he follow?" she asked.

"Yes, we bring things. He will be here very soon." He looked at her, and she looked a little older, a little tired. "Come," he said.

They walked to the edge of town and the boys followed. Halfway there, Kolonkan came running to the group.

"Her chores are done, and she was playing with her friends," Sogolon said.

Salt knelt down and opened his arms, and Kolonkan ran into them. He hugged her, and his heart warmed. "I have missed you most of all. You are growing so." He hugged her again.

"I am so glad you are back," Kolonkan said. "Did you bring me something?"

Salt laughed, "Yes, of course. Ahmed brings it." He held her arms and looked at her. "You have grown the most, my young lady. Let's meet him."

They walked to the edge of the village and could see riders approaching. Leading them were Ahmed and Azeez. They rode the usual large black mounts side by side. Behind them were many camels with riders on horseback flanking the caravan.

Sogolon's heart felt light and she wished they would move faster.

The boys and Kolonkan raced out to meet the group.

"Oh, my uncle, look at them," Azeez said.

Ahmed felt a lump in his throat and had to take a moment to swallow hard. "Yes, yes. Allah be praised," and he raised his right hand into the air.

The little group ran up to them shouting and singing. "Excuse me. Do you know where I can find a boy named Sundjata and his little brother Bory and their baby sister?" Ahmed asked in a serious manner.

"It is us! It is us!" replied the group. "It is us."

"No, no, that is impossible. They are small and young; they are not grown like you," Azeez added.

"It is us," Bory said.

"Yes, yes," said Kolonkan as she jumped up and down.

"It is too bad because we have brought them presents," Azeez said.

"It's us; it's us!" the group yelled.

Sundjata laughed and laughed.

"Wait, wait!" shouted Ahmed as he leaned over in his saddle. "Could it be?"

"Why, yes, I think it could be," added Azeez. He reached his hand down to Kolonkan and pulled her up into the saddle behind him." Kolonkan hugged him and his heart warmed.

Sundjata walked up to Ahmed and extended his hand. Ahmed grabbed and shook it. "My heart fills with happiness. For you too Bory," Ahmed let go of Sundjata's hand to touch Bory's. "Lead the way," he said.

The two boys turned and ran as Azeez and Ahmed followed at a trot.

Sogolon and Salt walked out toward them and met them half way.

"My eyes are happy now," Ahmed said looking at Sogolon. He dismounted, walked up to her and gave her hug. He kissed her full lips and looked into her eyes."

"I thought you forgot where I lived, old man," Sogolon said, kissing him back.

Ahmed laughed. "I am not that old... yet. Things have been crazy all around. Azeez and I have had to work hard to survive."

"I see that you have, but I never doubted that you would."

"The children look wonderful. It makes my heart soar."

"They have been a joy to me. They have grown so well."

Azeez came over and gave Sogolon a hug. "The spirits favor you still."

"A little less each day I fear, but I am well." She smiled.

"Have you been sick?" Azeez asked.

"Now and again, but I recover. This dry weather doesn't agree with me."

"You are too tough to kill," Azeez said with a smile.

Queen Massiran walked up to the small group. "I heard of your arrival. Thank you for bringing us things."

Ahmed and Azeez bowed.

"My pleasure. I hope what we have brought pleases you," Ahmed said.

"I will have my servants prepare a meal, and we shall celebrate your return."

The meal was prepared. All sat and ate in the center of the village. The sun was down, and the heavy air of the day became light and refreshing. Ahmed had brought several goats to be butchered so there was plenty to eat.

"I love my necklace," Kolonkan said to Ahmed. She adored the smooth gold twisted like a rope that lay against her dark skin.

"Those things are from Egypt," Ahmed said to Sogolon. She was looking at her necklace made of gold but had a pendant hanging from it with a green jewel in the center.

"These are too much but thank you."

"Nonsense, they are only so beautiful because it is those who wear them that bring out their beauty."

Sogolon smiled, shook her head and laughed at his flattery.

"The daggers I gave the boys have ivory handles. One never outgrows a good dagger." Ahmed stretched and then said to Massiran, "Sundjata tells me your guard is training him to fight and ride."

"Yes, he and Bory are both quick learners. They will grow to be fine men," Massiran said. "Thank you for the earrings." She turned her head from side to side. The copper and gold reflected the light of the fire.

"Has Sumaguru bothered you here?" Azeez asked.

"No, he is too busy raiding other places. I think he has grown bored with my brother now that he is a broken man."

"Yes, I am very sad about how things have turned out for him. "It is written," he said.

Massiran nodded her head in agreement. Her family had converted to Islam many generations ago; and as was their custom, they mixed Islam with their Soninke traditions. "It is so."

Azeez and Ahmed stayed a cycle of the full moon before they left. The entire village turned out to say goodbye to Ahmed, Azeez, Salt and the rest of his men. Hugs, smiles and tears were all in good measure that morning. Sogolon was sorry to see Ahmed go but understood it was his way of life. They stood there until the party disappeared over the horizon. Sogolon wondered if she would ever see Ahmed again.

*****

Kolonkan looked out the door and saw just a few thin clouds streaking the sky. She hoped Sundjata and Bory would return soon. Sogolon had come down with terrible fevers that would not go away. Kolonkan was afraid that her mother might die, and they would not get a chance to say goodbye. Sundjata and Bory were gone often between hunting and training with Massiran's guard. She looked back at her mother who looked pale and sweaty. "I think you should spend some time outside. It's nice out. It may help you."

Sogolon rolled over and looked at her daughter. "You have grown so big. How long have we been here? Where is Ahmed? Where is Kon?" The fevers kept clouding her head, and she would slip down paths she had traveled in the past. Everything seemed so real. When the fevers would lessen, she couldn't remember where she was.

Kolonkan shook her head, moved over and knelt beside her mother. "Eight seasons, eight growing seasons. It's been two seasons since Ahmed visited."

"Is Sundjata back?"

"Not yet," said Kolonkan as she helped her mother up. They moved through the door of Sogolon's house at a slow pace. "I will make you some Jalal tea," Kolonkan said. She sat her mother down on an ox hide in the shade of small tree that grew next to the house.

Sogolon quieted the voices in her head and watched her now big girl disappear through the doorway. The morning sun was climbing, heating up the day. The heat of the air felt good on her face and aching body. She saw the king's sister walking across the village square. "Massiran, have you seen my son?" Her voice had become weak and frail.

Massiran stopped her trek and walked up to Sogolon under the tree. "He was with the hunters last I saw him. I see you are feeling better."

"Yes, thank you. And thank you for helping my son on his journey to become a man these many seasons." Sogolon felt a great welling of emotion in her chest as she choked back tears.

"I am glad our Poro order is similar to your Komo order. After all, our clans still share many things." Massiran saw the emotion on Sogolon's face.

"Yes, your men act with great honor. It's sad what has happened to your brother and his kingdom. Do you think he will stay in Kumbi-Sahel? There is almost nobody left there?"

"It was written. Allah and the ancestors can't see us anymore. Sumaguru's power is very strong, but we survive," said Massiran as she looked into the distance. "I keep telling him to come here, but like a man he is stubborn; being a king makes it worse."

"True. I have never seen such power as Sumaguru's, but I know his magic will run out someday soon. I pray to the ancestors every day. Something is stopping them from seeing his evil."

"I pray five times a day, make sacrifices, and yet things around

243

us get worse."

Kolonkan came out of the house with Jala tea in a wooden cup. "Here, Mother." She turned and bowed towards Massiran.

Massiran looked at Kolonkan's bright face that looked so much like her mother's. "You are growing up to be a beautiful young lady."

"Thank you. Would you like me to get you something?"

"No, thank you. That is very kind."

*****

Sundjata crouched behind a stand of small trees that stood on a slight hill. Spear in hand, the iron head felt heavy, so he adjusted his grip. He could hear the men shouting. They drove the game through the tall grass, thick bushes and short trees towards him. The timing of the throw was everything. His hands were sweating, and his eyes searched the wall of green and brown before him. Now he heard branches cracking and hooves pounding the yellowish dirt. Standing with knees bent, he raised the spear ready to throw it. A large oryx like the one he once dreamed of burst from the thicket snorting and breathing hard. He waited till the beast was close and threw the spear hard; it stuck into the antelope's side. But the oryx was large and kept running. Sundjata dropped to one knee and picked up his father's bow with an arrow already knocked. The bow came up, he let the arrow fly, and it stuck into the charging beast's back leg. Now either the iron spearhead tearing organs or his mother's poison would fell the beast.

"Nice shot," said Kwame Nkrumah, head of Massiran's guard. He came through the tall grass followed by the rest of the guard. "If you track it and find it, I will butcher it, but if you can't find it you will butcher the next five animals we kill."

Sundjata smiled as there were many hiding places where an animal could lie down and never be found. "Yes, it will be easy," he said.

244

"Ha, he will find it before the sun moves half way down," Bory said walking over and standing next to Sundjata with arms crossed.

Sundjata looked hard at Bory.

"Okay, cheetah chaser. Get going." Kwame laughed.

"Will you stop telling that story?" Sundjata said giving Bory a push. "You will help me track, or you will be butchering those five animals with me, from the inside out!"

*****

"What is taking so long?" Fakoli asked Balla.

"They don't have much. They say it was a poor season, that someone else raided their stores," Balla said while walking up to a mounted Fakoli. He looked around then back to Fakoli and said, "These people are poor. How many people live here, maybe twenty or so?"

"Well, make sure you leave them enough to get by. We have more than we need. I don't even know why we are here." Fakoli realized he shouldn't have said that aloud. His uncle was becoming more stubborn every day, wanting more.

Balla looked at him surprised. He dared not say anything; but was glad to hear it. He had grown to like Fakoli very much as they often were sent on missions together. He wasn't like his uncle. Not as big and strong, but a better horseman. If Fakoli were king he'd be back in Niani for sure. "Things are getting crazy now that other clans are raiding."

Fakoli knew Balla was right. Clans were beginning to think they could do what they wanted. "Those raiders better be careful and not get Sumaguru angry. I hate to think what he would do if he caught them."

Balla shook his head and laughed. "Yes, he'd be wearing them."

Fakoli held back a laugh but let out a smile. "Get your horse. Let's go and meet Sumaguru on the trail. It may go easier for these people." He turned his horse, but it was too late. Sumaguru rode into the square.

"Where is my tribute?" Sumaguru asked, indignant.

"Uncle, they have very little to give."

"Your son is having our men load yams and grain in baskets now," Balla said.

A small group of donkeys came into the square led by his son.

"Four baskets, that's all?" Sumaguru said with disgust.

"They have been raided, and their growing season was poor. Many locusts as well," Fakoli said, attempting to calm his uncle.

"They can't protect their own village. They don't deserve to have it. How long ago were they raided? Balla, I want you to track them. Take my son and four men."

Balla was tired and wanted to go home and he let out a sigh.

Sumaguru saw the look on Balla's face. He charged him with his horse.

Balla realized he had made a mistake. He jumped sideways avoiding Sumaguru's horse but felt a slap across his head from the small leather whip that hung from Sumaguru's wrist.

"If I get off this horse you will be buried here."

Fakoli kicked his horse forward and put himself between his uncle and Balla. "He is tired, Uncle."

"Ahhh, you both act like women. Nephew, go with him since he is so tired and you are so concerned."

Fakoli also wanted to get home; he missed the beautiful brown eyes of Keleya and her soft laugh. He knew this look on his uncle's face, and to talk back would be a fight. Looking down at

Balla, he said, "Come, get your horse."

Sumaguru watched his nephew and Balla leave. He looked for the captain of his guard who was standing there watching him. "Burn this village and take these people as slaves. We will distribute them to the clans that support us."

"Should I send a man to make sure they do as you say?" asked the captain as he pointed in the direction of Fakoli and Balla. "How ungrateful they are."

Sumaguru turned his head and looked at his nephew and paused. "No, they will do as they are told." He hoped that someday he would not have to teach his nephew a lesson.

*****

"See anything?" Sundjata called to Bory. He wiped his forehead and noticed the sun getting low. He was worried he would lose his bet. He wanted to bring home something with strong nyama to help his mother regain her strength.

"Not yet."

Sundjata saw tracks of the oryx end in the sand, and before him stood large islands of brown grass. Some were small round tufts, but others were large enough to hide a large animal. Did the beast jump from island to island? He leaned on the spear that had fallen out of the beast.

"Here, here!" Bory called in excitement.

Sundjata ran towards him. "What?"

Bory knelt down and pointed. "Look. Over there."

Sundjata squatted down and he almost leaned on Bory's head. His brother had also grown tall in these past seasons. He followed Bory's finger and saw a hoof sticking up through a large island of grass. "Ahhh, I see it."

"It doesn't move. It's dead. I will go around this way, you the other." He took the spear from Sundjata and began to circle around with knees bent at the ready. Each step was soft yet deliberate, and his eyes were searching for any sign of movement.

Bory got around the island first and saw how the animal lay. "We got him," he said as he walked towards the large body.

Sundjata knew Bory's eyes were sharp. He stood up and walked towards him. The oryx with his last bit of energy jumped onto the island of grass but toppled over on his back. It died legs up. He felt excited to win his bet. This meant good food for the village, but most of all, something strong for his mother. Then he felt the usual small pang in his stomach after a kill. He knew it was the ancestors telling him to respect life. He remembered his father telling him that.

"Good eyes, brother."

"Here, look what I found," Bory said tossing something at him.

Sundjata caught it and looked in his hands. It was a lion's claw.

"Father sending us a message, I think."

Sundjata laughed and then smiled. "Yes, he is." This would be his new power item with his father's bow now too weak to use. "Go find Kwame and tell him to get ready to get his hands dirty."

*****

Dankaran paced back and forth in front of the palace altar. "This has to stop."

Sossuma looked down at the floor. "We must pay."

"They take too much. They should take only half. Also, Azeez and his uncle left. All the Islamic men we have hired have been unreliable."

"Ahh, I am glad they are gone. They helped your traitor brother and his witch mother leave. I heard it from many sources. We can't have traitors working for us."

248

"Your point is well taken, but good points don't fill our bellies or bring gold. The mansas of the surrounding villages complain at council that we don't fight back."

"Well, why are you are complaining? At least you are alive. Sumaguru's magic, and his men are powerful."

"We are many, we are strong, and I have the blood of the lion." With that Dankaran turned on his heels and walked out the door. "Come with me," he said to the two guards on either side of the door. He felt the anger surge through his chest as he could not take it any longer. He walked across the palace courtyard to the gate tailed by the guards. With each step he knew what he must do. He could see through the open gate Sumaguru's men with horses and donkeys loaded down with rice, millet and things they felt like taking. Dankaran yanked a spear out of the hands of a gate guard.

The lead man on horseback heard footsteps and turned to see the king. "We..."

Dankaran didn't wait to hear what the man had to say. He threw the spear with all his might and hit him square in the chest, knocking him off his horse. He drew his sword and slashed the man to the left.

Dankaran took the bow off his shoulder and nocked an arrow. He pointed it at the nearest man. "Leave one alive!" he shouted.

Dankaran's guards attacked the men. They shouted and smiled.

It was over very fast. In all the seasons they have been taking their tribute they never encountered trouble. Niani was always the easiest stop for them; their weapons were never needed.

Dankaran was smiling as he walked up to the lone survivor. "You will take back a message to Sumaguru."

Sossuma heard the commotion. She stood at the gate and saw the blood and dying men. She looked at her son and was so proud at that moment, but said aloud, "What are we to do now?"

"How is she?" Sundjata asked Kolonkan as they stood outside their mother's house.

"She is not getting better. Her fever goes but then returns. She grows weaker." She looked up at her older brother with a sad look on her face.

Sundjata hugged his sister and kissed her forehead. "Don't worry; mother is strong, as are her healing powers."

"I have never seen her weak like this." She wiped tears from her small bright eyes. "How was the hunting?"

"We had to travel far, but it was good. I got a big oryx. He had a piece of its tail sewn to his shirt next to a hyena claw and some buffalo tail. He pointed to it with pride. "We will eat well, and I have something to help mother."

Bory walked up to Sundjata and Kolonkan. "Is there anything to eat?" he asked, looking at Kolonkan.

"You are rude, Bory. You can greet me first. You just got back. You didn't even ask about mother," Kolonkan said.

Bory sighed. "Hello. Is there anything to eat? How is mother?"

Kolonkan shook her head, "You. Yes, and she isn't doing well."

"Ahh, how am I to know? She has been sick since we left."

"Come in and eat. I will put a curse on you someday; the Jinn here taught me how."

Bory made a face and went past her on his way inside.

Sundjata laughed. "You two are always fighting. I remember when you both got along so well."

"Well, I am not little anymore, and neither is that big head."

"Now, now, don't be like that. We are all we have."

"I know; come eat."

They went inside and saw Bory next to Sogolon. She was sitting up but looked sweaty with her hand on Bory's face.

"Mother," Sundjata said kneeling next to her.

"Boys, you have returned safe." Sogolon said in a weak voice, now touching both their faces.

"Mother, eat a piece of this oryx heart." Sundjata unwrapped the heart from a piece of cloth that he took from a leather bag over his shoulder. He handed her the piece of salted muscle. "It has much power and will help you."

She took the heart, chewed a small piece and forced herself to swallow. She didn't feel like eating, but her son was right about the heart having much nyama. It could heal her, but she felt it was too late.

"Eat it," said the mother voice. "Save yourself."

"The ancestors are calling you. Do not fight it," said the angry voice.

Sogolon didn't bother quieting the voices; at that moment she felt as though she were floating. She lay back down and said, "My son, you must honor the ancestors... always. Remember, the mansas are the key. They hold things together and talk to the spirits. Bory... have patience. My daughter, remember all I taught you."

"Rest, Mother, re-gain your strength," Sundjata said, "Don't talk like that."

"Yes," Bory added.

Sogolon was thinking of Kon, when they first met, also thinking of Ahmed's mischievous smile. How those two men loved her. She thought of the day her boy stood straight and strong, and when her beautiful daughter was born. Of course, she also thought of fiery Fanta. She had come a long way from being

251

laughed out of her village and rejected by all the men. To be queen, even for a while, was more than she ever imagined in her life. She smiled and closed her eyes.

"They are calling you," the mother voice said.

"Fight no more. Go to the ancestors." said the angry voice.

Kolonkan, Bory and Sundjata knelt next to Sogolon. They watched as her breathing became slow. Each was touching her now and remembering how gentle and kind she was. Always there, always encouraging, protecting and loving. Kolonkan was crying softly and leaning on Sundjata. Tears tumbled down Bory's round cheeks. He thought about his mother, Nama, and it made him miss her more. Sundjata wanted to cry, but he put his arms around Bory and Kolonkan and held them tight. Sogolon was quiet now, her breathing stopped.

"We must tell Massiran. We need to get the masks to lead her spirit out of the village. You know mother. She won't want to leave us."

*****

"They took off in different directions," Balla said looking at tracks in the dirt.

"Looks like in groups of three," Fakoli added while following a group.

"What shall we do now?" Balla asked wiping the sweat from his forehead.

"We shall go back and tell my uncle what has happened," Fakoli said with relief, turning back to Balla. "We can go home." He looked into the afternoon sky with a few fluffy white clouds. "We can camp around here and head back in the morning."

All the men were happy to hear this and smiled.

"There is a stand of trees over there where we can make camp. Gather wood, men," Balla said.

The night camp was a happy one. The men shot small game and gathered some fruit from a Baobab tree. They laughed and told stories as their large fire lit up the night. Dancing flames threw shadows while moths and beetles flew around them.

"What were Sumaguru's plans?" Balla asked Fakoli.

"He was going to drop those slaves off at some of our allies' then head home. We should move slow and not beat him back, so he doesn't think we didn't try."

"Do you hear that?" Balla sat up.

Into the camp rode one of Sumaguru's men. "What are you men doing here?" he asked with surprise.

"What are you doing here? Do you have the tribute from Niani?" Fakoli asked.

Balla's heart jumped hearing the name. If he could just get back...then he realized he was but a two or three-day ride away.

"King Dankaran fought back. He killed our men and sent me to tell Sumaguru that he takes too much."

It's about time, thought Balla with a smile.

Fakoli looked at Balla and saw the happiness on his face. You will ride and tell my uncle of this. I don't think you should go to Niani.

The happiness drained from Balla's face. He knew that Sumaguru's retaliation would be terrible. Balla shook his head and hoped Dankaran was ready for a fight. Sumaguru had most of his men with him collecting tribute. He had the army he needed to retaliate swift and hard.

*****

Balla stood at the base of Sumaguru's tower. If he could just find Sumaguru's power object he could be defeated, and he could go home. *If there is any home to go back to*; the thought

253

frightened him. He heard the drums begin to beat. Sumaguru was back. He walked to the meeting place in the middle of the square. *Aye, I will have to listen to more speeches of how wonderful Sumaguru is*, he thought. It was fifteen moons since he told Sumaguru about Dankaran and Niani. He worried about what he was about to hear or see. He was still angry at Dankaran for making him come in the first place, but he didn't want to see his skin or head hanging from Sumaguru's horse. He saw dust rising from the trail that twisted its way to the village. Sumaguru led the procession of horses, men and goods as they rode into the square. Women, children and the elders were also filling the square. They sang and clapped. Sumaguru had a look of supreme confidence as he rode in a slow circle while looking over the heads of his people. Then Balla saw Sumaguru's captain ride into the square. Trailing behind him on a small mare was a young woman who looked familiar. In an instant Balla's heart sank as he realized that it was Nana, Sundjata's sister. He ran up to her. "Nana."

Nana was staring into the distance, not making eye contact with anyone. She heard someone calling her name, and she looked down. "Balla, you are alive!" She jumped off the horse, and they embraced.

"What happened? What happened in Niani?"

"Dankaran put up a fight, but in the end, he had to flee. Mother gave me to Sumaguru, so he wouldn't burn Niani down."[33]

"Why didn't she come instead?"

"He didn't want her." Nana pushed her head in Sumaguru's direction. She could see him watching her.

"She is a handful, your mother. How are you? Are you okay?"

She could see the concern on Balla's face. "Nobody raped me. Even he didn't touch me. But I know he will. I can tell the way he looks at me. He thinks I don't notice, but I do."

Balla looked at her. "What happened to Sundjata? Did you

ever hear about him?" Emotions flooded his chest. He had kept all these feelings locked away, not thinking of his lion butterfly. If he had not he would have been driven crazy. He took a deep breath.

"No, he disappeared. There were rumors of him in Djedba but..." She made a face.

Balla caught himself. "It's so good to see a friend. My, what a woman you have become."

She smiled. "Even the dwarf palm grows."

Chapter 17

When the Roots are Deep There is No Reason to Fear the Wind

"What if someone recognizes us?" Kolonkan said to her brothers. She rode a small brown mare between her brothers' much larger grey steeds.

"Who will recognize us? Ahh, we are grown now," Bory said to his sister.

Sundjata laughed. "You think you are grown?"

"I am more grown than her," Bory responded while pointing his head at Kolonkan.

Kolonkan sucked her teeth at Bory, giving him an evil look. She began repeating words under her breath.

"What are you mumbling?" Bory asked of Kolonkan.

"I warned you; I am putting a curse on you."[34]

"Enough, we are here." They rode to a place along the Niger that was becoming a popular trading site. Selling stalls were being built along with more and more permanent structures. It was a chaotic affair, no central part of a town or village. People were coming and many staying. It was noisy, as men tried to gain the attention of others to come see their goods. Some men were Muslim, and others were of different tribes who worshiped their own gods.

The little group dismounted and walked around each selling stall. They looked at the colorful cloth, gold, copper jewelry, slabs of brown salt, brightly beaded baskets, painted pottery and tasty fish. Bush meat and animal skins lay out in the late afternoon sun.

"We should get something to eat," Bory complained.

"You only think of your stomach," Kolonkan said. She was hungry, but she wouldn't let Bory know.

"Yes, we should eat. We will stay the night and return to Massiran. Tell her that she was right regarding what she heard about this place," said Sundjata. "Let's look for food already cooked." Sundjata eye's searched for a food seller. Massiran had given them plenty of gold, so gaining supplies would be easy.

Bory walked away from the group, sniffing the air. His nose was the best in their village. He followed the smells and found a far stall where women were pounding grain and thin wisps of smoke rose from cooking fires. He backtracked and found his brother and sister. "Over here."

Sundjata heard his brother and turned to see him. He raised his head in acknowledgment and looked at his sister. They walked towards the stall; stopping and starting to let groups of people go by. "We need to feed and water the horses after this," he said to Kolonkan.

They caught up to Bory, who was standing off to the side of the stall. Sundjata held out his hand. "Give me the reins; you two get the food, and I will wait here." He handed Bory the pouch of gold dust. He moved the horses further away from the cooking stalls, and his horse released a long stream of hot urine. He felt the glare from the stall workers. He looked away from the hot stares and noticed a tall, muscular, young man staring at him. Sundjata looked at his face, and it seemed so familiar. He was strong and proud; his hair twisted into tight knots. *The eyes... these eyes I have seen before, but long, long ago. No, could it be, the blacksmith's son?* He mouthed his name, "Fara."

The man mouthed back, "Sundjata."

Fara's face broke into a large smile, and he walked over to Sundjata, not believing his eyes. "The spirits have blessed me." He was quite taller than Sundjata, so he leaned down to embrace him.

Sundjata embraced Fara and felt his body warmth. He could not believe he had found a member of his people again, a friend from long ago when things were so much better. It flooded his whole being, and he felt things he hadn't felt for a long time.

Kolonkan turned to see her brother in the embrace of a stranger. "Ahh, Bory, look."

Bory turned to see his brother hugging and talking to a stranger. "Come."

Sundjata heard Bory and Kolonkan. "Look, look it is Fara from Niani."

Kolonkan was too young to remember Fara, but she had heard of him.

"Fara!" Bory stared at him as if he was not real. "Why are you here?"

"I ask the same of you? Everyone thought you were dead. You disappeared. I know your brother was after you. Many thought he got you--or maybe Sumaguru."

"What has happened to my brother, Dankaran?" Sundjata asked.

"He is gone. He and Sossuma had to run away. She is back in her village. Dankaran like you has disappeared." He raised his arm and flicked his hand into the air.

"Why?"

"He attacked Sumaguru's men. He tried to stop them from taking things. We fought, but Dankaran was no real leader. We were defeated. Niani is small now, and the people are sadder than ever."

Sundjata could not believe what he had heard. He felt happy and sad all at once. Sossuma and Dankaran deserved what had happened to them, but he was still his brother.

"You, Sundjata... You... You must come back. You must be our leader. You have the blood of the lion. Your brother was false, but you could unite the people. Unite us like your father did. I want Niani to return to greatness. My forges are cold. I want fires burning in them once again. I can make weapons for you. The people love your mother. Where is Sogolon?"[35]

Sundjata bowed his head. "She is gone. She is with the ancestors now."

"I am sorry to hear that, but I know the people would follow you. There have been so many seasons of desperation, fighting and confusion that the people are ready for you."

Sundjata had not thought about going back in a long while. He had given up that thought and was ready to live under Massiran and find a wife. He was flirting with several women and was ready to start a family. "I don't know. It sounds good, but it will be hard. Besides, who will follow me? Who will even remember me? I was just a boy when I left."

"But now you return a man," Bory interjected. "People will follow if you lead."

Kolonkan added, "Yes, yes, let's go home."

"Do you even remember home?" Sundjata asked. "You have grown up away from Niani."

"I remember many things. I feel Niani in my heart, like I feel mother." She put her hand on her heart and then on her forehead.

"Come back to the village where we have lived all these seasons. The sister of the King of Ghana rules it; she is fair and kind. She will welcome you, and her tongue you will understand," Sundjata said to Fara.

"How far is it?"

"A three-day ride, not far," Bory interjected.

"I do not have a horse. I took the river and walked," said Fara.

"No worries. You can take Bory's horse," Sundjata said.

Bory made a face, and Kolonkan smiled.

"Fara is too heavy for sister's horse. You will ride with her."

Bory continued to make a face. He looked at Fara, who was taller than Sundjata and thicker than him and his brother together. Then he saw Kolonkan smiling in triumph at him.

* * * * *

They sat by the riverbank, gazing at the newest trading village. Sumaguru turned to look for his captain, who was still not back with his nephew. He shook his head in frustration.

Balla saw Sumaguru's anger was growing. He looked for a way to refocus him. "This new trading area may have some wrestling contests and your boy could make a bigger name for himself."

"True, you have done well with him. He is not as dumb and lazy as he once was. You shall be rewarded."

Balla knew better than to ask to leave. He had him distracted, and he didn't want to lose what he had gained. "Thank you."

"How about a wife?"

"I would like that."

"Then you don't have to sneak off with that blacksmith's daughter, the one with the small teeth." Sumaguru said.

Balla smiled. He couldn't believe how close he was still being watched. "She is a very sweet girl."

"Yes, I give her to you."

Balla turned to Sumaguru's son. "Go find where they wrestle."

The large boy turned his horse and rode into the trading village.

Balla heard hooves and turned to see Fakoli being led by Sumaguru's captain. Fakoli's face was twisted in anger.

"Finally," Sumaguru said. "Nephew."

"Uncle, why do you need me?" Fakoli said with exasperation. "What is going on here? I was told it was urgent."

Sumaguru just stared at him.

Balla waited for Sumaguru to explode, but he remained calm. He shifted on his horse, and a long smile came over his face.

"You are going to collect tax from this new place," Sumaguru said without emotion.

"Why don't you get someone from a closer village to collect it?" Fakoli said in frustration. "No one will steal from you. They are all afraid. We have more than we need already."

Sumaguru said, "Nephew, see your cousin wrestle, and let's see what we have here." Sumaguru turned his horse and rode towards the village.

Balla turned to Fakoli, and their deep brown eyes met in confusion. They had both expected Sumaguru to scold Fakoli, but nothing came. They waited till he could not hear them.

"That man never ceases to amaze me," Fakoli said.

"He is your uncle."

"If you ever escape I won't run after you. I am done with this man."

*****

The first two days of the ride everyone was often quiet. Even Bory and Kolonkan riding together did not fight, but they did tell Fara about their adventures. How they ended up so far away. As they got closer to home the idea of going back to Niani began to sink in. It had always been a hope, but it had seemed a remote one. No one ever dwelled on it. It would have made life too sad; however, their lives had been good once they found a home in Massiran's village. On the third day, it began to feel real and it no longer taunted them like a piece of fruit just out of reach.

Sundjata thought more and more about his father and mother's legacy. "You say people still talk about my father and mother?"

"Yes, all the time. Everyone remembers the good days when he ruled, how Niani prospered: the crops, the gold, the salt. Most of all, there was peace." Fara looked at Sundjata and continued, "...and your mother healing people."

"Sumaguru has Balla still?"

"Yes, as far as I know. Now your sister will become one of his wives," said Fara, shaking his head.

"Hmmm," Sundjata said, feeling anger well up in him. He reached deep down into his feelings. He remembered the day Balla left him, the day he walked away from Niani with his mother and sister. Season after season he kept those feelings buried, but they were running through him now. His chest was feeling tight, and he held back tears. He swallowed hard.

"It won't be easy," Fara said. "But if anyone could help, it would be you."

"How do you know this?" asked Bory.

"It makes sense; look at his father and mother. He escaped his brother and lived all this time to be found. Why else? You said you also escaped many dangers on your way here." Fara thought for a moment. "When the roots are deep there is no reason to fear the wind."

Bory nodded his head. "It does seem right."

"My father, before his death, had always hoped you'd come back. He told me how your father thought you would do great things one day," Fara said, looking at Sundjata.

"My father often asked your father for council," said Sundjata.

"This may be the only chance we get," Bory said excitedly.

"Do you want to go home, Kolonkan?" asked Sundjata.

"Yes, I do. I like where we live now, but our people are back in Niani. I want to raise children there."

I miss the green, the trees and the tall grass," Sundjata said. "The hill that overlooks Niani. I want to see it again."

"Yes! The hills! All this flat land is not so pretty," Bory added.

"If we do this, we do it together. Is Fran Kamara back in Tabon?"

"Yes, his father died, and he is now king," Fara replied.

"Is Kama in Sibi?"

"Yes, they will make good allies. They are no friends of Sumaguru."

"That is where we can start."

Chapter 18

From Many One

"The entire ride back people seem so suspicious of us," Kolonkan noticed.

"That's the way it is now. Between Sumaguru, the Fulani and whoever can get enough men. Raiding has become common." Fara shook his head in sadness.

"Those gates look the same," Sundjata said to Bory as they rode side-by-side, approaching Tabon.

"True," Bory replied.

Sundjata, Bory, Kolonkan, Fara and Kwame Nkrumah rode up to the low wooden gates of Tabon. Three men from Massiran's guard followed. The morning sun climbed into the blue sky. Two guards with spears leaned against the gates. They stood up straight only when the small group got close.

Sundjata looked over the gates and saw people moving about. He looked at the guard. "Tell King Kamara that his friend Sundjata is here to see him."

"King Sundjata," said Bory.

Sundjata turned around to see his brother and sister smiling. "Not yet."

The guard was suspicious and made a face. "I thought Sundjata was a cripple?"

"I was, when I was a boy."

The guard still made a face and turned to his partner. "Go tell the king."

"I suppose you could call yourself king, since there is no king in Niani now," Fara said. "And you have a king's guard with these four men."

"You have an army with us," said Bory.

"I can see Sumaguru shaking from here," said Fara.

Kwame Nkrumah laughed. "I don't doubt your will, but we have a ways to go before we have an army."

"Who said he is Sundjata?" a voice spoke out. "Who says such a thing?'

Sundjata turned around and saw Fran standing with hands on hips. He jumped down from the horse and faced him. They stared into each other's eyes.

Fran looked at this man who claimed to be his childhood friend. The face was so familiar. "Who won the rock throwing contest across the river?"

Sundjata turned and pointed at Fara. "Him."

Fran looked at the large man on a horse with his hair in twisted knots. That was Fara. He looked the same, just larger. "I can't believe you're alive," He stretched out his arms and hugged Sundjata.

Sundjata hugged him back. It was as if they were standing on the banks of the Sankranti all those years ago.

Everyone dismounted and joined the two men hugging. Fran saw Bory, and he released Sundjata and hugged Bory. "Is that Kolonkan? Oh, my. My father said all of you stopped here many seasons ago, but he made you leave. I am sorry. All of you."

"Your father was doing what was best."

"Who are these men?" Fran looked at Kwame Nkrumah and his men.

"They are here to help. Queen Massiran, the sister of the king of Ghana has allowed the head of her guard and three of his best men to come with me."

Fran acknowledged the men with a nod and by raising his right hand. "Come inside; we will celebrate." Fran touched his hand to Kolonkan's face.

They walked through the gates to his palace out of the sun into the coolness of the mudbrick. The eldest of Fran's wives, a beautiful woman, approached the group as they entered.

"This, my dear, is Sundjata," Fran said to his wife.

"Wonderful, Fran speaks of you often, and of your mother and father." She turned to her servants. "Bring food."

The group sat in a circle on palm mats. They looked at each other, not believing how they had been brought back together.

"This is the work of the spirits," Fran said. "What brings you here? Have you been to Niani?"

"No, we are on our way there. You are the first to know that I have returned," Sundjata said.

"Returned?" Fran asked.

"Yes, I am here to stay. I want to take Niani back. I need you to help me defeat Sumaguru."

Fran was surprised by Sundjata's words. "I like what you say, but that may not be so easy to do."

"Are you afraid?" asked Bory.

"Bory!" Kolonkan said.

"Some things never change," laughed Fran.

"I am here to return Niani to the way it was when my father was king. For it to be welcoming, as it was when my mother was queen. For it to be full of life, as it was when Azeez and Ahmed would bring caravans. When there was peace."

"That will be welcomed. You will see how things have changed on your ride back. You will see how everyone squabbles. They don't trust each other anymore. To make matters worse, Sumaguru has allies on the other side of the Niger. He gives to a select few, to those mansas with large villages, who will fight for him. He even allows them to raid if they want." Fran shook his head in sadness.

"Will you help me? Will you fight with me?

"I will, of course. I know you, and I know what kind of person you were as a boy. I will follow you now, but we must convince the others."

"His father had the blood of the lion. His mother had the blood of the buffalo. That will be a powerful force to remind the people what good leadership is like," Fara said.

"I have trained him in the ways of war," said Kwame. "He has gone through this ceremony to become a man. I too have assisted in that."

"That's good, but we must convince the other mansas," Fran said with a look of concern. "I am afraid that many mansas have been used to doing what they want to. Since Sumaguru took over, Dankaran did not have many council meetings. Nor did he visit them often enough; he let them each deal with Sumaguru themselves. Someone from among the villages may want to assert themselves."

"Are they the same men, or are their sons now in charge?" Sundjata asked.

"There are some older ones still alive, but many have passed on. Now their sons have taken over. I don't know their will. However, I only see the ones closest to me."

"If I should call a large council meeting do you think the mansas will come?"

Fran thought for a moment. "Most likely, many will come out of curiosity to see if it is you, the others out of respect for your family."

"If you do that, word of your return will reach Sumaguru's ears. That will most certainly provoke a response from him for which we might not be ready for," Kwame said with concern.

"True, we need to see Kama in Sibi also. Having the two of you at my side will convince many." Sundjata smiled.

"I should go to Selefougou and see my mother. I can see what is happening there and get us more support," Bory smiled. He couldn't wait to see his mother again. He missed her so. He hoped she was still alive.

"You will be close to the Sosso and their allies. You must be careful," Kwame said.

"We don't know if the king there is an ally of Sumaguru. You can't just ride in there," Sundjata said.

"I will send one of my men with him and we shall find out," Kwame offered.

"Last I heard he wasn't with Sumaguru," Fran added. "But best to be cautious."

"I am not wanted or even cared about. Dankaran didn't care about me. How many others even know I have been with you all these seasons?"

"That is true, but we have the same father, and you know how people gossip and make up stories. I can't afford to lose my brother. Sumaguru already has our sister. "

Bory looked at him with a serious look.

"You should go, but you must be quiet about it--which I know is difficult for you."

Kolonkan wanted to laugh, but she held it back. "Sundjata is right: you must be quiet."

"We will sleep on this; decisions must not be rushed," said Fran.

The sun was low, and Fakoli was close to entering his village. He and his horse were tired. The thought of home and Keleya had pushed him, and now the push would be worth it. Fakoli was now on the trail that would drop down and lead into his home. He looked over the houses and saw cooking fires and smoke. He rode to the stables. He saw a young man walking away from the corral of wood and brush and called out to him. "You there, come help me."

The young man recognized that voice. "Fakoli, ahh, you have returned." He had a worried look on his face. "Let me help you with your horse."

Fakoli noticed that the man acted in a strange manner. "Are you well?"

"Yes… Yes, I am well," he said looking away. He took down several pieces of wood and led the horse into the corral. "I will water him now and feed him in the morning for you." He took the bridle off the stallion, and several other horses whinnied at their arrival.

"He is my favorite. Please take good care of him. Are you sure you are well?"

"Ahh, sir, I, ahh… Your uncle's captain was here."

Fakoli was surprised. "What did he want?"

"He wanted your wife, Keleya."

Fakoli confused. "What? Why?"

"He was acting under orders from your uncle. He took her."

Fakoli felt as if he was hit by lightning. His weariness was replaced with rage. "And you and everyone let him take her?"

"The captain was with many men and took us by surprise. The captain said you would know why."

"AHHHH," Fakoli screamed. Stunned and angry he ordered, "Go get the others; I want a meeting right now."

*****

Sundjata was running as hard as he could, but the beast was too fast. He stopped and nocked an arrow. He let it fly but missed.

"Take your time, son. Watch your breathing, keep both eyes open, and release the arrow."

"Yes, Father," he said.

Sundjata took off running again. Then the beast stumbled, and he skidded to a halt. He caught his breath, nocked his arrow and let it fly. The arrow's path was true and sailed high. Sundjata smiled and felt a gust of wind in his face. The bright sky began to grow dark grey, and the wind grew stronger. The arrow began to turn up, and the wind tossed it like a leaf. Now, all around him was dark. He saw his mother sitting on the ground before him, mixing together leaves, grain and blood in a calabash. Then she took a mouth full of water and spit out into the air. The grey skies turned back to light when he heard Balla's voice behind him. He turned around, and he was in a stand of trees with his old griot.

"You will be great," said Balla.

Then he felt a pain in his back. He turned around expecting to see his mother, but it was Ahmed poking him with his sword.

"Remember that pain," Ahmed said with a smile

Sundjata opened his eyes, his heart racing. Even though he had been standing straight for many seasons, he often had stabbing pains in his back. It was wonderful to see everyone again. What a wonderful dream. He thanked the spirits of the land; this dream was a sign for sure. Balla... to see Balla again... he took a deep breath. The thought of Balla ran through him like an underground stream. It was deep down. The dream had poked a hole in him, and now the feelings flooded out into his heart. He knew that his dreams were telling him something important, and he would watch for more signs. He noticed Bory was already up and out. He was an early riser. Sundjata washed up and went to meet everyone in the palace.

Everyone was sitting where they were yesterday and eating breakfast.

"Did you sleep well?" Fran asked Sundjata

"Yes, yes, I did, and I dreamed of my mother, father, Balla and even Ahmed."

"That's a good sign," said Fara. "I dreamed of my father."

"I was thinking that having a large council meeting would be a good idea. The fear of Sumaguru coming here may make them fight with you even if they are not too eager to do so." Kwame said while having a piece of fruit.

"That is true; I agree. We can't beg them; they must want to fight with me. Fear of Sumaguru is better than fear of me."

"Fear is a good weapon, in the right hands," Kwame agreed.

"We will leave for Sibi as soon as we finish breakfast," Fran said.

"I want to go to Niani after we talk to Kama. Could you put the word out to the mansas around here to meet us there?" Sundjata asked.

"I will send men out, and I will have a force meet us in Niani. Just in case, I will have a few men with us today. If we run into trouble I want to be able to handle it. It isn't as safe traveling as it once was, but once we are in Niani we will be fine," said Fran as he stood up and stretched.

"Then why the larger force to Niani?" asked Bory.

"Well, Sumaguru may hear about this as well. We do not know where he is. What makes him so dangerous is that he is unpredictable. He raids even when it isn't harvest season." Fran called to some of his men to prepare his things for their trip.

"Maybe you should stay here," Sundjata looked at Kolonkan.

"No! I am going home. I traveled with you before when it was dangerous, and I was younger."

Sundjata smiled. "Yes, true."

*****

"He must keep his power object up there. If we can find out what it is, we can take it from him. We may weaken him," Balla said to Nana as they walked through the village towards the courtyard, not looking up at Sumaguru's tower.

"So, we are being watched?"

"Yes, all the time. You don't always know who, but he knows."

"Has he approached you about being his wife yet?"

"He asked, and he said if I didn't say yes he'd visit my mother." She grew angry and sad and hugged Balla.

Balla held her tight, not knowing what to say.

Nana's crying went to a sob, and she looked up at him. "If I were to marry him I could get into that tower. I could find things out about his magic, ways to defeat him." She wiped her eyes. "You have been here for many seasons. I fear I will be also, but maybe I can do something to cut this stay short."

"That is very brave of you."

They were closer to the tower. He looked into the courtyard and heard a rider coming in at full speed. The rider was shouting, and drums began to sound.

"What's going on?" Nana asked.

"I don't know," said Balla, becoming concerned. They walked

into the courtyard, and the drums kept beating. Men were coming with bows, spears and swords. Behind the low walls of the houses men stood with their weapons. They filled the courtyard. "It looks like we are being attacked."

Balla took Nana by the hand and they went up to one of the men. "What is happening? Who is attacking us?"

"Fakoli comes with his cavalry."

"Good, he will help us."

"No, he comes to attack us."

"Attack us! Why?"

"He stole from us. He took gold that didn't belong to him. So Sumaguru took his wife."

Balla made a face, knowing Fakoli well. He walked towards the tower, with Nana still holding his hand. He couldn't believe he didn't hear about this.

"Do you think he did it?" Nana asked.

"I know this man. No, he would not."

They stood by the tower watching the main street that Fakoli had to come down.

"Why don't they close the gates?" Nana asked.

"Look around. This village is in a valley. All the trees, houses and walls will give his horses a hard time maneuvering. The bowmen and spearmen have the advantage. As long as they hold the top of the ridges they have the advantage."

"Fakoli is Sumaguru's nephew. Do you think this family will fight each other?"

"I don't know? Fakoli's cavalry is excellent. Swift and hard hitting, great horsemen, but they are outnumbered. Fakoli's village is isolated; he hasn't worked on getting followers. He doesn't care about that."

It didn't take long for Fakoli to enter the village through the gates. Fakoli was at the front of a column of twenty men riding side-by-side. They rode hard into the courtyard, and as they stopped they raised a large cloud of dust.

"Uncle! Uncle, face me!" Fakoli yelled. He stopped in front of the tower with his horse moving from side to side. Fakoli looked around and noticed the men around him with bows and spears. He didn't care. His anger was boiling. If these people weren't of his tribe he would have attacked. Fakoli noticed Balla and a young woman standing by the tower.

Sumaguru came out of the tower—shirtless but with the human skin he took from the boy in Niani all those seasons ago tied around his neck. He wore it like a cape. He had a dismissive look on his face. Following close behind him were his two guards, each with a hyena held by a large chain.

Fakoli's horse became frightened of the hyenas and bucked, so he backed moved him away. "Easy boy," he said as he rubbed the stallion's neck.

"What brings you here, nephew?" said Sumaguru.

"Give me Keleya now, or there will be war," Fakoli growled.

Sumaguru looked around. "She is not here."

"Why do you do these things, Uncle?"

"You wouldn't fight your own people, would you?"

"When I am wronged I will."

"I have told you before. When you are called, you come. Ears that do not listen to advice accompany the head when it is chopped off. Besides my captain says you took some things that did not belong to you. Some gold, some salt. Is this not so?"

"You always get your share, and I come when you need me

274

most, Uncle. You do not trust me?"

"How can I trust you when you don't do as you are told?"

"Where is Keleya?"

"She is not here, and if you keep this up I will make her my next wife."

Balla saw the look on Fakoli's face, and knew he was going to charge Sumaguru. He ran towards him, hands up. "No, don't do this."

Fakoli spurred his horse forward, saw Balla at the last moment, and pulled hard on the reins to stop.

Balla hit the horse and bounced off it, falling to the ground in a heap.

The hyena to the right of Sumaguru saw Balla fall and got excited at the prospect of an easy meal. It jumped hard towards him. The guard holding him wasn't ready, and the chain slipped from his hand.

Balla looked up and saw the hyena coming straight towards him, mouth open and eyes fixed on him. He curled up in a ball waiting for the powerful jaws to bury into his flesh.

Nana saw the vicious beast lunge at Balla, and she let out a piercing scream.

Balla heard Nana screaming, then a loud yelp but only felt the animal bump him. He looked up and saw the hyena rolling in the dirt snapping at his body. Then another arrow struck the great beast. It yelped again, but it rolled over and was able to stand. Balla started to crawl away like a crab when he saw Sumaguru's son, his pupil, push a spear through the chest of the hyena. It growled and chewed at the wooden handle of the spear. But Sumaguru's son was strong and pinned the animal to the ground. "Shoot it," he said. Some of the men fired several arrows into it, and its head lowered to the ground.

"See what you have done!" Sumaguru yelled at Fakoli. "I loved that animal. Now you owe me a hyena!"

Balla was on his feet and at Fakoli's side, "He will kill her; you know it to be true. Leave now before it's too late."

Fakoli looked at Balla with rage. He turned his horse and rode out, and his column of men followed.

"That was wise," Sumaguru said to Balla.

Nana ran up to Balla. "Are you alright?"

"Better than him," Balla said, looking at Fakoli as he rode away. Then he felt a large hand on his shoulder, and he turned to see Sumaguru's son smiling at him. Wiping dirt and sweat from his face and with a look of relief, Balla said, "Thank you."

*****

"There are less people for sure, and fewer fields," Kama said, riding on the left of Sundjata with Fran on the right.

"It is sad," Fran agreed.

Sundjata remembered his childhood. Once there were farmer's fields, now everything was overgrown. The main trail into Niani that was once full of life, now was empty. "I remember those days; this is terrible."

"Then you will feel worse when you see the palace," said Fran.

The group rode on, larger now with Kama and the several men he had brought. Kama, like Fran, trusted their friend and was eager to help. Sundjata was leading the group and picked up the pace, wanting to see the palace. He recognized a few houses and longed to see the place of his childhood--the house he shared with his mother, sister and Fanta. The thought of Fanta brought tears to his eyes, and he spurred his horse into a gallop. The overhanging brush obscured his long view, but the walls of the palace he could now see, and his heart raced. Galloping faster and faster, he was well ahead of the group. The trail widened, and he turned to the left and saw the huge silk cotton tree. He pulled hard on the reins and stopped close to it. He looked at the palace and for the gate that once protected it, but now it lay in the dirt. The palace rose above the walls, and he could see large pieces of the mud plaster that covered the bricks missing. There were no covers in the windows. He dismounted and walked the horse through the opening in the wall and looked to the right to see his old house. The beams of the roof raised into the sky with the grass all gone, like bones no longer covered by muscle and skin. The wooden door lay on the ground where his mother's small garden once grew. He walked over and looked into the window; the floor was littered with grass and leaves. He remembered how his mother and Fanta pulled on him to straighten his back. How they both held him and loved him. The spirits blessed him even though he had lost everything, but he could change all that now. This was a test for sure. Sumaguru would be his biggest test--the last test, the last hill he would have to climb. He heard his group gallop into the courtyard. Then he thought about what his mother said to him: 'The mansas are the key.'

Kolonkan saw her old house, jumped off her horse and ran inside. She spun around looking at the fireplace, the old walls, her feet moving the grass, leaves and palm fronds. "It seems smaller." She looked at her brother.

"I know--because now you are bigger."

Kolonkan came outside and hugged her brother. Tears welled in her eyes. "We are home."

"You know, I didn't know I could feel this way again. I thought we would be away forever, but now that we are here I don't ever want to leave."

"Yes brother, it feels like a dream. Promise me we will stay."

He hugged her. "If the spirits will it, if the mansas can talk to them again, if they fight with us."

"I wish you were the only mansa," Kolonkan said, looking up at her brother.

"That would be interesting," said Sundjata while looking at the old house. "Let's sleep in the big house tonight. This one is a little breezy."

Kolonkan laughed and wiped her eyes as she ran towards the palace.

Sundjata motioned for Fran, Kama and Kwame to come to him. "Let's have a council meeting in six days. That should be enough for the people we need to arrive.

"And for people we don't," Kwame said.

"It also gives us time to prepare," Sundjata added.

The word of the return of Sundjata spread like fire through dry grass. People from the surrounding villages each day came to see if it were true. The young who heard stories about him and the old who remembered came to see his face. They filled the empty houses and old shops. Even though they could not all be in the council meeting they wanted to see if the son of Kon Fatta had returned. Could he be the new lion king? With the gate put back up Sundjata stayed within the grounds until it was time for the meeting. He spoke to a select few and thought about what he should do. He walked and held his power item, the claw of a lion Bory had given him. He wished his father's bow had not become so fragile. He wondered if Bory was safe. By the afternoon of the sixth day the sun was low, and the people gathered.

"The council area is too small. The meeting is now in the market place," Kwame said to Sundjata as they stood outside his old small house. He slept in the palace but felt drawn to the small round roofless house.

"Good. I want everyone there. Let the people be close enough to hear," Sundjata replied. "I didn't expect this kind of response, but if you could have seen this place when I was young. It was full of life. The whole area if you walked for days was full of life."

"I don't think we could stop them if we tried; there are so many. Your father and mother made a difference I can see. I hear much about them. There are many stories, and now the people are waiting for you."

"Where are Fran and Kama?"

"They are there."

Sundjata and Kwame walked out the gate past the houses and to the market place. All the mansas and chiefs, young and old, were sitting in a large group talking, until they saw him and became quiet. They stared at him as he walked towards Fran, Kama and Fara.

"Better turn out than we expected," Fran said.

Fara laughed. "I told you people would be happy to see you come back."

Sundjata looked at the group, and they looked at him with great curiosity. Then he looked up and saw the rest of the people all standing far back out of respect yet close enough to be able to hear. He stepped forward. "Good Mande people, I know things are hard. It was Sumaguru's dark magic that brought us down, that changed things, and now that is changing. He is losing his power. The spirits have now ended their slumber. They have allowed me to find Fara and open the door for me to return. I remember when my father ruled Niani. It was a place where people could live in peace. All the villages surrounding us had good crops and plenty of children. The forges were hot, and the Fulani lived in peace with us."

One of the younger mansas looked at Sundjata and stood up. "How do we know you are him? How do we know Fara isn't just wishing?"

"It is he, the blood of the lion and the buffalo run through him. I grew up with him, and this is he," Fran said. "You were too young to know him. You are mansa now because your father and grandfather have died. Now you should listen."

Kama stepped forward, "This is him from boy to man. He survived all this time with people after him. He has grown up; he has learned to be a man."

An older mansa, bent from years stood up, "You look like the boy I knew, and I knew your father and your mother. How do we know you are ready?"

Kwame stepped forward, "I am Kwame Nkrumah head of Queen Massiran of Ghana's guard. Sundjata has been taught the ways of being a man, and he has been taught how to fight. He is ready to lead. He has lived with me for many seasons, and I know that what is in his heart is good. He is strong."

"The kingdom of Ghana is gone. How do we know what you say is true?" asked the young mansa.

"I can show you if you like," said Kwame as he stepped forward with anger.

"I was there, where he, Bory and Kolonkan lived. I met Queen Massiran, and I can assure you he tells the truth," Fara said.

Sundjata stepped forward. "I am the true son of Kon Fatta and Sogolon. You know that deceit and lying does not live inside me. I see that since I have left people fight and squabble like jackals and dogs over a carcass. This is why Sumaguru is able to defeat us. We fight among ourselves. We lose sight of what is important. Remember, a fight between grasshoppers is a joy to the crow."

The council member from Sossuma's village stood. It was the large man who gave Kon Fatta problems all those seasons ago. He stood. "Why should we listen to you? You and your mother made things hard for Dankaran and Sossuma. You poisoned Dankaran's reign and tried to bring him down."

Mansas and chiefs began to laugh and grumble. The old mansa was still standing. "That is the funniest thing I've ever heard. We all know the only person that caused trouble was Sossuma. Sogolon did nothing but help people, and everyone here knows it." The group of mansas agreed and shook their heads. "I know that this young man would be good for the villages, good for Niani. No longer do I want my children to be hungry."

"I say we band together, all the villages again, and fight. We can defeat Sumaguru, but only if we do it as one. My brother Bory is finding out if Selefougou and the other villages by the Niger are with us. I know we can unite everyone on this side of the river at least."

"Who will lead us?" said a voice that rose from the group.

"I will, and I will have your captains and warriors with me," Sundjata said with confidence. "I have our captain here." Sundjata turned around. The captain of Niani's guard stepped forward, holding a leather vest with metal rings sown into it.

"I will follow this man. He has my sword and the men of Niani. I have spoken with him many days now, and he knows what to do. This is his father's vest that he will wear into battle."

Sundjata took the vest. "Speak to your diviners, your jins, your healers, but don't take too long. Sumaguru will hear of this, and he won't hesitate. If you want to fight Sumaguru's magic, there is something you must do. Do it and you strengthen our magic and please the spirits."

Fran, Kama, Kwame and the captain looked at each other. Sundjata did not share with them this part of the plan.

Sundjata's voice became heavy. "The spirits have not been pleased since my father died. I had to flee with my mother, brother and sister. To please them again, you must all give me your title of mansa. I will be the earth-surface master."

"Who are you to say such a thing?" said the man from Sossuma's village.

"I am the lion king; that is who I am. If you want to please the spirits of the land and restore our glory, this you must do. Everything else will remain as it is."

"The council and the chiefs?" asked the old mansa.

"Yes, everything will be the same. The district, compound and ritual chiefs all will remain. You have nothing to lose and everything to gain. If I am wrong and I can't defeat Sumaguru I will certainly die."

"And if you lose?" asked the young mansa. "What will happen to us?"

"We won't lose. Sticks in a bundle are unbreakable. I have already awakened the spirits of the land."

"That is easy for you to say," said the man for Sossuma's village.

"It's easy to complain, make excuses, and give into fear. You have the biggest village here. Why do you complain so?" said the old mansa to Sossuma's village councilman.

"I have the most to lose."

"And the most to gain," said the old man. "Your village has always been resentful that they do not have the council's trust. If the people of your village wouldn't act so full of themselves, they could send a king. You know this to be true."

"You insolent old man, how dare you--"

"Enough," shouted Sundjata. "This is why Sumaguru wins. In the end we always lose when we don't work together. You can continue to pay tribute to the Sosso and let them do as they please, or we can regain what we had under my father. Think about this and give me your answer in the morning." He turned and walked back towards the palace. Fran, Kama, Kwame and the captain followed him.

"Do you think the mansas will give up their title?" Fran asked.

"What made you think of this?" asked Kwame.

"I didn't, Kolonkan did. She made me realize that I had not

been listening all along. I was ignoring what was in front of me. I was ignoring the signs."

*****

Balla rode into Fakoli's village alone. It was early morning. The air was heavy and the sun above the horizon. It had been seven days since Fakoli had confronted his uncle. He rode into the square and dismounted. He walked his horse to Fakoli's house, which consisted of three round houses and a grain storage bin. The bin rested on a platform high above the ground. It was all surrounded by a knee-high wall. Balla tied his horse to a piece of wood protruding from the wall. He was taking the saddle off when Fakoli came out of the largest of the three houses.

"I am surprised to see you here," Fakoli said, stretching.

"Your uncle sent me to tell you there is a way back into his good graces, but I have more interesting things to tell you."

"Why did he send you?"

"He knows if he had sent one of his men you might kill him."

"And I won't kill you?"

"I'm still standing."

Fakoli smiled, "Well, when I kill him you can go home. I am going to find where he has Keleya first, and then I will kill him. I have men looking for her now."

"You may not have to kill your uncle yourself, and I may get to go home after all."

"What do you mean?"

"I mean when I lived in Niani I was griot to the son of Kon Fatta, the boy Sundjata."

"I remember him. He was a cripple and his mother a hunchback."

283

"He was a cripple when he was young, but he learned to walk even when you were there. We kept it a secret. Later, I heard he had to flee Niani. Everyone including myself thought he was dead, but he is back in Niani."

"Is he raising an army? Is it really him?"

"I hope so. People say his childhood friends are with him. I've only heard he is back. But what would you do?"

"Does uncle know about this? Could you be in danger? He could use you and Nana as hostages."

"He does know and acts as if he doesn't care, but I know he does. Nana is going to marry him. We have a plan; we will eventually have to run. Can I count on your help?"

"Of course, I will send a man to Niani and find out if it is him and what he is doing. If he is building an army we will join him. Think of what we can do. I know how my uncle fights, and my cavalry is better than his."

"The man you send to Niani. Have him ask the man who calls himself Sundjata what kind of branch helped him stand straight." Balla smiled.

"What kind of branch was it?"

"If the man answers custard apple, then it is he."

*****

Nana was close to the edge of the bed, and she looked down at the floor. She let out a few moans of false but believable pleasure. His pace quickened, and she felt his last push and heard his groan of pleasure. Then she felt him leave her, and he fell to the bed. She put a smile on her face and lay next to him, looking up at the grass ceiling in her house.

"When you have a child, he will claim Niani and lead it."

"Yes, we will have many children, and they will grow strong and

284

rule the land."

"I have many children already. I already rule the land. Don't you worry about your brother who has returned?"

Nana rolled over onto her elbow. "I never liked him, and he tried to kill my brother Dankaran. I'd rather have my children rule the land of my birth. Aren't you worried about him?"

Sumaguru began to laugh. "That would be like a buffalo worrying about a fly. I will swat him like the annoying bug that he is."

"What about Fakoli? You are gaining enemies."

"One will always have enemies. I doubt he can unite all the villages against me. Besides, I will be marching against him soon. I will crush a few villages, and the rest will stay afraid. I will catch this Sundjata and dispense with him. Besides, my nephew is too scared to move against me. He is like a whipped dog with his tail between his legs. He has become more woman than man. When he gives in I will marry Keleya."

"That you will," Nana said. She traced her finger around his chest.

"I remember when I met Sundjata. You were very young, and he was, well, bent. I even slapped his mother. I was glad I let them live. I will once again show how weak the line of Kon Fatta and Sogolon is. Why should I worry about him now? Nobody has been able to defeat me. This boy is just that: a boy."

"And your magic?"

"My magic is the strongest."

"Maybe one day I will show you why it is so strong."

"I must relieve myself." Sumaguru got up and went outside.

Nana watched him leave, and then she heard his stream. She rose and went over to his clothes and found a pouch. She could still hear his stream, and she opened the pouch to reveal a roosters claw. The stream stopped, so she closed the pouch, putting his clothing back. She stood up and walked towards him to meet him at the door.

"You are like your mother, only shorter."

Nana tilted her head and smiled, playing her game.

"You like power." Sumaguru walked over to his clothes." He put his shorts on and left.

Nana put the carved crocodile door back into place and leaned against it. She opened her legs wide and let his seed drip out. She reached down between her legs, pulled out a piece of cloth with honey and bitter fruit and threw it into the fire pit.

*****

Bory's heart leapt when he saw the hill overlooking Niani. He wanted to gallop forward but kept his pace, leading his mother and the group of men from her village. "Did you leave down this trail when you left Niani mother?"

"No, I left down the main trail."

Bory looked at his mother; she was still beautiful and youthful looking. "The place won't be the same without Sogolon and Fanta."

Nama looked at her son. She couldn't stop looking at him all the way from Selefougou. She never married again and had no other children. "To see you supporting your brother, I couldn't be more proud."

"Thank you. He is a great man."

Several men came out of the bush with spears and arrows, surrounding them on both sides. "Halt! Go no further," commanded one of the men.

"It is I, Bory. We come with help."

One of the men recognized him, "Ahh, good to see you."

"Good, Sundjata will know we are here," Bory said to his mother.

The column rode into the courtyard through the gate that had been put back up. Sundjata, Fran, Kama and Kwame met Bory, Nama and the new men.

"Welcome, brother. I am happy to see you again," Sundjata said, stepping forward to greet him. Then he noticed Nama. He was surprised and happy to see her. "Nama, mother, my heart is happy to see you. You look the same." He walked up to her, took her hand and kissed it. He helped her off her horse, and they hugged.

"My son, the spirits have blessed us. I never thought this day would happen. I am sorry about Sogolon. She will be missed."

Sundjata turned towards Bory. "What is the news from Selefougou?"

"You will be happy. They are with us. What is the news from here?"

"We, too, here are united. The mansas and chiefs have given their word. I have held council for several days and met with them all personally."

"You won't believe what they have done," said Kwame.

"What?"

"They have given over an important title. Sundjata is now the only mansa in all the land."

Bory stared at them in disbelief. "What? How?"

"He is like his father. He has the power to persuade," Fran said.

"From many we have become one," Sundjata said.

Chapter 19

Rain Does Not Fall on One Roof Alone

"I want you to lead a wave of cavalry and infantry towards Tabon," Sumaguru said to his son. "Threaten it but do not full out attack. I want you to draw Sundjata's forces there. When you get half a day's ride from it camp and make small attacks on the city till I get there." They stood outside the tower as the men mounted and waited for Sumaguru's son. "Before it rains you better go."

From a stand of trees Balla watched Sumaguru and his son at the base of the tower.

"You're sure he can't see us?" asked Nana.

"Yes. Now if Sumaguru takes me with him when he moves on Sundjata you must get away to Fakoli's and tell him about the cock's spur. There is a small stream you can use at night to get under the wall. Get back to Niani. I'm sure one of Fakoli's men will take you."

"Just over the hill facing the front gate and follow the road?" She had not been to Fakoli's village and didn't want to get lost.

"Yes. Let's hope he remains dismissive of Sundjata. You stay here till I get to the tower."

Balla circled around several houses so as not to be seen and reached the tower as Sumaguru's son was mounting his horse. "Don't get killed," he said to the son.

He turned to see Balla. "I won't. I'll do the opposite of what you taught me." With a smile he moved his horse forward.

"You will stay here while this little problem with Sundjata continues. Don't go to Fakoli's again, either. I will deal with him when I return. He's been sulking around since I taught him his lesson. I am bringing Keleya here today, and you and Nana will watch her while I am gone," said Sumaguru as he began to walk away.

"When are you leaving?"

Sumaguru looked at him. "Go to your wife." Thunder rumbled in the distance.

Balla shook his head and turned. He tried to keep his face looking disappointed until his back was to Sumaguru. This was perfect. He could escape with Keleya and Nana and allow Fakoli to join Sundjata. The problem was getting out alive.

*****

"Harvest time isn't for a while. Everyone is having the same problem. Nobody has enough food. Last harvest was poor. Even Sumaguru will be hungry," Fran said.

"His land isn't as good as ours," Kama added. "He didn't get much when he raided this past season."

"Well, the people have been generous so far." Sundjata said, looking back at the long line of men and horses and then into the sky. "You know it will rain as soon as the sun is at its hghest, so we need to move as fast."

"The scouts are coming back," said Fran.

It was early morning, and the sun was bright when it broke through the high puffy clouds. The sun was in Sundjata's eyes as he watched the scouts return. He put his right hand up, and he noticed Kwame leading the group. Kwame had taken a party across the Niger. They seemed to be in a hurry. The closer the group got, he could make out a familiar figure behind Kwame.

"Is that who I think it is?" Bory said, shaking his head, his sharp eyes knowing that skinny frame.

Sundjata, Fran, Kama and Bory rode out to meet them.

"Good to see you alive, my old friend," Sundjata said to Salt with a smile. His clothes hung on him as usual, but they were much nicer than in the past.

"Same to you both, I see you are following in your father's footsteps."

"Are Azeez and Ahmed still alive?" Bory asked.

"That is why I am here."

"We can always use their help. Are they close?" asked Sundjata.

"They are coming. When they heard the good news, they sent me. They are bringing supplies and men. I met Kwame this morning on the way to you."

"That is perfect. We will need food if we are going to fight."

"I have news," Kwame said. "Sumaguru is attacking Tabon."

"Those low gates are a problem," Bory said.

"Those gates will hold. They are low, so you can shoot arrows and throw spears over them," Fran said with anger.

"But then the attackers can throw them back," Bory said.

"Enough. Fran, many of your men are here. Will there be enough to defend the city?" Sundjata asked.

"There should be, but we should hurry all the same," Fran said anxiously.

"You go to Tabon. I will bring Azeez and Ahmed there," Salt said. "They will be happy to see you, as I am. We all hoped for this day," he said as he turned his horse and turned in the saddle. "But I knew it would come." He turned back and left.

"We should send some the cavalry ahead; the infantry will follow as soon as they can," Kwame suggested.

Sundjata nodded his head in agreement. "Bory, you bring the infantry. We shall move ahead and meet Sumaguru."

Bory made a face but saw the way his brother looked at him. "Yes, I will bring them."

"You will get your chance," Kwame said to Bory. "This won't be over in one fight."

"I was hoping it would be," Sundjata said with a laugh.

"Do you think this will be a long fight?" Fran asked Kwame.

"Yes, I do. I believe he is a crafty man, and his magic while weaker, is still strong."

"Kwame, take the lead please," Sundjata said. "I will join you."

Kwame nodded and moved forward.

Sundjata moved next to Bory. "You have half of the cavalry. Keep them out to protect your sides and your rear. Be careful; keep the men alert. Even though Sumaguru is in Tabon, he has friends."

"I know. Be careful," said Bory.

"Brother, we have come far together, and I will need you the rest of the way."

*****

In the early morning a guard from the tower stood at the door of Balla's house. "Hey, you," he called inside. "Keleya is in the house with wife Nana. She is your responsibility while Sumaguru is gone."

"When did he leave?"

"Last night. So, keep her here and out of Fakoli's house." He turned and walked back to the tower.

"I will be right back," Balla said to his wife. He hurried to Nana's house in the early morning sun, almost slipping and falling in the mud from the latest storm. It was a hot morning, and he was sweating when he arrived. The wooden door was not in the entrance, and he walked in. Keleya and Nama were sitting and talking, and he surprised them. They both jumped.

"Ahh, what's the matter with you?" Nana asked.

"Sorry, ladies, we are leaving tonight. Go to sleep early, and be ready when I come and get you. "

"She just got here," said Nana.

"And that is why we go now. Sumaguru will be a day's ride away, and we can be at Fakoli's by morning. We also know that he will be in Tabon. So, we can find Sundjata there as well and tell him about the cock's spur."

"That is his power item, his main sacrifice?" asked Keleya.

"Yes, we know now that it is," added Nana. "Are we still going to use the stream to get out?"

"Yes, the one that runs under the wall."

"I can't swim," Keleya said with panic.

"It is very shallow and running very fast. You won't have to. We've have had lots of good rain, and we will follow it and float down till we get away from the wall." Balla thought for a moment. "If it is dark and starts to rain for a while I will come and get you. It will be perfect cover."

"What about the man watching us?" Nana asked.

"I will take care of him. Then there is no turning back. Well, for you two it wouldn't be bad, but it would mean the end for me."

"Does your wife know?" Nana asked.

"No. Even though she is from another tribe, the less people know the better. I will see you later." Balla left for home.

"Do you think we can escape?" asked Keleya.

"I do. We have to. My brother has returned. He will defeat Sumaguru, and if my knowledge can help him I will try."

"You are one of Sumaguru's wives? What is that like?"

"Marriage is like a groundnut. You have to crack them to see what is inside. He has something about him for sure. He is attractive, but how he acts, ugh. He thinks his shit does not stink, so arrogant. Do you miss Fakoli?"

"Oh yes, what a wonderful husband. He is proud but humble, attentive but not in the house too much. He is…" She paused, thinking of how he looks at her and how he touches her.

"He sounds wonderful." Nana felt embarrassed.

"I'm sorry. I… I just… I am with child."

"That is wonderful. Now we have no choice but to get you home. Sumaguru rules harsh."

Keleya wiped her eyes. "He hasn't been rough with me, but he does scare me. I am used to Fakoli; he is stern but fair. This man does what he wants. Do you miss your home?"

"Very much, but things were bad. My mother ruined my brother Dankaran, and he wasn't strong enough to be a chief or king. I hope my brother Sundjata can change things. Are you hungry?"

"Yes, yes I am."

Nana got up to make something for Keleya. After the morning meal Nana took Keleya around the city. The highlight was the tall dark rough-hewn tower. They spent time going through the market looking at jewelry of gold and copper, bracelets of beads—and the many types of colorful cloth. Nana noticed Balla following them from afar, and she noticed a tall man following him. Everywhere they went the two men followed. She found herself walking toward the stream where they would make their escape. In a flash she changed course. They found themselves back at the tower and now Balla came to them.

"If I could get up there," Balla said.

"He has a large snake and an owl up there," Nana said with hope.

"An owl... He is an evil man. I would not want to be up there." As Keleya finished her sentence thunder rumbled and echoed and she jumped. "We must leave this place."

Nana looked up, a strong breeze began to blow the trees on the hillsides surrounding them. They rocked back and forth. Lightning flashed over the tree tops. "Let's get inside." They walked past the tower and past the round houses and low walls. People were rushing about seeking shelter from the storm. Arm-in-arm, at a fast pace, they walked and got inside as the rain began to fall. Nana put the door in its place. The sky turned grey, and a steady rain fell all day. Nana and Keleya lay down and drifted off to sleep. The sound of the rain on the grass roof and the rumble of thunder echoing through the sky relaxed them.

Balla knelt next to Nana and Keleya and rocked them gently. "Ladies, wake up, wake up,"

Nana woke up right away, lifting her head. "I'm ready," she said, sitting up and noticing it was now dark.

Keleya hadn't felt safe since her kidnapping. With Nana she felt secure and fell into a deep sleep. She was groggy and couldn't lift her head at first. "We go now?" She opened her eyes and couldn't see a thing.

"Yes, we must be quiet and move," said Balla in a hush.

"Is it still raining?" Keleya asked.

Nana had not put the wooden window in place, and she gazed out into the dark. Her eyes saw nothing at first, but she could hear the rain splashing into the puddles on the ground. The air was cool, and goose bumps rose on her arms and down her back.

She blinked and looked harder. Then she could make out shapes of the houses, walls and trees. She felt safe, as if they could just walk right out the front gate without being seen. She looked back and saw Keleya was up. "Come on. Let's go." She looked back outside, and saw something move. "Wait-did you take care of the guard?"

"Not yet, I was hoping to not have to."

"Well, someone is out there."

"Where?"

Nana pointed to the house across from them. "Over there."

Balla looked and saw a shadow move through the rain that had now become a mist. "Let's go out the back window. Stay low, crawl to the wall and with the house blocking us climb over the wall then follow me," Balla said.

Nana went out on her belly first, followed by Keleya then Balla. The mud stuck to them and made it hard to move, but fear and determination drove them. They kept low, and with the house covering them they scaled the wall then into a patch of trees.

"Come on. Stay low," Balla said.

Using the houses as cover they moved, slipping and sliding in the mud. Nana fell first, then Keleya, and Balla helped them up. He looked behind them and didn't see anything.

"Keep going. I will catch up," said Balla. He knelt in the mud, wiping the rain off his face. He looked to see Nana and Keleya moving away. He heard a splash. Turned around and pain shot through his head. With a groan he splashed into the mud. He got to his knees but was hit again, this time across the back, and fell hard. He felt panic but rolled towards his attacker and hit him in the legs. The attacker's knee went into his stomach, but then the attacker was thrown back. Balla rolled to his side and saw Nana on top of his adversary. He rose to his feet. Then Keleya jumped into the fight, kicking the man. Balla felt warm blood run down his face, and he felt dizzy. Taking a step forward he kicked a large stick. He picked it up and swung the stick as hard as he could. It hit the man in the head and knocked him out.

"That's the only guard in the tower, right?" Nana asked.

"Yes, all the rest are off to fight." He was dizzy but managed to keep his feet.

"Take her to the stream, and wait for me outside the wall," Nana said as she turned and ran towards the tower. She slipped and slid through the mud. She got to the tower and ran up its cold rough stone stairs. She breathed hard and paused when she got to the top. There was an oil lamp on the floor, giving a small flame. She lifted it into the air and saw the chain and empty collar of the beast Sumaguru's son killed. A long spear leaned against the rough-hewn stone. She picked up the spear and moved over to the wooden door with two snakes carved into it. She pushed on it and slipped inside. Something moved out of the corner of her eye, and she saw the owl and jumped. Fear ran through her, and she held her breath for a moment. She shook off the fear and moved toward the owl. She put the lamp on the floor and with the spear killed the owl. It screeched, and feathers floated to the floor. She wanted the snake. Searching the room with the lamp she saw a large basket under the table. Putting the lamp down once again she thrust the spear through the basket and did it again and again. The basket jumped and shook. She heard hissing and kept plunging the spear until she hit the floor again and again.
36

*****

It was near evening, and the rain had stopped. Droplets of water fell from leaves, and the smell of wet vegetation and rain hung in the air. Sundjata and Kama waited for Kwame and Fran to return from surveying the situation at Tabon. They had camped far enough away in a large stand of trees. Behind the trees was a series of hills that hid the horses. The two squatted down, using sticks and stones to make battle plans. They heard horses approaching.

Sundjata looked up. "Ahhh, they return."

Kwame and Fran rode through the trees as fast as they could.

"Do we need to attack?" Sundjata asked.

"They are under siege. They have infantry surrounding most of the walls and cavalry blockading the road and gate. Tabon is fighting back. Fortunately, it's getting dark, so it seems they are breaking off their attacks," Fran said.

"They are building fires and settling in for the night. They will attack in force in the morning. There were many scouts out so it's hard to get a closer look," Kwame added. "We are outnumbered until Bory gets here."

Sundjata thought for a moment. "They are lucky to find dry wood for fires."

"They bring their own my scouts tell me. They have a long train of pack animals," Fran said.

"We must help Tabon since they don't know we are here. We could surprise them when they send their main attack. They will be so busy trying to scale the walls and break the gates they will be vulnerable. Hopefully, it won't come to that and Bory will be closer with the infantry and the rest of the cavalry."

"Fran, it's your home?" Kama asked.

"I agree with Sundjata," Fran said.

"Let's make camp, but no large fires. Small ones if necessary, and wait till dark. I don't want them seeing any smoke on the horizon," Sundjata said with concern.

The men took the horses and tied them up for the night on long ropes. Finding dry wood behind the hills was proving difficult. For the first time in several nights it did not rain, but the ground was wet and slippery.

"I put some guards out," Kwame said, coming in out of the

darkness. "They are all tired, but we will be okay."

"It was a hard ride, but they seem ready," Sundjata said. "How long do you think till Bory arrives?"

"If they march fast, by tomorrow night or early the next day... If the rain holds, maybe a little sooner," Fran considered.

"Good. Well, Fara will help Bory keep them moving. Fara is very persuasive in his own right," Sundjata said, leaning on his saddle. He took off his father's vest and adjusted his palm mat to keep dry. "It's a good thing we brought these mats; they will help the men get some sleep. It was a good idea, Kwame." He lay his head down and closed his eyes. Soon his breathing became deep and slow; his head floated off to sleep.

"Wake up, Sundjata, wake up," Fran said, shaking him. "We are being attacked."

Spit hung from Sundjata's mouth and had pooled on his small saddle. He wiped his mouth and focused on Fran. "What?" The sun was just up; it was hard to see.

"Sumaguru is attacking us! Get to your horse." Fran picked up his saddle and ran.

Still kneeling, Sundjata heard men yelling, some screaming. He looked up to see Sumaguru's men moving through the trees, some firing arrows. An arrow zipped by his head, and then one hit his saddle. Kwame and Kama were using the trees as cover, firing arrows at the attackers. A man ran at him with a sword. Sundjata picked up his saddle and threw it at the man's feet. The man tried to jump over it, but it caught his foot. He fell to the ground hard. Sundjata grabbed his sword and chopped the man's neck.

"Go!" Kwame screamed at him.

Sundjata picked up his father's vest then his saddle with his left hand and ran. Arrows hit trees and flew past him. The ground was wet, and as he ran up the hill towards the horses his feet began to slip, and he fell to his knees. "This is like a bad dream," he said aloud. He jammed the butt of his sword into the ground and pulled hard. Another arrow hit his saddle then another into the ground next to him. He jammed the sword handle into the ground again and pumped his legs. An arrow sunk into his calf, and the pain made him lose his grip and slide down the hill. At the bottom he looked at his leg and tried to pull the arrow out, but it hurt too much. He let go of the saddle and saw a man with a spear running at him. The man thrust the spear at his chest. Sundjata swung his sword, hitting the blade and deflecting it, but not far enough. It caught his side. He grabbed the spear and swung his sword, chopping off one of the man's fingers. The man yelled, letting go of the spear, and stepped back. An arrow hit him in the chest, then another. The man dropped to a knee, and Sundjata finished him with a thrust to the throat. Sundjata's men rushed down the slippery slope and helped him to his feet. Many stood on top of the long arching hill, firing arrows, halting the attack. Kwame was by his side and helped him up the hill. The mud under their feet was slick, and they both used their swords to keep moving upwards. Finally, over the top of the hill they slid down to the horses. Another man brought his saddle and vest.

"We need to retreat," Fran said to him. "We are holding them for the moment."

"Lay me down, and push that arrow though if you can't pull it out," he said to Kwame. The men put him down.

Kwame knelt beside him and felt the arrow move. He held it tight while another man broke the arrow and made it short. Then Kwame pushed it through.

"Wait," Sundjata grimaced and the arrow was out. "Damn, that hurts."

Kwame took off his shirt and cut it with his knife. He tied it tight around Sundjata's leg. "That will do for now."

Sundjata looked at his side. The wound was a clean slice. "This isn't too bad; I can ride." Kwame tied the rest of his shirt around the wound then handed Sundjata the vest. He put on the vest, wincing from the pain of his wounds. The men saddled Sundjata's horse, and helped him mount.

"Why aren't they attacking more? Sundjata asked. "I'm sure they outnumber us."

Over the sounds of the fighting Kwame yelled to the men on top of the hill who were holding off the attack. "What do you see?"

The man who heard Kwame looked past the stand of trees to see men on horseback. He pointed towards the new attackers. He pointed, "Over there! Cavalry, they are coming; they are trying to outflank us."

Sundjata said, "They are trying to hold us here and come up from the rear."

"We need to get to the river and wait for Bory. We need more men," Kwame said. "Let's go!" he yelled to the men on the hill.

In groups of two they left to get their horses while the others kept the attackers at bay with their bows.

"You go. I will make sure our retreat is covered; I will catch up," Kama said.

"If we follow these hills we can outrun them, make it to the Bafing River and cross it. I know where there is a low crossing ahead," Fran said. "Once we lose them we can head back to the Niger."

Fran led the way with Sundjata and Kwame close behind. The men followed in groups of two and four.

Sundjata looked back and saw the men following. He realized he didn't feel any pain in his leg and side, but his heart was beating fast. Faster and faster they tried to go, but the ground was still slippery. The horses splashed mud as they went.

The hills on their right disappeared and the ground became flat. They could see Sumaguru's men racing towards them. It would be a race to the river.

"The crossing is shallow; we can ride through most of it, and the horses won't have too long a swim," Fran said to Sundjata and Kwame.

Sundjata turned back and couldn't see Kama. The wet ground had slowed everyone down, but soon they could see the river in the distance. As they drew closer to the river, the ground got better and they picked up some much needed speed.

Kwame yelled at Fran and Sundjata, "They are closing in on us!"

Fran looked back. "We will make it."

Sundjata looked at the men coming hard at them, and he could see Kama and the rest of their force. "Come on-faster."

*****

"The response is amazing. All these boats have saved us much time," Fara said to Bory while standing on the bank of the Niger.

"The news is spreading faster than we could have hoped," Bory said with a smile. "All these fisherman and traders coming here is fantastic."

"We have been lucky so far, but now that we are on the other side of the river I don't think we will find too many friends."

Bory nodded his head in agreement and saw his scouts return.

"Sundjata isn't at Tabon, but neither is Sumaguru. He stopped his attack," said the lead scout.

"Where did they go?"

"There are tracks leading everywhere, and a ways from Tabon we found some of our men dead."

Bory looked at Fara. "What do we do?"

Fara looked at the river rather than into the countryside. "We should find Sumaguru and hope Sundjata finds us."

"If he's alive," Bory said.

"He's alive. Sumaguru would have his body on display or his head at least."

"I hope you are right. Now we have to find Sumaguru."

"I'm sure he will find us before long." Thunder rumbled in the distance. Far off, storm clouds threw lighting and dropped rain. "I hope that storm stays over there. It's been nice that it hasn't rained in a while."

"Let's camp here for a day or two. We'll send out more scouts and see what happens." Bory looked around, worried.

Fara nodded in agreement, pleased that Bory was showing good judgement. "I will put out guards and have all the village commanders meet tonight. Then we will decide what to do next."

Bory wanted to get on his horse and ride to find his brother. He had to resist the urge and he rubbed his hands together in frustration. This couldn't be the end of him. *Am I ready to be king?* He shook his head and went to help organize things.

The rain did stay away, but thunder continued to rumble with lighting flashing all around them in the distance. Luckily, dry wood was found. Fires were burning and the men were eating. The air was heavy as darkness fell making everyone sleepy.

"I like the idea of giving each village the responsibility of guarding a certain area," Bory said to Fara as they stood by the bank of the river.

"Just having Sundjata back has given the people hope, and they will to work together," said Fran.

"He better be alive. I don't know if they will follow me." said Bory.

"They will if you act like a leader, like your brother does. You can be a little..."

"I know, I know. I am aware of my faults."

"But your energy and your blood line will inspire them."

"I hope Ahmed and Azeez come with supplies soon. We should have enough men. Our ranks have swelled just marching up here. We have enough spearmen now," Bory said, throwing a rock into the water.

"I was worried about that too. We have gathered many new shields and more arrows from the new villages joining us. Now I wish Sundjata had taken his bow," Fara said with worry.

"We need to sleep. Who knows what will happen tomorrow." Bory said to Fara.

*****

Sumaguru sat by a large fire alone while servants waited in the darkness for him to speak. He sat on palm mats and a leather skin. He chewed on some goat and sipped some palm wine. The information about Balla, Keleya and Nana's escape reached him as the sun went down. He would now have to kill both Balla and Fakoli. His son walked out of the darkness towards him with a smaller man his hands tied behind his back. The son pushed the man to the ground in front of the fire.

"What do you know, son? Who is this... wretch?"

"We chased a group of cavalry men to the Bafing River. We almost caught them. We killed many and we managed to catch this one. I sent a hundred men after them."

"Excellent. Was Sundjata with them? Is he dead?" Sumaguru sat up, excited.

"Speak," said Sumaguru's son. "You know who this is."

The man's head and lower lip bled. A bandage stained with

blood around his arm. He looked at Sumaguru with contempt.

Sumaguru's son kicked the man. "Tell him."

Sumaguru looked at the man. "Tell me what you know, and I will let you go. You will live. I am not afraid of you or Sundjata."

The man winced in pain, then looked at Sumaguru. "He was there."

"He is dead?" Sumaguru asked.

"I do not know. An arrow hit my horse. I fell and was not awake. I did not see him cross, but I did not see his body either," said the man as he bowed his head in shame.

"It is true about him and his horse," Sumaguru's son confirmed. "The trap almost worked; we almost had him."

Sumaguru laughed and clapped his hands. "He has tasted my power again. How many men does he have, and where is the rest of your army?"

The man looked up. "We have more men and horses than you. Where they are I don't know. I am here. And if I did know, of course I would not tell you."

Sumaguru's son took his sword and raised it above his head. "When I take your hand, you will tell us."

Sumaguru raised his hand. "No, leave him. I doubt you have as many men as I do, but you do know where they are." He sipped some wine and thought for a moment. "Free him. Let him go. I do not care. Get him out of my sight."

Sumaguru's son lifted the man up and cut the ropes, freeing his hands. The man was amazed, as he thought he would die for sure.

"Oh, you can even tell whoever you like: I am headed for Krina and then to Do."

"Father," Sumaguru's son said with alarm as he held his sword to the man's throat.

Sumaguru waved his hand. "Let him go."

Sumaguru's son called one of the servants. "Take this man and have several soldiers take him far out of camp." The servant took the man and left. "Father, you take too many risks. And why are we going to Krina and Do? Shouldn't we cross the Niger and crush them?"

"We will, but first we have to deal with your cousin Fakoli and your teacher Balla."

Sumaguru's son was taken aback. "Father, what?"

"Balla has escaped with Keleya and Nana, and of course he will go to Fakoli's. I must teach them a final lesson."

"Father, you know I love you, but don't ask me to kill either one of them. Please! We have fought together, and they both have taught me."

Sumaguru looked at his son's face and smiled. "You disappoint me."

His son knelt by the fire.

"I will do it, son. I will marry Keleya and get Nana back. The other two must die. I will not be disobeyed--ever."

His son stared into the fire. He felt awful; this could not be happening. He loved both men, and he hoped maybe after his father calmed down he could save Balla. After all, Balla was a slave. He could make Balla his.

"I know what you are thinking. You can't save them. Rain does not fall on one roof alone," Sumaguru said.

* * * * *

"It's been three days. We need to move. We need to find

Sumaguru," Bory said to Fara. They stood by the fast, flowing river in the afternoon. The sky was heavy and grey. The threatening rain made everyone feel worse about the situation. "What are the company commanders saying?"

"They, too, are becoming anxious. For now they look to us. They feel their men may lose their will to fight if Sundjata doesn't come back soon. They and I agree we should move and stay close to the river, keeping it near so we only have to worry about attack from one side." Fara looked at Bory shaking his head.

Bory looked at the river, thinking... *But which way? Up the river or down?* At that moment he felt trapped in its current. "There are several spots Sumaguru can try to cross. I would think he would try to cross and move to crush Niani." The thought of Sumaguru getting his hands on his sister and his mother frightened him.

"It will take him most of the day to get his men and horses across. The river is high and fast. He won't have the boats we had. Everyone has agreed not to help him." Fara looked up and down the river. "We could split our forces. Guard the two main crossings and catch him when he tries."

"I don't know about splitting up. Remember what Kwame said about that. If either one of us runs into his main force we could be wiped out," Bory said with concern. "Maybe we should have stayed on the other side and waited for him."

Chapter 20

The Battle for the Bright Country

The rain ended before dawn and the air was cool. Everyone was uncomfortable as the sun rose in the sky of patchwork clouds. Slight rays of light peaked in and out as the men were breaking camp. It was time to move and find Sumaguru and Sundjata.

"We are alternating companies of bowmen and spearmen as we march," said Fara.

"If the company commanders feel safe moving that way," Bory said. "I'm glad last night we all agreed on moving together. Splitting up would have been bad."

Bory and Fara stood silent looking at each other, knowing the task at hand would be difficult. They turned and went to do what must be done.

By late morning the men had lined up and began to march alongside the river. They had decided to attack the Sosso homeland directly.

Bory rode at the head of the long columns of men while Fara rode with the cavalry to protect the rear. Mounted scouts were sent out ahead while sentries to the sides and the rear kept them safe from a surprise attack. Now the clouds parted, the sky began to clear. A strong wind started to blow. Bory looked back at the men with their tall spears high in the air, the sound of shields and bows clacking together. Seeing the sun and getting on the move lifted his spirits as well as the men's, and he could hear them begin to sing. The bright rays on the red dirt and the rivers surface showed why it was called the bright country. *I know my brother will return; I know it; I will have faith,* he thought to himself. He rode while singing a song his mother taught them, but he had forgotten some of the words and laughed. He noticed where the sun was in the sky and wondered when they should stop. He wanted to march until he saw the walls of Sumaguru's home. Bory was lost in thought when he heard a cheer from the men. The cheering got louder and louder. Bory turned his mount around to see what was happening. As he rode past the men he noticed they were breaking ranks and were jumping up and down as several riders were coming towards him. Bory's keen eyes made out the shapes and his heart leapt. "No, it can't be." He kicked his horse hard and galloped as fast as he could. "Yes, Yes, Yes, Yes," he said.

As Sundjata rode past the men they cheered, jumped and clapped. Kwame, Fara and Kama were with him, as well as Azeez, Salt and Ahmed.

"Were you going to let me do all the work? I would have killed Sumaguru for you," Bory said, riding up to Sundjata.

"You think I would let you have all the fun?" Sundjata reached out and he grasped his brother's hand. "I brought some friends."

"I've never been so happy to see all your ugly faces," Bory laughed, "now what happened, damn it? You guys scared the shit out of me."

"We were attacked and chased," Sundjata said. "We were lucky to lose them and found Ahmed and Azeez on our way back to you."

"Did you lose many men?" Bory asked.

"Yes, twenty-five in all. It was bad. It was my mistake leaving the main body like that," Sundjata said.

"Do not look where you fell but where you slipped," Ahmed said. "It is alright now."

"Where were you going?" Azeez asked Bory.

"We were going to attack Sumaguru's home. We waited, hoping you'd show up, but we had to move."

"What happened to Tabon?" Fran asked.

"Sumaguru broke off his siege and withdrew," Bory explained.

As they spoke, a scout rode up to the group. He had a man sitting behind him. When the scout saw Sundjata he smiled. "We found one of our men."

Fran recognized him right away. "You... You were with us at the river. What happened to you?"

"Sumaguru captured me, and he let me go. He even told me where he was going."

All the men in the group looked at each other. "What did he tell you?"

"He said he isn't afraid of you or anybody and that he is headed for Krina then Do."

"This is crazy. All felt lost a moment ago, and now this," Bory exclaimed.

"That is war," Ahmed said, "organized chaos."

"Krina is only a two-day march from here. If we send out riders we can see if this is true," Kwame said.

"Isn't there a river crossing not far from there?" Kama asked.

"Yes, and it is a good place to fight--tall hills surrounding a large flat valley," Kwame added.

"What if it is another trap? What happened at Tabon felt like one. It was like he knew we were there," Kama said with concern. "His magic is still strong."

"We are all together now, so I say let him come," Sundjata said with confidence.

Bory noticed a bandage on Sundjata's leg. "Your leg, what happened?"

"An arrow, I am fine."

"The spirits are with us," Bory said.

"Men, I say we move towards Krina. Any objections?"

All the men nodded their heads in agreement.

"One more thing, it was stupid for all the leaders to go to the same place at once. We need to be more careful. That was my fault for letting it happen. I see where I slipped," Sundjata said nodding at Ahmed.

Ahmed smirked, "You exhibit traits of your father."

"Thank you. Now, let's get moving," Sundjata said. He reached and touched his power item on his belt. He and Bory rode to the front of the men.

"Those amulets Kolonkan made for us worked. She did learn something from mother," Bory said. He had a string of beads on his wrist blessed by her.

Sundjata raised his arm showing Bory he also had his. He thought about his sister and missed her.

"I thought you might be dead when you didn't return. Our scouts found dead men and everyone gone."

"It was close. I got cut in the side as well, but everything is healing. At the river crossing we lost many men, and they chased us for a day. Often I thought we were finished."

Bory looked skyward. "The men were beginning to lose faith without you. You are what holds us together."

"But they stayed these days under you and Fara. Good leadership is important. If nothing else, our father showed us that."

"When we win, what will we do?" asked Bory.

Sundjata smiled, thought, and then said, "We will return Niani to what it was when our father ruled it. With Azeez and Ahmed behind us we can bring back the trade."

"With a victory you will be the king. The council will want that for sure, but the elders may want their titles back."

"As long as we win, they can have their titles."

"What about the Sosso?"

"They will not bother anyone again. We will crush them." Sundjata's confidence was growing. He could feel everything coming together.

Sundjata and Bory led the men, but they sent their cavalry under Kwame and Fran ahead to block the pass to the river at Krina. On two hundred horses they doubled up with spearmen and bowmen to give the appearance of a larger force. Azeez accompanied them with a force of fifty Tuareg fighters. They dressed in blue with black or white turbans, some on camels, and some on horses. For two days, through hot sun and strong winds the ground rose. Marching became harder. When news of Sumaguru's men collecting at Krina came from their scouts they moved even faster. They were happy the rain did not return.

"Those must be our fires," Sundjata said to Bory. The sun was going down. The wind blew hard pushing long clouds through the darkening sky.

They soon came upon their sentries who let them pass with smiles, waves and cheers. They directed them to the main camp with Fran and Kwame. Ahmed, Salt and Kama followed. The camp sat on top of a large hill looking down into the valley. They tied their horses below and climbed the hill through brush and grass. They heard voices above them.

"This hill is steep," Ahmed complained.

"Why must you complain?" Salt added.

"Try it with an arrow wound in your leg," Sundjata said. His leg was sore but healing fast.

"When you get to be my age, come see me," Ahmed said to

Salt.

"You will be dead. I will live a long life," Salt laughed.

"True. I climbed a hill like this once with your father," Ahmed said to Sundjata.

"Yes?" Sundjata asked.

"The only difference is we killed most of the people at the top," Ahmed laughed.

Sundjata was first to the flat top of the tall hill. As he waited for the group, he looked to his sore leg. Ahmed was last up as Salt helped him. They looked towards a large fire in a stand of trees. People half in shadows and half in orange light were standing around it talking, but stopped when they realized someone was there.

Sundjata and the group walked to the stand of tall trees. The shadows faded and the orange dancing light bathed the scene. When Sundjata drew closer he stopped in his tracks; he couldn't believe his eyes. Was it a dream?

"My old lion butterfly, you are alive and well I see." Balla stood before him in the firelight.

Sundjata walked over to Balla and they embraced. Balla's arms held him tight and he squeezed back.

"I can't believe you are alive, my griot, my friend. It has been too many seasons. I know now the spirits and the ancestors have awoken." Sundjata looked at Balla, older but still strong, his smile and bright eyes the same. Sundjata wanted to cry but held back the tears. His chest swelled, and he swallowed hard. "How have you survived all these years?"

Balla saw the emotion on Sundjata's face. He too wanted to cry, but took several deep breaths. They looked into each other's eyes. "Sumaguru liked to show me off like a prize. He made me teach one of his sons, like I did for you."

Sundjata looked to see his sister.

Nana rushed forward and threw her arms around him. "Brother, it is good to see you. It has been too long."

He smiled, "It is I who am glad to see you. Your other sister is in Niani. Our family will be back together when this is over. This is a present from the ancestors."

She laughed, "It is I who bring you a present. We can break Sumaguru's magic."

"How is this possible? We have sacrifices ready, and the signs keep showing in our favor."

"Before we escaped I climbed into his tower and found his magic, and I know what he keeps for a power item."

"This is true. I had been in that tower often, and what Nana has brought is his," Balla said.

"His power item is the cock's foot with spur. I killed his owl and snake. They are in a sack and a leather bag hung in a tree below." Nana smiled.

"When he sees what you have of his he will be weak," said Fakoli who came up behind Sundjata.

Sundjata turned to see Fakoli and was confused, speechless. He looked at the others.

Balla, Nana and Fran laughed.

"My uncle stole my wife and often accused me of being disloyal. I will no longer serve him. My cavalry is yours. I left a sizable force behind to protect my village, but the rest is yours," Fakoli said. "I am sorry for what happened in the past."[37]

"I am glad you are with us," Sundjata said taking Fakoli's hand.

"This man is nothing like his uncle. He is fair and just," Balla said.

"Do we have enough men? Can you help us defeat him?" Sundjata said with concern.

"Yes, I know how he fights and how he thinks," Fakoli added. "I noticed below saddles on your horses. Does most of your cavalry have saddles?"

"Yes. Not all, but many," Sundjata replied. "Why?"

"My cavalry, his cavalry, doesn't have them. They do the usual, cut the backs of the horses and use the blood to stay stuck to their mounts. This leaves them easier to dislodge and weakens the mounts. I found this out when we fought against some Tuareg on horseback. Many of my men were defeated or dismounted. Saddles are a great advantage.

"This is great to hear. What will the terrain be like when we fight tomorrow?" Sundjata asked.

"We got to the pass just as he did, and we blocked the road. We've been able to scout the valley below as well as the roads and trails," Fran said. "We have the hills to the left and he has the hills on the right. We put up a line of men in the valley. We didn't want to engage until you got here with the rest of the men.

"I know the trails and roads here. This is good ground to fight on. My uncle is full of himself. He underestimates you, all of you. This will be to our advantage; if you can break out of the valley you stand a good chance," Fakoli said with confidence.

"Well, he has never lost, so he has good reason to be full of himself," Sundjata said with a smile.

"True, our victory is not guaranteed. He is great on the battlefield. His son, who he trained," Fakoli said pointing at Balla, "is a very capable warrior."

"If any one of you gets into a fight with his son be very careful. He is dangerous. He is very strong," Balla added. "He looks like his father, but even taller and broader."

"Once we put more troops out in the valley he will come and face us," said Fakoli.

"What about being outflanked? Can he use the hills?" Bory asked.

"The hills he holds are steep and wooded, hard to fight on. He may try to go around us on our right. There is a tight winding trail on the other side of the hills. We need to put more men there," Fakoli explained. "The rest of the grounds beyond that trail are jagged hills, tight and wooded. It's like that all the way to Krina, very hard to move through."

"I will take my men and the Tuareg to guard that pass. With them I have two hundred," Ahmed said.

"The trail there is narrow, so you can guard it with that many. Bowmen on the sides shooting down into the road will be a big deterrent," Fakoli said, looking at Ahmed.

"In the morning you will see the valley and where the rest of the men will go," Fran said.

Sundjata looked out across the valley. He saw the fires of his men and Sumaguru's men through the trees on the tops of the hills and in the grassy valley below. The bright moon hung in the sky making it easy to see. "We are lucky this moon is to our advantage. It would be hard to sneak attack us. Do we have a lot of sentries out?"

"Yes, we are guarding against a night attack. We have men and fast horses to alert us," Kwame said.

"We should sleep and be ready. Tomorrow will be a big day," Azeez said.

"Yes, you are right," Sundjata said.

Azeez and Ahmed made their way down the hill. "Did you ever think this would be possible, uncle?"

"It is written. Things like this don't just happen. It's a miracle,"

Ahmed said.

"If we win, that will be the second miracle," Azeez replied. "This young man seems like his father. We need to win if we are going to get things right here."

"Allah is with us, my boy. Seeing Sundjata is like seeing his father again."

Sundjata, Bory and Balla stood on the edge of the steep hill, looking out over the dim lit valley.

"I don't think we will lose tomorrow..." Sundjata paused. "...and I don't think I will ever flee again."

Bory looked at him and thought about what he said. "I remember when we left Niani and we pledged to never run again."

"I remember. I don't mind retreating to fight again. But if all is lost... I am not running."

"Lions don't run," said Bory.

"That's right. Lions don't run."

"I agree with you both; we should never be parted again. But I must confess I thought this day would never come. Seeing you both again is like a dream come true." Balla touched his right hand to his heart. "It's not that I gave up, but to survive I had to bury the memory of you. It lived inside me, asleep."

Sundjata smiled. "I know. I felt the same way. If I thought about everything that happened I would have been angry always. I could not do that. I hoped that the spirits would favor us again. All that you have taught me kept me alive. Ahmed, Salt and Kwame added to your teaching. But, if not for your beginning, I would have come to an end."

"I always knew this day would come," Bory said. "I was sure of it."

"It's true; he never shuts up," Sundjata laughed.

"Nothing has changed I see," Balla added.

Fakoli and Keleya were lying down together on a skin by a fire not far from a string of horses below the hill. Fakoli had his arms wrapped around her. Nana was lying down across from them on her own skin. She looked up at the stars and the bright heavy moon.

"If you meet your uncle on the battlefield will you kill him?"

"Yes, he took you. He insults me. There is no turning back from that."

"You must be careful tomorrow. You are fighting for more than just me."

"I know, of course. This is for everyone back in the villages."

"And someone new."

"New?" He paused and thought for a moment. "Are you with child? You're sure?"

Keleya turned her head to look at him. "Yes."

Nana listened to them and smiled and laughed at Fakoli's excitement. In the short while with Keleya she had grown to like her. She had a sweet and gentle nature. Fakoli was everything that she said he was. Nana tried to make sense of everything. Everyone was united again, but tomorrow could change everything back. She laughed, and even wanted to see her mother again. Even though Sossuma had caused so much trouble, she missed her.

Sumaguru's son stood on a hill overlooking the valley. He looked at the fires from Sundjata's camp. "I told you we should have moved faster. We would have crossed the river and been on our way to Niani."

Sumaguru reclined by the fire, rubbing his power item, the

cock's foot. He pierced his finger with the spur dropping his blood into the fire. "You worry too much. I would rather destroy them here now, instead of having to chase them all over. I figured if that fool we let go found them, we could fight them where the ground is good. We hold the large part of the valley. The hills close them in."

"True, their ground is small, and if we can keep them from breaking out we can crush them. I want to lead the first attack tomorrow."

Sumaguru looked at his son and thought for a moment. "Okay, you may lead the attack. I let them mass their army here. They have fallen for the trap, and we outnumber them according to our scouts. I want to destroy them now. Do not fail."

His son walked over to the fire and took the knife strapped on his right arm. He sliced the arm dropping his blood into the fire. "When this is over, father, I want Balla as my slave. Do not kill him."

"Balla is over there with your traitorous cousin. He may not survive past tomorrow. After that, you will be the ruler in Niani."

"Yes, but I take Balla with me if he survives. I understand about Fakoli. I will not kill either one of them. I tell you again. They have broken no law in my eyes. Balla should have tried to escape seasons ago, and you did take uncle's wife. Be angry with me if you want."

"How would you rule being so soft? You make me think twice about letting you lead the attack tomorrow. Stop being like a woman; you act like the hen not the cock. You must not hesitate. You must not waver. I thought you had learned. I don't know what I will do with you." Sumaguru looked into the fire and was quiet for a moment. "True, Balla was a slave, and to run I understand. But your cousin's loyalty must never waver."

"You have been hard, but you still have uprisings."

"How many, really? Dankaran was a joke and now this. A few

squabbles season to season. If I were soft, it would happen often. Mind my words, son. Now sleep, and prepare for a victory tomorrow."

Sleep was fitful for both sides, the coming day's action on everyone's mind. There was a feeling in the air of excitement and fear. The sky had been clear and the wind had died down. It was a comfortable night. Then the first rays of the sun cracked the hold of night, and the transition from evening to morning had everyone up.

Ahmed, Balla, Bory, Fran, Kama, Kwame, Salt and Sundjata looked down into the triangle-shaped valley, able to see details with the sun rising. Their hill, the tallest, was where the two lines of tall wooded hills converged. The hills to their right stretched out with their steep sides and then turned hard to the right. Those Sumaguru held. The hills they held on the left were a bit shorter and rounder. The valley floor was raised as hollows cut by small streams ran along the bases of both groups of hills. There was a patch work of trees on top of most of the hills, while the sides had been cut down for fire wood for Krina. Tall grass and shrubs covered the hillsides. The grass in the valley was grazed short by animals both wild and domestic.

"We need to break out of the small part of the valley we hold," Fran said. "We can be sure Sumaguru is keeping most of his forces out of sight."

"Balla, can you command the archers on our hills?

"Yes, it will be my honor. Have all the holes been cut through the branches so we can shoot to the other side?"

"Yes, they are ready," answered Fran. "You have a hard job. You must keep shooting towards the hills. You must protect our side, as he may send men into the trees to outflank us. But most important, you must put pressure on Sumaguru's lines that face us."

"I will get it done. Excuse me. I will prepare." He looked at Sundjata and Bory, "I will see you after."

"After," said Bory.

"After," repeated Sundjata. He and Balla touched each other's shoulders. Balla left the group.

"See the hollows running along the hills? I sent men in there while it was still dark," Fakoli said. We can use them to attempt to break out of our end. Of course, they will try the same thing from their side."

The group looked down. They saw men blocking the road below and some lying against the ground in the hollow.

"They can't be seen by Sumaguru as long as they stay down," Fakoli said.

"I will join my nephew on the trail," Ahmed said to the group.

"We shall see all of you after. May the spirits be with you, my friends," Ahmed said.

"And Allah with you," Sundjata responded.

"Our troops in the hollow will follow along with our line to protect them. Spearmen with strong shields should do the trick."

Sundjata looked across the valley and saw Sumaguru's infantry massing. "I'd thought he'd send his cavalry first, but we shall see."

Kwame turned to the group. "I will take the center, if you don't mind."

"I will take the right," Kama said.

"That leaves left; I'm good with that," Fran said.

Bory was about to say something, but Sundjata stopped him. "You and I will be behind them with the cavalry. If there is a break we stop it. I will fight better from horseback with my leg. As Fakoli said, use your saddle as an advantage. You have stirrups to hold your feet. They don't. Stay close to me." Sundjata looked at

Bory with a serious look.

"I will hold in reserve with my cavalry and men. I'll watch the hollows on either side. Remember, he may appear to overpower one side of a line but then throw his might to another when we overcommit. He's sneaky that way," Fakoli said.

Sundjata turned as the smell of death filled his nose. Nana was standing behind the group with Keleya. "Ahh, you have it, very good. I can smell the death through that bag. Good thing we show him this now."

"Yes, it smells pretty bad." She handed the bag to her brother. "Be safe, my brothers," Nana said, looking at them and smiling with tears in her eyes.

"There he is, on the closest hill," Fakoli said.

The valley road separated the steep hills as Sumaguru walked out of a stand of trees then stood in the open. He wore a leather vest and shorts to his thighs. On his left arm a large knife was strapped and another strapped to his right leg. He held a spear and a sword hung from a leather belt.

"Go now to your positions," Sundjata said. The group broke up. "Bory, I will meet you at the bottom of the hill. Have my mount ready."

"Sundjata," Sumaguru called in a loud voice. "I will give you a chance to surrender. Are my nephew and your griot with you?"

"Yes," Sundjata said in a loud clear voice as he stepped out of the trees.

"Give them to me and you may survive this day...maybe."

"They will meet you but as the men that they are. Not the slaves you wanted them to be."

Sumaguru laughed. "You are brave for such a young one. I have heard things about you, that you are even greater than your father."

"Thank you, but I could never be as great as my father."

"Then I will defeat you even easier. Give up now and your people's lives."

"That is where you are wrong. I have an advantage today that my father did not have."

"All your friends and allies will not save you."

"Your magic cannot defeat that of the lion." Sundjata put the leather bag on the ground and reached into it. The smell grabbed his throat. He felt like throwing up, but he held it down. The snake was wrapped in cloth. He pulled it out, uncovering it. He still held the cloth, not wanting to touch rotting flesh. He held it above his head. The large snake's head and tail dangling in the air. "This is from your tower. Your magic is weak. This flesh rots like your rule. It smells and makes everyone sick." Sundjata threw the snake off the side of the hill. He went back into the bag and picked out the owl by the talon. "This symbolizes your fall today. This bird is the messenger of war and death, and today death comes for you." He threw the bird to the ground and spit on it. "And your power item, your cock's foot." Sundjata laughed. "Lions don't fear the cock. My sister killed your beasts, and today I will kill you. No longer will you trouble this land or the Mande people."

Sumaguru could not believe his eyes. He felt fear, something he had not felt in a long while. Then the fear turned to anger. "You will pay for your insolence today. I will now kill your griot and all your allies. I will have my army take your sister and pleasure themselves with her. And you, I will save for last. I will even make you watch all of them die, so you can tell your feeble ancestors what happened here today. Your disgusting witch of a mother, I should have killed her that day." Sumaguru turned towards his troops, raised his spear and pumped it up and down. He then turned back towards Sundjata. "If you are a man I will meet you down there." [38]

Sundjata turned and ran across the hill, through the trees and down the steep hill. His leg hurt, but he did not care. At the bottom of the hill was Bory with his horse, sword, bow and a quiver full of arrows. The bow and quiver were tied to his saddle. Men were streaming past them in columns four men wide through the pass between the large hills. They spurred their horses alongside them and into the valley floor. Fakoli was with his men jammed up behind them.

"They must push them forward," Sundjata said to Bory.

Kwame was in the middle on his horse, Fran and Kama on each side. "Sumaguru is going to try and push us back, keep us from maneuvering. Keep on the attack," Kwame said.

Fran and Kwame rode to their positions.

"Men, forward!" Kwame yelled. He stood still as his spearmen three rows deep went around him. Sumaguru had committed his spearmen first, so they would be a wall of iron-headed spears against each other. The men held their wooden shields high with their spears tucked firmly under their arms.

Now the frontlines met as the sides of the hills kept Sundjata's forces bunched. Both sides attacked with spears stabbing into shields. This would be a battle of patience and strength with each man trying to find an opening, breaking the others' shield, piercing them, and opening a hole in which riders or swordsmen could break through.

In the hollows spearmen opened their wall of shields to let men rush forward. Men clashed, some swung clubs and fought others with short blades. The water at their feet began to turn red.

Sundjata watched the men move forward, line after line. He began to move his horse forward. He heard men screaming. Then the line on his left turned. Sumaguru's men in the hollow leapt out to break up the attack. They had broken through.

"Bory, look," Sundjata spurred his horse, and Bory and their men followed as men parted for them to move.

323

Sumaguru's swordsmen ran into the line of Sundjata's spearmen. Their long weapons did not allow them to turn. They began to fall like tall grass being cut. Sundjata and Bory with a line of cavalry rode into the swordsmen, knocking some down with their horses while cutting down others.

Sumaguru watched from above as the lines crashed together, pushing and stabbing. He signaled for his archers to fire. He hoped to deplete Sundjata's rear ranks, weakening their resolve. They hadn't fought in a while; he knew they feared him. He must exploit that fear.

When the arrows started to rain down onto the rear, Balla gave the command. "Archers, go! Go!" Row after row of men with bows rose to the top of the hills where the trees parted or cleared and began firing into Sumaguru's men. Others used the trees for cover and fired across the valley.

Sumaguru's arrows fell into the first row of Sundjata's spearmen, and the line began to open. Sumaguru's men surged forward. Men behind the line tried to protect the men in front of them with their shields high in the air.

Ahmed and Azeez stood behind their men and heard horses advancing towards them. Archers were on the slopes of the hills and as soon as they saw the riders they let loose. The arrows hit their marks and men fell from their mounts. The leader of the Tuareg looked at Ahmed and Azeez and smiled. He put his royal blue veil over his face and moved his mount forward. The Tuareg mounts were small and fast. They hit Sumaguru's men like a crashing wave as iron and horse hit each other. They easily dismounted and halted Sumaguru's men on the tight trail. The archers moved forward firing arrow after arrow and Sumaguru's men stopped in the trail.

Holding their respective hills, Sundjata's and Sumaguru's archers continued to fire at each other through the gaps in the branches. Others hid behind trees or on the steep grassy hillsides to weaken the lines of the other. The trees kept both sides from concentrating their attack. Arrows flew across the valley from hill to hill while others flew into the line of men below. From Ahmed's position Salt took a group of fifty men up the steep hill to attack Sumaguru's archers. They carried shields, bows and swords.

Fakoli sent a second wave of men and filled the hole in the line, stopping Sumaguru's surge. Fakoli watched the second line do their job. He rode towards the men in their hollow. "Forward!" he yelled. The men were shoulder to shoulder in the hollow. Then Sundjata's men had the advantage. They rose out of the hollow and crashed into the first line of Sumaguru's men. The attacking men had short stabbing swords and some clubs. They cut and pounded their way into the line. Men screamed and blood splashed all around.

Sundjata, Bory and their men broke the attack out of the hollow. Into the hollow they went and surged out onto flat ground and towards the line of archers in Sumaguru's rear as they were forming to fire.

Sumaguru's son waited in reserve and saw riders smash into his archers. "Forward!" he yelled at several companies of swordsmen.

The arrows lessened on Sundjata's spearmen, and they began to break the shields of Sumaguru's men. They broke a hole in the line. The rain of Sundjata's men's arrows had taken its toll. Spaces began to open, and as men tried to fill them arrows took them down.

Fakoli sent a company of men from Selefougou to the left along the small hills. He needed to keep pressure on Sumaguru, protect his flank and support the archers with Balla on the hills above.

Sundjata, Bory and a hundred men were slashing into the archers. Their ranks began to break. Horses pushed over their bodies and hooves smashed bone.

Fakoli noticed the side where Sundjata went was open. He turned to his second in command. "I'm taking half the men to follow Sundjata. You fill gaps if needed. Spread the word." Fakoli took off with men in tow.

Sundjata swung his horse and his sword left then right, knocking men down. He slashed and stabbed into them. An arrow hit one of the small tight rings on his father's vest, and it bounced off into the air. This stunned the offending archer. Sundjata rode over and cut him down. After this happened several times, Sumaguru's men began to grow scared.

Bory was swinging his sword but not moving his horse fast enough. A group of men leapt up, grabbing his reins and pulling his horse to the ground. They stabbed at him. His vest protected him, but his face and arms were being cut.

Sundjata's frontline broke Sumaguru's lines, and they began to retreat. Fran took his rear reserves of men through the opening on the left. His swordsmen ran forward yelling and moving into the wider part of the valley.

Sumaguru's son's reserve men met Fran's men, swords clashed and shields smashed. An arrow hit Fran's horse in the neck, and it reared up, dumping him to the ground.

As Sundjata's men pushed forward the widening valley gave them room to maneuver. Fakoli rode into the open space and saw his nephew far away on his left. He saw Bory on the ground and he moved to help him.

Bory was swinging and stabbing his sword, pushing the circle of men back. Blood ran down his arms and face. Fakoli killed two men, and Bory got to his feet. "Be careful," he yelled at Bory.

The archers attempted to regroup and started shooting arrows towards Sundjata and his men. Fakoli's men charged the archers, further breaking their ranks.

Fran's men had broken Sumaguru's first line of reserves. Sundjata and his men caught them from behind and killed them as they tried to retreat. Fran fought on foot.

Sumaguru's son noticed that the hollow Sundjata had ridden

through was open. He turned to his father's captain and had him take a group of men up the hills to break the enemy archers. The captain dismounted and took his men to where the hills were not guarded. They moved along, using the trees and brush as cover until they were close enough to attack. Archers from both sides tried to nock arrows and fire faster than the other. When they ran out of arrows they fought hand to hand.

Alerted to the attack on the hills, Balla brought up men to stop it. They used the trees for cover. Arrows began to fly past him or slam into trunks. Balla was careful to not use up what arrows he had left. He saw a man to the right and was about to shoot at him when one of his men put an arrow through the man's neck.

Sumaguru's captain killed an archer and knelt down and looked through the trees. Men were screaming and fighting around him. To his delight he saw Balla by the side of a tree. He took the bow and arrow from the man he killed and aimed for Balla's head. He let it go excited at bringing Balla's head back to Sumaguru. He saw bark fly and Balla fall.

Sumaguru's son took his men into the open hollow. Most of Sundjata's men were now up on the valley floor. His horse trampled the wounded.

Several of Salt's men held a wall of shields to protect themselves. Archers would peek out from behind them, hitting Sumaguru's unprotected archers. They moved out of the open into the stand of trees and found groups of archers shooting through gaps in the branches, attacking silently sneaking up on them and fewer and fewer arrows flew into the valley.

Sundjata rode over to Bory protecting him as he got back on a horse. The archers and retreating men were defeated. Sundjata saw Sumaguru bring the rest of his forces up. They emerged into sight from around the line of hills that turned sharply right. He looked behind him and saw that his original line of men began to reform under Kama's orders. The hills were now far enough apart and their men could maneuver. They had broken out pouring into the open, but the day was not yet theirs.

From his horse Sundjata noticed how much blood covered Bory.

Bory saw the look on his brother's face. "I am fine."

"We need to move some troops even further left here and not let him get around us," Sundjata said. He looked around and saw Kwame forming men into fighting lines.

Sumaguru's son and his men launched themselves out of the hollow. At Sundjata's rear Sumaguru's swift attack caused panic, and the men broke their formation, making it easy to be killed.

Salt and his group cleared out the archers, slowing the rain of arrows to their rear. Many of his men gathered around him as they looked below. On the steep slopes they saw archers hiding in the tall grass, firing into the valley. "Run at them, break them, follow me!" Salt ran down the hill with his men behind him. Being light, Salt covered ground without much sound. He caught a lone archer in the back of the head with his sword.

An archer heard a man scream and turned to see a skinny man moving through the tall grass at him. He let an arrow fly, but the man dropped into the grass.

Salt could see the archer before him was nervous. He dropped to the ground and an arrow flew over his head. Salt stood up, taking a battle axe out of his belt and threw it. The ax spun end-over-end and caught the man in the shoulder as he pulled back his bow. The arrow few and hit Salt, and he fell into the grass.

An arrow skimmed the side of tree next to Balla's head and bark flew into his face. He dropped to a knee and ducked behind the tree. "Damn it," he cursed and cleared the bark from his eyes.

"Are you okay?" one of his men called to him also behind a tree. "In front of you to the left, I see who fired at you." He fired an arrow at the man. "I missed." He held his hand out pointing at the man.

As the captain stepped forward an arrow flew close to his

head. He ducked behind a tree and caught his breath.

Balla knelt down, bow at the ready, guided by his man. His eyes watered, and his breath was heavy. Then he saw a face peak out, and he let the arrow fly.

The captain bent down low to see who shot at him. As he peaked around the tree an arrow flew into his eye and stuck in his brain.

Balla saw the arrow hit the man in the face. The body fell to the ground. Balla moved low and towards the man he killed. The man looked familiar to him, but everything happened so fast. Close to the body he kicked it over and saw the face of Sumaguru's captain. He smiled but wondered where Sumaguru's son was. He didn't want to meet him.

Sundjata's men rallied from their original panic. No other troops could follow Sumaguru's son, and he realized he was in trouble. He and his men were cut off and formed a battle circle. But spearmen advanced towards them and stabbed at their horses. One by one they fell to the ground to be swarmed by a storm of swords. Sumaguru's son was the last to fall. His bloody mount gave a scream and fell sideways. He hit the ground, but the dead horses and men gave him time to get to his feet. He grabbed a man who lunged at him, taking his sword and using him as a shield. His left arm held the man's neck, and he swung at anyone who stepped near him. He turned left then right and around to protect his back. Sweat ran down his face as he turned, spun and swung. *If I could just reach the hollow*, he thought. With his sword he caught one man in the arm and another in the head, but a spear thrown into his back sunk deep and it made him flinch while lifting his sword arm. Anger and pain flooded his body, but in an instant he felt no pain. Everything stopped, the world grew dim and he could not catch his breath. He didn't see the man who rushed forward, thrusting a sword under his arm into his chest, piercing his heart. The body of the son of Sumaguru went limp, and he fell to the ground.

The Tuareg had routed the men on the tight trail and the

constant stream of arrows pushed the attackers off. Ahmed and Azeez braced for a counter attack.

Keleya and Nana stood on the tall hill arm-in-arm, tears streaming down their face. They looked out across the valley as their troops fanned out in lines three deep. Cavalry filled in the gaps between them. The enemy also began to form row after row. When they looked down, bodies lay in piles or littered across the ground. Some horses lay motionless. Others tried to get up, kicking their legs and making the terrible sounds that dying things do. Some wounded men crawled out of desperation, while others cried out. It was all a terrible scene.

"So much blood," Nana said. "It soaks the ground, the grass; I have never seen so much." It was horrible, but she could not look away.

Sundjata realized Sumaguru was moving slow and that his frontline had few spearmen. A thought grabbed him. "Bory, get Fran and Kama, and meet me by Kwame." He rode over to Kwame. "Have the cavalry get spears, and let's charge his frontline on the left. It will weaken the whole front. With the spears we can ride right through the swordsmen. He has almost no spearmen there. Look, his archers are still forming."

Kwame looked at the situation and saw Sumaguru's mistake. "Yes, it could work."

Bory rode up with Fran, again on a horse, Kama and Fakoli. "Get your cavalry to take the spears from the spearmen. We will charge their left; it is weakest. Do it quick, and rally on Sundjata."

Sumaguru rode up and saw that Sundjata had broken out of the valley. Turning to a commander on his left, he asked, "What is taking so long? Get these men formed up." He shook his head and regretted letting his eldest lead the first attack. His son had failed him. "That boy," he said aloud. He saw confusion in his ranks, and he began to yell at his men to assemble faster. "Where is the cavalry?"

More and more men began to gather around Sundjata. Each

mounted man now armed with long spears. "Quick, quick!" he yelled. Bory tossed him a spear.

Balla stood on the hills and saw Sundjata lining up with his cavalry, and he turned to some of his men on his right. "Get most of the men with what arrows they have left, we must support the men on the field. Leave some to protect our left."

Sumaguru saw mounted men amassing on his right. He looked for his cavalry and turned to see them just now coming up. But they were not where they should be.

Sundjata felt satisfied he had enough men to charge. "Kwame, you stay and command the middle." He saw Fakoli and rode to him. "You stay behind us, and when we break their line then you come." Fakoli nodded in agreement.

Sundjata rode in front of his men and raised his spear above his head. "We end this now. Follow me." He turned his mount and headed straight at the left side of Sumaguru's line of swordsmen. Excitement filled his chest, and Bory, bloody but smiling, was on his right. He began to yell, and his men yelled behind him. The line of swordsmen got closer and closer, and he could see the fear on their faces. One by one they began to turn and run, knowing they could not stop the onslaught. His spear caught a man in the back, and the man fell to the ground. He pulled out his sword and began hacking at the men running.

Fakoli saw Sumaguru's left line collapse. He spurred his horse, and his men followed him through the breach. "Uncle, I come for you." They moved fast over the ground. Once into the hole he turned right, and his several hundred men followed.

Kwame could not believe his eyes as he saw Sundjata ride into the enemy's rear. Panic gripped the enemy, as men were now behind them as well as in front. Kwame pressed his attack forward.

Keleya and Nana stopped crying and cheered as they saw Sumaguru's forces beginning to break and run. Some formed groups and stood and fought, but most ran. "Oh my," Keleya exclaimed. The girls hugged and began to clap, sing and dance. "We are victorious. This is our day, and Niani will rise."

Sumaguru could see men running as row upon row of men broke. Some formed circles to fight, but men began to stream past him. "Stop, stop!" he yelled. "Fight! We will not lose!" He managed to stop large groups and formed them up. "Forward." Sumaguru spurred his horse forward and began to fight. Seeing him, the men were inspired and counter-attacked.

Sundjata and Bory hacked and slashed, bringing down men even though they were exhausted. They stopped and surveyed the scene of panic. Bory's keen eyes picked out Sumaguru.

"Look, there he is," Bory pointed.

Sundjata looked and saw Sumaguru taking down men with a battle axe. More and more of his men began to fight with him. Sundjata still had his bow tied to his saddle with several arrows. He sheathed his sword and released his bow.

"Kill him," Bory said.

Sundjata gave his reins to Bory. "Hold him still." Sundjata took several deep breaths and nocked an arrow. "He's far away."

"Just kill him," Bory said.

Sundjata took a deep breath and held it, and then he released the arrow. It flew straight and strong but missed Sumaguru by a small margin. He took another arrow, but this time he aimed for his horse. The arrow struck the horse in the neck. The horse reared up, dumping Sumaguru to the ground. Sundjata threw the bow to the ground and rode forward as Bory followed. He pulled his sword and saw Sumaguru stand up, swinging his axe. Men fighting got in Sundjata's way. Bory reached Sumaguru first and knocked him down with his horse. Sumaguru's men attacked Bory and he had to defend himself.

Sumaguru found himself on the ground. He rolled over. When he stood up he saw Sundjata before him on horseback. He raised his axe. Sundjata was fast, and his sword caught Sumaguru in the left shoulder. Sundjata rode past him, and Sumaguru fell to a knee.

Sundjata saw Sumaguru on one knee. He turned his horse and charged him again. He swung but missed as Sumaguru rolled out of the way. Sumaguru's guards rallied and pulled Sundjata off his horse to the ground.

Bory saw Sundjata get pulled off his horse. He charged forward, striking one man in the skull, making a loud cracking sound. Then he swung at a second man who stepped back to defend himself.

Sundjata took the knife that was strapped to his arm and plunged it into the man who fought Bory. The man screamed and stepped back, tripping over a body and falling to the ground. Still on the ground, Sundjata found his sword. Sumaguru lunged at him, but Sundjata rolled to the side and slashed Sumaguru in the knee. Sumaguru let out a scream and was down on one knee again.

Sumaguru stood up and ran towards Sundjata, swinging the axe at his head.

Sundjata swung his sword, and it smashed Sumaguru's axe aside. He stepped back as Sumaguru swung again. Sundjata pressed the attack as Sumaguru countered the blows. They hacked at each other again and again. Sundjata's leg hurt. He was angry yet controlled.

Sumaguru thought each blow would finish Sundjata, but he would not fall.

Sundjata moved in close. His sword and Sumaguru's axe met, and they stopped and looked into each other's eyes. He could see the fear and anger in Sumaguru. This made Sundjata feel stronger. He pushed upwards, and as Sumaguru's axe went skywards he slashed Sumaguru's leg. Sumaguru yelled in pain and dropped to a knee, his axe on the ground.

Bory could not believe his eyes. Sumaguru's head snapped down as his brother's sword smashed into flesh and bone. Sumaguru's neck was broken, and his body fell lifeless onto the ground.

Chapter 21

To Build an Empire

Drums were beating as the sun cracked the horizon. The word had gone out that it was time to celebrate Sundjata's great victory and to hear the decision of the council. The morning sun bathed the soft brown of the palace. Everyone was dressed in their finest, Sundjata, Bory and Balla walked through the courtyard to the silk cotton tree.

"This is the biggest gathering of elders anyone can remember," said Balla.

"Do you think they will ask for their titles of mansa back?" asked Bory.

"I told you I don't care. Everyone supported us, and that is all that counts," Sundjata said.

"You will be king either way," Bory smiled.

Sundjata smiled. "Yes, I will."

"You were right to give the land of the Sosso to Fakoli. He will not disappoint you." Balla said looking at the brothers.

"He fought bravely when it counted, and he kept you and my sister alive. He should be rewarded," Sundjata said while nodding his head.

Under the silk cotton tree mats were covering the ground. Elders, chiefs and sub-chiefs filled the meeting area. Men and women lined up behind them, packing every open space.

Sundjata, Bory and Balla walked through the crowd to a spot by the wall where a low chair sat on the ground. Nana and Kolonkan were waiting by the chair. There they met the oldest elder. The elder raised his hands, and the crowd began to quiet down. When there was silence he spoke. "With your great victory you have freed us from the tyranny of Sumaguru and the Sosso. You have united all the people, and by our decision you shall be king, like your father."

"I accept and am ready to return your title of mansa to those who claim it," Sundjata said in a loud clear voice.

"No, you must keep it; the spirits are pleased. Talk to our ancestors. The sacrifices today will further please them, and the kingdom will rise as it did when your father ruled."

"I accept and will speak to them as long as they are willing to hear me. Let's fight no more and listen to each other's stories again, raise families, grow crops and make the market full once more. The council is wise, and I will not disappoint. Let us celebrate this day," Sundjata said, raising his hands high. Fran and Kama came forward to shake his hand.

The crowd cheered and clapped, then broke into dance.

Sundjata looked to his right and were greeted by Azeez, Ahmed and Salt.

"How is your arm?" Sundjata asked Salt.

"Sore but I will live."

"Azeez, you will have your old job back. Ahmed please start bringing things as fast as possible. I have sent men to talk to the people who run the goldfields at Bure." Sundjata shook their hands.

"You are the true lion king, my friend," Ahmed said. "I have known your mother and father, and you make them proud. You have their good heart."

"Thank you. I would not be here without either of you. Allah has smiled on me."

"You are learning," Azeez said. "With what has happened here today this place will grow even bigger."

Sundjata saw Kwame behind Salt and motioned for him to come close. "I want you to stay if you like, but I will understand if you want to return to your queen."

"I will return, but with what you can build here the queen will be pleased, and we shall all benefit."

"Thank you for your all your help," said Sundjata as he shook his hand. Kwame stepped back. Sundjata turned to his sister. "I will not punish your mother, but she is not welcome here in Niani...ever. She must stay in her village."

"Thank you, brother. That is very generous. I know she is trouble from head to toe."

"That she is. After all we have been through I want to rebuild what father had made and more if we can."

Bibliography

Books

Concrad, David C. Sunjata *A West African Epic of the Mande People*. Narrated   by Djanka Tassey Conde. Indianapolis: Hackett Publishing, 2004.

Doubma, Naomi and Adama. *The Way of the Elders: West African Spirituality   & Tradition*. Llewellyn Worldwide, Ltd, 2004.

Johnson, John William. *Son-Jara The Mande Epic Mandekan/English Edition with Notes and Commentary New Edition,* Text by Jeli Fa-Digi Sisoko. Bloomington: Indiana University Press, 2003.

Niane, D.T. *Sundiata Revised Edition.* Translated by G.D. Pickett. Edinburgh Gate, Harlow, England: Pearson Education, 2007.

Reid, Richard. *Warfare in African History*. New York, Cambridge University Press, 2012.

Shillington, Kevin. *History of Africa.* Third Edition. New York: Palgrave Macmillan, 2012.

Journals

Manzon, Agnes Kedzierska. "Humans and Things: Mande "Fetishes" as Subjects." Anthropological Quarterly, Vol. 86, No. 4 (2013): 1119 -1146.

Endnotes

1. John William Johnson, *Son-Jara The Mande Epic*, (Bloomington, Indiana University Press, 2003) 290.

2. D.T. Niane, *SUNDIATA AN EPIC OF OLD MALI*, (Edinburgh Gate, Harlow, Esssex, Pearson Education Limited, 2007) 5.

3. Niane, *SUNDIATA*, 5.

4. Ibid., 5.

5. Johnson, *Son-Jara*, 291.

6. Niane, *SUNDIATA*, 4.

7. Ibid., 10.

8. Ibid., 10.

9. Ibid., 10.

10. Ibid., 10.

11. Ibid., 10.

12. Ibid., 10.

13. Ibid., 10.

14. Ibid., 10.

15. Niane., 11.

16. Ibid., 10.

17. David C. Conrad, *SUNJATA A West African Epic of the Mande People*, (Indianapolis, Hackett Publishing, 2004) 64.

18. Ibid., 61

19. Ibid., 64.

20. Niane, *SUNDIATA*, 13.

21. Ibid., 13.

22. Niane, *SUNDIATA*, 24.

23. Ibid., 24.

24. Niane, *SUNDIATA*, 38.

25. Niane, *SUNDIATA*, 19.

26. Niane, *SUNDIATA*, 20-21. / Johnson, *Son-Jara*, 286.

27. Conrad, *SUNDJATA*, 82-87.

28. Niane, *SUNDIATA*, 31.

29. Niane, *SUNDIATA*, 30.

30. Ibid., 30.

31. Ibid., 30.

32. Niane, *SUNDIATA*, 33.

33. Niane, *SUNDIATA*, 57.

34. Conrad, *SUNDJATA*, 129.

35. Niane, *SUNDIATA*, 45.

36. Niane, *SUNDIATA*, 58, 64.

37. Niane, *SUNDIATA*, 42.

38. Niane, *SUNDIATA*, 60.